THE PARTING TREES
A Savior's Beginning

By:
K. Gilbert

To my love, my everything; you made this happen.

Chapter 1 The Great Escape

It was just another ordinary day for Regina and Tyler Baylon. The sun was rising up for the morning to begin, the trees were swaying in the wind and the Baylon siblings were attempting their fifth escape from the house this month! Regina, the eldest, was gently letting out the tied up sheets as her brother was clinging on for dear life on the other end. Tyler opened his bright blue eyes once he could feel the cool touch of the grass below his feet. He untied the sheet from around his waist and waited for his sister to toss down a few items.

"Reg!" whispered Tyler as his sister was leaning out the window reeling in the rest of the sheet, "Don't forget my shoes."

Regina tossed down Tyler's shoes and began tying the sheet rope to the bedpost and the other end around her waist. She grabbed her light blue backpack filled with food and clothes, tied up her long brown hair and began climbing out the window. Tyler was waiting nervously below. He brushed away the dirty blonde hair that was blocking his view of the street. He looked back up at his sister and saw a light come on in the far left corner of the house.

"Regina, hurry, she is up!" Regina's heart started beating heavily in her chest. She could hear stirring in the other room.

Their legal guardian, Lady Dumontet, was a cruel and hateful woman. She would spend her days watching television as she made the children clean the house from top to bottom every day. Often the children would be scrubbing on their hands and knees for hours on in before Lady Dumontet would allow them to take a break. They were fed cans of soup twice a day and bread for dinner. Lady Dumontet watched them eat their soup as she gorged herself on her own personal supply of food. She would also never allow Regina and Tyler outside; their only reprieve from Lady Dumontet was on Bingo Thursdays at the recreation center which fortunately shared the building with the public library.

Regina took full advantage of their time in the library, reading as much as she could and teaching Tyler along the way; this was the only form of education that they would ever receive. Luckily for them, Lady Dumontet would spend hours trying to win big in Bingo and during this time Regina would also use the computer at the library to research laws on child care, how to tie different knots and survival skills for the wild all while Tyler acted as their lookout.

Yes, Lady Dumontet was quite terrible, but nothing frightened the children more than hearing her walk down the dark hall running her fingernails along the wood. The sound of her long nails scratching against the wood would give both of them chills. In fact, she did this so often that the wall had groove lines from where her fingernails had been dragged across. There was one thing Regina never understood, the old lady never seemed to age. The four miserable years Regina and Tyler were under her care she had never added a wrinkle, extra grey hair or even a single digit to her age. She had a hard look to her, like she had smoked for years (which she did), but only that of a woman in her fifties. She would always brag how good she looked for being 99 years old and she never got a day older.

Regina hurried out the window tossed the backpack down to Tyler and started making her way down the side of the house. She had almost reached the bottom when she felt the sheet tug from the top. A wrinkly old hand grasped the window seal and another reached for the sheet. Lady Dumontet's head appeared outside the window. Her coarse, black hair was extra bushy from just waking up and she had a scary crazed look in her eyes as she began pulling Regina back up into the bedroom. Regina turned pale when she felt the sheet tugging at her waist pulling her higher and higher from the ground. Halfway from the floor to the window Regina thought it was best to untie herself rather than ending back up in that room with her.

So she quickly untied the sheet from around her waist and fell hard on the grass next to her brother.

Lady Dumontet yelled furiously "I will get you little brats back one way or another!" She disappeared from the window to call the Sheriff and Tyler started to take off running.

Regina grabbed him before he got too far. "No." she said in a breathless voice, "Let's go right this time. We will run behind the house and cut through the trees."

Tyler gave Regina a wary expression. "You want to go through the woods?" He looked passed his sister into the dark tree lines and shook his head no. "There is a good reason why we don't go that way."

Tyler hesitated. He could feel his body leaning in the other direction; towards the safe and familiar route. The way that they always took when they tried escaping. He was ready to argue the point when he heard keys jingling inside the house and her heavy footsteps were clambering down the stairs.

He took in a deep breath and resigned to the plan of heading into the scary woods. "Alright. I'll follow."

Regina lead the way. They ran as fast as they could so they could take cover behind one of the trees. Regina knelt behind a tree and caught her breath. She glanced around to see if there were any wolves. The Baylon children had never gone in this direction before mostly because every night they could hear wolves howling at the moon, but Regina knew it would be worth the risk if it threw Lady Dumontet of their tracks.

Regina and Tyler peered around the tree, when they heard the loud crack of a car backfiring. Dumontet looked to the left first, the usual way Regina and Tyler would run off to, and then she looked to the right, which was the road that ran along side the woods. The two of them held their breath waiting to see which way she would turn. She made a left and disappeared down the road. They both breathed a sigh of relief. Regina got up and dusted herself off; Tyler did the same. They took one last look at the house before they made their way through the woods.

They had been running for a while through the woods before they found themselves approaching a dirt road. They had to cross it if they wanted to continue running out of plain sight. Regina and Tyler inched their way closer to make sure it was clear before they crossed. Tyler, being the smallest and less easy to spot, slowly made his way out from behind a trees when he saw a car approaching in the distance. He hid behind the tree line again and waited for the car to pass. Once it had disappeared down the road he gave a thumbs up to his sister to let her know the path was clear.

They began walking along the other side of the road in the cover of the trees when Tyler noticed a little bit of blood on the backside of his sister's arm. He pointed at the cut and asked, "Are you okay?"

Regina hadn't noticed; the pain had been subdued by all the adrenalin and the overall rush of their escape. She shrugged it off and told Tyler "I'll be fine. It doesn't even hurt."

They continued walking for what seemed like several hours. Regina could see that her brother couldn't go much further; his feet were barley coming off the ground and his pace had become that of a snail's.

"How about we take a break?" Regina said realizing how exhausted she was as well.

Tyler nodded his head in agreement and found a large stump to sit on. Regina grabbed from her backpack a bottle of water and handed it to her little brother. She looked around and wondered how far they were from the house. They had never gone this far before, it usually only took an hour for the sheriff to find them. There was something about this time that made them both determined to get out of that house for good. Regina thought back to the crazed look Lady Dumontet had when she tried pulling her back in and shuttered for a minute.

Tyler looked into his sister's hazel eyes and had noticed her far off stare and knew what she was thinking. "I know," he said softly, "she really scared me too. We had to get out of there. I was afraid of what she had planned for you after she caught you stealing some of her food for us." Tyler's eyes began to water.

Regina was tall for a fifteen-year-old girl which made it easy for her to reach up into the cupboard and grab the good food that Lady Dumontet kept for herself. Last night Lady Dumontet had forbid Tyler from having dinner as punishment for not refilling her drink fast enough when she had finished it. Regina knew her brother was starving and she couldn't let him go without a meal so she decided to steal Lady Dumontet's food like she had done several times before; except this time, she got caught.

Regina threw her arms around Tyler and tried to comfort him. "We will start a whole new life together." She said this trying to convince herself as well. "We will find a loving family that will takes us in and care for us. We just have to be brave in the meantime." She helped her brother up. "Come on, let's get going before the sun starts to set." As Regina felt her stomach sink a little as she said this. Night would approach sooner rather than later. She had no real plan for where they would stay. She always hoped they would successfully escape, but she never really knew what would happen if they did.

With every step they took their shadows grew longer and their cover was getting smaller. The woods were starting to thin out; they would have to take their chances being exposed along the dirt road. They walked in silence, constantly looking over their shoulders, for about twenty minutes before they heard something coming up behind them. Regina quickly looked around for somewhere to hide. The closest thing to them was a small bush about five feet ahead of them. They had no choice, they raced towards the bush and dove for cover.

Regina peered through the leaves, as the car got closer. "Crap, it's the Sheriff!"

"Do you think he saw us?" Tyler asked nervously.

They both watched from behind the bush as the car drove past them. It didn't look like the sheriff was slowing down to stop. They hid behind the bush for another minute or so to make sure the sheriff was far enough ahead. Regina was about to stand up and continue down the road when they heard a *Crunch* a few feet away on the other side of the bush. They both turned back around to look through the leaves again, but it was too late. The Sheriff was standing over them with a big grin on his face.

Regina knew they were caught so she stood up from the bush and smiled at the Sheriff. "Sheriff Tucker, what a lovely day to take a stroll, don't you agree?"

He looked down at them with his dark brown eyes and his sunglasses hanging low on the bridge of his bent nose. "You know I was having a wonderful breakfast this morning when a call was dispatched; a fifteen-year-old girl and her ten-year-old brother had run away from home and I thought to myself, 'who could that be…" The Sheriff scratched his chin looking upwards pretending to ponder. "…oh yes, the Baylon kids!' So I figured I would finish my chocolate chip pancakes before I came looking for you two. You know, to give you a head start and all. I do have to say you two sure did get far this time."

Tyler looked up with a big smile on his face, "So what is our prize?" The Sheriff gave them a stern look for half a second. He pulled his hands out from behind his back and revealed a chocolate candy bar in each of them. Tyler quickly grabbed the bar and began to devour it. He said with a full mouth "Fanks bor the bocolate 'enry!"

The Sheriff let out a big laugh that shook the brown curls on his head. "Alright, you guys know the drill into the truck you go." Sheriff Tucker opened the door for the kids to slide in the front seat with him and called into the police station letting them know they could call off the search. "What is this, your third or fourth attempt this month?"

Regina with a sulked face told the Sheriff, "Our fifth." She couldn't help but think how close they were to getting away this time and she dreaded the thought of seeing Lady Dumontet. How she would pretend to be so happy and relieved to find them in front of everyone, but afterwards, she would throw them in their rooms and wouldn't let them come out for days.

Henry felt sorry for the Regina and Tyler kids. He had tried so many times to find a way out for them, but Lady Dumontet wasn't breaking the law (that he knew of) so his hands were tied.

"Cheer up kiddo, it can't be all bad. Three more years and you are free to leave." He knew there was nothing he could say to make this situation any better for them. "Wow, you two made it so far out that I am unfamiliar with this area. So there might be a good chance we will get lost along the way. Maybe we will have to stop at that diner on the left there." He turned and gave them a wink. "I don't know about you, but some waffles with some whip cream and strawberries sure do sound good right-"

Tucker cut off midsentence. His hands tightened around the steering wheel. A deer galloped onto the road. Its black eyes starred them down as the young buck froze in front of them. It was too late for Tucker to brake; he had to swerve in order to avoid the deer coming through the windshield. He managed to go around the deer, but he overcorrected. The truck's left tires lifted off from the ground. Tucker knew what was coming. He placed his right arm across Regina and Tyler. Tucker's body tensed as the sky turned sideways before him. A notepad and pen slid across the dash. His cold coffee spilled from his lap to his face. Their bodies shifted in their seats. Up became down.

There was one final thud before Regina dared to open up her eyes. She felt dazed and pressure was starting to build as the blood began rushing to her head. As the dust settled around them it had become clear to Regina that they were all hanging upside down. Regina turned to Tyler who was looking back at her.

"Are you alright?" She looked her brother up and down; there were no serious injuries to be found.

"Uh, yeah, I think so. Are you okay?"

"I don't see anything wrong. How about you Tucker? Tucker?" Regina glanced over at an unresponsive Sheriff.

She reached for her buckle and managed to get out of her seat and helped Tyler out of his seat as well. They both climbed out from the broken windshield of the vehicle; carefully avoiding the sharp shards of glass that were scattered across the ground. Regina then went back to the driver's window and looked at Sheriff Tucker, who appeared to be okay as well, just unconscious.

Regina reached in to check his pulse. "He is still alive." She turned to Tyler, "Run ahead and look for the name of that diner." She searched for The Sheriffs cell phone and found it laying in the dirt. The screen was cracked, but it still worked.

Tyler came back panting. "It is called..." he took a few breaths, "Betty's Diner."

Regina made a call to 911 and told them their location was next to Betty's Diner. They both waited a few minutes to make sure the Sheriff was truly okay. Regina then placed the phone next to the Sheriff as he began to wake up. Henry made a few moans, but was starting to become aware of what just happened. Regina looked at her brother and debated whether to stay or run.

Regina jumped as the Sheriff grabbed her arm. He looked up at her with some pain in his eyes and told her "Run!" Regina looked scared and confused, both her and her brother liked the Sheriff very much and neither one of them wanted to leave him. Henry told her again, but this time in a stern voice, "RUN! I will be fine. Just RUN!"

Regina didn't hesitate the second time. She grabbed her brother and headed back towards the woods. In the distance, they could already hear the sirens. The red lights from the ambulance began to glow in the darkness of the setting sun. Doors slammed and cops were talking on their radios. Regina and Tyler picked up the pace when they heard dogs barking; without saying anything to one another they knew they had to run far and fast to get away from the cops and their dogs.

Voices started caring through the trees "It looks like they went this way!"

A few seconds later, *BAM!* A loud sound echoed through the woods that sent chills up and down Regina and Tyler's spines; it was the sound of a car backfiring, which told them that Lady Dumontet had arrived.

They could hear the police gaining on them and somehow Lady Dumontet had caught up with them as well. Her shrill voice was calling out for them, "Regina, Tyler please come out! I have been so worried!" Her concerned pleads didn't even fool the police, but she kept on going.

Regina and Tyler were growing tired and their pace was slowing. They couldn't keep running, not after the long day they had. The police and Lady Dumontet were right behind them now and they both knew they couldn't out run them anymore. Regina and Tyler saw that to the left of them the ground dropped off into another part of the woods. Regina gave a signal and they quickly veered towards the drop. It wasn't a gentle slope down, but luckily it wasn't that far of a drop. They began their descent when Regina's foot slipped on a rock. She tumbled down the hill and lost track of her brother. She looked up to see where he was, but she only saw flashlights at the top of the hill.

Regina heard footsteps approaching her from the bottom of the hill. Tyler was running towards her.

"No!" She whispered, "Go hide somewhere."

Tyler stopped and looked around for somewhere to hide. He saw a hollowed out tree a few feet ahead of him. He glanced back at his sister before he climbed in. Regina glanced back up at the hilltop; the flashlights were moving away from their location. The last of the lights were fading, Regina was ready to make a break towards her brother when she heard a scratching noise. The familiar sound made Regina's skin crawl. Her heart began to race in her chest, it was coming in their direction. Lady Dumontet's finger nails ran across the bark of a tree that was next to the one Tyler was in. Regina hid behind a nearby stump on the hillside and watched as Lady Dumontet inched her way towards Tyler. She got closer and closer to the tree, almost as if she knew he was hiding there. She began running her nails down the tree gradually getting closer to the opening. She dug her nails deeper into the bark; Tyler closed his eyes and waited for her to grab him. Lady Dumontet started peering in through the hole. Thump! A noise echoed behind her. Thump! Again, but this time a little further away. Dumontet hesitated, but ultimately turned her attention to noise that came from behind her. Thump! This time the noise came from atop of the hill and with a sudden swiftness she followed the noise and disappeared over the hill.

Regina ran to her brother. "I can't believe that worked." Her heart was pounding in her chest.

"What worked?" Tyler moved over so his sister could climb in.

"I was sure she had spotted you. Out of desperation, I threw a few rocks just past the tree to distract her. I guess she thought we had slipped by her." Regina joined her brother in the hollowed out tree. "Hey!" Regina grabbed at her arm.

"What happened?" Tyler asked.

"Its nothing. The edge of the bark just scratched my arm a little, but who cares. I think we did it Tyler. I think we lost them at least for now."

They took a moment to breathe; it had been a long day and they were both tired. The sound of leaves rustling in the trees grew louder than the voices that were calling for them.

Tyler looked up at his sister. His eyes were weary and his body ached. "Do you think we can stay in here?" Regina knew they could not out run the cops or Lady Dumontet so she agreed to stay there until the morning when hopefully everyone would have moved on.

The sounds of chaos moved further away into the distance. Tyler began to fall asleep in her lap and soon, there were no sounds at all. Regina's eyelids grew heavy and she decided it was safe enough to let herself fall asleep. Before she let herself sleep, though, she made the same wish she had made every night since they found themselves living with Dumontet, "Please let us find our way home." She closed her eyes and let herself drift into a rather deep sleep.

    A streak of sunlight hit her face, rousing her from the dream she was having. She began to panic when she didn't see Tyler in her lap and all of the previous day's happenings hit her at once. Regina quickly climbed out of the tree and found Tyler playing with a bug. Her eyes lit up once she had realized he was okay and that there was no one around to take them back to Lady Dumontet.

    Tyler saw his sister and ran towards her. "We did it Regina! We escaped!" She embraced him in open arms and thought that finally things might work out, but once the moment had passed over them, they both looked around realizing something was not right.

    "I know it was dark, but I could have sworn there were more than just these three trees." Regina looked around still very confused when she had noticed the hill, rather the lack of a hill. It was flat land all around them. "What happened to the hill we came down from?" Regina held her brother close "Where are we?"

Chapter 2 The Fox Tree

    Standing in the middle of a wide-open field with only three trees was not how they remembered things from last night. Tyler went back to the tree in the middle where their backpack was still inside. He grabbed the outside of the tree to balance himself as he reached in for the backpack. The tree felt oddly smooth where he had laid his hand. He looked under where his hand was placed and noticed that there was a carving on the tree. He ran his fingers along the grooves and traced out a figure.

    "Look Reg! There is a fox on this tree." Regina came over to have a look. Perfectly carved into the tree was a white fox sitting with its long bushy tail wrapped around the front of it.

"Wow!" Regina momentarily lost her breath. "This is beautiful."

Tyler called from the tree next to it. "This one has a carving too! An owl, it's an owl!" Regina went towards the last tree to see if it had one as well. She saw what looked like a wolf on the tree, but it was a little hard to tell. Tyler shouted to his sister, "What does that one *have* on it?"

"I think it is a wolf," Regina called back to her brother, "but it is hard to tell. It has scratches over it like if someone wanted to rip it off." The two of them stared at the tree for a while before they realized that they were still lost. "Right, we are probably just a little disoriented from everything that happened last night." Regina was still trying to make sense of things; she grabbed her brother's shoulder, "We should try to retrace our steps and head back to the road and maybe try to get some food from the diner." The two started trudging along back towards the direction which they thought they had come from.

After an hour of walking they came across a lake, but this was no ordinary lake. Along the shoreline laid thousands of rocks; some were blue, others yellow and a few were white. They looked as if they were mimicking the sky. The water was crystal clear and shimmered brightly in the sun. Just as the two children walked closer to the lake, there was a break in the surface and out raised an odd looking head followed by a long neck. This magnificent looking creature stunned Regina and Tyler; the hard skin of the creature had a light purple tinge to it and it seemed to just glide through the water. It swam towards a tree that had a branch hanging over the edge of the lake. The creature stretched out its neck to grab a low hanging apple from the tree. It had become perfectly clear to Regina and Tyler that they were no longer in the same place as they were twenty-four hours ago.

Tyler looked up at his sister, "This is so cool! Where do you think we are? Germany, Spain? No! This must be Florida!"

Regina was utterly confused, but she couldn't help, but be amazed with all the beauty surrounding them. "Tyler, I don't know where we are. We must be in some kind of dream. None of this could ever be possible!"

A whistling sound came from the direction of the apple tree. A brawny looking man, pushing a wheelbarrow, came from behind the tree whistling a delightful tune. The man was hauling a full case of moving dirt that would fling pieces of soil every few seconds. The man reached for an apple and the kart kept moving forward without the man pushing it from behind. It was as if an invisible ghost was pushing the kart along.

None of what was happening seemed to have phased Tyler; he went running towards the man, "Excuse me sir, can you tell us where we are?" Tyler looked up at the man with a naïve cheerful expression on his face; all while watching the wheelbarrow push ahead of the strange man.

He gave both of them a good onceover, noticing their tired faces and tattered clothes. The gleaming smile on his face quickly turned to sadness. He could tell that these children hadn't had a good meal in days if not ever; which was thoroughly true.

In a big booming voice, the man said, "This is the Kingdom of Nahtovia, of course." After a moment of thought, he looked troubled and asked, "Ya all didn't escape from Ka-Kazny did ya?" He waited, holding his breath until Tyler gave an answer.

"N-no sir." Said Tyler, not understanding why the man looked so concerned. "We are from-"

"Great!" breathing a sigh of relief as the man interrupted Tyler "Ya don't want anything to do with that place. It is very dangerous and there are many, uh unsavory people who live there." The giant man bent down to introduce himself, "Hi I am Reynold Porter, and ya two are?"

"Hi Reynold! I'm Tyler Baylon…" He said with such excitement, "…and this is my sister Regina."

Reynold stood back up, "Nice to meetya. You two look exhausted. Where are your par…" he paused, looking at their unnourished faces and realizing that the two children probably didn't have any parents. "How about ya come with me? My wife should be fixing up some food right now." He told his kart to follow and waved for the two of them to come along as well.

There was something about this man that seemed trustworthy. He had a sense of kindness in his eyes and a charming smile. He brushed some dirt off his salt and pepper hair and mustache. Regina didn't know why, but she felt like this man would become a big part of their lives. So the two children followed Reynold in the hopes to fill their bellies and find out more about this strange land called Nahtovia.

After a mile or so they came to the edge of a hill overlooking a busy town below. Businesses in cute little cottages lined the cobbled stoned streets. The roads were a hustle and bustle of people weaving in and out of the shops. It started to become clearer, as they walked into town, that there was some kind of holiday sale going on. Regina and Tyler overheard shoppers haggling with different street vendors. "There is no way this is worth twenty Figgles! I will give you ten."

"If I get all three of these dream catchers can we work out some kind of deal?" Said a large hairy man talking to a merchant.

A lady called out from another vendor, "Argent potion! Come get your Argent potion!"

"What does that do?" Regina asked.

Reynold said in a low mumble "It keeps werewolves from turning into, well ya know werewolves. She is going to have a tough time selling that today. There won't be a full moon for weeks!"

Tyler and Regina looked at each other and Regina whispered to Tyler "Werewolves?"

They both shrugged and continued to watch all the amazing things and people around them. There was a short man with long finger nails and big droopy ears, waiting in line for *Tommy's Green Pie and Toads*. There was a group of children, in matching gray and blue uniforms, skipping through the streets all caring bags that said *Potions, Potions and more Potions!* As they turned the corner Regina almost screamed when she saw a woman with bright red hair and tips that looked like they were on fire. Regina couldn't understand why no one was concerned that this lady's hair was on fire. It didn't even seem to faze the woman; she ran her fingers through her hair and nothing happened. There was something very strange about this place and Regina couldn't figure out if any of it was real or not.

They continued their way through the town and past several more bizarre people and places. The street lights started flickering on as they left the town and it wasn't long before they reached Reynold's house. The house was two stories tall and had a beautiful wrap around patio on the second floor. The age of the house was showing in the small chips of white paint on the outside and the few shingles missing from the roof, but the yellow lights shining through the windows gave it a warm and inviting feeling. Reynold had several crops on the side of his house, but none that Regina had ever seen before. They were all so colorful and swayed gently in the night breeze. Next to the plants was a light blue barn. The kart that had been following behind them this whole time made its way next to the barn and tilted its contents along the side. Then it moved to the front of the house and rested itself against the wall.

Reynold smiled and waved his hand in a dismissing matter towards the kart, "I will deal with that arbunk thief tomorrow."

They stepped through the gate of the white picketed fence and followed Reynold through the front door. Regina and Tyler raised their noses in the air; the smell coming from the kitchen was intoxicating and made their mouths water. Reynold called out to his wife "Ann, Annabel I'm home and I brought some…um…guest."

A very short woman, at least compared to Reynold, came to the front door to greet her husband. Her long blonde hair flowed from the breeze coming through the entrance. "Oh honey!" she said with a slight shiver in her voice. "Close the door that wind is chilly." She had a pink polka-dotted dress on, with a white frilly apron wrapped around the front of it, and it was marked up in what looked like strawberry jam. To Regina and Tyler, she had seemed the most normal out of all the people they had seen today. She smiled brightly at Regina and Tyler and extended out her hand for them to shake. In what sounded like a slightly southern accent she introduced herself. "Hello there! I'm Annabel Porter, but y'all can call me Ann. Where are y'all from?" Before Tyler could answer a loud bell went off in the kitchen. "Dinner is ready! Ya two are joining us for dinner aren't ya?" Regina could feel her stomach ache with hunger as the smell of the food wafted in the air. She didn't have to be asked twice to enjoy a good meal, even if it was coming from complete strangers.

They entered the kitchen and watched as plates full of food floated their way from the stove to the table. Annabel looked at her husband "Thank ya sweetie for setting the table."

The kitchen like the rest of the house was small, but had a quaint kind of charm to it. The shelf along the back wall had tiny elf figurines singing and dancing upon it. There were even a few that had tiny mugs in their hands swaying back and forth as they walked along the shelf. The walls were painted a light yellow and the kitchen windows had soft blue curtains on them.

The last plate had placed itself on the dining room table as they all sat down. Tyler began shoveling the food into his mouth as quickly as he possibly could. Regina was a little hesitant eating food that had just placed itself onto a plate that flew across the room on its own.

Regina looked up from her plate at Reynold and Annabel, who were staring lovingly into each other's eyes, she couldn't hold back her questions anymore and she needed to know how any of what happed was even true or possible. "Is this all part of a show or something? How is any of this even real? I mean plates don't float across the room and silverware doesn't just dance its way onto the table and how can a lady's hair be on fire, but it does not burn her? None of this makes any sense!"

Reynold gave Regina a strange look and then gave a deep bellowing laugh, "Hahaha ya must mean Laney, yea she always has some kind of extravagant look going on. As far as the table setting itself, it didn't I made it do that. I am a sorcerer and sorcerers like to do magic. Haven't ya ever seen magic before?" Tyler and Regina looked at one another and then back at Reynold and shook their heads in bewilderment. "Ya don't have magic where you come from?"

"Yip!" Annabel let out a small shout of excitement and her light brown eyes lit up. "Oh my goodness, ya two are like me. I grew up in Georgia; my husband forgets that not everyone has grown up in a realm full of magic!"

"Realm?" said Tyler in a confused voice "So this isn't Florida?"

"Florida? Oh heavens no, ya are in a place of magic, where creatures ya only read about in story tales live, and everythang is enchanted. It was a huge shock when I first heard about this place. Ya see, my grandparents are from this world. They fled when-" Ann paused looking around and leaned closer to whisper, "When the King's sister went mad and started terrorizen villages and torturing anyone who wasn't her supporter. She even took over the castle at one point." Ann walked towards the kitchen window and pointed out towards the distance. "If ya look just above that hill you can just barely see the point of the east tower. It has been empty for decades though."

With a mouth full of food Reynold added to Ann's story as she headed back to the table, "Yeaf bor firwenty free bears-" Reynold swallowed his food and continued, "Sorry, twenty-three years it has been empty of any royalty."

Ann sat back down and elbowed her husband in the ribs "Don't talk with your mouth full. Anyways, yes there are a few loyal members of the King who still occupy the castle, but it is a large castle to upkeep and most of the castle has become run down and creepy. It scares the living daylights out of most who go in there."

Regina had decided it was okay to eat after all and was taking the news of this new magical realm they were in quite well. It didn't seem to bother Tyler at all as he was listening excitedly and helping himself to the strawberry filled pie in front of him. Tyler, swallowing the large piece of pie he shoved in his mouth and asked "So what happened to the King and his sister?"

Annabel grabbing a slice of pie as well continued with her story "Well, that's the thang, no one is really sure what happened to the King and his family. The most common belief is that the Mad Sister killed King Amos and Queen Esme and their son too, Prince William. Another theory is that they are still in the castle and letten people believe they died, and some believe that the Foxguards had taken refuge in our world with the rest of those who fled. There are a few families who have since returned after the Mad Hysteria, that is what many are calling the Mad Sister's take over, but there are several families, like my grandparents and parents, who refuse to come back."

Regina had finished what was on her plate and was in awe with everything, "Sooo what do you believe? What do you think happened?"

Ann started gathering the empty plates. "Let me get that sweetheart." Reynold snapped his fingers and the dishes started dancing their way to the sink and began washing themselves. Tyler gave a small clap of excitement, and at that moment, the suds in the sink started to overflow and turn green. Reynold's eyes grew large as the suds came close to hitting the celling. "Woah! That has never happened before. I will fix this. Keep telling the story dear."

Ann looked back at her husband as he was trying to get things under control with the soap. "I like to believe the royal family were able to escape to our realm. Before you ask why, here is my theory. It took a lot of sorcerers to keep the Mad Sister and her loyal band of Carnagers from getting into the castle. It was a long, violent and blood-" Ann looked at Tyler playing innocently with some of the bubbles that had made their way to the table, "Let's just say not many people made it through that battle. When the Mad Sister made it to the front steps she only had a handful of her Carnagers left. After a few weeks had past the royal supporters were able to gather some more sorcerers to try and rush the castle they even got the help of a giant. It didn't take much effort for them to get into the castle and once inside they were shocked at what they saw. The Mad Sister was weak and alone; the Carnagers had left her there to die. Anyways, after some much thought and consideration the King's council had decided to let her heal and then banished her to our world, or I should say the non-magical realm."

"Didn't they worry she would come back or that she would use her powers to hurt people in our world?" Regina said in a scared voice.

"Since magic no longer exists in our world, sorcerers have no power. Plus, she was sent over weak and with very little power left in her." Regina sat there shocked, this whole time she had never knew any of this could be possible; she even pinched herself to make sure she wasn't dreaming.

"So if she is no longer here-" Regina continued, "then why are there so many families who are still afraid to come back?"

Reynold had finally contained the overflow of suds and had managed to get the dishes back to cleaning themselves. "It is the same reason why many people here are still cautious." Reynold said as he sat himself back down next to his wife, wiping off his wet hands on his shirt. "The same reason why I made sure ya two were not from Kazny, not that ya two look very threating anyways. The Mad Sister's followers were insane and many of them were pretty powerful. Most were sent off to prison, some were killed during the Mad Hysteria, but there are still several who have made refuge in Kazny where the Mad Sister ruled as their Duchess. It has been several years since any of them have tried to cause any problems, probably because they have all become very weak since the Mad Sister left. It was a funny thing really, when the Mad Sister was sent over to your world, it was as almost as if she took a lot of her followers' powers with her. But before that, anyone who was terrorized by her Carnagers felt the full brunt of their powers and many did not come out of it unscathed. So those who left probably still fear that they will be attacked by them if they were to return. There was so much betrayal and loss of life when the Mad Hysteria happened; I don't blame them for staying in your world." Reynold looked down and shook his head, "My parents were killed during the…I-I was only ten; luckily I still had my grandparents to take me in."

    Ann saw the somber look on his face and grabbed for her husband's hand and interlocked her small fingers with his thick long ones. She looked up and continued the story for him. "The Mad Sister did a lot of horrible thangs, she even performed one last dirty trick before she was banished; she put a curse on the Parting Trees, well at least on two of them." Ann answered Regina's question before she could even ask it. "The Parting Trees are the passage ways between the two realms. There are three trees to represent each one of the sorcerers who created this realm. There is the owl tree for Katherine Aves who ruled Broadcove. The second, is the Fox Tree which is for

Dravick Foxguard who ruled Nahtovia, but eventually took over Kazny as well and lastly is the wolf tree, which represents the original King of Kazny, Zeev Wolfhound. Anyone can use the Parting Trees to go across the realms, but ya are to use the tree that ya are most loyal to. For instance, if ya are truly loyal to Nahtovia then ya must use the Fox Tree, same with the Owl Tree and the Wolf Tree."

Tyler was starting to look sleepy sitting at the dinner table and with a big yawn he asked "What happens when you try using a tree that you are not loyal to?"

Reynold, who was looking a bit more cheerful now, responded, "Well they get hit with a scorching hot pain that brands them with an 'X' on the shoulder. They call it the traitor's mark."

"None of that matters now, however." Ann continued, "The Mad Sister put a curse on the Parting Trees before she was banished. She made it so no one could ever use the Fox Tree! She also put a freeze on the Wolf Tree that would only thaw upon her return. This all ties back into my theory. The Mad Sister wanted to be banished and knew the King's council wouldn't make the decision to kill her without the King's consent, it was still his sister after all. So that is why I think the Royal supporters found her weak and alone when they entered the castle. She needed time to create this powerful curse and it made her weak in the process."

Regina finished off the last bit of her pie; content and completely enthralled by the story. Regina thought for a moment, "Ann, how did you make it to this realm?"

"Since many families fled this world during the Mad Hysteria the people of this realm feared that those families would never be able to return or that they could never go to see them. So they asked the wise and powerful Grand Master for help. The curse on the Parting Trees was the strongest curse he had ever seen. He removed the loyalty charm from the Owl Tree, the only Parting Tree that had not been cursed." Ann gave off a long yawn, "My grand pappy has told me that story several times, along with many other amazin stories about this place, so naturally I came lookin for the last remaining Parting Tree."

Reynold threw his arm around his wife and gave her a kiss. "The Grand Master also did an anti-curse on the Fox Tree,

> 'Let the legend be told,
> that the true Foxguard heir,
> will save this tree's soul,
> but when the darkness once again flares,
> she will be the savior who will take the toll,
> to save our throne,
> so let it be known.

Many believe this to be a prophecy, that the next female heir to the Nahtovia throne, will come and save the kingdom and stop the Mad Sister once and for all."

Ann let out a big laugh, "Yeah, I am sure there are people out there waitin for this 'savior' to come through the Fox Tree, a Parting Tree that has not let anyone pass through since the curse, and she will save us all from the Mad Sister's return. Ha!"

Tyler suddenly became very alert; he leaned over to his sister and whispered, "But we came through the Fox Tree!"

Chapter 3 A New Home

BANG, BANG! Two loud knocks came from the front door. It was clear that Reynold and Ann were not expecting anyone, based on the surprised looks on their faces. Another loud knock, BANG! Followed by a muffled voice, "Reynold, Ann open up!" Ann and Reynold both seemed to have recognized the voice coming from the other side; they both quickly got up from their chairs and ran to the front door. A beautiful tall woman in a bright red blazer stood on the other side of the door. The wind coming in felt much colder than before and the dark haired mystery lady was shivering from head to toe. She was an attractive woman, maybe in her mid to late thirties, Regina thought, and her light colored green eyes really stood out amongst her dark complexion.

Ann waved her in, "Nita, come in! Come in! You look completely frozen. What are you doing out so late?"

Nita had clearly rushed over to the house as she was still trying to catch her breath. Nita's tight slicked back bun had become disheveled and a few hairs had strayed from her hair tie. She looked as if she had seen a ghost. She tried to speak between breaths "T-he, the pro-p-prophecy." She bent over to clench her side.

"What?" said Reynold, looking completely confused, "I don't understand what ya are trying to say?"

Nita had finally caught her breath. As she stood back up she had noticed the children for the first time. Ann had caught Nita's gaze and looked back towards Regina and Tyler, who were both peering around the corner of the kitchen. She elbowed Reynold who was still very unware of what was going on. He turned around, "Ah!" He began walking back to the kitchen, he looked over his shoulder gave a wink to Ann and said "I will be back in a minute."

He bent down to be eye level with Tyler. "Hey, um it is pretty late. Ummm, how about ya stay here tonight and we can sort things out in the morning?" Tyler let out a big yawn and nodded his head yes. "Great! Ya two can stay in the study across the way from our bedroom."

Reynold lead Regina and Tyler down the hall and to the left. He opened the door to a small room filled with what looked like a chemistry set. A table in the corner had a bunch of vases filled with all sorts of different colored liquids, some looked like they were in the process of turning colors, others were foaming to the brim and some even were boiling without a flame underneath. "Oops, it looks like Ann forgot to put away her brews. She is trying to teach herself." Reynold waved his hand over the brews and commanded them to put themselves away. Just like the dishes, the brews floated from the table and neatly put themselves back into a cupboard.

"All right, one of ya can sleep on the bed and I think we have-" Reynold was reaching under the bed for something. "Here we go, and one of you can use this sleeping bag." Regina and Tyler both cringed at the dusty, old sleeping bag. They watched Reynold as he opened it up. He gave it a few shakes before he laid it on the ground; a dust cloud hovered in the air momentarily before Reynold snapped his fingers and sent it flying out the window. Tyler gave the sleeping bag a double take; it was now laying atop a mattress about the same size as the other one in the room, he rubbed his eyes to make sure he was not seeing things. It was filled with lots of pillows and the blanket on top, that was the sleeping bag just a few seconds ago, looked clean and not old at all. Tyler climbed into the sleeping bag bed and cuddled a stuffed dragon he found hiding underneath the blanket.

Regina had a big smile on her face. She looked up at Reynold, "This will do."

"Perfect!" Reynold said with a chuckle. "If ya need anything at all, Ann and I's room is across the way. Have a good night." Reynold quietly closed the door behind him. Regina rushed to the door; she listened to his footsteps heading down the hall. She tried to listen to their conversation through the door, but could only hear whenever someone got overly excited. Regina jumped at a sound coming from behind her. She turned around quickly and watched her brother place a leg through the open window. "Tyler, what are you doing?"

"I want to hear what they are talking about too." He was already half way out the window and Regina was just as curious. So she grabbed the blanket off her bed and followed her brother out the window.

Regina wrapped the blanket around Tyler and herself as they made their way around the corner of the house towards the kitchen where the lights were still on. Luckily, the wind had died down so it wasn't as cold as it was before. They crouched down past the first window and made their way towards the second window next to the dining room table where Reynold, Ann and Nita were all siting.

Once they had reached the window Regina turned to her brother, "I will go around to the front and throw a rock or something at the front door. When I do that I want you to crack the window open slightly so we can hear what is going on." Regina snuck around to the front. She was searching the ground for something to throw when she heard footsteps coming up behind her. Before she could turn around to see who it was, she felt an arm around her waist and someone pulling her back.

Tyler whispered into the cold dark air "They are coming!" Regina and Tyler ducked behind the bewitched kart just in time. The front door swung open, Nita came out first followed by Reynold, who was now wearing a thick jacket and a scarf.

"We shouldn't be long." Nita was trying to comfort Ann, who looked very worried. "The Parting Trees are not that far."

"Hold on." Nita was noticeably shivering again. "Let me get you a coat." Ann rushed back inside.

"Why would the Fox Tree be glowing?" asked Reynold. "Do ya really think it is working again?"

Nita shook her head, "I'm not sure, but I told Thomas to guard it to make sure no one tries to go through it."

Ann came back with a thick pink coat. "Here this should keep you warm." She handed the coat to Nita, who gave her a thankful nod. Ann stood on her tippy toes to give Reynold a good-bye kiss. "Please be safe." Reynold gave Ann a reassuring smile before he and Nita rushed out into the cold dark night. Regina grabbed her brother and knew this was their cue to head back to the room.

Regina gave Tyler a boost through the window and then climbed through herself. She quietly shut the window behind her, crawled into bed and pulled the covers up to her chin. She watched her brother cuddle with the stuffed dragon again as he quickly went into a deep sleep.

Regina's head was swimming with the day's events. She closed her eyes hoping sleep would come to her soon.

***

    Regina was standing in a long dark hallway that seemed endless. She ran forward searching for the end of it. Lights flickered above her with every step she took. She ran for what seemed like miles. Regina stopped dead in her tracks; she heard a faint sound coming from behind her. She listened closely as the sound grew louder and louder. Her heart began to race, there was something familiar about the sound. It was almost as if, as if it were nails scratching along the walls. Regina could feel the panic and fear raising within herself. A lump formed her throat and her hands became shaky. She was frozen in place as the scratching came closer and closer; her legs felt like they were sinking in quick sand. Lady Dumontet's figure was becoming visible under the flickering lights. Regina found her legs and began to run down the hall again. After a few feet, the scratching stopped. It was eerily quiet. Regina quickly turned around, but there was no one there. Confusion swept over her; there was no way she had just disappeared. Determined to still put some separation between her and the direction where she thought Lady Dumontet was coming from, Regina continued running down the hall. The end of the hall was finally coming into sight… she then realized she was no longer in the hall, but back in the woods where Tyler and she were running from the police and Lady Dumontet. Regina saw the tree that Tyler was hiding in and ran as quickly as she could towards it. She reached out for the hole in the tree, she looked behind her and then back towards the tree only to find Lady Dumontet in her way. Dumontet grabbed Regina…

    Regina awoke, kicking and punching the air. She sat up straight, breathing heavily, trying to focus on the strange room in front of her. Regina's memory came back to her, still panting hard, she looked at the bed where her brother fell asleep and found it empty. Regina swiftly removed the sheets from atop of her and rushed for the door. She reached for the handle when she heard laughter coming from the other side. It was Tyler and Ann laughing together, about who knows what. Regina sat back down on the bed and ran her fingers through her hair. Her dream felt way too real. She took a few deep breaths and reminded herself that she was no longer living with Lady Dumontet, she wasn't even in the same realm as her.

Regina shook her head trying to clear her thoughts. She took another deep breath, but this time she inhaled a wonderful smell that told her breakfast was being made. Her tummy gave a small grumble in reaction to the smell and Regina felt it was not worth dwelling on her dream anymore. She jumped off the bed and decided to join the others in hopes of enjoying another tasty meal.

Regina walked into the kitchen wafting in more of the delicious smell coming from the stove. A spatula was turning over bacon frying in a pan while eggs were cracking themselves into a bowl by the stove. She then turned her attention to her brother and Ann standing over something in the middle of the kitchen.

"Okay, really concentrate." Ann said in an excited voice. "Ya want to be precise. Think about what ya want to do, take aim and let your hands do all the work."

Regina walked closer to get a better look at what Tyler and Ann were doing. They were standing over one of the elf figurines that Regina saw dancing on the shelves from last night. The elf was looking very disgruntled and a little tired from last night's activities.

She watched her brother standing over the elf with a very concentrated look on his face. He stretched his arm out, his hand was tight in a fist; he opened his hand and quickly wiggled one finger at a time and closed his hand again. The elf's legs began jerking left and right and then he broke out into a jig. Tyler and Ann clapped their hands in a rhythmic pace as the elf sloppily danced across the kitchen floor. His legs and arms were moving gleefully, but the disgruntle look on his face remained. Tyler repeated the hand motion he did before and the elf stopped dancing.

"Tyler, did you just do magic?" Regina stepped in closer. "Wow! That is amazing!"

Ann and Tyler looked up at Regina with huge smiles on their faces. The elf took this opportunity to scurry away and made his way back up onto the kitchen shelves.

"Tyler is doing exceptionally well." Ann ruffled Tyler's hair, "It took me a couple of days to get that one down. I have been tryin to teach myself magic ever since I came to this realm; Reynold has been a big help as well."

"So can anyone use magic?"

"Well, I think so? I mean, everyone here can do magic, but then again they all come from magical families. I have not met anyone who can do magic and not have ties to this realm. I-uh-I am not sure." Ann paced around the kitchen scratching her head, "Wait! What about your family are they from this realm?"

Regina and Tyler looked at each other, finally faced with the question that would have inevitably come up. Regina, wishing it was not now that she would have to explain the tragic death of her parents and the horrible living situation her and her brother just escaped from two nights ago, she took a deep breath and started to explain everything to Ann.

"Our parents died in a car accident four years ago." Regina leaned against the wall and looked at the ground. She began fidgeting with her fingers before she continued her story." We were moving for the second time that year; the car was fully packed with our stuff and ready to go. It started to drizzle as we climbed into the car with the last of our things. The further we drove away from the house the harder the rain came down. The sky turned black and we couldn't even see ten feet in front of us. Dad knew there was a small café a few miles ahead and was planning to wait it out there for a while in hopes that the rain would pass. It was only a few moments after he had said this that the car jerked hard to the right, like something had hit us on the side. Our dad was able to keep us on the road, but something hit us again. That is when the car swerved off the road and down the side of a hill." Regina took a minute to keep herself from crying.

"The next thing I remember is waking up in a hospital bed. An older woman, whom I had never seen before, claimed to be a distant relative of my dad and she now had custody over me and my brother. She took us to her home and took care of us while we were still healing from the accident. She had seemed nice enough, but it wasn't until we got better that things started to turn south. She wouldn't let us out of the house and well it was not long before her true self came to the surface." Regina explained to Ann how life was like living with Lady Dumontet for the last four years and how they had ran away. Regina omitted the part about coming through The Fox Tree; she still was not sure what it would mean if they were the ones who had broken the Mad Sister's curse.

"So that is how we escaped from Lady Dumontet and how we ended up here." Reynold had come around the corner with tears in his eyes, he had been apparently listening to Regina's story the whole time. Ann had a handkerchief to her face, dabbing at the tears rolling down to her chin. Reynold looked at his wife and nodded his head which Ann had done in return. He walked towards Regina and crouched down to grab her hands. His huge hands had engulfed hers.

"We would be honored if ya two lived with us."

Ann placed her hand on Reynold's shoulder "We understand if y'all need time to think about it. We know that ya don't know us, but we promise we will never do anything to hurt ya."

Tyler ran towards Ann and threw his arms around her waist. It was clear to Regina that Tyler had obviously made up his mind already. Tyler looked up to his sister awaiting her response. All eyes were on her. Regina knew that Ann and Reynold, who were offering up their home, were kind and wonderful people who would be true to their promise, but she still found herself hesitating. She looked again into her brother's eyes and saw how relaxed and safe he felt here.

It was quiet, but Regina gave an audible "Okay." Reynold stood up and threw his arms around her. Regina, who was not expecting the hug and didn't really care for personal contact, had her arms dangling down her sides. Reynold gave her a big squeeze and was going to let go when he found himself being pulled back in. Regina had decided she was not ready for the hug to be over and threw her arms around him. Ann and Tyler came over and they all had one big group hug.

They all sat down to enjoy the breakfast that had been making itself in the background. Reynold was overflowing his plate with heaps of bacon. "How about I take ya on a tour of your new home after breakfast and maybe go into town for a few supplies. Sound good?"

Regina and Tyler both nodded their heads in excitement. Regina looked around the table and watched her new family laugh and fill their bellies with delicious food. Regina couldn't remember the last time she was this happy. She dug into her food wishing that this feeling would never end.

Chapter 4 Sparks of Magic

After breakfast Reynold gave them a tour of the rest of the house. "Well ya are already familiar with our kitchen and the study, let me show ya the living room."

Reynold lead them down the same hallway that took them to the study, except he was heading the opposite direction, towards the front door. Just to the right of the front door was the stairs and on the left was the living room. The large windows brought a lot of light into what otherwise would be considered a dull and rather untouched room. There was a small brown sofa against the wall and a few chairs in the far corner of the room. Next to the chairs Regina swore there was a television on top of a coffee table, but there was something different about it. Tyler noticed it too. "You have televisions in this realm?"

Reynold let out a small chuckle, "No it is not a television. Ann told me about those things. This is called a Deception Projection, my grandparents got this during the gargoyle feud. If an intruder comes into the house, the DP gives the appearance to the intruder that the home is torn up and abandoned. The intruder than leaves realizing that there is nothing there for them."

They moved on from the living room and made their way towards the stairs. There were several pictures hanging on the wall. A few were of Ann and Reynold, but the others looked like they were pictures of Reynold's parents and grandparents. Reynold greatly resembled his father and his grandfather. Both were very tall and burly men who towered over their wives. Reynold's father even seemed to have had salt and pepper hair at a young age. His parents looked young and could not have been any older than twenty-five in the picture. They looked like a happy family; a young Reynold Porter was sitting on his father's lap with a huge grin across his face. His mother and father were holding hands and laughing as if Reynold had just done something funny.

Reynold noticed Regina starring at the picture. "I had just caught a fropper and my parents were laughing at how pleased I was with myself. Fropper are really hard to catch." Sure enough, Regina looked at the picture again and noticed a small yellow creature that greatly resembled a frog with horned scales all along its back.

They reached the last step of the stairs, Reynold pointed to the two rooms to the right. "Those are our two spare bedrooms; I will let ya two decide who gets what room." Reynold pointed to another door. "There is a bathroom through there. And in this room…" He led them to the last remaining room. He opened the door with such an excited look on his face. "…is our library." Regina had never seen so many books in her life. "My parents and grandparents left me a lot of money when they passed. So

Ann and I decided to build this big library and fill the shelves with as many books as we could possibly find."

Almost every inch of the walls were covered with bookshelves that ranged from the floor all the way to the ceiling and each one was completely filled with books. There were several comfortable looking reading chairs and a few built-in reading nooks placed against a long window. But the best part of the room was the French doors that opened up to the wrap around patio that overlooked the castle. Regina was now understanding why the living room was untouched; in her eyes, this room was absolutely perfect.

"We even have several books from your realm. I really like the one with the man and the whale." Reynold looked off for a moment trying to remember the name of the book. "Anyways, ya can use this room as much as ya want."

Regina walked over to one of the reading nooks and ran her fingers along the soft pillow that was leaning against the window. Regina picked up the pillow and saw from behind it through the window a dark shadowy figure. The window was smudge, but she clearly saw something disappear into the colorful plants. She let out an audible gasp.

Reynold ran towards her, "What is it?"

"I don't know. It was dark and…"

"Ugh, it must be that darn arbunk, trying to steal my crops again. Come on, let's see if we can catch it before it gets away. Good eye Regina!"

Regina looked back at the window again and shivered; whatever it was down there just gave her the heebie jeebies.

They all raced down stairs and outside towards the crops. Reynold bent down next to the enchanted kart and scooped up a handful of the dirt that the kart was hauling yesterday. "Tyler grab the dirt and start spreading it through the middle. Regina, ya and I will spread the dirt along the edges of the crops. Arbunks are not that big but they have a nasty bite so keep a good look out. Regina we have to be quick. Spread lightly and I will meet ya on the other side."

Regina was spreading the dirt as quickly as she could all the while trying to keep an eye on her brother. She had no idea what an arbunk was, but she knew what she saw wasn't one. Regina let the reddish dirt slip through her fingers. She glanced up every few steps to see if she could spot the dark figure in the crops, however, the plants were thick and bushy. About halfway down the line she was able to catch a glimpse of her brother. She noticed the plants shook above where he was standing, but they were also moving a little further back from Tyler's position.

"Tyler, have you see anything?" Regina shouted to her brother.

"Uh, nothing yet." He shouted back.

Regina looked at the spot again where the plants had been moving, but they were still now. She quickly scanned the plot, but only saw movement above her brother. Regina rounded the final corner of the plot; Tyler stepped out of the middle and Reynold had just rounded his corner of the plot. Regina and Reynold continued to spread their dirt until they met up in the middle where Tyler was standing.

Reynold dusted off his hands. "The dirt is meant to grab the arbunk and keep it in place. I think we surrounded the crops before it was able to escape. So if we search through the crops we should be able to find it before the dirt wears off." Reynold walked into the plot first. "Remember, the arbunk will bite so don't get close if ya see it first."

Reynold instructed them to spread out and search. It was not long before Tyler shouted from the middle of the field, "I think I found it!"

Regina rushed to meet Tyler. When she found him he was holding a fluffy black creature no bigger than a football. It had large doughy eyes and white and brown stripes across its back. As Regina stepped closer to her brother she could hear a slight purring sound from the arbunk. Tyler looked just as confused as Regina, "This is an arbunk? This is what was stealing your crops?"

Reynold yelled out to Tyler from around the corner, "Don't be fooled by their cuddly looks, arbunks are mean and..." Reynold stepped into view as the arbunk began nestling into Tyler's arms, "Whoa, is th- is that thing purring?"

Tyler put the arbunk down so he and his sister could pet it. Tyler put his face close to the arbunk's face. "No Tyler! Don't put your face nex-" The arbunk began licking Tyler's nose. Reynold scratched the top of his head. "Wha- I, it can't, I have never seen one of these things ever be this nice. I can't believe it."

The arbunk began walking towards Reynold, who started backing away in fear. It began to hiss and growl at Reynold. "Daisy, no! Be nice." Tyler commanded the arbunk to sit, which it did obligingly.

"Daisy?" Reynold said in a confused tone.

"Yeah I decided to call her Daisy"

"Uh, Tyler, I'm not sure ya should be naming the animal." Reynold was holding a defensive pose.

"Oh, she seems to like me though."

Regina saw the concerned look on Reynold's face, "Tyler, I don't think it is a good idea for you to keep, uh, Daisy as a pet." Tyler expression went from complete excitement to a very somber look.

"But why not? She listens to me and I promise to take great care of her."

"Tyler you can't kee-"

Reynold interrupted before Regina finished her sentence. "Alright, ya can keep Daisy. Maybe we can use her to keep other arbunks away from the crops."

A voice from the distance called out. "Reynold, is that you in the crops."

"Yeah, Nita it's me." All three of them emerged from the crops; with Tyler still holding Daisy in his arms.

"Are you cradling an arbunk?" Nita had the same confused and frightened look on her face that Reynold had a few moments ago.

"Uh don't ask." said Reynold. "Nita I would like ya to meet Regina and Tyler Baylon. Nita runs everything in Nahtovia."

Regina noticed Nita looked much more put together than the last time she had saw her. There was not a single hair out of place and her bun was tightly wound. Nita bent down to shake Tyler's hand, "How do you do?" And she repeated the gesture to Regina, but Regina felt like Nita's handshake with her lingered just a little longer than she had with Tyler's. "I'm sure you two remember my intrusion last night. Again, Reynold sorry to barge in on you like that."

Reynold let out a chuckle, "No problem at all Nita."

"I actually came by to give you an update on the, uh, on the situation." Nita's eyes kept darting to the side, gesturing to Reynold she wanted to speak to him in private.

"Right. Why don't ya two play with, uh, your new friend Daisy, while I just…" Reynold's voice faded off as he moved closer towards Nita. Regina was still very curious about the matter with the Fox Tree and so was Tyler. Fortunately for them, Nita and Reynold were not as quiet as they thought they were being.

"So did ya figure out how to test the tree?" Reynold asked Nita.

"Well, sort of…" Nita began to fidget with her hands.

"What do ya mean sorta?"

"As you know, no one has even dared to touch The Fox Tree ever since Oliver tried to use it several years ago."

"Yea of course. That poor kid, he still has a limp."

"Right. So after you had left last night Thomas and I kept trying different things, but kept coming up short. That is, until Oliver showed up."

Reynold had a stunned look on his face. "No, he didn't."

"He did. Apparently, word had already spread that the Fox Tree was glowing and Oliver so happened to be at Eddie's Tavern when the word reached him. I guess he downed a few drinks before he made his way over to the tree. By then a crowd had gathered; I began letting everyone know about the situation when Oliver decided to sneak up behind me and the crowd. He started to crawl into the tree. Before anyone had realized what was going on, it was already too late. Thomas ran to the tree and poof he was gone. Needless to say, we were all shocked and frightened that it might have been a one way trip for poor Oliver, if you know what I mean. After several minutes went by, we all kind of lost hope. Then all of a sudden, Oliver comes stumbling out of the tree and says 'sorry everyone, but I wanted to have proof that I had gone through to the other side.' He had a rock in his hand."

"How did that prove anything?"

"It didn't, but we all saw him disappear and come back through. The Fox Tree works Reynold! I even went through myself. It really works!"

"That is amazing Nita, but why does the tree work now?"

"Well if the prophecy is correct that means the next female heir of Nahtovia has arrived." Nita looked very serious now. "Reynold, I had a few people ask around to see if they noticed any new faces in the area, but no one has seen anyone new except for..."

Nita's voice got really quiet and neither Tyler nor Regina could hear what she had said, but Regina didn't need to hear, she already knew that she had meant them.

Reynold walked back towards Regina and Tyler as Nita waved goodbye to all of them. "Alright are ya ready to head into town? I'll show ya the barn later."

The three of them headed off with Tyler's new friend following closely behind. "No Daisy, stay here." Said Tyler.

"Can ya also tell Daisy not to eat my crops?" Reynold shook his head. "We just have a few things to pick up. Plus, we can get some pie from Tommy's!"

The sounds of people hustling and bustling filled the air as they stepped into town. Reynold took them back down the street that they had come through only just yesterday. Regina took note of the street sign: Tuttle Road. She looked at the several shops that lined the cobbled stone road and each one of them had similar flyers up on their windows:

COME *DISCOVER* HOW LOW OUR PRICES GO!

***FIND* GREAT DEALS FOR THAT SPECIAL SORCERER IN YOUR LIFE!**

WE HAVE GIFTS FOR SORCERS, GLINTS, GARGOYLES, WEREWOLVES AND MUCH, MUCH MORE!

A large shop for animals had a sign on their window too:

EVEN YOUR PETS LIKE GREAT DEALS TOO!

Reynold pointed to the pet shop "We need to go into Ellie's Pet Emporium. She will have everything that we need." Out of all the shops that they had passed Ellie's Pet Emporium was by far the most crowded. A chime went off as they walked through the doors. Regina and Tyler walked through the shop looking at the different kinds of animals that were there; very few in which they had recognized. Children ran from one station to the next yelling at their mothers or fathers to come look. Regina walked towards a nearly empty station. A red bushy tailed fox was frolicking along the fence. A small pig-tailed girl came running up behind Regina to get a better look.

"Oh what is it? What is it?" The little girl came into view of the fox. "Oh, darn. It is just a red fox." With her head down, the pig-tailed girl walked away with such a disappointed look on her face.

A lady's voice came from behind Regina. "No one ever appreciates the cunning beauty of the red fox." The strange lady stepped closer to the station next to Regina. She was an older lady with several wrinkles in her face, but she had a strong look to her; like she could take on Reynold if she had to. The square glasses on her face accentuated her light brown eyes. "D'you want to hold her? She is very friendly." The lady reached down and handed the fox to Regina. It was amazing to have such a beautiful creature like this in her arms. In Regina's world a fox would never be this friendly and if someone was in the presence of one they wouldn't shrug it off as if it was your everyday run of the mill pet.

Regina gently stroked the fox and watched her roll onto her back and present her belly. "She really likes you; they don't usually expose their stomachs like that." Regina rubbed the fox's belly as the lady handed her a rope. "Here, she loves to play with this." Regina grabbed the rope and played tug of war with the fox. Regina noticed something had caught the lady's eye. She glanced towards the front and made her way over. Regina looked over her shoulder, Reynold and the lady seemed to be having a secretive conversation. They glanced around to make sure no one was looking and they made their way into the back room of the store.

Tyler joined his sister, "Where did Reynold go?" The fox ran over to Tyler and started rubbing herself against his legs.

"I saw him go in the back with some lady that works here. They looked like they were trying to not be overheard."

"Reg, we should tell them that we came through the..." Tyler lowered his voice to a whisper. "You know, through the Fox Tree."

"Did you just say Fox Tree?" A boy, about the same age as Tyler, with short brown hair and hazel eyes started talking to the two of them. "So I take it you heard about the tree working again. It is so crazy after all these years it finally works again. My mom thinks that the Mad Sister finally died on the other side and that is why the tree is working." Regina began to say something but was interrupted by the kid again. "But I think she is not dead and the savior came through. What do you think?" This time Tyler went to answer, but was again interrupted by the boy. "I think we should go on the other side and look for the Mad Sister. She shouldn't be too hard to find based off the pictures I have seen. Yuck!" The boy stuck out his tongue and made a sour face. He took another breath to keep talking, but didn't have the chance to get a word out. An older boy, whom the younger one looked like, placed his hand on the younger boy's shoulder.

"Sorry about my brother Lars. He can be rather talkative, especially if he is hopped up on sugar flies."

Lars pulled a gummy candy shaped like a fly from a bag and lifted it up to offer to Regina and Tyler. "Wants some?" The sugar fly's wings were flapping and it seemed like it was trying to escape. Regina tried not to look disgusted and shook her head no, but Tyler seemed to have no problem with it. He took the sugar fly from Lars and popped it in his mouth.

The elder brother reached out with his hand. "Hi I'm Gramm." Gramm shook Tyler's hand and then Regina's. His hair was a darker brown compared to his brother and his eyes were more green than brown. He was tall and a little lanky as if he was still growing into his own body.

"This is my brother Tyler and I'm Regina."

Reynold walked up from behind them with a large sack slung over his shoulder. "I see ya met the Wyatt brothers. They live next door to Ann and me, oh I guess now, next to ya two as well." Gramm gave Reynold a confused look. "They are new to this realm and they are staying with us." When Lars and Gramm heard Reynold say "new to this realm" both of their eyes got big. Luckily, Regina and Tyler were the only ones to notice.

Reynold shifted the large bag to his other shoulder, "My hankering for a pie is getting pretty strong. Let's head out shall we?" The older lady that Reynold was talking to, picked up the fox and put her back in her station. Reynold waved bye to her. "See ya Ellie." Ellie, Lars and Gramm stared as they left the store and Regina had a particular feeling that they were mostly staring at her.

"Ellie? Is she the same Ellie that owns the store?" Regina asked Reynold.

"Actually, Ellie's grandmother, Ellie, is the one who opened the store many years ago." Reynold jerked to the left to let through a bunch of kids chasing one another. "Ellie inherited the store and her grandmother's name."

Regina turned her attention to the kids chasing each other as they continued their way down the street. A few kids up ahead were controlling paper airplanes with their magic. One plane was colored red and was doing loops around another. Regina sighed and longed for the life she knew before her parents died and before she had Lady Dumontet as their guardian. Regina had high hopes for this new life and though things finally seemed to be getting better, she had this new found weight pressing down on her chest.

"*Could it really be true?*" Regina thought, "*Am I this so called savior? The next heir to the Nahtovia throne? And how am I going to beat the Mad Sister?*"

They stopped at Tommy's Green Pie and Toads where they met up with Ann. She was carrying a few bags and had already placed an order for two pies to go. Reynold gave her a kiss and tried to help her out with the bags she was carrying.

"Thank you sweetheart, but I can carry them." She threw him a suspicious look.

"I'm just trying to help."

Ann scoffed, "No, ya are just tryin to see what I got ya for Founders' Day."

"Me? Never." As innocent as Reynold tried to act, it was not fooling anyone.

"Here." Ann handed him a bag. "This one does not have anythin in it for ya." Reynold looked in the bag that had Potions, Potions and More Potions labeled on the outside and saw more brewing potions for Ann.

"What's Founders' Day?" asked Regina.

"Every year on June 26th we celebrate the three creators or 'Founders' of this realm. It used to be a tradition where all three Kingdoms got together and celebrated, but with the Mad Sister and all the craziness…" Ann began to trail off. "Well each kingdom celebrates on their own now. So on the anniversary in which this realm was created we like to celebrate with lots and lots of magic."

Reynold pointed to Ann's bags "Somewhere along the way, it became a day to buy presents to spoil your loved ones."

"Cool! Two Christmases! Shouted Tyler.

Reynold laughed "Yeah basically."

"Here are the two pies you ordered sir." A man in a green shirt with a toad on it handed Reynold the pies and they all headed out.

On the way back to the house, Ann was showing Tyler how to fly a paper airplane. Regina watched her brother control the plane with his hands. It was hovering ever so gently above them. Every now and again it seemed to falter and drop, but Ann would help Tyler before the plane ever hit the ground. Ann called Regina over. "Why don't ya give it a try."

Regina felt ecstatic. She had wanted to attempt to do some magic earlier after watching her brother make the shelf elf dance. Ann handed Regina the paper airplane. "So what ya wanna do is hold the plane with your hands flat. Concentrate on levitatin the plane and then use your hands to control it. Got it?"

Regina did exactly what Ann had said. She held the plane with her hands flat and concentrated real hard, but nothing happened. Regina repositioned the plane in her hands and tried again. Still nothing.

"Umm, why don't ya try to close your eyes and really concentrate this time?" Ann patted Regina on the shoulder.

Regina closed her eyes and really tried hard to think about the plane levitating before her. She opened her eyes and saw that the plane was slowly lifting from her hands. It was barley floating but the plane was now in the air. Reynold smiled and was about to say something when all of a sudden a few bright sparks came from the tips of Regina's fingers and the plane dropped to the ground.

"I've never seen that before." Ann glared at her husband for what he had said. "I-I mean, it happens. Pssh, no big deal." The rest of their walk to the house was done in silence.

When they arrived at the Porters' home, Nita was standing at the front door. Her arms were crossed and she seemed to be flustered. Ann looked very concerned. "Uh, why don't y'all help out Reynold while I put these bags away and I start making dinner?"

Ann grabbed the bag of potions and pies from Reynold and hurried off towards Nita. Regina, Tyler and Reynold made their way to the barn. Regina looked back to see what was going on; Ann had grabbed Nita by the arm and shoved her into the house. Nita looked completely stunned by this. Muffled shouting ensued.

"Are they going to be alright?" asked Regina.

Reynold nervously glanced over his shoulder. "Yea, I'm sure everything will be fine."

They reached a crate attached to a harness outside of the barn. Reynold dropped the large bag that he got from Ellie's onto the crate. Regina began to read the description on the bag when she heard Ann's voice get really loud "Nita ya need to back off!"

Reynold, still looking nervous looked towards the direction of Ann's voice. As he did this, he noticed the Wyatt brothers walking by. Reynold waved them over. "Ya two mind giving us a hand?" The Wyatt brothers gladly walked over to help. "I need to load up a few tools and the kart onto the crate and then raise the crate to the second level of the barn to store it away." Everyone pitched in and loaded the crate. "All right that should do for now. I don't want to overload the harness. Gramm can ya grab the other rope and help me pull the crate up to the top? Regina he can probably use your help."

Gramm and Regina walked over to the other rope. "So how do you like it here? I mean in this realm."

Regina watched her brother and Lars play with Daisy. She had a big smile on her face, she knew her brother was very happy, in fact, this was the happiest they had ever been in a very long time. "We really like it here. I'm excited to learn more about this place."

Reynold, Gramm and Regina began pulling on the rope. Regina could still hear Ann and Nita arguing inside the house.

"So how old are you? I just turned sixteen a few months ago." Gramm said brushing the hair from his face with one hand and pulling the rope with the other.

"Oh, I turn sixteen next month." Regina watched the crate rise slowly to the halfway point. She noticed that the rope on Reynold's side was starting to fray.

"Hey Reynold, we should stop. Your rope is star-"

Regina was interrupted by an angry Nita storming out of the house. She was quickly making her way towards Reynold and Ann was following closely behind.

"What's that?" Reynold's head jerked towards Nita. A nervous crinkle formed on his forehead and he turned back towards the crate. "Just keep pulling." Reynold and Gramm gave another tug to the ropes. The crate was very high now and Regina watched Reynold's rope fray some more.

"Reynold stop!" Regina shouted.

Nita was now next to Reynold and the three of them began to argue.

"We need to know which tree they came from!"

"NITA! Not now!" Reynold yelled back.

Reynold and Gramm pulled on the ropes again not noticing that the rope was unweaving itself. Regina rushed over to Reynold.

"Why not?"

45

"There just kids Nita. Besides it doesn't look like she can even do magic." Ann responded trying to diffuse the situation.

Regina was about to push her way through when she heard a yelp coming from the direction of Tyler and Lars. Lars had accidently stepped on Daisy's tail and now the arbunk was running towards the barn. Regina turned again to yell at the arguing adults.

Reynold and Gramm gave one final tug to the ropes. Tyler was running after Daisy towards the barn, directly under the crate. The rope snapped and Tyler was directly under it now.

"Tyler!" Regina closed her eyes and shouted for her brother. She stood there silent waiting for the crash, waiting for the cries of pain. She waited, but nothing happened. She slowly opened her eyes afraid of what she would see.

Still hovering in the air was the crate and all of its contents. Regina looked around and noticed that everyone was staring, but not at the crate or at Tyler, no, they were all staring at her. Regina followed the white jet of light that was holding up the crate back down towards the source of it. Regina was the one who was controlling the crate; she was the one who had saved her brother. Regina wasn't sure how, but she slowly pushed the crate through the open window of the barn on the second level.

Once the crate was securely placed into the barn, Regina turned back around towards Reynold, "The rope was fraying." Regina took a breath, her face grew red and flushed, her entire body clenched. She directed her attention to Nita, "And yes, we came through the Fox Tree!"

Chapter 5 Fox Squad

A full minute went by before anyone said anything. Tyler grabbed Daisy and stood by his sister. Ann was the first person to snap out of her shock. She walked towards Regina and opened her mouth to speak. Regina prepared herself for the worst. She figured she and her brother would have to pack their stuff and leave. Regina stared at Ann and waited for the backlash to unleash. "Regina, I-I can't believe it. Ya-ya… " Regina looked for the anger in Ann's eyes, but it wasn't there. "Ya just did some pretty powerful magic right now. I have never seen anythin like that in such a young person." Regina felt the sense of relief wash over her. "I guess the prophecy was right. Ya will be the one to defeat the Mad Sister!" Regina's sense of relief was now replaced with overwhelming pressure.

"I'm not even sure how I did that. I mean, my eyes were closed. I wasn't even looking at what I was doing. Ann, you watched me fail at controlling the paper airplane. I couldn't even get it to float. How am I- there is no way I can beat the Mad Sister."

Ann looked to Nita and Reynold for support. Reynold still looked shocked and Nita appeared to be searching the pockets of her red blazer. Nita found what she was looking for and made her way over to Ann and Regina.

"Take this." Nita handed Regina a pen. "After what I just saw, you should have no problem making this float."

Regina grabbed the pen and placed it flat on her hand like she had done with the paper airplane. She stared and concentrated as hard as she could, but nothing was happening. She tried closing her eyes and still nothing. The pen didn't move an inch and sparks didn't even bother coming from her fingertips this time.

"This isn't going to work." Regina handed the pen back to Nita and walked away. She stopped halfway towards the house. "I don't know what you expect of me, but I am not this Kingdom or any Kingdom's savior." She turned back on her heel and went inside.

Regina felt it was best to try and burry her thoughts into a book. She grabbed a random book off one of the shelves, made herself comfortable in one of the reading nooks and pretended like she could concentrate on what she was reading. The cover of the book had a scary looking gray and black wolf on it with its hair standing on end, its sharp teeth bared and ready to strike. The title across the book read *How to Tell If You Are a Werewolf*.

Regina could feel the tears forming in her eyes. She had absolutely no idea how she saved Tyler and where all that power came from. She felt scared and alone. She thought to herself *"Two days in this strange new world and already all the joy and fun has been sucked out of it and it has been replaced with this overwhelming sense of responsibility to save these people from a very powerful psycho."* Regina was left alone to sort out these very complicated thoughts racing through her head.

An hour later, the door finally opened to the library. Regina was expecting Ann or Reynold to come through the door, but she was very pleasantly surprised to see her brothers face peak through.

"Thanks for saving me." Tyler looked abashed as he made his way towards his sister. "Are you okay?"

"Yeah, Tyler I'm okay."

"Good. So Nita, Ann and Reynold were talking and they figured out how to get you fully up to speed with your magic."

"No, Tyler. I'm not going to do this; I can't do this. I don't know magic and I don't know how to be a savior."

"But you already are."

Regina turned away from her brother and stared out the window "Tyler, stop."

"What you did out there, what you did to get us here and away from Lady Dumontet and what you have been doing ever since I was born was you being you. There have been so many times that you could have just walked away and times where you would have been better off doing so, but you don't. You have never turned away from a fight and just because you have always fought for me doesn't mean you can't do it for everyone else."

"But we don't even know if any of this is true. That would mean mom and dad were royalty, that would mean we are royalty and that is-that is insane! That's what it is!"

"You…" Tyler grabbed his sister's hand. "You have always been my savior."

Regina looked away from the window and back to her brother; the tears in her eyes were on the verge of spilling over. "I'm scared and I don't think saviors or heroes are supposed to be scared."

Ann, who had been listening to their conversation the whole time, came out from behind the corner and made her way over to Regina and Tyler. She too had tears in her eyes, but she was smiling. "I would be worried if ya weren't a little bit scared. Being scared just means you have somethin to live for; somethin to fight for. I knew the moment ya walked through that door that you were a force to be reckoned with. So prove your brother and myself right." Ann grabbed Regina's hand and looked her square in the eye, "Ya won't have to do this alone."

Regina looked out the window once more. Her head was swimming but everything else seemed to be moving slowly. The plants outside were swaying ever so gently in the breeze. The different colors of the plants meshed together and pulled apart with the wind. Lars was still outside playing with Daisy, chasing each other around the barn. Reynold placed a tall ladder to the window of the barn where Regina had guided the crate to earlier. He reached the top of the ladder and climbed through the window. Nita and Gramm were guiding a few tools up with their magic to Reynold. He grabbed the tools to fix up the rig after the rope on the crate snapped. He looked up after the last twist of the wrench and made eye contact with Regina. He gave her a kind smile. Regina returned the smile and knew that these people who took her in were worth fighting for.

Regina turned back to Ann and Tyler, "Okay, let's do this!"

Lars and Gramm went home after checking in on Regina. After their goodbyes, the five people left, gathered around the kitchen table to discuss a plan. On one side of the table Ann was helping Tyler with his magic; practicing on the paper airplane. On the left side of Tyler was Reynold, who seemed to be carving a bear out of a small piece of wood. Regina was sitting on the other side of the table trying to make one of the shelf elves dance in front of her, but nothing was happening. One little spark shot from her finger tips in the second attempt, which made the elf laugh and mock each attempt afterwards.

Nita was communicating to someone in a mirror on the far side of the kitchen. She had waved her hand in front of the mirror and said "Thomas" the name of whom she wished to speak with. The mirror vibrated on the wall while Nita waited for the person on the other side to appear. Eventually, a balding heavy set man showed up on the other side. Thomas had a hard face, with dark bushy eyebrows and a small scar on his upper lip. Regina could not hear the conversation, but she watched Nita's small frame shift its weight from one hip to another; her arms folded and her black heel was tapping slowly with annoyance. Thomas' face, however, did not change at all. His lips and eyebrows seemed to stay furrowed throughout the entirety of the conversation.

After a minute or two Nita ended her communication with Thomas. The mirror then proceeded to fold itself into a smaller compact which could fit neatly into her purse. Everyone's attention shifted to her as she made her way to the end of the table. She somehow looked worried and confident at the same time. Her facial expressions and her body language were saying two very different things.

"Thomas is setting up a team. It should only take us a couple of weeks to get there." Nita was now leaning over the table looking very serious. "Word got around quick about The Fox Tree. I'm sure people from Kazny have heard about it by now. So we need to stay vigilant. There are very few people we can trust. We have a slight advantage right now; people are aware of The Fox Tree but they still don't know who is responsible for it."

"Are you going to tell us where we are going?" asked Reynold slightly annoyed.

"No, but only because I'm not entirely sure where it is. I can tell you, however, who we are going to see."

Ann had a frighten look on her face. "No! There is a reason why no one has found him since the Mad Sister was forced from this realm. It is too dangerous!"

Nita grabbed Ann's hand, "He is our best shot at getting Regina up to speed with her magic. Without him, all we can do is hope she can do it on her own. Besides we don't know what her inclination is yet."

"Inclination?" Regina asked.

"Oh, right." Reynold looked at Regina like he had forgotten she was there. "Basically, a sorcerer's powers tend to favor one thing over the rest. For instance, Ann's powers are more inclined with brews, mine is with plants and it might be too early to tell, but I think Tyler's is more inclined with creatures."

"Cool!" Tyler looked outside at Daisy who was sitting by the window.

"What is the Mad Sister's inclination?" Regina was hesitant to ask, but felt it was necessary to know. "I mean, I should know what I am up against, right?"

Nita, Reynold and Ann all gave nervous glances to one another. "Umm, well…" This was the first time Regina had seen Nita stumble through her words. "The Mad S-Sister, she umm."

Reynold interrupted, "She can pretty much do everything." Regina watched for any kind of sign that Reynold was joking, but the silence in the room told her he was not. "I'm not saying she is great at everything, but it seems like she can do it all. As much as I would like to fly, I can't and there are some out there who can; the Mad Sister being one of them. I would also like to be able to move heavy objects, but I can only get them an inch off the ground. The rumors make it hard to pinpoint exactly what her inclination is. I personally don't think she has one."

"The Mad Sister is extremely powerful. A lot of people believe she is the most powerful sorcerer alive." Said Ann. "My Grand pappy said that during the Mad

Hysteria, there were murmurs that she had been able to do some mind control as well."

"Don't be ridiculous Ann!" Nita found her confidence again. "There is not a single sorcerer out there who can control minds. It is impossible!"

Ann shrugged off Nita's comment. "Anyways, she is really powerful and we don't know how long we have before she comes back.

"Exactly!" Nita chimed in again, "That's why it is important we get you fully functional as soon as possible."

"Are we even sure that she will come back?" Regina asked hoping for a better answer than yes.

"No we don't." Regina was somewhat comforted by Nita's words. "But I don't want to be unprepared for her return. This is why we need to find him right away."

"Find who?" Regina looked at Nita and waited for her answer.

Nita looked Regina square in the eyes and with a straight face said, "The Grand Master."

***

To avoid attention, Reynold, Ann, Tyler and Regina left the house after the sun went down and the stores in town had closed. They were meeting Nita at her office on the far side of town. Regina looked into the different shops along the way; most had empty shelves and cleaned out racks. With only a few days left before Founders' Day, last minute shoppers were making sure everyone was checked off on their list.

They approached the steps of a grand white building with beautiful but strange markings along the entryway. Reynold looked around to make sure no one was close by before they made the short climb up the stairs. Once inside, Reynold and Ann didn't appear to be so tense anymore. Regina and Tyler followed Ann and Reynold straight back to the large office directly across the front entrance. Regina couldn't help but admire the craftsmanship of the building; from the white marble floors to the chromed covered railings and the glass ceiling, everything about this building was beautiful. There were several cherry red wood desks in front of other offices; all were perfectly organized. In front of the mayor's office, in which they were heading, sat a large crest in the flooring. It was the same fox as the Parting Tree's that Regina and Tyler had gone through. The colors here, however, were much bolder and vibrant, its blue eyes glimmered in the moon light shining from above. The fox was encased in a large black circle with the words *Composuerunt Potentia Ab Intellectu* arched above the Fox's head.

Nita opened her office door before Reynold had the chance to knock. It was exactly eight o'clock, the agreed upon meeting time, but Nita was the only one in her office.

"Where is everyone?" Reynold asked in a frustrated voice.

"Right here." A man's voice echoed through the room. Heads were scanning Nita's office, but there was no man in sight. Regina saw movement out of the corner of her eye and quickly jerked her head in that direction. A puff of blue smoke appeared and out from it stood a tall lengthy fellow. He wore a black and gray uniform with several badges pressed upon the shoulders. He had jet black curly hair and dark brown skin.

"This is Ravi Chaaya. As you can see he has mastered the magic of camouflage." Nita had a smirk across her face.

"I don't think I have." Said Ravi, "This lovely young lady saw me before I appeared. Strange." Ravi gave Regina a small frown.

"Hey Ravi." A woman's voice came from the other side of the room. "Do you think you can reveal the rest of us?"

"Right." Ravi snapped his fingers and three other blue puffs of smoke appeared from where the woman's voice had come from. "At least you couldn't see them."

"This here is Maggie Smith." Nita was pointing to a younger woman with bright shoulder length, curly red hair. She had on a white long-sleeved blouse and high waist black pants. She had two knives hoisted on her sides and a number of other weapons in various places. "As you can see, she is our weapons specialist."

Maggie gave a wink and said "Magic is great, but a knife can be just as good if used properly."

An older man smoking an old wooden pipe stepped forward. His hair was dark gray and he had strips of white by his temples. He bowed forward in his nice coal colored suit and introduced himself. "My name is Thack Wallace."

Reynold leaned over to Ann and whispered "He's kinda old. Why is he on the team?" Reynold looked up and realized he had been overheard by Thack who was now glaring at him.

Red sparks and smoke covered Thack. When the smoke cleared a large gray wolf with flecks of white was growling in the place where Thack had just been.

Nita gave a smug chuckle, "Thack is a werewolf. He just turned 120 and he has been with the Royal family for a very long time. He also has become very skilled at controlling when he can change forms." There was another poof of red smoke and Thack was back in his human form.

"Last, but not least we have Vaul…" Nita paused and looked at Vaul as he purposefully cleared his throat. "Do I have to?" Vaul gestured with his hand for Nita to continue. In an exasperated voice Nita announced, "Vaul the King Dwarf." Nita shook her head and turned away as Vaul began flexing his arms in different positions.

Vaul wasn't much to look at. He was about as tall as the desk next to him and almost just as wide. He had a long bent nose and ragged brown hair. Regina noticed he had a few missing teeth and the teeth he did have left were yellow and crooked. Regina was starting to wonder why he was on the team at all until she watched him pick up a large bronze statue of the founding sorcerer of Nahtovia and lifted it straight over his head with one hand. He then proceeded to do reps with the statue in one hand and a giggling Tyler in the other. Ann, however, quickly grabbed Tyler and put a stop to Vaul using him as a weight.

"Yours no funs lady." Said Vaul in a gruff voice.

"I have personally hand selected everyone on this team. They can be trusted to carry out this mission with 100 percent confidentiality." Nita seemed to be pleased with herself almost as if she was patting herself on the back. "Regina, Ravi, Maggie, Thack and Vaul…" Nita mumbled *the King Dwarf* part. "…will be leaving in five days during the Founders' Day magicworks display."

"Excuse me Nita, but I think ya forgot to include the three of us." Ann pointed to Reynold, Tyler and herself. "We can't just send her off with a bunch of people she doesn't know."

"Forgive me for being so blunt, but I believe you and Reynold are strangers to the girl as well. Besides we need things to remain normal and if you two go with Regina others might become suspicious about your sudden disappearance."

Regina was starting to wonder if Nita was purposefully being harsh or she just didn't realize how her straight forward comments were being received. Either way, Ann and Reynold looked like angry rattle snakes and were ready to strike at any moment. Even the team Nita had assembled were all wearing the same uncomfortable look. Nita not noticing the looks on Ann and Reynolds faces or anyone else's continued speaking.

"We should probably take the boy as well. He might be of great use."

"Can you please stop talking about my brother and me as if we are not here? I think we should have a say in this too." Regina, now feeling fed up, continued. "Also, Ann and Reynold from here on out should be considered as family and nothing less. They took us in and treated us like family why would my brother and I think of them as anything else." Nita was taken aback by Regina's comment.

"Very well. When the team comes to get you-"

"Actually…" Ravi interrupted "…the team would like it if you would refer to us as Fox Squad."

55

"Alright, Fox Squad will meet you at your house on Founders' Day as soon as the magicworks display begins. This will act as a cover for the team- I mean-for Fox Squad to get out of town unnoticed. You will have until then to decide who all will be going."

The following morning was not very pleasant in the Porter household. Ann and Reynold had been arguing since they awoke this morning about who should stay and who should go. Regina was happy that her and her brother moved into the empty rooms on the second floor; otherwise they would still be in the room next to the kitchen hearing every upset word crystal clear. Regina could only hear muffled words from her new room, but she knew she didn't want to get caught up in that hail storm. So when Regina and Tyler made their way to the kitchen they made sure to make a lot of noise coming down the stairs so Ann and Reynold could hear them coming.

"Good morning!" Ann said in a cheerful voice trying to hide her disgruntled demeanor. "I'll start breakfast. Why don't y'all go help Reynold; he has somethin cool to show ya."

Reynold directed them back towards the entry to the kitchen "Right this way."

Reynold lead them outside and to the light blue barn. Daisy ran up to Tyler and rubbed against his leg. Reynold gave Tyler a whole ear of corn to give to Daisy. Tyler motioned Daisy to sit before he gave her the corn.

"Wow! That is impressive. I tried feeding Daisy earlier with that same corn and she just stuck her nose up at it." Said Reynold still looking amazed. Reynold turned back to the doors of the barn. "I can't wait for ya to see this!" He did an opening motion with his hands and the heavy barn doors opened out slowly.

It was a rather cool morning, but the inside of the barn felt humid and hot. Regina stepped closer and felt a hot breath blowing from inside. Regina moved in a bit closer to see what was causing the hot breath of air that was hitting her face.

"I can't see anything." Regina said in a confused voice to Reynold.

"Eydis light please." Reynold called out to the darkness. A blue ember appeared in the middle of the barn; it burned soft at first, but with each step they took, the light burned brighter and brighter. Regina stopped in her tracks when the light finally got bright enough to illuminate the dark black scales along a long winged back. She couldn't believe her eyes.

"Is that a dragon?" Regina said almost not believing her own eyes.

"She sure is!" Reynold was grinning ear to ear. "Her name is Eydis. She is one of the eighty or so dragons left in this realm. Isn't she beautiful?" Tyler and Regina were hesitant to approach the massive creature. "Don't worry, she is really friendly. Here I will introduce her to ya." Reynold turned to the dragon. "Eydis, I would like you to meet Regina and Tyler."

As if Eydis understood, she stood and gave a deep stretch before she walked towards Regina and Tyler. They both held their hands out in front of them; unsure of what would happen next. Eydis slowly bent her large head down towards them and pressed her nose against their hands.

Eydis was not as large as what Regina had imagined a dragon would be. The beautiful scaly creature was about as tall as an elephant and almost twice as long as one. She was black from her head to her tail, except for the bright red tips of the spikes that ran along her spine. Eydis stepped back to get a better look at Tyler and Regina. She tilted her head and looked at them curiously with her green almond shaped eyes that softened her face, but all of a sudden those eyes turned into something fierce. She let out a roar bearing her many large sharp teeth and released a few blue sparks from her mouth.

Regina and Tyler ran back to the barn doors. They peaked their heads from around the corner and watched as Eydis pulled her foot off a large rake that she had just stepped on. She kicked the rake across the room, it hit the wall and broke in two. She then looked back towards Regina and Tyler with the same kind face she had before.

"Eydis that is the third rake this month. Ya really need to watch where ya are stepping."

Regina and Tyler came out from behind the doors and slowly walked back towards Eydis. Once they were close enough, Eydis nuzzled up against them again and laid back down. She let Tyler climb on top and straddle her just above where her spikes began. He lifted his arms up to the side, closed his eyes and pretended like he was flying. Reynold grabbed Regina and put her on top of Eydis as well.

"Hold on tight!" Reynold said with huge smile.

"Wait! What!" It was too late Reynold signaled Eydis to take off and before Regina could argue Eydis galloped out of the barn and up into the air.

Regina's eyes were sealed tight and her grip was even tighter. She wasn't so much afraid of heights just the unfamiliar dragon that had complete control of whether she would plummet to the ground or not. Regina was determined to keep her eyes closed, but a quick drop by Eydis made them quickly wrench open. The dragon then decided to do a hard right that lead into a fast loopy-loop. The fresh cool air running through her hair and the sun shining on her back, made Regina forget all about a potential fall into the abyss. Once her dangerous thoughts floated away, she noticed the happy giggles coming from her brother. Regina didn't know what to expect when they ran away and came to this strange world, but seeing how happy her brother was made everything worthwhile.

Eydis touched down and made her way back into the barn. She tilted her wing to the floor to let Regina and Tyler slide down from her back. Regina rubbed Eydis behind the ear and the sweet dragon thumped her back foot in pleasure.

"Reynold she is amazing!" Regina said in surprised delight.

"I'm glad ya think so." Reynold responded. "I wanted ya to meet her because I think she would be useful for your, um…trip."

"I think that would be a great idea!" Regina fondly placed her hand on the dragon's chest and felt the mighty beating of her heart. "I don't think anyone would want to go up against her."

The days leading up to Fox Squad's departure to find the Grand Master, were more or less the same. Ann and Reynold would argue when they thought Regina and Tyler were out of ear range. The Baylons would practice their magic daily and Regina, most days, did her best to avoid answering questions about who should go and who should stay.

Regina didn't want to answer that question for multiple reasons. She knew whomever she picked the person who had to stay behind would have their feelings hurt. She also kind of agreed with Nita, that it would draw too much attention if everyone left. Regina had a bigger concern though. She spent most of her time contemplating if her brother should go or stay behind. She knew that no matter what would happen her brother would probably get swept into this whole mess of battling the Mad Sister, so Regina thought it would be a good idea if Tyler was at full strength with his powers as well. On the other hand, Regina wanted to delay any danger to Tyler for as long as possible. Plus, he was already way ahead on learning how to use his powers than most sorcerers would be just starting out.

Reynold had been right about Tyler's inclination and it had become even clearer in Tylers hours of practice at Ellie's Pet Emporium. There Tyler would work in the back of Ellie's store practicing commands on snakes, fropper, a hawk and even a wild baby wizzly that Ellie had adopted.

The wizzly was an odd looking animal. Its head and paws were large and powerful like that of a Grizzly bear, but the body was built like a wolf's. His brown thick fur was soft and his eyes were narrowed and focused. Regina could tell a full grown wizzly would be a scary force to reckon with.

On the last day before they had to find the Grand Master, Regina was really starting to enjoy her new life. Besides Ann and Reynold's occasional arguments, things were pretty pleasant. Her days were starting to become routine, breakfast, helping Reynold with his crops and Eydis, Tyler's practices at Ellie's, lunch in town, a few hours in the library, Regina's magic practices with Ann (with no real success), dinner and back outside to hang out with the Wyatt brothers before it got dark. Regina especially enjoyed her time with Gramm. She found herself anticipating the moment that he came through the front gate. They would sit on the porch and watch Tyler and Lars as they played with Daisy.

The last day was no different. Regina had even made a decision about who would be going with Fox Squad. She had also finally come to terms with her new found role and she was actually feeling pretty sure of herself. She had said one last goodbye to Gramm before she and Tyler went back inside. Regina noticed a lingered hug from Gramm that night. She closed the door and headed up the stairs to do some light reading before bed. She reached the second step of the stairs when there was a knock on the door.

Regina's heart fluttered thinking it was Gramm wanting one more hug. She raced to the door and swung it open. Regina paused for a moment, a smile crept across her face and she flung her arms around him, but it wasn't the same him she was expecting.

"Regina who is that?" Reynold came around the corner looking very concerned. Ann joined her husband and was wearing the same worried face.

Regina could hardly contain her glee, "I'm so happy to see you."

Chapter 6 The Wolf Queen

Tyler sprinted down the stairs, side-swiped Reynold and ran to the door with open arms. "Sheriff!"

Ann and Reynold looked at each other "Sheriff?"

Sheriff Henry Tucker was standing at the Porter's front door. His left arm was bandaged, he had a few cuts on his face and a small bruise on the bridge of his nose. He looked a little worn, but the huge grin on his face said otherwise.

"I was so worried leaving you behind after the accident, but you look good…" Regina looked at his bandage, "Well as good as can be I guess. I'm just glad you are here." All of a sudden Regina remembered where 'here' was. "Wait, why are you here and how did you find us?"

"It is my job little lady. My duty is to track you two down wherever it is you may go. It has been ever since the first time you tried to escape from Lady Dumontet. As soon as I was released from the hospital I went back to where I last saw you. I had read the report and noticed at one point one of the cops saw Lady Dumontet head down a hill. I searched and searched for any sign of where you had gone to. I was about to go back up the hill when I noticed scratch marks on a tree. I followed the marks which lead me to a hollowed out tree. I looked around for any signs of where you went from there, but there was nothing. That is until I noticed a small piece of fabric snagged on the inside of the tree." Tucker handed the piece of fabric to Regina.

"My shirt. I had felt a tug when I got in, but I didn't even notice it had torn." Regina examined the fabric.

"It was exactly the clue I was looking for. There was just one problem, I still had no idea what happen to you next. I stayed until nightfall hoping I could recreate your steps. I walked back to a nearby stump looking for more clues. When all of a sudden a man came from out of the tree."

"That must have been Oliver." Said Reynold

"Yeah, I questioned him for a while, but he was plastered so I figured it was no use. I'm not even sure he realized that I was there. So I let him go, hoping he would show me how to get through. Sure enough, that drunk man picked up a rock from the ground and climbed into the tree. Poof he was gone. I followed shortly after with a rock in my hand." Tucker glanced at Reynold as he tried to hold in a chuckle.

"No one noticed ya comin through the tree?" asked Ann.

"Luckily, everyone seemed to be excited about that Oliver fellow going through the tree that they didn't even notice me coming through shortly after."

"Wait. You have been here for four days? Why are you just showing up now?" asked Regina.

"To be honest, it took me a little while to figure out what this place is and to come to terms that I am not dreaming. I am a sensible man and a place like this shouldn't exist, but here I am." Tucker still seemed apprehensive, but he continued. "I spent the last three days tracking down your location. It was not an easy task. Then I spent most of today making sure, uh…" Tucker bent down and whispered to Regina and Tyler "I wanted to make sure these people were safe." Tucker looked around from the Porter's front door. "But it appears you have made a new home of this place."

"Oh right, Henry Tucker I would like you to meet Ann and Reynold Porter." Regina just remembered Ann and Reynold had no idea who this man was. "He is the reason why we didn't escape from Lady Dumontet sooner." Regina smiled at the Sheriff.

"It is a pleasure to meet ya." Reynold reached out to shake Tucker's hand. Tucker returned the gesture, but in doing so, he strained his injured arm.

"Ouch."

"Let me get my healin brew." Ann said as she rushed off to the back room.

A few moments later Ann returned with a bubbling pink brew. Regina took a deep breath and inhaled the intoxicating scent of roses and something else that had a sweet scent to it, but Regina couldn't quite put her finger on it.

"Here." Ann handed her brew to an unsure Tucker. "This should heal you right up."

"No offense ma'am, but I don't really believe in that herbal remedy stuff."

"Umm, this is somethin else. I do have to warn ya though…" Ann's nose scrunched up, "It has a bit of a nasty taste to it."

Tucker looked to Regina for approval. She gave a slight nod and Tucker downed the whole brew.

"That wasn't so bad, taste like cherries and roses. I think that was pretty tast-" Tucker's face turned green before he could finish his sentence. Reynold ran into the kitchen and came back with a cup of water.

Tucker yanked the glass from Reynold's hand and didn't stop drinking until the water was all gone.

"That was awful! Did you mix moonshine and some kind of pepper that you found in the garbage?" Tucker was doing his best to keep the brew from coming back up.

"That has to be your best batch yet." Reynold said with a smile.

Tucker was on the verge of yelling and potentially vomiting, when he noticed all the pain in his body was gone. He unwrapped his bandaged arm and moved it around. He walked towards a mirror and watched the last bit of his cuts disappear from his face.

"Wow! That stuff is amazing!" Tucker just realized that he had insulted Ann's brew and his southern hospitality urged him to apologize. "Sorry, I didn't mean to insult you ma'am."

"Please call me Ann."

"Right. Thank you Ann." Tucker turned back towards Regina and Tyler. "Well I came here to bring you back with me." Regina was getting ready to protest the Sheriff, but before she could begin he raised up a hand; signaling to Regina that he still had more to say. "...but, I don't plan on taking you back to Lady Dumontet."

"After all this time, what has made you change your mind?" Regina always knew that the Sheriff didn't like bringing them back to Lady Dumontet, but he always obeyed the legality of her guardianship.

"I knew she was a poor caretaker to say the least, but there was something about her that night that scared the bejesus out of me. I saw her when she first pulled up and she had this fierce look in her eyes; not of stricken grief or despair, but of rage and anger. I watched her put on an act once a cop came up to her, but I still couldn't forget that look. I knew if I found you two that I wouldn't take you back to her."

"Where would you take us then?" Asked Tyler.

"Well, I was thinking you would stay with me."

Regina was happy and upset at the same time. All she ever wanted to hear just came out of Tucker's mouth, but she was furious that it took him so long to say it. Plus, she liked Reynold and Ann and she had finally accepted her responsibilities as the savior. "*Savior!*" Everything came rushing to the fore front of Regina's mind.

Regina explained everything that had happened from the moment they got to this realm to Tucker. She explained about magic, about their royal background and about her job as the savior.

"That is a lot of information to take in." Tucker stood there trying to make sense of everything.

"Yeah I know." Regina said with an unenthusiastic tone. Regina looked at Reynold and Ann. "I have made my decision about who should go." Ann looked like she was about to say something. "Before you interrupt, please hear me out." Ann thought for a second and agreed to let Regina finish. "I don't want either of you to come."

"But..." Reynold tried to dispute.

"Please try to understand. It's not because I do not trust you I just can't ask you to put your lives at risk for me."

Reynold put his arm around his wife. "We would do anything for ya."

"I believe you, but I also think Nita is right. It will be too suspicious if either one of you are gone for a long time. Not many people know we have been staying with you or that we have any connection to you both and I want to keep it that way."

"I will go." Tucker stepped forward. "I may not have any powers…"

"Ya might." Ann interrupted.

"Okay, well I may or may not have any powers, but I will do my best to protect you from any harm."

Regina smiled, "I was just about to ask you if you would join. As much as I would like to have Ann and Reynold come, I just think it is better this way. It will be nice having someone on the team that I can trust."

"What about me?" Tyler looked upset that Regina hadn't considered him.

"As much as I would like to protect you, I can't always be there to do so. I want you to decide if you want to go? Don't answer now. I really want you to think about this. We will probably run into trouble out there and I need to know that you are fully prepared for it. Let me know tomorrow how you feel."

Tyler hated waiting to answer, but he understood.

"Well I can't say I am happy to be staying behind, but I'm glad ya have someone there who ya can trust all the same." Reynold gave Tucker a rough pat on the back. "Come join us for dinner and ya can stay in the room down the hall."

"Thanks!" Tucker leaned over and whispered to Tyler and Regina. "Do they have normal food here?"

Regina and Tyler looked up at Tucker and laughed.

The day had finally arrived. The house was a buzz with excitement; it was Founders' Day! Regina and Tyler woke up to the wonderful aroma of chocolate chip waffles being freshly made in the kitchen. They quickly rushed down the stairs ready to see what joys this holiday would bring.

Ann had already put up a few decorations a couple of days ago, but this morning the house looked completely different. Ann was explaining Founders' Day to Tucker as Regina and Tyler walked into the kitchen.

"So each kingdom decorates their homes with the colors that represent their founding sorcerers. Nahtovia's colors, as ya can see…" Ann gestured to all the decorations. "… are blue, gold and white. Kazny's colors are black, red and white and Broadcove's colors are silver, purple and white. Each kingdom is united by sharing white as one of their colors. Kazny changed it for a while, but it was changed back once the kingdom of Nahtovia took over. There is actually a white building atop of white grounds that functions as the neutral precinct where anyone from the three kingdoms can claim refuge there and will be protected, it is called the White House."

"Really?" Tucker laughed.

"Yea, technically they stole the name from us."

On the kitchen table, there was a very fascinating decoration. Three figurines, the founders, were all dressed up in their kingdom's colors with their hands stretched out towards the sky. A small piece of land was forming above them; Regina watched as the land grew and grew. Once the three kingdoms had been created, the founders began creating a force field around it. Once the force field had completely enclosed, magicworks would shoot off inside of it. Then the whole process would begin again. Regina was not the only one fascinated by this decoration, Tyler sat at the table and watched the whole process again from start to finish.

Regina walked over to Tyler and pointed at the founders. "Pretty cool, huh!" Tyler walked away without saying anything. Regina just assumed Tyler didn't hear her and shrugged it off.

Reynold walked into the kitchen with his hands behind his back. He stood next to his wife with a big grin across his face. "Happy Founders' Day!" He brought his hands out in front of him and waved two boxes, neatly wrapped, in front of Regina and Tyler.

"Just a little somethin from the two of us." Ann was just as excited as Reynold.

Tyler grabbed his gift first and quickly tore into it. Regina watched the excitement on her brother's face; it had been a long time since either one of them had received any kind of gift. Tyler pulled out a large black board with small red stripes across it. Regina and Tucker stared at the large board and the smaller box it came in. There was no possible way that board could have fit in that box under normal circumstances.

Reynold noticed the confused look on Tyler's face. "It is the latest wingboard, Speedster 300! Just set it on the ground and stand on top of it."

Tyler did as Reynold said; he placed the wingboard on the ground and stood upon it. Straps came shooting out from the board and wrapped themselves tightly around his feet. Once Tyler was securely in place the wingboard slowly came off the ground.

"Ya tilt the board up to go higher and shift your weight to go either left or right."

Ann chimed in "Basically, it is the same concept as a snowboard, but with no snow and in the air. Ya will figure it out."

Tyler practiced shifting his weight on the wingboard while Regina started opening her gift. Regina reached in and pulled out four small metal balls. There was one green ball, another one was blue and the remaining two were bright red.

"Sorry, Regina, but we gave ya a more practical gift considering…well…ya know." Reynold looked abashed. "Ann made some brews and put them in these metal containers, they are called brew balls. We wanted to make more, but we were kinda pressed for time."

"These are a great way to defend yourself in case ya run into any kind of trouble. Tucker ya should probably come learn about these as well." Ann waved Tucker over. "The green ball will let out a thick layer of gas that will make your enemies pass out, but don't worry I got bits of hair from everyone on the team including everyone in this room."

"What is the hair for?" Tucker stroked his own, "I don't remember giving you any of my hair."

Ann gave a sly smile. "I have my ways. Don't worry, I only grabbed a single strand so the gas won't make ya pass out. Any who, the blue ball places a five-foot radius force field around ya and the team. The two red ones are pretty impressive if I do say so myself. This red baby will spring up duplicates of the team. This other red ball plays off the first, it sets of a scent forcing the enemy to go after the duplicates. Just make sure you throw both at the same time."

"Thanks Ann." Regina was very appreciative of the gift, but was a little disappointed it wasn't something fun like Tyler's present.

Ann placed a solemn hand on Regina's shoulder. "I really hope y'all don't have to use these."

The room was silent as everyone tried not to say aloud what they were thinking. The Porters desperately wanted to keep the small amount of innocence left in the children, but they were powerless to do so. They all knew what must be done for the greater good, but each one of them wanted to post-pone the inevitable just a little while longer.

The tension broke with a loud single knock on the front door followed by a click of the locking mechanism turning open. Nita blazed through to the kitchen looking rather frazzled and upset.

Ann turned to Reynold, "We really need to get better about putting the locking spell on that door."

Nita flicked her wrist and Regina heard the front door slam closed. "There has been a change of plans and we need to move now!"

"What do ya mean? What is going on?" demanded Reynold.

"Ravi was being followed. We believe that this same person may be after Regina and Tyler."

There was a small poof of blue smoke that appeared next to Nita. Ravi was now standing next to her pointing a finger towards the kitchen table. Regina notice that Ravi's appearance was much less showy this time around and not as dramatic.

"It was him!" Ravi gave a hard glare towards Tucker. "He was the one who was following me."

"Are y'all talkin about Henry?" asked Ann.

Ravi threw his hand forward towards the Sheriff who instantaneously became shackled to his chair.

"What the-" Tucker was thrown off by the surprised attack by Ravi. "Yeah I followed you!"

"So you admit it?" asked Nita.

"Yes, I just said I did." Tucker answered in a very sarcastic tone. "Let me explain."

Nita was reluctant to listen, but Ann forced her to hear him out. Tucker explained his connection to the Baylons and how he had been trying to track them down since he made his way over to this realm.

"Sorry about that chap." Ravi snapped his fingers and the shackles vanished into thin air.

"Tucker will be going with us on our trip." Regina added.

"Absolutely not!" Nita interjected. She looked towards Tucker, "No offense Sheriff, but I don't know you and I don't allow unknown factors into my planning."

Reynold, Ann and Tucker all started in on Nita at once. Every word that came from their mouths were all objections to Nita's 'unknown factor argument,' but not a single word was heard because they were all trying to talk over one another.

Regina gave a loud whistle to break up the argument. The room fell silent and all eyes were on her. "He is going! Tyler and I trust him and that should be all that matters." Nita looked annoyed at Regina's defiance. "Nita, Ann and Reynold are staying behind, you still got what you wanted. No one knows Tucker so no one, in this realm at least, will notice he has gone missing."

"And what about your brother? Have we decided on that as well?" Nita asked trying not to sound bitter.

"I don't know. Why don't you ask Regina?" Tyler stormed out of the room and ran up the stairs. Regina was shocked at Tyler's sudden outburst. They had never really fought before and worst of all Regina did not know what she had done wrong.

Regina followed her brother out of the room and made her way up the stairs. About half way up she remembered Tyler had ignored her earlier. She slapped her palm to her forehead.

"How could I not notice?" She said aloud to herself.

She knocked on Tyler's bedroom door and slowly entered before he could answer. Tyler was sitting on his bed making his paper airplane fly through the room. He was facing the window in his room and didn't even bother to turn around to see who had come through the door.

"How could you not automatically think to have me go with you?" Tyler turned to face Regina, "We have been through everything together. How is this any different?" Tyler sounded truly hurt.

Regina, understanding how her brother felt now, took a moment to think before she responded. "I-I didn't want to put you in harm's way. I just wanted to protect you. Anything that we have ever gone through together my first priority has always been to keep you safe and away from danger. I hope you understand that this will not be a guaranteed safe trip; I would actually be shocked if we didn't run into any trouble. Do you get why I wanted you to make this choice?"

"There was never a doubt in my mind that I would let you go without me. I am ready for this." Tyler smiled, "Besides, *I* can use magic." He really emphasized the *I* to tease his sister.

Regina threw a pillow at her brother for being a smart mouth. She sat next to him on the bed and hit him again with the pillow. They laughed and laughed; enjoying this brief moment in time were they were just brother and sister and nothing else.

The time to leave was quickly approaching. They had spent most of their day enjoying the warm summer breeze floundering about with Daisy and Edyis; Lars and Gramm came over briefly, but Regina did her best to avoid Gramm fearing she would let out her plans to leave tonight. It hurt her to do so, especially after she noticed the glum look on his face, but she knew it was for the best.

The sun began to set which meant it wouldn't be long before the magicworks display would begin. Everyone headed inside to prepare for Fox Squads arrival. Regina, Tyler and Tucker had packed earlier in the day, but they each did a once through of their stuff to make sure they didn't forget any essentials.

They all gathered their bags and waited patiently in the kitchen. After a moment or two of tense silence, Reynold snapped his fingers; clearly remembering he had something to do. He stood up from his chair and walked out of the kitchen. He quickly returned holding two identical silver lockets. On the outside of each locket was a beautifully embroidered $\mathcal{P}$.

"These are family heirlooms. My grandparents enchanted these lockets as a way to secretly communicate with my parents during the Mad Hysteria."

Reynold opened the lockets to show them the inside. On one side of the locket was a small mirror and on the other it had three sections inscribed along with a notch that moved above the sections. Reynold pointed to the side of the locket that had the different sections on it. The first section read '*Safe,*' the second was '*In Distress*' and finally '*Resting.*'

Reynold started to explain how the lockets worked. "The locket notch will automatically detect which one of the three categories ya are currently experiencing. The mirror on our locket will display one of the three categories ya all may be experiencing and ya will see ours. If the team is in a sticky situation…" Reynold held his thumb on the mirror in the locket, it flashed green and then Reynold spoke into it. "…send help quickly!" The other locket vibrated and flashed green until Reynold opened it. In that lockets mirror Reynolds faced appeared relaying the message he just sent from the other locket. "If this ever happens, we will send Eydis in a flash."

"I thought Eydis was coming with us?" Tyler asked Reynold. Regina looked at her brother sharing the same confusion.

"Oh no. Eydis is much too big! There is no way Fox Squad could be stealthy with Eydis following ya. She is good, but not that good."

Regina nodded in agreement. She held in a laugh as she pictured Eydis trying to hide behind a tree from an enemy.

Reynold handed the locket to Regina and told Tyler and Tucker to grab it as well. "Okay, the three of ya hold tight, I need to enchant the locket so only the three of ya can open it up." Regina, Tyler and Tucker each held tightly onto the locket as Reynold waved his hands above them mumbling something under his breath. Regina felt a prickly surge of energy run through her arm as Reynold finished his enchantment. Tyler and Tucker both shook out their arms, trying to get rid of the same prickly feeling. "There that should do it. Keep this on at all times. Ann will hold onto the other one."

Reynold placed one of the lockets around his wife's neck and gave the other to Regina. She placed the locket around her neck and hid it under her shirt. She patted her chest where the cold metal of the locket laid.

CRACK! There was a loud noise that came from outside. Ann pulled back the curtains from the kitchen window that faced the castle. They watched as two more loud cracks went off. The night sky lite up as purple and blue foxes shot up into the sky and danced amongst the stars.

"Oh no! The magicwork display has started! Why has the team not shown yet?" Ann looked from Reynold to Regina and then to the kitchen entrance. They all stared at the kitchen entrance waiting for Fox Squad to walk through, but nothing happened.

"Wait here!" Tucker pulled out his gun and headed for the front door.

"Let me come with ya." Reynold joined Tucker to see if they could find out what was going on.

It was only a few minutes later that Tucker and Reynold ran back in through the front door with panic stricken looks across their faces.

"T-th-there are screams coming from the town!" Regina had never seen Tucker like this. His face was pale and she could see the horror in his eyes.

Regina could hear the distant screams. The cries of pain seem to call to her. An urge to help began to grow inside her and without realizing she was already heading for the door. She rushed passed Reynold and Tucker, who both tried to stop her from getting hurt. She could hear the small pounding footsteps of her brother and Tucker calling out for her. Soon the rest of them were running to the town, towards the horrible screams and the cries of torment.

Regina made her way to Tuttle Road where the screams were getting louder. She turned the corner and nearly knocked over Maggie. "Hey, watchit! Oh, good it is you. We could use your help. There are Carnagers causing problems" Maggie handed Regina a long black cudgel. "Here. This cudgel was forged by ancient Glints. It will guide you. Now go help the others!"

Regina ran off to help the others, but she was unsure of what Maggie meant by *'It will guide you.'* Regina approached a Carnager who was breaking into one of the shops. He wore an evil looking black wolf's mask to cover his face. Regina swung the cudgel at the man's legs. She caught one of them causing him to trip and fall to the ground. He quickly got up and lunged towards her. Regina could feel the cudgel forcing her hand to swing it forward and clock the guy across the face, knocking him out cold.

"That is a neat trick!" Regina smiled at the cudgel and continued on to the next person. Tyler joined her along with Ann, Reynold and Tucker.

"Ann!" Reynold called over to his wife. "Go check on Nita." Ann rushed off in the direction of Nita's office.

"I will go with her." Tucker yelled over his shoulder to Reynold as he followed Ann.

There were several Carnagers causing havoc all over Tuttle Road. Shopkeepers, who were surprised by the attack, were doing their best to fight of the masked villains; each of whom, were all wearing the same black wolf mask. The assault was unorganized and chaotic, but it was clear that the Carnagers had only one goal in mind, destroy everything in sight.

Reynold stepped in front of two Carnagers who were about to mug Laney.

A snarky laugh came from one of the Carnagers. "Are you really about to try and fight the both of us?" He elbowed his comrade who in turn gave a snorted laugh.

They both attacked Reynold at the same time, but with his large stature and brute strength he was able to take them on with ease. After a few devastating blows, the Carnagers ran away as fast as they could with Reynold following closely behind.

Tyler spotted his sister fighting a Carnager and snuck up behind them. He used his levitating trick, the same one used to fly a paper airplane, and was able to make the masked figure slightly hover off the ground. Regina took advantage of the Carnager's confusion and did a gut check with the cudgel. They continued their fight against the Carnagers with Tyler doing what little magic he knew how and Regina would tag in by attacking them with the Glint cudgel.

Ann soon returned with Nita, Thack and Ravi; all of whom looked a little war-torn. The Carnagers had the element of surprise on their side, but it did not take long for the people of Nahtovia to have the numbers against them. The Carnagers began running off once they realized they were fighting a losing battle. Those fighting off the masked invaders cheered as they began to retreat; others tried to pursue. But one Carnager, with a red wolf mask, had a trick up his sleeve. He threw out a black powder in front of Ellie's Pet Emporium. The black powder turned into smoke and the street went dark. Regina felt around for her brother. She could hear movement all around her, footsteps were pounding the cobbled path, the Carnagers were making their escape. The smoke began to clear. Regina reached for her brother's hand as soon as she was able to make out the top of his head.

There was a blood curdling scream. Regina jumped at the sound and like everyone else she looked for the source. All eyes landed on a trembling Ann; her face was pale and ghostly; her unsteady finger pointed ahead of her. Regina followed Ann's finger towards the window of Ellie's shop. On the window written clearly in blood read, *The Wolf Queen has returned!*

Chapter 7 Midnight Smoke

Ann, still trembling, managed to explain her ghastly scream. "I-I s-s-saw the whole thing."

"Whata ya mean ya saw the whole thing? It was pitch black." Reynold walked towards his wife to comfort her.

Ann took a few steps back from her husband, recoiling in fear of what she just witnessed. "I managed to throw one of my brew balls right as the smoke began to billow. The brew ball was supposed to illuminate the whole area, but it malfunctioned and only illuminated the area in front of me leading up to the store. The Carnager with the red wolf mask, grabbed Ellie from inside her store, it pulled off its mask and r-re-revealed…"

"What did you see?" Regina asked Ann, restraining the fear that was now bubbling up inside of her.

"It's face; it was an actual wolf's face!"

"That is preposterous! Werewolves can't choose to change only certain parts of their body." Thack spoke defiantly. "I should know; I have trained for years just to learn how to control my transition."

"I know what I saw, okay!" Ann too was now responding with insolence. "It had a wolf's head and a regular sorcerer body. I know it was a wolf's head because I saw him bite Ellie with his large fangs and used her blood to write that message! Then he ran off with her."

Nita walked over to Ellie's shop. She placed her hand on the window and let out a deep sigh. "I guess it is true."

"What are ya talking about?" Reynold asked.

Nita looked around and shook her head. "Not here. We need to go back to my office." Nita reached into her pocket and pulled out her compact mirror. Once again it unfolded itself into a larger mirror and floated in front of her. Nita waved her hand over the mirror and called out "Thomas." The mirror vibrated in midair and after a second or two the same bald bushy eyed man Regina saw through the same mirror several days ago, appeared, except for this time there were heavy bags under his eyes. "Thomas I need you to dispatch a second group of Shamans to Tuttle Road."

"They are on their way." Thomas disappeared and the mirror returned back into a reflection.

Nita was putting the communication mirror back into her pocket when the Shamans appeared out of nowhere.

"Okay, great. We can head back to my office now."

Each Shaman carried with them wooden staffs with white crystals attached at the top. They all wore blue capes that seemed to hoover slightly over the ground. The capes waved gracefully behind them as each Shaman went from one injured person to the next pointing their staffs at the different wounds. The Shamans would lower their heads and hum a soft beautiful melody. Regina watched in amazement as a cut or a bruise would slowly fade away. A few Shamans were repairing damages done to the buildings and the road. Regina continued watching the Shamans as they all walked back to Nita's office. She was particularly fascinated with the different symbols that laid upon each Shaman's forehead; each more unique and colorful then the next, they even glowed slightly as the Shaman performed an act of healing.

"Madame Mayor, I know I am new to this realm and what not, but what the heck just happened back there and who is this Wolf Queen?" asked Tucker.

"Well Sheriff, those masked sorcerers back there were all supporters of the Mad Sister, I assume you are familiar with her. The Wolf Queen is what the people of Kazny and the Carnagers call her." Nita answered back snobbishly, clearly still upset about Tucker joining the group.

"Not all Kazny residents supported the Mad Sister." Ann interjected. The color had finally returned to her face.

"Well most of them did and still do! The people of Kazny are rotten people."

Ann rolled her eyes; tired of listening to Nita's prejudice and her overall superiority. The rest of the walk back to Nita's office was done in silence. Once they had reached the grand white building, the town's city hall, the silence had finally broken.

"We will be safe to talk in here." Nita announced to the line that formed behind her as they walked through the doorway. A few Shamans were still lingering after, what Regina assumed, to be a fight that went on inside the building.

Before Regina could ask, Ravi began to explain. "There was about ten of them who came rushing through here." Ravi looked over to Thack. "Thack and I took them on while Vaul protected Nita in her office."

"Where is Vaul?" Maggie asked.

"We told him to stay here just in case any more of the Carnagers came back." Ravi answered.

Ravi opened Nita's office door and SMACK! Ravi was knocked sideways by a giant fist. He slid down the door holding his hand to his head.

"Vaul! What is wrong with you?" Ravi yelled at Vaul who quickly bent down to help him up.

"Sorrys, I thoughts yous was one of those masked Carnagers."

"Well I'm not!" Ravi rubbed the side of his head.

Everyone clambered into Nita's office. Nita being the last one in, closed the door and strode to the seat behind her desk.

"Perfect no one can hear us in here."

"How do we know that no one is listening on the other side of the door?" Tucker asked in a suspicious manner.

"This building had a strong enchantment placed on it once it was completed. No one can eavesdrop on a conversation that they are not included in." Nita displayed her haughtiness once again.

"Okay, so what is it that ya wanna tell us?" Reynold asked.

"Ever since the word got out about the Fox Tree, I thought it would be best to start gathering information from Kazny. Thomas had sent some of his very best to go press on some informants. Well Thomas kept coming up empty handed, which was unacceptable. So I ordered him to keep increasing the pressure on these informants."

Tucker leaned over to Reynold and whispered "I'm sure she enjoyed that." Nita threw a harsh glance in Tucker's direction, but luckily for him she did not hear his comment.

"It wasn't long before someone finally cracked." Nita continued. "One of the informants told us that there had been some chatter as of late. Some sorcerer families left Kazny on the rumors that the Mad Sister had returned."

"So the message is true?" Regina asked.

"We can't say for sure, but there has been a lot of movement going on in Kazny and it is not looking good. We all thought it would be a while before she returned, but I guess we were wrong."

"I'm sure that is a first for you Madame Mayor. You know, being wrong and all." Tucker said sarcastically.

Nita choose to ignore Tucker's comment and continued speaking. "Regardless of what has happened tonight, we are still moving forward with our plan to find the Grand Master. Ravi will put a camouflage spell over Regina and Tyler…" Nita looked in Tucker's direction and cringed her nose. "…You should include the Sheriff as well. Reynold and Ann can follow them back to the house. Maggie, Thack and Vaul the King Dwarf will leave twenty minutes after you do to avoid suspension. Good luck to you all."

"Regina may I speak with you for a moment?" Regina waved to Tyler and the rest of them to go ahead, as they all turned to look at her when Nita made her request. She gave a small smile to Tucker, who lingered by the door, that she would be alright on her own.

Regina sat in an empty chair on the other side of Nita's desk. "I just want you to know how much everyone appreciates you doing this. It is a lot to ask of someone, especially as someone as young as yourself. Despite what it may seem, I do concern myself with the safety of the team. Here…" Nita handed Regina what looked like a small yellow marble. "…this will help you find your way if you ever get lost. Use it wisely because you can only get one shot."

"Thanks Nita." Regina was surprised by Nita's unusual compassion. Regina left to join the others, but she looked back at Nita as she reached the doorway of the office, Nita gave a slight smile and a wink as Regina walked out the door.

Regina was finally saying her goodbyes to Reynold and Ann. All of Fox Squad had arrived and Regina, Tyler and Tucker were ready to go. Ann held back tears as she gave her third last goodbye hugs. Although, Regina's time staying with the Porter's had been brief, she still considered them as her family and the house as her home.

They began their journey heading towards the run down castle of Nahtovia. The moon in the night sky had reached the peak of its ascent and shone brightly above them as if it were their guiding light. Yesterday marked the first official day of summer which was the only thing keeping them from freezing at night. The weather in Nahtovia, Regina noticed, was very mild and even for summer the days were only slightly warm.

Regina guessed that the trail they were taking was hardly frequented based on the condition of the barely visible dirt path that they strode along. After the small battle on Tuttle Road, Regina still felt a little shaken; a sentiment that both Tyler and Tucker had shared. Regina watched her fellow team members; not a single one of them looked tensed. She couldn't understand how they looked so relaxed. They just fought off several Carnagers and the fate of Ellie was still unknown. When they arrived at the house, Ravi briefly mentioned that Nita had sent out a small search team for her, but they expected very little to come of it.

They must be true professionals, Regina thought, which made sense because Nita would only accept perfection from a team she handpicked herself. Obviously Thack was the oldest of the group, followed by several decades age gap between him and Vaul, so they probably had the most experience. Thack and Vaul probably fought during the Mad Hysteria the first time around and maybe even other battles before that. Maggie and Ravi, however, looked like they were in their early to mid-twenties. *"How much experience could they possibly have?"* thought Regina. Well despite their age, Ravi and Maggie like Thack and Vaul were all perfectly unperturbed by the Carnagers incident that happened only hours ago. Like most professionals, they were still on guard and aware of their surroundings, but they continued on like nothing happened.

Regina glanced over to her brother making sure he was still able to keep up. He was dragging his feet and looking like a zombie, but he was still moving along. Regina glanced back up at the moon and guessed they had a couple more hours before the sun would rise. They were approaching the run down castle when Thack broke the silence.

"We will stop at the castle and rest there. I have a friend inside that will keep us safe and will probably have plenty of food waiting for us." Everyone's spirits raised at thought of bountiful food waiting for them. Thack, liking his lips, continued. "He wants us to meet him around the back. Follow me."

"I can place a camouflage spell over everyone, but since there are so many of us I can only keep it up for maybe ten minutes give or take a few seconds." Said Ravi. "We have to be quick, but we also have to be quiet."

Ravi snapped his fingers, everyone disappeared into the background. Regina could hear breathing next to her that was the only way she knew her brother was there. They each grabbed at the air to link arms with the person next to them.

"Why didn't we link arms before?" Tucker asked in a hushed voice.

"Yeah, sorry. I guess I didn't think that through." Ravi called out somewhere left of Regina.

"Hey that is *NOT* my arm!" Maggie said smacking away whoever was trying to grab onto her.

"Oh, sorry my dear." Said Thack.

Regina felt a small hand grab her arm. Tyler was the last one to link up.

"Okay, everyone has an arm?" Small "uh-huhs" followed down the line in response to Thack. "Great! Let's get moving."

Regina was tugged forward. She followed along as best she could without stepping on the person in front of her. They rounded the corner of the castle and entered a back gate that was clearly left unlocked for them. It was eerie to look at the overgrown vines that covered most of the walls and parts of the floor. Everything was dirty and untouched except for a set of footprints that came around one corner and went around to the other side. Regina was sure those footprints belonged to a single guard that kept watch over the castle. Regina followed the line that was leading them through the courtyard or what used to look like a courtyard. The water fountain in the middle had water dripping from a small spout that came out of a sorcerer's crown. The dripping water had made a divot on the back of a stone fox that stood next to the sorcerer. Regina guessed that the stone sorcerer was supposed to be the founder of Nahtovia, Dravick Foxguard.

They had just passed the fountain when Ravi's camouflage spell wore off. Ravi swore and looked disappointed with himself for not holding the spell for longer.

"We just need to get to that door. There really is no need to be sneaky anymore. There is no one to hide from in here." Thack made a good point. The castle was deserted. The outer walls stretched high into the sky and every entrance was reinforced with thick steal walls. Even the small walk through gate that Fox Squad went through was extremely difficult to open. Regina was pretty sure Vaul broke from the line to help Thack open the iron gate. Regina could only imagine how much work and power it took for the Mad Sister to break through.

The door that they were heading to slowly creaked open. An old man came hobbling out supporting himself with a cane. His kindly face was smiling as he waved to Fox Squad from the entrance of the doorway. He had a slight hunch to his back that kept him from standing up straight. The old man's hair was completely white, that is, in the few places on his head that he still had hair.

"Barnabas!" Thack happily called out. "It is good to see you. How have you been?" Thack gave his dear friend a hug.

"As spry as a spring chicken and still younger and better looking than you." Barnabas laughed along with his friend.

"Everyone this is Barnabas." Thack introduced him to the group.

"Oh please, call me Barney." One by one each of them shook hands with Barney and introduced themselves. Regina watched Tucker introduce himself when something had caught her eye. Tyler was walking over to a portrait that was directly behind Barney. Barney turned to introduce himself to Regina, but she was no longer standing next to him. She had joined her brother. There in front of Tyler and Regina was there father.

"I've almost forgotten what he looked like." Said Tyler.

Regina nodded. She stood there and examined every bit of the man that was in front of her. His light brown hair laid under a large golden crown. Although the crown was large it was very modest. There were no emeralds, diamonds or rubies; just engraved designs and a single blue sapphire that rested on the front of the crown. Their father had very defined features that made him look handsome and strapping. His bright blue eyes stood out amongst the dark canvas background. Regina looked down at the golden name plate: William Foxguard age 15.

Regina turned to her brother, "It is weird to think that our real last name is Foxguard."

Tyler thought for a moment, "Yeah that is weird to think about. So where did the name Baylon come from?"

"Maybe it was our mother's."

Barney joined Regina and Tyler. He looked up at the portrait and back down to Tyler. "You look so much like your father."

"Did you know him?" asked Tyler with excited curiosity.

"Oh yes. I knew him very well." His eyes glazed and a wide smile spread across his face as if he was remembering a fond memory. "It was my duty to look after your father. He was a very kind and smart young man. Overall he was a good kid, but he liked to sneak out a lot."

Regina and Tyler looked at each other and laughed; even Tucker let out a chuckle from across the room. It felt good to share this connection with her father. Regina looked at his portrait again, but her lingered happiness turned into sadness. She had forgotten how much she had missed him and her mother. Tyler and Regina spent so much time hating Lady Dumontet that the pain of missing her parents rarely came up. It always sat in the back of her mind that if her parents were still alive she wouldn't be under the control of a mad women, but Regina's time and energy went towards protecting her brother and figuring out new ways to escape the hellish prison she wished she didn't have to call home.

Regina's face became serious and asked the question she had been dying to know, "Do you know how the royal family escaped from the Mad Sister?"

"Yes I do, well sort of." Barney said with a frown.

Regina was intrigued. If she knew how they made it out of the castle, then maybe she could figure out what happened to her grandparents. She became ecstatic at the prospect that her grandparents, King Amos and Queen Esme, could possibly still be alive. She listened intently as Barney began his story.

"I remember that day very well. The Mad Sister and the Carnagers had reached the castle just two days before. Your father had urged me to leave, but I couldn't abandon him. He was like a son to me. King Amos was commanding his troops and planning attacks from the Royal Brigade tower. He didn't want to abandon his people, but he also didn't want any harm to come to his family. Royal guards were running about the castle making sure every passage way remained sealed from the outside. Your father wanted to join the fight, but the King would not allow it. Your father was the only heir to the throne. If the Mad Sister were to take over, he figured his supporters would rally around his son to take back the kingdom. Of course he also cared for his son very much, but he always had a hard time showing it."

"It was late afternoon, when a small breach had just occurred. The Mad Sister didn't make it in, but Midnight Smoke did."

"Who or what is Midnight Smoke?" Regina asked. Everyone had gathered at this point and was just as enthralled by Barney's story as Tyler and Regina were.

"Nobody really knew who Midnight Smoke was. People would tell stories of terrible attacks where Carnagers would take orders from this sorcerer who would linger in the darkness. The most terrifying story I had heard was from a Royal Guard. He was out on a routine patrol with his fellow guards, just surveying the hills surrounding the castle. It was a bright sunny day. The war had just begun and most attacks were being held at the lake and there hadn't been any talks of movement. The guards were making their last round before they headed back to the castle when a sorcerer appeared up on a hill top. They didn't think much of it at first, but then the sky began to rumble. In an instant, dark clouds covered the sun; thunder boomed through the air and then **CRACK**! Lightning struck behind the mysterious sorcerer. The sorcerer's body turned to smoke and a group of Carnagers came charging down the hill. The Carnagers followed the mist of smoke to the battle grounds. The unsuspecting guards bellow didn't stand a chance. In a matter of minutes, the Royal Guards were defeated, but before the last blow could be dealt; Midnight Smoke intervened. The smoky mist of the sorcerer whispered into the guard's ear. He was spared, but only so he could tell all of what happened that day. So others would know the name of Midnight Smoke."

"Rumors were that Midnight Smoke was the Mad Sister's second in command. That is all I believed it to be, just rumors, I didn't think anything so terrifying could exist, that is until the breach happened. Once word reached Queen Esme, she grabbed her son and myself and headed to the secret passageway that lead out of the castle and out towards the Parting Trees. The three of us had just reached the secret entrance when Midnight Smoke appeared at the end of the hallway. He or she just stood there and watched us. It felt as if time itself slowed down; we watched Midnight Smoke and Midnight watched us. A thundering boom came from behind Midnight Smoke. Everyone flinched but not Midnight. The Mad Sister was breaking her way through, I knew we had to leave right there and then before it was too late. I turned to open the secret entrance. I looked towards Midnight Smoke, still just standing there, I blinked and-and…"

"Whats happened nexts?" Vaul asked sitting crossed legged on the floor holding his head up with his thick meaty hands.

"…And this mist or smoke, I'm still not sure what it was, stood in front of me. I tilted my head to look behind it and a light trail of a blackish purple mist was floating in the air. Midnight Smoke had traveled from the end of the hall to a few inches in front of me in the blink of an eye. Then something crashed down on my head. The last thing I saw was young Prince William's face; he was laying me down on the floor where broken bits of ceramic still swayed from just hitting the ground."

"Midnight Smoke must have hit you over the head with a vase or something." Maggie suggested.

"Yes I believe so. The next thing I remember is waking up in my house with my wife standing over me padding my forehead with a wet cloth. I can only assume Queen Esme and Prince William made it out somehow because how else would I end up in my own home. And before you ask, my wife has no idea how I ended up at the house either."

"What happened to Midnight Smoke?" Tyler asked.

"Midnight Smoke hasn't been seen since that horrible day."

Everyone was silent and Regina felt disappointed. She was no closer to figuring out what happened to her grandparents than she had been before.

"Let's come along now. I have lots of food waiting for you in the dining area. We don't want it to get cold." Barney led the way; walking surprisingly fast for an old man with a walking stick.

The hallway was dark and dingy. Spider webs laid across every nook and cranny. Dust layered on table tops, portraits and the floor; basically, anywhere that had not been touched in years. Regina expected the rest of the castle to look more or less of the same as the hallway.

They walked through what was clearly a back entrance to the dining room. Unlike the hall, this room sparkled. Not a single web in sight. The golden chandelier that hung above was lit with candles that burned a beautiful blue that seemed to cascade down to the floor. Portraits of past kings and queens lined the walls; generation after generation after generation. Regina examined each and every single portrait closely. She wanted to imprint the images of her ancestors deep into her brain so she could never forget.

Blue, white and gold lights twinkled on the celling and in the air. Founders' Day decorations hung about. But nothing was more beautiful than the delicious spread that laid across the long cherry wood table. It did not take long for everyone to grab a plate and start stuffing their faces with the tasty food. Stomachs were full and faces were smiling all around the table. Sleepy voices gave thanks to the gracious host.

"Not a problem." Barney replied delightfully. "Would anyone like a tour of the castle?"

"I would be ever so happy if you can show me a bed mate." Said Ravi, holding in a yawn. Several others nodded in agreement.

"Sorry, dear friend, but I wouldn't mind a little shut eye myself. I can show them where to go." Thack walked out the front entrance followed by Ravi, Vaul and Maggie. Regina, Tyler and Tucker stayed behind for Barney's tour.

Barney pointed a hand to the same door Thack and the rest of them had just gone through. "Shall we?"

The rest of the castle was just as unimpressive as the dark dingy hallway that they first walked through. Regina could tell that under all the dust and grime hid a lovely place, but it would need some serious cleaning in order for it to turn back into its former glory.

"Regina do you know if your mother was from this realm?" asked Barney.

"Uh? So you did not know my mother?" Ever since Regina had found out about her and her brother's royal past, she had assumed that her mother was some kind of royalty herself; arranged to marry her father at birth. "I thought royals could only marry royals?"

"Ah yes, I believe that is a common practice in your world, but we know happy kings and queens are better rulers and it is a lot easier to keep someone happy if you let them marry whomever they like."

"Oh! Then I am not sure if my mother is from this realm or not." Regina now had a billion questions about her mother and who she really was, but there was no one who could answer these questions for her.

Barney noticed the sadden expression that grew heavy on Regina's face. "What did your mother look like? Maybe I knew her and I can tell you who she was based on your description."

Regina tried hard to remember every detail about her mother. She closed her eyes; fleeting images ran swiftly through her mind like watching the night sky for shooting stars. She scanned her brain and waited for an image to stand still. Finally, an image from when Regina was about six or seven, popped into view. Her mother had just finished making Regina's favorite snack, peanut butter on bananas. She placed the plate on the table and watched Regina eat each slice of banana. Regina remembered her mother laughing; the peanut butter on her fingers had smeared across her face as she attempted to wipe herself cleaning with a napkin. Her mother grabbed a paper towel, wet the corner of it and dabbed the bits of peanut butter from her face. Once she was done, her mother starred and smiled at Regina. She said in her soft sweet voice, "There is my beautiful princesa!"

Regina let out a big smile. She began to describe her mother keeping her eyes tightly shut so the image of her would not leave. "She had long dark brown hair. I remember she was constantly sweeping it out of her face because she had so much of it. Her lips were pouty and they always look like she had red lipstick on even when she didn't. Her nose had a slight bump on the bridge of it. She looked shorter than she actually was. I think it was because her hips were so curvy. Her eyes were hazel like mine except hers like to change colors. When she wore eyeliner the green in her eyes popped. They also did this when she looked towards any kind of light or when she had tears in her eyes. And no matter what time of the year it was her skin radiated her bronze complexion. Her smile would make any room bright. She was fun, loving and kind. My mother was absolutely beautiful in every way." Regina opened her eyes. Tyler, Barney and Tucker all had far off looks, but they were all smiling as if they could see what Regina was seeing.

"Your mother must have been a wonderful person. I am sorry I never got the chance to meet her." Barney tried to look cheerful as he said this. He continued the tour and decided it was best to change the subject. "Well let me take you to your rooms."

Barney walked them across an outdoor atrium that had a large clock on the floor. As they stepped over the gold rimmed clock it flashed red and the hands on the clock began to spin rapidly.

Tucker jumped and tensed at the sudden movement of the clock. He threw his fist up prepared to fight anything and everything. "What is it doing?" he asked.

Barney looked just as alert as Tucker. Panic had stricken his face and sweat formed above his brow. He watched as the hands of the clock still moved quickly around and around.

"The clock only does that when an intruder has entered the castle. The hands of the clock will point…" Barney paused as the hands of the clock slowed to a stop. Both the small and big hand were pointing at twelve o'clock. Regina knew that was not the correct time. She turned to Barney and watched him look to the clock and then up to where the hands were pointing to. He continued saying "…they will point to the direction of the intruder."

Regina, Tyler and Tucker looked straight across from where the hands of the clock were pointing to, but there was nothing there.

"There." Barney said in a loud whisper.

They followed Barney's gaze to the top of the atrium wall. Regina saw something moved from the shadows. She thought out loud "It can't be."

Tyler heard his sister's quiet remark. "What is it?" he asked her.

Regina thought back to the day they had caught Daisy. She remembered seeing a shadowy figure from the library. That shadowy figure was now standing before her.

Regina stirred from her memory at the sound of Tucker shouting "Hey you! Freeze you are under arrest!"

The figure cast a dark smoke over the atrium and when it cleared the shadowy figure was gone.

Regina and Tyler glared at Tucker. Regina said what they were both thinking, "Freeze? Really?"

Tucker looking abashed raised his shoulders and said "Sorry, force of habit." Tucker turned to Barney, "Who was that?"

Barney's face was pale as if he had just seen a ghost. His hands were slightly trembling and the beads of sweat that had formed above his brow earlier were now streaming down his face. He grabbed a handkerchief from his pocket and dabbed his face with it. He finally found the words to speak, "That was the resurrection of Midnight Smoke."

Chapter 8 Cannipers Colony

Thack was awoken by a loud bang on the door. He could hear distant knocks on other doors down the hall. Knowing something was wrong, Thack quickly put on his clothes and prepared himself for whatever was thrown his way. He was the first person in the hall followed, by Maggie, Vaul and Ravi who was still wearing his pajamas.

Maggie glanced over to Ravi who was staying in the room next to hers. She let out a small laugh and said "Nice jammies!"

Ravi peered down at himself and tried to cover up the green and orange froppers that were printed on his pajamas. "I-I like froppers, okay!' He said trying to display confidence while suppressing the rosiness that was coming through his cheeks.

Maggie had managed to put on her black slacks and grabbed a few knives, but she was still wearing a black tank instead of her usual white blouse. Vaul was wearing small glasses that he quickly tucked away once he noticed he still had them on. His hair was a mess as usual and he hadn't managed to grab the patched up brown coat that he always wore. Thack, on the other hand, was wearing his coal suit, his hair was perfectly slicked back and he had his wood pipe in hand. He lit the end of his pipe and took a few puffs.

"What seems to be the problem?" Thack asked casually, still smoking from his pipe.

Regina explained to everyone what had just happened and how she thought she saw the same person at the Porter's.

Thack raised an eye brow "hmm, I see." He did not say anything else he just paced back and forth by his door.

"I guess we should let Nita know what happened." Ravi said this as he went back into his room. A few minutes later he re-emerged, but this time he was wearing his black and gray uniform. He pulled out a compact that was similar to Nita's. It unfolded and hung in midair. A few seconds later, Nita was on the mirror. Ravi gave her an updated report. Regina could clearly hear Nita demanding to speak with her.

"You saw Midnight Smoke before and you didn't say anything?" Nita's face furrowed. Creases were forming on her forehead.

"Calm down Madame Mayor!" Tucker interjected.

"Nita, I wasn't sure what I saw or if I had really seen anything at all. Why would I bring up something like that?" Regina defended herself knowing it would do little to settle Nita down.

"From now on, I want to know everything even if you are not sure!" Nita paused to let her statement sink in. "Is that clear?"

"If you wanted to know every single thing that was going on you should have come along." Tucker's face had turned red. Clearly furious with Nita's demands. "We will give you an update when we feel like the update is needed."

Regina had never seen anyone so angry before. Nita was nearly shaking with rage. Nita started yelling at Tucker. Regina could almost see the fire spitting from her mouth.

"What's that? I'm sorry, but I think you are breaking up." Tucker waved Ravi over as he turned the mirror around.

"Mirror connections don't break up! What are you doi-"

Ravi broke the connection and folded the mirror back up. Tucker patted Ravi on the shoulder and gave him a nod of appreciation. "You're a good man."

Most of the team was indifferent about Nita, but an occasion like this made them lean more towards the disliking side than liking. Even Ravi, who seemed the most loyal to Nita, was frustrated by the berating she just gave out. He, however, felt it was always best to hear Nita out because she usually made a good point.

"No problem, there was no need for yelling." Ravi responded to Tucker. Ravi had everyone gather in his room. He was effectively the team's leader even though he was probably the youngest besides Regina and Tyler. Ravi waved his hands over the closed door a couple of times before a wave of blue light encompassed the entire room.

"I just placed a spell to block any one from eavesdropping. I figured we need to come up with a plan to make sure we are not being followed when we leave this place." Ravi looked around hoping someone had a decent plan.

"Whys don't we just beat ups anyones who follows us?" Vaul suggested.

"We can't just fight whoever is following us. What if they have back up? That can get us into trouble. I want to throw them off; make them think we are heading in a completely different direction." Said Ravi.

"What if we split up?" Maggie proposed.

"Splitting is usually not a good idea." Tucker chimed in.

"Hear me out. What if we have Barney pull a cart or something and have Ravi underneath it with some random stuff. We will send him out first and whoever is following us will follow Ravi and Barney. After a while the rest of us will go on our way with no one watching us. Barney can distract them for a mile or two before he reveals he has nobody in the cart with him; Ravi will be using his camouflage of course. After that, Ravi can meet up with us at the rendezvous point."

"Why don't we just have the random stuff under the sheet? Why do I have to be there?"

"In case Barney runs into any trouble you can help him out." Maggie explained. "Someone else should probably go with you as well."

"I'll go with him." Regina volunteered.

"Take this with you." Maggie handed Regina her cudgel. "You can keep it. I saw how well you did with it during the attacks on Tuttle Road."

"Thanks, but are you sure you want to part with it?"

"Don't worry, I have a spare." Maggie gave Regina a little wink.

"Perfect! We will leave at sunset." Ravi said a little sarcastically; not feeling too keen about being the bait. "Now, kindly get out of my room." He said as he watched Vaul peer through his belongings.

"Best if we get some rest until then." Barney said leading everyone out of Ravi's room.

The sun was just starting its descent into night when Fox Squad gathered to execute their plan. Barney had already set up a small wagon and attached it to a couple of creatures that Barney called oxirds. The body of the animal was thick and muscular with tall legs that could move expeditiously for an animal of that size. One of the oxirds was a steal grey and the other was a tan and white combination. They were covered in feathers although they could not fly.

Barney clambered onto the seat on top of the wagon and waited for Ravi and Regina to climb in. Already camouflaged, Ravi and Regina tucked themselves into the corner of the wagon that was filled with the same dragon feed Reynold used for Eydis.

"Do you have a dragon?" Regina asked Barney.

"No, I make different kinds of feed here and sell them at different markets. There is plenty of space at the castle to grow lots of different crops."

Once Ravi and Regina were completely settled into position Ravi gave a small knock on the wood to signal Barney. Barney then grabbed a blanket that was next to him and threw it over the wagon from his seat. Barney directed the oxirds to a large brick wall. He raised both of his hands together and then separated them. He proceeded to make the same gesture a second time, but he mumbled something under his breath as he did so.

Regina thought she heard him say "Open Apesame." The brick wall parted to let them through and then swiftly closed as the last bit of the wagon went through the opening. After twenty minutes or so went by, the second group left the castle; following a path that was perpendicular to the wagon's.

The ground for the first part of the ride was rough, Regina's small frame was being tossed around with every bump they hit. Regina was grateful that the rest of the ride was on a much smoother road. After another ten minutes or so, Regina noticed that the sunlight grew dim and the air became brisk. It wouldn't be long before Barney would stop and remove the blanket from the wagon.

The wagon came to a sudden stop. The oxirds gave a loud neighing sound and lurched backwards. Barney shouted "WHAT AR-" he paused and sat silently. Barney's breathing became heavy as footsteps neared the back of the wagon. The little light that remained in the sky disappeared and was replaced with dark almost suffocating smoke. The blanket was pulled from over Regina and Ravi. A woman in a dark purple hooded cloak was standing over them. Her long jet black hair peaked through her hood. Her lips were smirking and scowling at the same time. Her amber colored eyes flared as she looked at the contents of the wagon and only saw junk. She began rummaging through the stuff almost grabbing Regina's feet a few times. Regina starred at the woman before her and couldn't help but feel that there was something familiar about her. Regina felt angry with herself because she couldn't help but see a beautiful wild woman instead of the murdering beast that she really was.

The woman stopped searching all of a sudden and smiled. Regina felt like she was staring directly into her eyes. *"Have I been seen?"* Regina thought, but even as she thought this she knew it was impossible. The hooded woman gave Barney a wink and disappeared as quickly as she came, leaving clouds of midnight behind her.

Barney whispered softly, "She is gone."

"What the- how did-who was that?" Ravi asked still trying to figure out what just happened.

Regina answered for Barney. "That was Midnight Smoke."

"She is a she? I didn't think it was possible for Midnight Smoke to be a sorcerer. I was sure it was a thing a creature of some sort." Ravi said, sounding very surprised.

"It appears she is not." Barney replied.

It was night now or maybe it was just remnants of Midnight's dark smoke still lingering in the air, either way Ravi felt it was safe enough to remove the camouflage spell. They said their goodbyes to Barney and thanked him for his help. Barney handed Regina a few snacks for their journey that she tucked away in her blue backpack. Ravi and Regina headed off to meet with the others, but before they got too far Barney called Regina back.

He hugged her with a grimace look on his face. "Please be careful on your journey. Midnight is dangerous. She killed your grandfather and I don't want her to do the same to you."

Regina shocked by this new information, did her best to hold Barney's gaze. She was sure he was told not to say anything about her grandfather's fate. Her suspicions were confirmed when Barney looked over her shoulder at Ravi. He looked at Regina again, but this time he was smiling. "You have your father's spirit that I am sure of." She hugged him one last time and ran to catch up with Ravi. She turned to watch Barney head back to the castle and disappear into the night. She was grateful to him for telling her the truth and treating her as an equal and not as a child.

Ravi placed the camouflage spell on Regina and himself again to make sure that they could meet up with the rest of the group undetected. It did not take them long to reach the meeting place where the rest of the team was sitting around waiting for them. Regina and Ravi told the rest of Fox Squad about their run-in with Midnight Smoke.

Some were relieved to hear that Midnight was fooled by the diversion. Others, however, appeared to be more anxious and more on guard, particularly Vaul.

They continued with their journey to the Grand Master's after everyone had a few minutes to rest up. Regina signaled her brother to hang back from the rest of the group. She slowed her pace enough to be just out of earshot; she leaned over towards her brother and whispered into his ear. She told him about Midnight killing their grandfather and how Barney told her in secret.

"Why would they keep something like that from us?" Tyler looked at the group of people walking in front of him. He slowly shook his head and turned back to his sister. "They have been pretty truthful with us so far. It doesn't make sense for them to start lying to us now."

"Yeah I hope you are right. I just don't understand why Barney couldn't tell us in front of everybody else."

Tyler shrugged and jumped onto his wingboard. He sped off ahead and did a few jumps along the way. Regina admired her brother; he still knew how to be a child even after everything they had been through. He was smart and mature when he needed to be, but childish and carefree all other times. He had wisdom beyond his years with some of the things he said. Tyler really knew how to handle the cards that life had dealt to him; to them. Regina saw greatness in her brother that others may not have seen.

Night turned into dawn and Fox Squad was looking for a good place to setup camp. They reached a forest's edge before the sun peered over the horizon. Grabbing a small package from his pocket, Ravi threw it towards the tree tops and watched it expand. Small green huts popped up in the trees, ladders extended to the ground and an invisible barrier was placed around the three trees that had the huts in them. Each hut fit two people comfortably, but since there were seven of them Regina, Tyler and Tucker crammed into a single hut.

All the huts were laid out the same and each were colored green on the outside to help blend in with the tree leaves. Each hut had two single beds, a bathroom and not much else. They were meant to be bare and tight to keep travelers from becoming too comfortable in them. Regina had no clue how the bathroom had running water or where the pipes lead to after the water was used. Like most things in this realm, if Regina did not understand it she just chalked it up to magic.

    Tyler pulled out the sleeping bag he had slept on the first night at the Porter's. Tyler spread the sleeping bag out in between Regina and Tucker's beds. The sleeping bag turned into a small bed that fit perfectly in its spot, but left little room for each of them to walk around in. Tucker volunteered to take the first watch to avoid being crammed in the hut.

    It was an uneventful shift for Tucker and anyone else who took look out shifts for the next couple of days. It wasn't until their sixth night into the journey that they ran into trouble again. No one in Fox Squad knew exactly where their end location was or even the path to get there. Regina was pretty sure Thack didn't even know the direct path to the Grand Master and he was the one who was handling the map. Thack would turn into a wolf as they would set up to leave. He would lead the way sniffing the ground as they went. Every now and again he would pull out this map that had moving figures on it. Regina would only see glimpses of the map, but one area in particular glowed softly. It did not pinpoint one spot or another but gave a general region in which they were heading to.

    On that sixth night Thack abruptly stopped. His long black nose lifted from the ground and sniffed the air. He transformed and quickly reached for the map.

    "Ravi the Huts!" Thack's sense of urgency sent a wave of fear through the group. It didn't take long for everyone to get up the trees and into the huts.

    In a hushed voice Tucker asked what everyone was thinking. "Thack what are we doing up here? What is going on?"

Thack looked at the map again and said aloud to himself "I knew we would be close to it, but I didn't think we had to go through it." Thack's voice shaked a little and the creases in his face indicated fear, which said a lot coming from the werewolf that was always calm and collective.

"Go through where Thack?" Maggie asked with frustration and concern.

Thack looked up from the map and said "The Cannipers Colony."

Maggie and Ravi looked at Thack hoping he would say something else. While Vaul slammed his fist against a branch and made most of the leaves on it fall off. "Are yous kidding mes? I didn't comes all this ways to get eats."

"I'm sorry, but did you just say 'eats'? Are we in danger of getting eaten?" Tucker asked with a scared look upon his face hoping he had heard Vaul wrong.

"Uh yes." Thack answered slowly. "We are not far from the Cannipers Colony. They are deformed indigenous people who like to find outsiders and do sacrifices for the gods. Other times they eat the outsiders hoping to gain healing powers from their healthy bodies."

"So if they capture us, we are either going to be sacrificed or eaten? I don't like either of those outcomes." Tucker swallowed trying to clear the lump in his throat.

"It is actually rather interesting, babies who are born free from deformities learn how to become Shamans by the elders in their colony. Unfortunately, most of the Shamans leave after they realize their healing powers can't help the Cannipers. Actually, only real Sham…" Thack trailed off after he looked around and noticed he was the only one amused by his anecdote.

"Do we have a plan to get passed those revolting Cannipers? Is there no other way around them?" Ravi asked.

"I'm afraid not." Thack responded. "Their colony blocks the only path that will take us to the Roaming Caverns."

"The caverns are real?" Maggie asked in disbelief.

"Yes, they do exist; I have been there myself." Thack answered. He pulled out the map and placed it in front of him. He pointed to the glowing area labeled *Roaming Caverns.* "The glowing part of the map became smaller and smaller as we went. I was hoping it would not lead us here, but there is no denying it anymore. We need to go through the Cannipers Colony to get to the Grand Master."

"Okay, but we still need a plan." Tucker urgently interjected.

"Vaul you can take them on, right mate?" Ravi joked as he watched Vaul back away cringing at the thought of it all.

"I say we get as close as we can to the colony and we will just have Ravi camouflage us all. Will move quick and quietly; they will never know that we were there." Maggie suggested looking around the group for any other ideas. That was the best thing they could think of so everyone agreed that this would be the plan.

Ravi was the last one down the latter. He tucked away the package that contained the huts into one of his pockets. They crept along the path trying to make as little noise as possible. Vaul lingered in the back, he was clearly in no hurry to get to the colony.

Thack signaled the rest of the group to stop by raising a closed fist in the air. He then signaled them to gather behind some bushes not far from where he was standing. Learning from last time, they all linked arms before Ravi put the camouflage spell on them.

"Stay linked and be quick we don't have that muc-" *CRACK!* Ravi cut off mid-sentence. The sound of a twig snapping pulled their attention towards the road from which they came from.

"I think it came from behind us. It sounded like it was a few feet away, somewhere along the path that we just came from." Maggie said in a low whisper.

A young child walked forward from the path. His back was hunched, his black hair looked like it had never been combed and he wore a tattered loincloth. Like the Shamans, the young boy had a colorful symbol upon his forehead; a half crested sun with purple waves on either side of it. His bare body was a canvas of art, but only a dark red was used to draw in the different designs. His timid presence made Regina question the ferocity of this boy and his fellow Cannipers. The boy moved from the shadows dragging his left foot along the dirt path. It wasn't until he bared his teeth that Regina finally understood the fear that came across the group earlier. His yellow teeth were jagged and pointy. He snarled and let out a nasty call "Voota-barr! Voota-barr!"

Before any of them could react, hands were grabbing them from the other side of the bush. There were too many of them to fight off. They had been watching them and the young boy was just a distraction. Regina kicked and punched but nothing seemed to make contact; they were too fast. Loud cracking sounds echoed around her. She watched as the Cannipers swung clubs and knocked out each member of Fox Squad one by one. Regina heard the final thud. Her head throbbed in horrible pain. She began to see black dots. She fought to clear her vision, but the black dots had now become complete darkness and she could feel herself slipping out of consciousness.

Regina jolted awake, but didn't move an inch. Her arms were wrapped around a wood plank buried deep into the ground. She tried to slip her hands out of the binds, but they were too tight. The splitting pain in her head was now a continuous throb that sent waves of dull pain on every other beat. She looked in both directions and noticed she was the first to regain consciousness. On a wide tree stump that laid in front of Regina were all of Fox Squad's weapons and many other items of value.

A large fire burned below with several Cannipers surrounding it. They bent to their knees and began to praise the fire. Pink dust was thrown into the flames and onto the dirt surrounding it by a large woman with a colorful leaf headpiece that fit tightly around her large head. She hummed a melody and danced around the fire as she sprinkled more and more pink dust into it. The melody was the same one the Shamans hummed but when she hummed it there was much more emphasis on certain parts and her tone was harsh and almost hateful. There were no noticeable deformities to this woman and she acted with purpose. Regina remembered what Thack had said and made the connection; she must be an elder.

    Regina knew she had to be right. Whenever the grey haired woman in the leaf headpiece came close to the Cannipers worshiping the fire, they would reach out and kiss her feet. Two elderly men, who looked like they were twins, joined the woman dancing around the fire. The twins danced in opposite directions throwing yellow dust and joined in the woman's singing. The twins were old, older than the woman and their eyes were steal grey with a bit of film over them. They both had long white hair and the same wide ears. They were identical in every way except one of the twins had a deep scar that ran diagonally across his chin.

    Drums began to echo through the crowd. Cannipers in the back were pounding and swaying in place on their drums. One them was missing his left ear another an entire foot was gone, a female drummer had a patch over her eye and the front of her nose was missing. Regina scanned the sea of Cannipers, many of them had brown blotches all over their bodies, some had complete limbs missing and others were lucky to still be alive. Regina began to feel sorry for them that is until, one of them bared their sharp teeth at her and clamped his teeth together making a shredding motion with his mouth.

    The sound of the drums grew louder and louder and then complete silence. A very large man appeared from behind the drummers opposite from where Regina and the rest of them were tied up. He signaled with his hands to direct all attention towards him and out of the silence came a loud booming voice. Regina couldn't understand what the man was saying although she was sure he was their leader; he held a staff in one hand and gestured vigorously with the other. His very colorful leaf headpiece had flecks of gold that shimmered brightly from the light of the fire. He was covered from head to toe with dark blue designs and symbols. He was plump with folds that layered themselves under his chin; they rippled with each word that came from deep within his lunges and reverberated out from his throat. The sound of his voice stirred awake Vaul and Thack who were the only two still unconscious at the time.

    Maggie, who was tied up to a stake that was slightly in front of Regina, was wiggling suspiciously. Most of the weapons on the stump were Maggie's, but apparently she still had one hiding up her sleeve, literally. She shimmied the blade down her white blouse sleeve and caught the tip of the blade with her fingers. She pressed the blade to the rope and moved it up and down. Within a few seconds she was able to break her hands free. While the Cannipers were still distracted by the leader's speech, Maggie untied her feet as well and moved to Tucker, who was the closest person to her. She just finished untying Tucker's feet when one of the Cannipers shouted at her. She stood still and looked towards the tree stump that was several feet away. She knew it would be a race to see who would get there first, but she was confident that she would win.

    Maggie made a mad dash to the stump and directed Tucker to release the others while she fought the Cannipers off. She reached her weapons just in time. The first Canniper took a swing with his club, aiming directly for Maggie's head. She ducked, swung her sword around and chopped the club in two. Dumbfounded the Canniper grabbed the other half of his club from the ground and tried putting it back together.

    "Oh good! They are not very bright!" Maggie said with a laugh and excitement gleaming in her eyes. She gave a hard kick to the chest and made the Canniper topple over. Another one came from behind, but Maggie was too quick for him. She moved side to side dogging every blow sent her way. She grabbed another sword from the stump and hit the Canniper hard on the head with the hilt knocking him out cold.

Tucker ran into trouble himself as he attempted to untie Tyler. A Canniper jumped on his back and tried to take a chunk out of his ear. Tucker managed to grab the angry female Canniper by the arm and fling her off his back. The Canniper hit the ground hard. Tucker made another attempt to free Tucker, but two Cannipers clenched his arms and dragged him backwards. Maggie tossed a dagger and hit the shoulder of one of the Cannipers grabbing onto Tucker's arm. With his one arm free, Tucker gave an upper cut to the chin of the other Canniper knocking him out of the way. Tucker grabbed the dagger from the Canniper's shoulder and managed to get Tyler free, but was immediately tackled by another Canniper; the force knocked the dagger from his hands and slid its way over to Tyler.

Tyler picked up the dagger and made his way over to Regina. Lucky for Tyler, he was small enough to go unnoticed and was able to free his sister before any of the Cannipers saw him. Regina reacted fast and grabbed her cudgel from the stump. She swept the legs of a Canniper who jumped out from behind them; knocking her to the floor.

"Use that dagger to free the others." Regina pointed to Ravi, Vaul and Thack who were struggling to get out of their bindings. "Once everyone is free I'll use these to get us out of here." Regina picked up the two red brew balls that Ann had given her.

Tyler gave an understanding smile and left to help free the others. Regina went to go help Maggie, but found, to her surprise, that Maggie did not need any help. She was taking on three or four Cannipers at a time. Regina was thoroughly impressed with Maggie's strength, agility and her ability to use her surroundings so affectively. Maggie grabbed the rope that was used to tie her ankles and wrists together and used it to clothesline the

Cannipers. Regina went to go help Tucker instead, seeing that he was in much more need of her help than Maggie was.

Regina fought by Tucker's side until only Thack was still tied up. Tyler had not reached him yet, but Thack was one step ahead and started to turn himself into a wolf. His transformation made the ropes loose around his narrow paws which allowed him to escape. Regina grabbed for the red brew balls right as a giant boulder flew past her head. Vaul had thrown the boulder with precise aim that it landed exactly between Tucker and the Cannipers. There was another whizzing sound by Regina's ear and another landed next to the first boulder; Vaul was throwing the boulders ferociously trying to create a barrier between them and the Cannipers. It worked but only temporally. Fox Squad managed to shake off the Cannipers that they were fighting and moved in closer to one another.

They were going to make a run for it, but the Cannipers, in large numbers, started to vault over the boulders, others were simply going around. The Cannipers were closing in; there were too many to fight. Regina gestured to the team to start backing up. She was surprised to see them do so without any hesitation. Tyler joined his sister's side, she handed him one of the red brew balls.

"On three." Regina said quietly. Tyler smiled and waited for the count. "One. Two." Regina glanced over her shoulder to make sure she knew where to run afterwards. THREE!"

The brew balls landed at the feet of the first row of Cannipers. Perfect duplicates popped out from the first ball. The Cannipers were becoming confused and frustrated as the duplicates taunted them while the real team was only standing a few feet away. The duplicate Vaul flexed and roared at the Cannipers. The fake Maggie shifted her weight back and forth and swung a sword from side to side. Ravi's doppelganger kept disappearing and reappearing with his camouflage spell and Thack's wolf double growled ferociously. Tyler and Tucker's copies kept pacing back and forth holding rocks in their hands. Regina's replica just stood there, gold sparks buzzing at her finger tips.

The second ball had already released its scent and the smell was slowly wafting in the air. Cannipers held their noses upward and breathed deep relentless breaths. The leader slammed his staff hard into the ground, giving the signal to attack. That was also the cue for the real Fox Squad to get away. Regina looked back one last time at the Cannipers before they disappeared, she saw powerful bolts of energy coming from her fake twin. Regina didn't understand, the powers displayed by the copies were realistic to their owners own powers except for hers. She stopped and watched the other Regina for a little while, none of the attacks were actually real by any of them, but hers certainly stood out the most.

Regina snapped out of her gaze after she heard her name being shouted from afar.

"Reg! REGINA!" Tucker was running back to get her, desperately calling out for her.

Regina caught up with the rest of the team as they were heading towards the winding road that would lead them to the Roaming Caverns.

Chapter 9 Racing the Sunlight

It was a narrow escape from the Cannipers Colony, but Regina and the rest of Fox Squad were feeling exhilarated.

"I cannot believe how well that worked!" Ravi exclaimed, trying not to sound too surprised.

"Ye have little faith in Regina's abilities or Ann's?" Thack asked Ravi with one eyebrow raised.

Ravi did a small throat clearing sound. "It wasn't that I…umm…well it's…"

"He's just pulling your chain Ravi." Maggie called out from the back of the group.

"Right, I knew that." Muffled laughter made its way through the group. "Well, it went brilliantly none the less."

"Hey do you think we can setup camp soon?" Regina asked aloud after watching her brother let out a long yawn. She looked around at the rest of the group as well, the excitement from the harrowing escape was the only thing keeping their feet moving forward while exhaustion laid heavily on their faces.

"I second that idea." Said Tucker.

"Rest sounds goods." Mumbled Vaul.

"Yes, a break would be pleasant, but where would you like to stop?" Thack addressed the small road that hugged the mountain side. "We can't exactly setup camp here in the middle of the road and the map doesn't show any other place nearby." Thack flashed the map for all to see the flaw in their plan.

Vaul stomped ahead and grabbed the map from Thack's hand. "Let mes sees this." He demanded. He searched the map and muttered to himself "Wheres it?" He slammed his thick sausage like finger on the map. "Yes! Heres!" He pointed to a bend that was not too far up the road. Vaul marched forward still holding the map in his hand.

"Where are you going?" Thack looked dumbfounded. Ravi shrugged his shoulders at Thack and followed Vaul's lead. Thack stood aside as the whole team followed Vaul. His face turned into a sour frown and he reluctantly followed.

It did not take them long to reach the spot Vaul had pointed out to them on the map. Vaul stood as far back as he could from the mountain side and scanned the wall of the mountain.

"Great, you lead us to nothing." Thack said unenthusiastically. Vaul's eyes were still searching; his face scrunched in slight frustration. A smile cracked and Vaul thrusted the map into Thack's chest. He had found a small slightly out of place pebble on the mountain wall. He removed the pebble from the wall which revealed a key hole. He patted himself down looking in the many pockets that his tattered old coat had. He pulled out a small book and his glasses.

"Are those glasses?" Ravi asked.

"No there nots!" Vaul grunted back loudly and Ravi backed off immediately.

Vaul finally pulled out a key from an inside pocket deep within his coat. He placed the key in the hole and gave it a turn. Clicks came from inside the wall. He pulled the key out and waited a few seconds as the key began to change shapes. He placed it in the hole again and turned it once more. More clicks came from the wall; only slightly louder. He pulled the key out again watched it change one last time and then repeated the process. Several loud clicks went off at once which meant the mountain wall was now unlocked. He glanced around to make sure there were no strangers watching. He placed the pebble back over the whole. He then pushed the mountain door in a tad and then slid the door to one side. Once everyone was in, Ravi tried to close the mountain door, but it would not budge.

"I's gots it." Vaul grabbed the door with one hand slid it back over and closed it shut.

They walked down a dark stairwell lite by yellow burning lanterns. It was cold and a bit drafty. Escaping light framed a wooden door at the bottom of the stairwell where they could hear muffled noises coming from within.

"Where are we?" Maggie asked. Her arms were folded and held close to her body, trying to keep the warmth in.

Vaul pointed to a rusted sign above the door.

"The Bear Hug Tavern?" Tucker read the sign aloud.

Vaul shrugged. "Wees likes bears." Vaul said smiling.

"Who is we?" Ravi asked.

Vaul opened the door to reveal a tavern full of dwarves. "This is wees."

Thack grabbed Vaul's shoulder. "How do we know if we can trust these dwarves?"

In unison every dwarf in the tavern turned to face Vaul and chanted "Vaul the King Dwarf! Vaul the King Dwarf!"

Vaul raised his hand and directed it towards all the smiling faces that were staring back at him and cheering his name. "This is hows I's knows."

Vaul shook hands and waved to all the dwarves he passed on his way to the bar. Each dwarf was more eager than the next to touch him or to greet him and those who got a response in return seemed to gleam and boast afterwards.

Regina walked up next to Vaul at the bar "Are you really a king?" Regina was just as confused as the rest of the group; they had all just assumed that Vaul liked giving himself a fake title.

"Unofficiallys, yes I's am their king." Vaul turned to the bartender and held out two fingers. A small man with brown hair pulled back in a braid, handed Vaul two drinks. Vaul tried handing the man some figgles, but the bartender waved him off.

"It's on the house my liege." Vaul raised his glass to the young man and took a long gulp of his drink. He handed the other to Regina.

"I'll take that." Tucker grabbed the drink from Regina and looked into the glass. The liquid was a deep dark brown. Bronze swirls spun about on top of the dark liquid. It was almost mesmerizing to watch.

"Drink up my friend." Vaul finished the last of his and ordered another. He wiped his mouth with the sleeve of his brown coat and let out a loud belch. Maggie and Ravi ordered some drinks for themselves and joined Thack at a corner table. Tucker let go of any ill-conceived notions and took a swig of the drink as he sat down at the table.

"This is really good. It tastes like coffee and caramel and some other spices that I can't put my finger on."

"It is called a Wakenaught Stout and they are absolutely delightful." Ravi finished up his first glass and ordered another.

"You should take it slow." Maggie placed a hand on Tucker's; who was reaching for his already half empty glass.

"I can handle it." Tucker waved off Maggie and drank some more of his Wakenaught Stout.

"Alright, suit yourself." Maggie sighed with slight agitation.

Thirty minutes later Ravi, Tucker and Vaul were laughing loudly with a group of dwarves on the opposite side of the tavern. They were playing a card game called Sorcerer Scramble.

"So how the game works, *hiccup**..." Ravi was explaining the rules of the game to Tucker. "...you want to be the first person to get rid of all your carfs, karps, *hiccup** cards. Everyone takes turns laying one card down at a time, *hiccup** towards-a the middle of the table. Different cards mean different things, *hiccup** Ace through 6 mean nothing you just keep piling them on top of one another. If you pull out a 7, you get to pick the lucky person who has to pick up seven of the cards on the table. If an 8 is drawn you don't want to be the last person to hit your hand on the card, otherwise you have to pick up the ca-cards, *hiccup** that are laid in the middle. 9s and 10s makes the person across from you pick up two. The jester lets you pick someone to skip a round, *hiccup**. The queen makes the person who drew it skip-ss a round. Whoever draws a king lets them give up two cards to the pile. And finally, *hiccup**," Ravi pulled a single card from the deck that had a picture of a male sorcerer in a red cloak on one half and a female sorcerer in a blue cloak on the other. "This beautiful card, the Sorcerer card, lets the person who draws it switch their deck with someone else's."

"What's-s the name of the ga- game?" Tucker asked.

"Sorcerer Scramble!" Vaul gave an excited shout. "Losers haves to chugs theirs Wakenaughts."

Thack looked back at the loud group as he sulked at the bar and smoked from his wood pipe. Maggie stayed at the table with Regina and Tyler, who was laid across the booth cushions, fast asleep even with all the noise going on at The Bear Hug Tavern. Maggie had just finished her first drink and ordered a second. Regina sat across from her contemplating on a couple of questions she had been thinking about since their escape from the Canniper Colony.

"Maggie, can I ask you a couple of questions?" Regina half expected her to brush her off.

"What do you want to know?" Maggie smiled and answered with no hesitation, but they both turned their attention to the Sorcerer Scramble table when Ravi let out a loud snort.

Ravi, Vaul and a couple of dwarves were sniggering; trying their best not to let out a laugh, Ravi especially. Vaul placed down a 2 and started bawling in laughter with the rest of the table.

"What's so funny?" Tucker asked not understanding why everyone was laughing except for him. Vaul pointed to Tucker's card that he had just placed, it was a jester card. "Wait I get to pick someone to skip a turn!"

"Not anymore." Ravi said with fits of laughter.

"Pick on the n-new guy." Tucker frowned, but was now determined.

Maggie shook her head and turned to face Regina again.

"Back at the Canniper Colony, when we were all tied up, how come no one used magic to undo the ropes?"

"Those were unbreakable ropes. Only enchanted items, like my weapons, can break through them. Trying to use simple magic against them would not have worked." Maggie paused and took a sip of her drink. "That is why Tucker was struggling to free your brother until he used my dagger."

"Oh, I guess that makes sense." Regina hesitated again. "I guess the reason I ask is because I noticed you didn't use any magic to fight off the Cannipers. Why is that?"

A small frown graced her lips. Maggie looked around to make sure no one was listening. Ravi, Vaul and Tucker were still playing Sorcerer Scramble on the other side of the tavern; Thack was still at the bar smoking his pipe, but he was now in a conversation with an attractive female dwarf; and Tyler was still asleep at the booth.

Maggie took an especially large gulp of her drink, "Nobody knows, not even Nita." She took a deep breath. "I can't do magic." The words hung in the air. A moment or two passed before the silence was broken.

"But I thought everyone in this realm could do magic?" Regina asked trying to make the question sound as casual as she possibly could.

"It is extremely rare; I have only met 2 others who are like me."

"Can your-Do they- um, is your family magical?" Regina was unsure of every word that came out of her mouth. Maggie usually kept to herself and the last thing Regina wanted to do was upset her.

"Yep, my mom, my dad and my brother can all use magic. They are the only ones who know, well, and now you I guess. Promise you will not say anything. I don't want to become a pariah of sorts."

Regina probably knew better than anyone else how Maggie was feeling. "I promise I won't tell anyone." Maggie smiled and she knew Regina meant it.

Tyler popped his sleepy head up from the booth cushion, "I promise I won't tell either." Tyler's head disappeared under the table once more and fell asleep.

Regina and Maggie looked at one another and laughed. It was a good honest laugh that brought them closer together.

From the other side of the room Ravi stood from his chair and shouted. "I got it! I got the Sorcerer's card."

Tucker chimed in "Ravi only has one card left and we all have a lot more cards in our hands, does he still have to trade?"

"Yeps!" Vaul answered.

"Wait! What?" Ravi was still dancing with the card in his hand. He stopped and asked Vaul the same question again. "I still have to trade?" Vaul nodded. "But I don't want to trade." Ravi's elated face turned sour. He looked at the different decks and choose to switch with Tucker, who had the smallest of all the other decks. Tucker gladly handed his deck to Ravi and Ravi held a firm grip on his last card.

"This is your last card chap; you better hope it is a good one." Ravi said starring at his now much larger deck. Tucker flipped his last card onto the table, a 6.

"I won! I won!" Tucker was now mimicking the silly dance that Ravi was just doing only a few seconds ago.

"Beginners luck." Ravi tossed his remaining cards into the middle of the deck and reached towards his full glass of Wakenaught.

"Oh that is right!" Tucker flashed a wicked grin. "Losers have to chug their drinks." Tucker fully reveled in his victory.

Thack kissed the hand of the attractive dwarf he had been speaking to and bid her farewell. Vaul grabbed the female dwarf's hand as she walked by. "Gooiea yous look wonderfuls tonights." She pulled her hand out from Vaul's, rolled her brown eyes and walked away. "She is in to mees." Gooiea cracked a smile as he said this.

The night went on and the bar began to clear out. Thack, Maggie, Tyler and Regina attempted to get some shut eye, but were constantly awoken by different renditions of "Where the King Roams" sung by Ravi, Tucker, Vaul and the rest of the remaining dwarves.

"There once was a fellow who left his home
Roam-roam did he go
He traveled the land with his helmet of chrome
Roam-roam did he go
One day he came across a troll

Roam-roam did he go
The beast demanded for his soul
Roam-roam did he go
The fellow had the strength of ten or more
Roam-roam did he go
It was a fatal swing aimed for the core
Roam-roam did he go
The troll fell down from his throne
Roam-roam did he go
And that is how we ended up with a king of our own.

With each passing verse, more words were stumbled over and each note grew increasingly out of tune. Eventually the singing died down and so did the men. Regina awoke to find Tucker sprawled out on the floor, dead asleep. She stepped over Tucker only to witness a very unsightly scene; Ravi was curled into a ball with a large hand slung across his shoulder and laid firmly on his chest. Regina walked around Ravi to see who the hand belonged to; Vaul had cozied himself up to Ravi and used him like a child would use a stuffed bear to cuddle with. Maggie and Thack joined Regina; all three of them were standing over Ravi when he awoke.

"Good morn-" Ravi paused when he noticed the hand on his chest. He grabbed the thick hairy wrist of Vaul and flung it off as quickly as he could. "Why are you so close to me?"

Vaul grumbled in a half dazed fashion and said, "Yous looked cold." Vaul turned over and fell back asleep.

The morning stretched into the late afternoon before Vaul and Tucker were fully awake. They gathered up their belongings and sat together to eat a delicious meal that the tavern owner, Gooiea, had made for them. They had finished up their meals and were ready to leave when the young bartender, from last night, rushed through the wood door entrance.

"What's the matter Borge?" said Gooiea.

"There is some movement going on at the Cannipers Colony. We are not sure what it is or who it is, but it looks like they are heading this way." Borge wiped beads of sweat from his forehead. "It might not be safe for you to leave my king."

"We cannot afford to stand around waiting." Thack interjected. "We need to leave now."

Gooiea ducked behind the bar and removed a wooden panel from the floor. She pulled a dusty tap lever that connected to a trap door that was hidden under the wooden panel. "Go through here. This will take you further up the mountain. When you come out on the other side you will be far ahead of whoever it is that may be looking for you."

"Thank you!" Regina said to Gooiea as she climbed down into the hidden tunnel.

"We were never here." Said Thack. Maggie rolled her eyes and followed Thack down the ladder.

Vaul was the last to leave. He grabbed Gooiea's hands and looked deep into her eyes. "Thanks Gooiea."

She kissed him on the cheek and whispered in his ear, "Good luck." Vaul's cheeks turned red. Gooiea watched him disappear down the ladder before she shut the trap door.

"She's a keeper Vaul." Ravi smiled and wrapped his arm around Vaul's shoulder. Ravi looked at his arm, frowned and quickly removed his arm, wiping the side of it against his body.

The tunnel was dark, humid and every little sound echoed loudly throughout. There were several stairs that lead up a steep incline; Regina was already starting to sweat and they were only halfway through. Cracks in the mountain wall at the top of the staircase let in bits of sunlight. The light coming through was dim and pink indicating that the sun was starting to set.

"The sun should be completely gone by the time we reach the top. Hopefully this will take us close to where we need to be." Thack said fanning himself and trying to contain the sweat dripping through his suit.

They reached the top of the staircase, opened the mountain door and took in deep breaths of the fresh cool air. Thack pulled out the map to locate where the tunnel had lead them to. Regina looked over at the map and noticed that The Bear Hug Tavern and the hidden tunnel they had just gone through were now marked on the map.

"How much further?" Maggie asked.

"We are fairly close now. That tunnel was a nice little short cut." Thack examined the map more closely. "We are half a day ahead of schedule." He laid the map down on a nearby bolder. "See those black dots? That is us." He then pointed to the glowing circle that he had been following this whole time. "This is where we want to go."

Tucker scratched his head. "That is a pretty big area that you are pointing to. Where exactly in that circle do we need to head to?"

"The thing is…" Thack folded up the map and concentrated on the ground. "You see, um I don't know where the entrance is exactly."

A collective, "What?" came from the group.

"As most of you know already, the entrance to the caverns moves every day."

"Yeah but you said you had been there before. We assumed you knew a way to find the entrance." Maggie threw her hands up waiting for Thacks response.

"Um well, I didn't actually find the entrance, I mean technically I guess I did, but I found it when I was in wolf form." Ravi, Maggie and Vaul all grunted with frustration.

"What does that mean? What does you being in wolf form have to do with anything?" Regina looked confused and just as frustrated as the rest of them.

"Whenever someone is in wolf form they usually don't remember what happened during that time." Maggie was now pacing back and forth. "Correct me if I am wrong Thack, but I assume you found the caverns before you learned how to control your change."

"That is correct."

"I thought so." Maggie turned to face Regina, Tucker and Tyler. "Once Thack learned how to control his change he also learned how to keep the memories while in wolf form."

"But he originally found the caverns before he could control it so he has no idea how he got in or where he found the entrance. Got it." Tucker helped summarize the situation.

"So what now?" Regina asked.

"Well, I hoped the map would tell us where the entrance is, but it doesn't look like it will. So we will have to search the area in hopes that we will find it on our own." Thack responded trying to take back control of the situation.

"That could take days. Worst case scenario we never find it. Great!" Ravi didn't hold back any of his sarcasm. "How long will it take us to get to the glowing area on the map?"

"A couple of hours, maybe even less. The map at least gives us a search area so we aren't going in completely blind."

"That is a comforting thought." Said Maggie.

Ravi grabbed the map from Thack. "Let's get going."

They continued up the mountain path. Thack usually lead the group, but this time he hung back and avoided eye contact with everyone. His shoulders were slumped and he dragged his feet along the dirt road, creating dust clouds that lingered behind him. Regina thought he was the saddest man she had ever seen in a suit.

"Why didn't you just tell us in the first place?" Regina asked Thack trying to match his pace. "We would have understood."

"I was hoping it would all come back to me and there wouldn't be a problem." He paused for a second and thought hard about what he was about to say. "I like being in control. I've always been that way. And when I got bit...well obviously that did not sit well with me." Regina could tell that the rest of the group was listening in on the story now. "I was very miserable when I could not control my change. I would often wake up in strange places having no idea where I had been and how I had gotten there. The worst mornings, were when I woke up with blood on my face. There was no way of me being able to tell if it was from an animal or a human." Thack buried his face in his hands. "To think that I had fated someone to a life of my own, I couldn't bear the thought of it."

Thack was no longer a mystery to Regina. She understood now why he constantly looked sharp, why he always wore a suit, why he was upset when Vaul lead them to The Bear Hug Tavern; losing control made him relive all those terrible memories. Regina could even see it now. The way Thack's hands trembled slightly was like him slipping back into a world that he could no longer control.

Ravi walked back towards Thack to hand him the map. "Here, you should take the lead again."

Maggie grabbed Ravi's hand before he could give the map back to Thack. "You need to learn how to live without always being in control. Life is unpredictable, it's not always going to behave the way you want it to. You should know that better than anybody else." Maggie released her grip on Ravi's hand. Thack reached for the map, but looked at Maggie before he grabbed it.

"Maggie's right. Ravi you hold onto the map." Thack, still however, took the lead again. Maggie threw Thack a dirty look. "Baby steps my dear, baby steps."

They had finally arrived at the glowing area on the map. They all agreed it would be best to search for the entrance in daylight, so they set up camp for the night.

They began their search at the first break of daylight. They broke up into two groups: Vaul, Thack and Tucker in the first group and Ravi, Maggie, Tyler and Regina in the second.

Maggie handed Tucker a small pouch full of green sand. "If you get into trouble or you find the entrance throw this into the air. Green smoke will rise up into the sky and we will come running."

"Won't that give our location away to any enemy who might be in the area?" asked Tucker.

"We have the twin pouch, we are the only ones who will be able to see the smoke and vice versa." Maggie pulled out her identical pouch from her pocket.

"Let's meet back here at noon." Thack said taking charge again.

The two groups went their separate ways searching for the entrance to the Roaming Caverns. Their task was difficult considering that they had no idea of what they were looking for. Regina found herself removing stones all over the place thinking the entrance would open like a hidden door.

"How do we know if the entrance is in plain sight?" Regina asked as she pulled up another rock.

"Well we don't know." Ravi responded clearing overgrown vines from the mountain side. "Not much information is available on the Roaming Caverns.

Maggie pulled a familiar device from her bag. She dragged her finger up the screen searching for information on the Caverns.

"Is that a tablet?" Regina was not sure she believed her eyes.

"Yes it is."

"Put that away Maggie, it is embarrassing." Ravi looked around nervously.

Maggie didn't even bother to look up at Ravi; she continued looking through the information on her tablet. "A lot of sorcerers refuse to use tools that come from the non-magic world; they like to think their magical items are far superior." Maggie lifted her nose into the air as she said it; mimicking the way a snobby person would say something. "There are several non-magical items, like a tablet, that really come in handy, especially when someone uses magic to add some cool features to it." She selected a game on her tablet. It projected itself out and Regina was able to play it using her own body as the controller.

"Cut the vegetables with your knife before they hit the ground." A holographic type knife appeared in front of Regina. She grabbed the image of the knife and started attacking the falling vegetables.

"This is awesome." Regina handed the knife to her brother and let him finish up the level. Maggie tapped the screen again, the knife and vegetables disappeared. After a few more seconds of searching on her tablet a wide smile spread across Maggie's face.

"What is it? What have you found?" Ravi asked.

"Are you asking me? I thought the tablet was embarrassing you? I don't know if I want to share this information with you; this AMAZING information I found on my NON-magical item." Maggie waved over Tyler and Regina. They huddled together as Maggie whispered the new bit of information to them.

"Oh yeah that is good." Tyler helped Maggie taunt Ravi.

"You are right; I don't think we should tell him." Added Regina.

"Fine I won't tell you my brilliant idea then." Ravi was trying too hard to look like he did not care.

"I think you are bluffing. I don't think you have any brilliant ideas. Come on guys lets go tell the others what our new information is."

Ravi could not take it anymore. "Oh please tell me. I'm sorry I made fun."

"Alright since you asked nicely. It says here that the entrance is rumored to reveal itself in the twilight hours. So there is no point to search for it now. We should let the others know." Maggie began walking back to look for the others.

"Wait! Don't you want to hear my idea?"

"You actually have something to share with us?" Maggie turned around in surprise.

"There is a small lake just around the corner, anyone fancy a swim?" Ravi wiggled his thick dark eyebrows with excitement.

Maggie checked her watch "We still have three hours before we have to meet back up, but shouldn't we let them know? Isn't it kind of mean for us to let them search for something they can't find?"

"They never have to know." Ravi replied.

Maggie was hesitant, but Regina and Tyler gave her the biggest puppy dog eyes that they could muster up. Even Ravi joined in. Maggie placed her hand over Ravi's face and pushed it back gently. "Oh, alright. Let's go."

The four of them, led by Ravi, ran as fast as they could to the lake. No one even bothered to take off their clothes. Maggie removed her weapons and a few water sensitive items and jumped right in with the others.

It was a nice relief from the warm summer day. The weather had steadily increased in heat since they had left the castle. Each day seemed hotter than the last.

"The water is perfect." Ravi was gliding through the water on his back.

"Woohoo!" Tyler had gotten out of the water and jumped off from the small dock that was nearby.

"Who wants to play invisible Marco Polo?" asked Ravi. Cheers of agreement rang through the group. Ravi snapped his fingers and all but Maggie was invisible.

"I guess I am it." Said Maggie as she glided through the water. "Marco!"

"Polo!" Invisible responses came from all around her.

They splashed and played until it was almost noon. Ravi pulled the water from their clothes with a flick of his hand and shot it back out to the lake.

"That's a cool trick." Tyler said rubbing a hand over his completely dry shirt.

They met back at the meeting spot a few minutes later. Tucker, Vaul and Thack were covered in mud.

Regina quickly pulled back her hair, hiding her wet tips that were missed by Ravi's spell.

"Uh, what happened to you?" Maggie asked.

"You don't want to know." Tucker responded. "We obviously did not have any luck finding the entrance. How about you?"

"Umm well sorta, we searched all around, but could not find a thing. So I thought I would give a quick search on my tablet and found this bit of information." She started to hand over the tablet to Thack but his hands were filthy so she pulled it back towards her and decided to read what she found instead. "It has been rumored that the entrance does not show itself until the twilight hours."

"I guess that makes sense how I managed to find the entrance as a wolf. Alright, I think it will be best to set up camp and wait until sunset to start our search again."

A large piece of mud fell off of Vaul when he walked forward.

"There is a small lake just up ahead if you chaps would like to get cleaned up." Ravi pointed to the lake.

Vaul grunted as he went by and the three of them slowly made their way to the lake, making squashing sounds with every step they took.

They all ate and napped before they went to search for the entrance again. Regina checked on her locket, the mirror read safe. She tucked it back into her shirt and was happy to know everything was okay with Reynold and Ann. Regina had sent them a message after they had escaped from the Canniper Colony. She could feel the locket move when she was tied up and figured the notch was changing from "Safe" to "In Distress;" she thought it was best to send them a message through the mirror to let them know that they were okay.

Nightfall came and they began their search for the entrance to the Roaming Caverns again, but this time they did not split up. Thack pulled the map out to double check that they were in the right area; seven dots were displayed just within the glowing circle on the map.

"That is still a pretty big area to search. How accurate is that map?" Tucker asked as he looked over Thack's shoulder.

"This map is 100 percent accurate, I will have you know!" Thack's agitation kept Tucker from asking any more questions, at least questions directed towards himself. "If everyone keeps an eye out, we should find the entrance before morning."

They searched for hours, checking every nook and cranny they came across. At some point in the night Vaul began picking up rocks from the mountain side out of pure desperation.

"I think I found it." Tucker called out to the rest of the group. They quickly gathered around, holding their breath in excitement. "Oh wait, never mind." Tucker turned around and slumped off after realizing he had come across another arbunk hole.

"Tucker that is your third false alarm. I might punch you the next time." Maggie walked away from Tucker feeling just as tired and anxious as the rest.

Thack pulled a pocket watch from the inside pocket of his suit. He flipped it open and let out a small sigh. "We have an hour before sunrise. We are running out of time." He stood in front of the group and looked at each member of Fox Squad with a long expressionless frown. "I do not want to be doing this all over again tomorrow." Defeat had taken over him, but after a few seconds a jolt to the brain made Thack revive his spirt. "Let's pick up the pace everyone."

Thack was the only one who got a second wind, meanwhile, the rest of them were still dragging their feet. Sunken and tired faces were searching high and low, but still nothing was to be found. Ravi pulled out his thermos full of coffee and passed it around. Thack was the only one who willing did not drink any and Tucker made sure to keep it away from Tyler.

"I only want a sip Tucker." Tyler reached for the thermos as it passed hands.

"Unless you want to stay that tall forever, you will not be drinking coffee anytime soon." Tucker handed the thermos back to Ravi.

"I think we have to call it tonight Thack. The sun will be coming up any moment now." Ravi patted Thack's shoulder.

"I suppose you are right. Shall we set up camp then?"

Regina could feel the stress lay heavily upon her shoulders. Tired beaten bodies swayed with the night breeze as they waited for Ravi to pick a place to set up the huts. Regina was just as desperate as the rest of them to find the entrance, maybe even a little more so. She knew the longer it took them to find the Grand Master the more likely it would mean danger for the people back home. Regina thought about Reynold and Ann and how quickly she grew to like them and call them family. She missed Eydis, Gramm, Lars and Daisy, she even missed Nita.

"Nita!"

"What about Nita?" Thack jumped at Regina's sudden outburst.

Regina pulled the small yellow marble from her backpack and held it up to her face. "Nita said 'this will help you find your way if you get lost' I only just remembered I had it."

"How does it work?' Asked Tucker

"I'm not sure, but Nita said we can only use this once." Regina looked around for some kind of confirmation.

"Uses its then." Vaul gazed at the marble enchanted by it possibilities.

"Umm anyone have any ideas how to make this work?" Regina held the marble out in front of her. It rolled gently on the palm of her hand and then fell to the floor. A collective gasp echoed as the marble bounced on the ground. The marble rolled a few inches and then stopped. A crack split through the middle and out from it came a beautiful yellow butterfly.

"Wows, its wonderfuls!" Vaul gawked at the fluttering bug.

"Well I guess that is one way to open it. What now?" Ravi asked waiting for something else to happen.

"Can you show us the entrance to the Roaming Caverns?" Regina hesitantly asked the butterfly. It buzzed around Regina a few times and then took off leading them up a hill.

Everyone ran to keep up with the butterfly. The hill got steeper and steeper as they went along. Regina looked over her shoulder and saw that the sun was beginning to rise.

Thack shouted from the back of the group, "We already checked this hill."

"Just follow the damn butterfly Thack!" Ravi shouted back.

They reached the top of the hill and ran into the same mountain wall they had searched before. The butterfly paused and waited for the rest of the group to catch up. Once everyone had gathered the butterfly flew straight through the mossed covered wall.

"See there is nothing here. We already checked this area. That stupid bug lead us nowhere." Thack bent forward trying to catch his breath.

"Wait there has to be something here." Regina rejected the idea that the butterfly mislead them. She starred at the moss wall looking for any kind of clue. The sunlight was now only a few feet away from reaching them. Regina headed towards the wall.

"Give it up Regina. It is not there." Thack's frustration had reached its peak. He kicked a rock and started to make his way back down the hill.

Regina ignored Thack and placed her hand against the wall, but it fell through. She hurriedly pulled her hand back towards her unsure of what just happened.

"Did you see that?" Regina asked. She reached out again and her hand completely disappeared behind the wall. She continued moving forward through the wall until she was on the other side of it.

"Regina!" Tucker frantically called out to her.

"Yes?" Regina stepped forward from the wide entrance that was now clearly visible. With a huge smile on her face she said, "This is the entrance! It must have been covered with some kind of cloaking spell, but this is it! The cloaking spell must have disappeared when I went through it, but the caverns are just on the other side." Regina went through the entrance followed by Tyler and Tucker.

"Ravi go get Thack!" Said Maggie before she walked with Vaul to the other side.

Ravi leaned over the edge of the hill and called out to Thack, "Come quickly, we found the entrance."

Thack raised his eyebrows and hurried up the hill. He was almost to the top when Maggie yelled from behind the wall. "Hurry! The sunlight has hit the top of the entrance and it is starting to close."

Ravi could hear the door closing, they only had a few seconds before the door closed all together. Thack stumbled as he reached the top of the hill. Ravi bent over to help him up, but instead he watched as Thack continued to roll until he was on the other side of the entrance.

"What?" Ravi yelled, but there was no time for him to be dumbfounded. He ran towards the entrance and slid through just before the door closed completely.

"Good job Ravi!" Thack began but Ravi just glared at him. "What?"

Chapter 10 The Truth Lies Beneath the Surface

"I can't believe we all made it." Maggie said as she helped Ravi dust off his back.

Regina placed a hand at the entrance door, it was solid and she knew there was no going back, at least not while the sun was up. Regina turned to face the wide open caverns. She had pictured a dark, dirty, infested cave that would be enclosed and hard to navigate through, but the Roaming Caverns were something more than magnificent.

Metallic stalactites hung from the ceiling, bits of sunlight peered through cracks from above and the water reflected all the colors of the cavern; Regina felt like she was in a painting.

"This is unbelievable." Regina reached down to touch the water with her fingertips. "The water is even at a perfect temperature."

"Where do wes goes nows?" Vaul asked as he pointed to the three different paths that laid in front of them.

"Shouldn't we seeet uuup camp first?" Tyler let out a big yawn in the middle of his sentence.

"I'm with Tyler." Ravi stretched his arms out and began setting up the huts.

Thack pulled out the map and studied it for a bit. He kept glancing up from the map and back down at it. "It looks like we will be heading down that middle path."

"Oh, you mean the darkest of the three paths? Well that is fantastic." Tucker looked down the middle path and then at the paths on either side; they were well lit and the water seemed to sparkle vibrantly down those paths.

"You sound a little cranky Tucker, maybe you should get some rest?" Regina grabbed Tucker's arm and took him to the hut.

"Yeah you're right. I need some sleep." Tucker and Tyler leaned on each other for support as they sleepily walked into the hut and made their way to their beds.

After several hours of well-deserved rest, the team was refreshed and ready to go. Ravi packed away the huts, Thack examined the map again and Vaul was doing one handed push-ups by the water's edge.

Tyler was flying around on his wingboard when a thought occurred to him, "How are we going to get through the water?"

Everyone looked up from what they were doing and stared at the water.

"We can swim through." Ravi recommended.

"Uh, I-s can'ts swim so goods." Vaul said bashfully.

"Well Tyler can use his wingboard, so that solves the issue for one of us…" Maggie looked around the cavern contemplating. "Look! There is a boat tied up in the far corner over there."

"Do you think that will be big enough to carry all of us?" Asked Regina.

"Well there is only one way to find out." Maggie dove into the water and swam to the boat. She climbed in and rowed the boat back to the group. She stepped off carefully avoiding to slip on the puddle of water she had created.

"Ravi, do you mind?" Ravi snapped his fingers and the water dripping from her clothes flew back into the water. "Thanks!"

The boat was larger than it had appeared from far away and much sturdier as well. One by one they climbed into the boat. It wasn't until Vaul stepped in that the boat began to sink. He quickly jumped out and the boat went back to its normal buoyancy. They had almost managed to fit everyone in the boat including Tyler.

"Hey Tyler, do you think two people can fit on that thing?" Tucker asked about Tyler's wingboard.

"Uh, I think so." Tyler got onto his wingboard with Tucker. The board was unsteady and did not hoover as much as it had with just one person on.

"What if we sit on the board so we both aren't trying to balance on it?" They sat on the board with their legs hanging off on either side. The balance had improved and only the bottoms of their feet skimmed the water. Tucker smiled, "I think this should work."

The boat was now minus the weight of Tucker and Tyler which helped accommodate for Vaul's weight, although, the boat still sank a little after he got in. Vaul grabbed a paddle in each hand and began to row. Each stroke was strong and made their strides long, which made it a struggle for Tucker and Tyler to keep up.

"Vaul, there is a fork up ahead make sure you go left not right. Got it?"

"Ayes, ayes captain." Vaul said sarcastically to Thack.

The middle path was not as dark and gloomy as it seemed from the outside. The roof here too was covered in the metallic stalactites and the reflective metal gave the illusion of stars in the night sky. As they got further in, there were more cracks and actual gaps in the cavern walls that let in a lot of light. Regina enjoyed the breeze from Vaul's quick rowing and the warmth of the sunlight when it hit her cheeks. Regina was so entranced by the beauty of the caverns that she could almost hear the walls sing to her. Regina realized that the singing was real when everyone else on the boat was now humming the same tune.

"Where is that music coming from?" Regina looked around for the source.

"What music?" Thack asked.

Regina saw the confused looks on everyone's faces. "The music that you are all humming along to."

"What are you talking about Regina? We are not humming." Maggie continued humming the tune as soon as she finished her sentence.

"Is this a joke? Do any of you recognize that you are humming or that there is someone else out there singing this melody?" No one responded to Regina this time. Their eyes were glazed over and the music that was being played from afar grew louder and louder. Afraid, Regina grabbed Maggie by the shoulders and shook her hard, but Maggie still had a vacant expression across her face.

"Whoever is playing that music stop! Stop it right now!" Regina yelled but the music continued to play. Regina grew frantic as Vaul started rowing them in the wrong direction, he was heading to the right side of the fork.

Regina tried shaking the others on the boat, but still nothing was happening. "STOP! STOP THAT MUSIC!" Regina cringed her nose and took a deep breath. She raised her hand and slapped Maggie across the face as hard as she could. Maggie awoke from the trance and clutched her cheek.

"Ouch! What was tha-" Maggie broke off midsentence. She quickly realized why after she looked around to the others. "What is going on?" Maggie helped Regina wake up the rest of the team. Everyone on the boat was awoken and no longer hypnotized by the song, but it was too late for Tucker and Tyler whom were still under the trance. The wingboard was now floating on the water and it got caught up in a fast current that was sending them further and further down the right side of the split.

"Where did this current come from?" Ravi shouted over the noise of the rushing water.

Vaul steered the boat in the same direction Tucker and Tyler were heading down; he had to use some daft maneuvers to keep the boat from hitting rocks and from crashing into the side of the cavern walls.

"Watch out!" Regina shouted to Vaul, who narrowly missed a boulder. He had already reacted to the next boulder before Regina could warn him again. She was thoroughly impressed at how quick Vaul was able to weave in and out of the oncoming obstacles.

They were desperately trying to reach Tucker and Tyler. They were unconscious now and were slowly slipping off the wingboard. Fortunately, the wingboard was small enough to avoid most of the obstacles, but they knew it would only be a matter of time before they would crash and fall off the board.

Regina extended her arm and reached out for her brother's green shirt. She managed to grab the collar and began pulling her brother into the boat. A rip in the shirt caused Regina's hand to slip and she toppled backwards into Ravi.

"You alright?" Ravi asked as he attempted to get Regina back on to her feet, but Regina didn't answer. She climbed back to the front of the boat, her elbow ached from the fall and the back of her wrist was bleeding. The water was moving faster and Regina could see a dead end up ahead. If she couldn't get to them soon they would run straight into the jagged rocks.

Regina leapt off the boat and onto the wingboard. She tried to wake her brother but he was in a much deeper trance then the rest of them had been. She managed to slow the wingboard with her extra weight which allowed the boat to pull up next to her. She grabbed the boat with one of her hands and helped Thack get Tyler into the boat with the other.

"Looks outs!" Vaul pointed to a boulder that was in the middle of the stream. Regina pushed away from the boat to avoid hitting the boulder head on, but it was not enough. The back of the wingboard made contact and knocked off Regina and Tucker, who was still unconscious.

Regina's head bobbed in and out of the water. She caught glimpses of Tucker just in front of her. He began to sink below the water's surface. On quick instinct she dove in after him. The current was still pushing them forward which made it difficult for Regina to keep a steady swim towards him. She managed to grab ahold of his flannel shirt and pulled him closer to her, but as she did so she could feel something pulling back on the other end. Regina had managed to grab hold of Tucker around his chest and she swam with all her might, but she was not getting any closer to the surface. Regina looked towards Tucker's feet to see if he was caught on something. Glimmering scales rushed passed her face. She turned around to see what it was, but nothing was there. She tugged again and felt that there was no longer any resistance. She swam to the surface as fast as her legs would let her. Regina could feel the breath in her lungs escaping, the pounding of her head increase and the darkness began to swallow her vision.

"GHUAHH!" Regina broke the surface of the water and gasped for air. She took in deep breaths as she struggled to keep herself and Tucker above the water. Regina heard shouting in her head, but it kept getting muffled with the water flowing over her ears. The black dots that were blocking her vision started to clear and she realized the shouting was not in her head but it was coming from the boat. She could not make out what they were saying, but she saw them point to something behind her. She turned her head and saw the jagged rock wall getting closer and closer. The current was sweeping them fast towards it, but she had nothing around her to stop them from hitting it. They were only inches away from the wall now. Regina closed her eyes and waited for the inevitable.

Regina and Tucker hit a wall, but it was not the wall she was expecting to hit. She felt the rushing water forcing her into to a pliable cushion. Regina opened her eyes and saw that the real wall was still inches away from them.

All of a sudden the water became still and Tucker awoke. He looked around confused and coughing out the water he most likely swallowed when he went under. "What happened?"

Tyler came over with his wingboard and helped Regina lay Tucker across it. Vaul rowed the boat closer to Regina so she could get back in. Ravi pulled the water from Regina and Tucker's clothes. Regina's hair was still a little wet so Maggie handed her a towel. Regina settled into the boat and wrapped the towel around herself before she noticed everyone was gawking at her.

"What? Why are you all staring at me?"

"You were about to die, twice in front of us." Maggie said in a shaky voice.

"You went under for quite some time. I had jumped in after you, but I couldn't see where you had gone." Ravi paused for a moment. "We thought we had lost both of you."

"Then you surfaced and we were happy for two seconds before we realized you two were heading straight for the jagged rocks." Thack looked to the others, "We had no time to react."

"Yous blinded us with bright golds lights." Vaul finished the rest of Thack's thought.

"What do you mean I blinded you? I didn't do anything."

"Regina, you did it again. You used your magic." Tyler smiled glowingly at his sister.

"Oh I see." Regina looked down at her feet while the rest of the group rang out in praises.

"We had no idea your powers were so strong."

"And how they come so instinctively."

"I-s never seens anythings like its."

"It is truly remarkable."

The chatter continued on. Regina listened to their words echo throughout the cavern. She felt her stomach boiling and her face grow warm. Her powers were not amazing and she did not deserve their admirations.

"Enough!" Everyone was startled by the suddenness of Regina's outburst. "How can my powers be so amazing if I can't even control them? You don't under-"

A giant colorful coral rose from the water. Upon the top of the coral was an enchanted woman with a crown on her head and as the coral continued to rise there were more enchanted women and men. Their upper bodies were that of a human and the lower bodies were of a fish. Regina saw the glimmering scales and remembered the thing that had passed her underwater.

The beautiful woman with the crown spoke, "I am Zahari, Queen of the sirens." Her voice was deep and it resonated clearly through the cavern. "We do not take kindly to trespassers especially those of the sorcery nature." The sirens below hissed when Zahari mentioned sorcery. "Your kind have entered these caverns before. They came with promises, but all we got was betrayal and deceit!" The anger in her voice made the stalactites tremble above and bits of lose rocks fell into the water.

Regina was taken aback by the vicious faces that were now glaring back at them. The loveliness that was once there turned into savage hate. Their sparkled skin turned to a pale green and their eyes blazoned an ice blue.

They chattered their teeth so they could show off their sharp fangs.

"Leave now before I let my beauties attack." Queen Zahari had her hand raised ready to signal an attack.

"Okay we are leaving." Thack pointed to Vaul to get back to the oars so they could take off.

Regina noticed how exhausted Tucker was and told him to switch spots with her on the boat. Once he was safely in the boat Regina stepped onto the wingboard with her brother. Zahari caught sight of Regina as she made the switch. Her thin eyebrows raised and her face softened a bit. The sirens below followed suit and turned back into their charming enchanted selves.

"Wait!" Zahari whispered to the young male siren next to her. He jumped into the water and swam towards the team.

"Please we don't want any trouble." Thack pleaded.

"I only want the girl. The rest of you can go." The young male was now by Regina's side. Regina noticed as he got closer that he looked a lot like Zahari. He grabbed the wingboard and began to drag it back to the coral, but not before he pushed Tyler off.

Ravi jumped in the water and resurfaced by the wingboard. "You will not take her!"

"Arturo do not attack." Regina had not noticed but the siren that had been dragging the wingboard had swum around to Ravi as soon as he had resurfaced. Regina looked back at the rest of Fox Squad and saw that they too were ready to fight.

Maggie raised her sword in the air. "You will have to fight us to the death if you think you are going to take Regina."

"Very well then." Zahari signaled the sirens to attack. Each siren flung themselves into the water. Their fins glided them quickly to the boat and before the team could respond the boat was tipped over. Vaul who was struggling to stay afloat in the water had no choice but to surrender right away. Tucker was still weak from before, so he was overtaken quickly and it was not long before Tyler and Thack suffered the same fate. Maggie was the only one who was still fighting the sirens when Regina spoke to Zahari.

"I will surrender to you if you promise that no harm will come to my team."

"You are not really in a position to negotiate."

"Regina don't do it!" Maggie managed to get in one more punch before she was taken down.

"Yes, but whatever it is that you want from me will be much easier for you if I corporate." Regina faced her brother. He shook his head no and pleaded with his eyes for her to not go willingly. She quietly said, "Sorry" and turned back to face the Queen.

"So do we have a deal?" Regina waited for Zahari's response.

Zahari gave a slight nod. "I will hold them prisoner until I feel satisfied with the information that you will provide to me." Zahari signaled the sirens once more. "We will take you to our city at once. I suggest you take a deep breath now."

Regina barely managed to take a breath before Arturo pulled her under. Water rushed passed her face and the rest of her body; she could hardly keep her eyes open. They went through a small hole at the bottom of the cavern floor. A couple of twist and turns and they came out through a large opening. Regina noticed that they were no longer in the caverns. The sky was completely visible and there were no walls on either side of them, just open water. The sirens took them to the surface so they could take a breath.

Out in the distance Regina noticed an apple tree by the shore and the same long necked creature reaching out for one of the tree's fruits.

"What is that?" Regina asked Arturo.

"That is Fimby. He helps protect our city."

Regina took another deep breath before they dove back in. Lights emanated from the far distance and more life became visible as they got closer to the city. Regina's ears began to pop and the light from the sun grew dimmer as they went. A dome covered the city of the sirens. Arturo, still holding onto Regina, was the first one to lead them through the dome. As they went through, the jelly like substance clung to their skin and contorted until they popped out on the other side. Each member of the team was escorted through the doom with a siren and up towards the surface of the city.

"Welcome to Rapantheon." Zahari no longer had a tail. She walked to her throne made of shells and sat upon it. She crossed her legs with a definitive purpose and flung her dark black hair, with streaks of blue throughout, from her face. Her white glittering dress clung to her shapely figure and the gold bracelets around her wrists only added to her dark illusive beauty.

Zahari directed them to sit at her dining table. The team tried to stick together which was not difficult because the sirens were trying to do the same thing. Arturo, however, made it a point to sit next to Regina.

Zahari stood from her thrown raised her hands by her head and clapped twice. "We shall feast." The queen seductively made her way down the throne steps and to her chair placed at the head of the table.

Regina watched the sirens that were around her. Every single one of them glowed with splendor and grace. Regina had never seen more attractive people in her life. Every movement was done with sophistication, even the way they ate was alluring. Regina, however, concentrated on the ugliness that came from their anger; the vicious looks on their faces. She did not want to become enchanted by their charm. She knew it would be important to keep a sharp mind around the sirens.

Zahari touched Arturo's cheek with the back of her hand and slowly moved it down towards his chin. She then grabbed the bottom of his chin and smiled. "My handsome son. You have done well today. Regina I believe you have already met my son Arturo." Zahari had a devilish grin on her face.

"Yes I have." Regina knew she did not have to respond, but did so anyways.

"So you are the savior?" Zahari said this loud enough so the rest of the table could hear.

Before Regina could respond, servers placed large plates filled with food on the table. Crabs, oysters, clams, lobsters and a few other fish Regina did not recognize were laid out in abundance.

Tucker pulled something from his mouth. "Is this a gold pearl?" He rose the shiny gold colored pearl up to his face to examine it more carefully.

"You can keep it; we have plenty of those." Zahari's waved off the pearl as if it were no big deal.

Zahari turned her attention back to Regina. "I thought the savior would be older. You must have a strong inclination, what is it?"

"I umm, I'm not sure."

"I do not take kindly to liars. We had a deal, remember?" Zahari kept a calm composure, but the tone of her voice said otherwise.

"She is not lying." Tyler defended his sister.

"Do not speak unless spoken to boy." Zahari threw a nasty hiss at Tyler that made him jump in his seat.

"Hey, don't talk to my brother that way!"

A glimmer of recognition flashed in Zahari's eyes. "I see. The prince had two children that is interesting. Tell me child, how old are you?"

Tyler felt unsure and hesitated to answer. "Uh I'm ten almost eleven."

"And what is your inclination?" Zahari was now directing her questions towards Tyler.

"They think my powers are animal related. Why?"

Zahari did not answer. Her eyes became vacant and the wheels in her head were spinning. She stood up without any warning and walked away from the table. She walked passed her throne and straight to a guard standing outside a door. She leaned over to the man and whispered in his ear. She winked at the guard and continued through the doorway he was guarding. Once the door was shut the guard made his way back to the dining table.

"Miss Regina, the queen has request your presences after you have finished with your meal." The guard did a quick about-face and walked back to the door he was guarding. Arturo followed the guard back to the room and joined his mother inside.

"What was that about?" asked Maggie.

"Yeah she got real curious about Tyler after she found out he is your brother." Tucker added.

"I don't know. I have no idea what Zahari wants from me. I mean, what possible information can I give her that she doesn't already know about?"

Vaul shrugged and the rest of the team sat there contemplating the matter.

"My dear, just be careful. If there is something she wants I think she will do anything to get it." Thack hung his head and took a deep breath. "Unfortunately, there are many people out there who would like to see you dead. Don't let anyone get that opportunity."

Ravi leaned in close so only the team could hear him. "If at all possible, avoid telling her…" He looked around to make sure no one was listening in. "About the Grand Master."

"What do we do if she keeps us here?" Tucker did his best to contain his anxiety about their situation.

"Sirens are honest creatures. They don't break their word. Our only concern is how long we are going to be here for?" Maggie did her best to reassure the group.

"Did you notice we are in Lake Kahuilla? I hope they take us back to the caverns after this otherwise we have to start all over again." Thack was fiddling with the chain of his pocket watch. "Darn Sirens, there was a reason they were banished in the first place."

"Oh don't start that Thack. Everything can't be like the 'good o'l days.' Things change, people change. Just let it be." Ravi rolled his eyes. His contempt for Thack's comment was thinly vailed.

Tucker gestured his head towards Ravi and Thack. He looked at Regina hoping she could shed some light on their argument, but Regina just shrugged. She was just as confused as him and they both knew it was best not to further question the subject.

Regina took her time finishing up her meal. She was in no rush to meet with Zahari. However, she thought it would be best not to keep the Queen waiting for too long.

"Wish me luck." Regina pushed her chair from the table and walked towards the door that Zahari had gone through about thirty minutes ago. Regina kept glancing over her shoulder, hoping something would happen to get her out of this, but she inevitably reached the door and had to walk through to the other side.

"I'm glad to see that you have decided to join me. I was starting to think I would have to send a guard to go and fetch you." Zahari gave a small laugh. Her laugh was as deep as her voice and did not seem at all sincere. Regina politely smiled back and waited for the Queen to direct the next step in their conversation.

"Please come join me. I promise I won't bite." Zahari had submerged herself in a small circular pool. Her tail was back again. Regina could tell that the water made Zahari feel at ease. There was less stress in her voice and her facial expressions seemed more relaxed.

Regina walked slowly through the Queen's room. White and pink pearls decorated the room. Regina passed a giant pink pearl spinning in a water fountain that had depictions of sirens drawn on the base. As she got closer to the pool, Regina realized that it was connected to the outside lake. She could see other sirens swimming way below with fishes and other creatures. Regina took off her shoes and let her feet soak in the water.

Zahari had waited for Regina to sit before she said anything else. "So, you are planning to see the Grand Master are you?"

Regina couldn't contain the surprised expression that came across her face. She was sure Zahari knew more than she had lead on, but she didn't think she knew about this. "How, uh, how did you know?"

"Child, it is obvious. You don't know how to use your powers; there is only one person who can help you with that." Zahari examined her nails; she let out a small sigh and then looked back at Regina. "It's a shame too. The powers that are hiding within are immense beyond belief; true greatness unlike any other."

"How do you know these things?"

"Give me your hand child." Regina slowly extended her hand towards Zahari. Once in reach, Zahari wrapped her hand around Regina's wrist and yanked it closer to her. Zahari took her sharp fingernail and slashed it across Regina's palm. Blood drew out slowly from the fresh cut. Regina winced at the pain, but she did not pull back her hand. Zahari moved her face close to the blood spilling out from the cut and took a deep breath in. Her head flipped back and her eyes were icy blue. Zahari's whole body vibrated. The grip around Regina's wrist grew tighter. Then it all stopped. It was only a moment, but Regina was absolutely terrified by what she had just seen.

"What just happened?" Regina was now the one who was shaking.

"That, child, was a vision. I saw two possible outcomes to your future."

After a moment or two of silence, Regina spoke. "Well are you going to tell me?"

"It is best if one does not know too much about their own future. That being said, I ask of you to listen carefully to what I have to say next." Zahari took a deep breath and continued. "Your worst enemy may be closer to you then you may think. If this is so, the outcome will be fatal." Silence hung in the air like a sharp knife. At any moment that knife could fall and Regina did not want to be under it when it did.

Regina did her best to gather her thoughts, but her mind was racing. She felt like she could pass out. The only thing that brought her out of her dazed confusion was the painful throbbing in her hand. "Zahari, you must tell me who this enemy is."

"I cannot my child." Zahari's words were emotionless and cruel.

Regina felt the anger rise up through her body. A lump sat heavily in her throat as she opened her mouth to speak. "Why did you bring me here? I don't understand what you want from me!" Regina was now practically screaming at Zahari. "You are evil and I hate you!" This outburst did not seem to bother Zahari at all. She just stood there and waited for Regina to finish so she could move on to something else. "You want the Mad Sister to win, don't you?" Regina saw a shift in Zahari. She was no longer indifferent to what Regina had to say. Regina noticed the anger in Zahari's eyes. She now wanted to infuriate the Queen so she kept on poking at the subject. "You are probably helping the Mad Sister. You are collecting information for her like a good little pet. Aren't you? You wouldn't want to disappoint your master, would you?"

"Enough!" The anger flared in the Queens eyes. She had turned into the evil creature and took a swimming lunge towards Regina; knocking her to the ground. Zahari's lower half was still in the water, but her upper half laid on top of Regina. Her arms were pressed tightly on Regina's shoulders and her face was only inches from her own. She had Regina pinned. Zahari snapped at Regina with her sharp fangs and then she slid herself back into the water.

"I would never help that vile creature." She lingered on the last word as her face became normal again. "Nor do we wish to help your kind."

"My kind?"

"Sorcerers! Your kind came to blunder the caverns. They killed anyone who got in their way and in the end they left with most of our treasures, but that was not the worst of it. The princess at the time, was young and naïve. She claimed to have fallen in love with one of them and that he loved her in return. But when the rest of them left he followed, leaving the young princess pregnant and alone. The princess fled Rapantheon to search for her love."

"What happened to her and the baby?"

"Our guards searched for her, but she and the baby were never found. That was the first time sorcerers defiled our world." Zahari paused for a moment.

"The Mad Sister was the second. During the Mad Hysteria, that creature ordered her fleet of sorcerers, the Carnagers, to destroy our city. Many of my people were killed trying to protect this kingdom. Now that she is back, we do not plan to fall victim to her tirades again."

Zahari's eyes began to fill with tears. Regina, who had admired the Queen's strength, was surprised to see her showing a sign of weakness. But even in this moment of faultiness she did not allow a single tear to escape from her watering eyes.

"I'm sorry. I-I didn't know." Regina regretted taunting Zahari like that.

"You and your friends are free to go. I will have Arturo and a few of my royal guards take you back to the caverns." Zahari refused to look at Regina.

"Thank you Queen Zahari." Regina did a little curtsy before she left the pool side.

"My child, I wish you the best of luck."

Regina grabbed the door handle, but she did not turn it. She looked back at Zahari, "I still don't understand why you asked me here. You already knew everything."

"I needed to see your future."

"But I still don't understand, how does knowing my future help you?"

Zahari finally faced Regina. She had gathered her composure once more and even managed to let out a sly smile. "Because, my child, I needed to know what kind of war to prepare for. This will not be the last you will see of me. I can guarantee it." Zahari gave a menacing chuckle before she dove under the water and disappeared.

Chapter 11 Leaps of Faith

Zahari kept her word. She released the team and had them escorted back to the caverns. She even gave the group extra supplies and a secondary boat before they left. Regina told the team what happened in Zahari's pool. She told them how she already knew about their mission to go see the Grand Master and about Zahari reading her future. Regina, however, purposefully left out the part about 'Your worst enemy may be closer to you then you may think.'

"So she didn't even give you a little bit of information about the visions?" Tucker was trying to make sense of Regina's encounter with the Queen siren.

"Nope. Nothing more than the possibility of two different paths and she wanted to see what kind of war was coming." Regina didn't like lying to the group, but if Zahari's vision was true, her enemy could be anyone of her team mates. "The only reason why she wanted to see my future was so she could prepare herself accordingly."

"Did she indicate which way it would go?" Maggie was just as frustrated as Regina was with Zahari's lack of communication.

"Not really, but maybe she just needed to know when it was coming or if it was coming at all?"

"My dear, we all know war is coming and I think it is fair to say it will reach deep into every corner of this realm."

"Not if I can help it." Regina couldn't help but feel some resentment towards Thack's statement and without even realizing it the resentment started to grow inside of her.

The boats rowed with one in front of the other. They back tracked their way to the fork and headed up the left side. They rowed for several hours with Regina getting more and more agitated by the minute. At one point Vaul accidently splashed Regina which seemed to send her off the edge. "Will you watch what you are doing?"

"Sorrys."

Regina scoffed and rolled her eyes. "How much further before we rest, I am tired of being on this boat.

"Right, I guess we shall stop and rest up here for the night." Ravi pointed to a small strip of solid rock that was just up ahead.

Regina got off the boat as soon as it reached the side of the rock, nearly knocking over Tyler in the process.

"Are you alright?" Tyler touched his sister's shoulder.

She shrugged him off and said, "I'm fine." She walked away a distance before she looked back at her brother. His eyes were sad and he wore a small frown. Regina immediately regretted her reaction and walked back over to him. "I'm sorry, I guess I'm just tired."

"It's alright. You almost died twice today, plus you had to deal with that crazy Zahari."

Regina grinned and threw her arm around her brother. "She was crazy." They both laughed and in that moment she thought it was best to tell her brother about Zahari's vision. "I need to tel-"

"Okay the huts are ready to go." Ravi interrupted Regina before she could finish telling her brother. "Tucker, why don't you join Maggie and me in our hut?" Ravi gave a suggestive nod as he waited for Tucker's response.

"What are you doing with your head?" Tucker gave Ravi a strange look.

"Ugh, will you just stay in our hut tonight?" Ravi whispered into Tucker's ear as he came around.

"Oh, well why didn't you just say so?" Tucker turned back around to address Regina. "Hey Regina, I'm going to use Ravi and Maggie's hut for tonight so you and Tyler can get some sound rest."

"Thanks Tucker." Said Regina.

"See, that wasn't so hard. Plus, this will give me a chance to get to know Maggie a little better." Tucker told a gapping mouth Ravi.

They all sat around a camp fire and ate dinner like they usually did, except the conversation this time around was awkward and cautious for the sake of Regina's new attitude. It did not take long for the group to split off and break into their own personal conversations.

Regina looked around at the group, most of these people were new to her, but yet they had all become close. Tucker had taken advantage of his new sleeping arrangement and was sitting and chatting with Maggie. Ravi sat alone next to Regina glowering over at Tucker and Maggie's conversation. Thack and Vaul were having an animated discussion across from Regina. Vaul was making several hand gestures and the volume of Thack's voice raised as they got further into their talk. Regina was enjoying the company of her brother and in that moment she had decided to let go of all thoughts of betrayal. Each of them had made some kind of sacrifice in order to help Regina because they believed in her. There was no way that any of them would willing turn on her.

Ravi abruptly stood up, "I think I will be heading to bed now." He looked at Maggie and Tucker one last time and walked away to his hut. Regina ran after him.

"You need to tell her how you feel."

"Sshh…" Ravi looked around to make sure no one heard Regina. He waved her inside the hut so they could talk in private. "I don't know what you are talking about."

"Please, I have seen the way you look at her. You were practically foaming at the mouth right now, watching Tucker flirt with her."

"I can't tell her how I feel. I am a professional and we are on a mission right now. If I told her how I felt and she did not feel the same way…that would be terrible." Ravi kicked at the ground.

Regina smiled and placed a hand on Ravi's shoulder. "Or she could feel the same way and that would be amazing."

"I do really care for her. She doesn't smile very often, but when she does it makes my heart flutter. She is tough and beautiful and smart. I even love how she tells people how it is and does not apologize for it. She is the whole package. But I can't risk the mission all because I could not keep my feelings to myself. There's just no way I could tell her."

"Fine, if you don't tell her at least let Tucker know how you feel. He will back off and if he doesn't I will make sure he does."

Ravi smiled and agreed to talk to Tucker. He hugged Regina, "Thanks for the chat. Do you think anyone else knows?"

"I'm pretty sure Tucker is the only one who has not noticed."

"Wait! So does Maggie know?"

"I would be surprised if she didn't know." Regina patted Ravi on the back and walked out of the hut. "Hey Tucker! Ravi wants to talk to you?"

Regina switched places with Tucker and after a few minutes, Ravi and Tucker came out from the hut laughing with their arms over each other's shoulders.

"What is that about?" Maggie asked Regina.

"I have no idea." Regina was half telling the truth as she watched Ravi and Tucker do some kind of hug arm shake; she was baffled by their male bonding.

The night soon wound down and everyone headed to their respective huts. Regina and Tyler had the hut to themselves and Regina thought it was best to let Tyler know now about Zahari's vision before any other interruptions could happen.

"Tyler, there was something else that happened at Rapantheon that I didn't want to share with the rest of the group."

Tyler looked at her quizzically. "What is it?"

"Zahari said 'Your worst enemy may be closer to you then you may think. If this is so, the outcome will be fatal.'" Regina let what she said sink in. "I did not want to say anything just in case someone from the group was…you know…gonna betray us."

Tyler sat up in his bed. "You really think one of them is working for the Mad Sister?"

"I don't know. I don't know what any of it means. I asked Zahari to tell me more, but she refused."

"I have a hard time believing any of them would betray the group. Maybe Zahari was just trying to mess with you or maybe that future will never happen. She did say she saw two possible futures, right?"

"Yeah, maybe she was just trying to get in my head or like you said maybe the other future will happen, whatever that is. It's hard to shake this feeling, I have been on edge ever since we found out about the Mad Sister and how that puts us in danger." Regina took a deep breath; her hands were slightly trembling. "I have never missed mom and dad more than I do now."

"Me too. At least we still have each other." Tyler grabbed his sister's hand and smiled. A minute passed before anything was said. "Are you going to tell the rest of the group about Zahari's vision?"

"No, I think it is for the best if this stays between the two of us. I can't see any good coming out of it if I tell them." Regina was trying to convince herself that this was the right choice.

Tyler picked up on his sister's hesitation. "I think you should tell them. They have done a lot for us already. If someone was going to betray us I think they would have done it by now. We are too close to the Grand Master's now; it would be a lot easier for the Mad Sister to win if you never learned how to use your powers, so I'm pretty sure everyone here is in the clear." Tyler pulled the sheets over him and laid his head on the pillow. "Just think about it, okay?" He turned off the light and let the silence fill the night air.

Regina listened to the water gently hitting the rocks outside. She thought about what her brother said and knew that he was right, but something deep in the pit of her stomach was telling her otherwise. She let the sound of the water wash over her as she drifted off to sleep.

Morning had come faster than Regina had wanted it to. She glanced over to her brother's bed that was already emptied and neatly made up. The inviting smell of coffee filled the room along with the chatter from outside her hut. Everyone sounded cheerful and happy after a good night's rest. Regina went to the bathroom to wash her face and got dressed. As the water splashed over her face Regina wondered where the water was even coming from. The entire trip they always had water, but they had to gather food when it was running low.

Regina joined the others outside and grabbed a plate full of eggs and bacon.

"The sirens gave us the eggs and bacon before we left." Maggie responded to the look on Regina's face.

"About that. How come we have to scavenge for food when we are low, but we never run out of water?" Regina asked as everyone was stuffing their faces with food.

"We can only use the things that already exists around us, well as far as material things go." Thack said enthusiastically.

"And what does that mean?" Regina asked still confused.

"Water has been in one form or another around us this whole time. Whether it is in the air, underground or in an ocean we can use that water."

"But you can't drink ocean water."

"Well that is when we use our magic to turn it into useable water." Ravi finished Thack's response.

"What about food? It exists already." Regina asked again.

"Food is a little trickier. Plants and animals are living things and living things put up a fight if we try to extract it with our magic. So we have to do things the old fashion way when it comes to food. Of course you have food like cheese that is not necessarily a living thing, but the cheese is there because somebody made it and then at that point we are just stealing." Said Maggie.

"The laws of magic are taught to children when they are in school. I'm sure Reynold has a book somewhere in that massive library of his that explains all the rules. You and Tyler should read up on it when we get back." Said Thack in a matter of fact tone.

"You mean if we are not in the middle of a war." Said Regina.

After breakfast, they packed up their stuff and headed back out. The water had remained calm and easy to navigate after Fox Squad's run in with the sirens. It was pretty clear that the sirens had set up a trap for whoever traveled through the cavern.

"We should be a couple of hours out from the exit of the cavern." Thack was studying the map as he spoke. "From there it should not take too long before we get to the Grand Master's."

"Whats is 'nots too longs'?" Vaul asked suspiciously.

"Umm...about a half a day's hike." Thack's voice was small and hardly audible over the sounds of the oars splashing into the water.

"How terrible is this hike?" Ravi asked, joining in on Vaul's suspicion.

"We are hiking down into a ravine, the rocks are pretty jagged and the path is very narrow."

"Lovely." Ravi said sarcastically.

The rest of the boat ride to the exit was done in silence. The group was feeling ragged and worn. Their journey had been strenuous and had been met with many challenges. The end was almost near but they all knew in their minds that there was still much more to come.

They had reached the end of the cavern sooner than they had expected.

"This is a pleasant surprise. For once something is going our way." Tucker immediately regretted his words.

The caverns exit lead them to a very steep and narrow stair way. Somewhere far up the stair way it made a sudden left turn and disappeared out of sight.

Tucker wiped some sweat off his forehead. "I guess I spoke to soon." A collective sigh came from the group as they began their ascent.

Broken wood steps and flimsy railings made things extremely difficult for them. Twice they had to make dangerous jumps up onto the next safe set of stairs. Once they reached the left turn, they were able to see the path that lead them to the outside world.

"Thats does nots looks goods." Vaul grabbed at a stitch on his side and took in a few deep breaths.

"We should probably only allow one person to go at a time." Maggie looked at the rotted out planks and ropes that lead to the top.

"Wait, look over there." Tyler pointed to a strange looking mechanical box.

"Is that a lift?" Ravi asked walking closer to it. "It is a lift!" Ravi could hardly contain his excitement.

"Someone must have built this recently. It is in great shape." Maggie stepped onto the platform and waited for the others to join her.

"Where is the button?" Tyler looked around for something to push.

"Button? What do you mean? I think we just shut this gate and it will take us up." Thack closed the gate behind him and sure enough the platform began to move out towards the center.

Once the lift reached the center it came to a stop and a male's voice came from somewhere above them. "What is it that you seek?" He had a bouncy pitch that made Regina want to laugh. "Only honesty will let you pass."

Maggie gave Regina a nudge. "You should be the one to answer."

Regina looked around to the rest of them who were all nodding in agreement.

"Okay." Regina said quietly to herself. "We seek the uh…Grand Master."

The voice spoke again. "What do you want from the Grand Master?"

"We are here for his wisdom and guidance. So we can defeat the Mad Sister." Regina responded to the voice.

There was complete silence. Regina waited for the lift to move upwards, but nothing happened. The voice spoke again. "Remember, only honesty will let you pass."

"Hey she's telling the truth! Let us up!" Tucker shouted back into nothingness.

The voice did not speak again. The lift finally began to move, but it was moving back towards the edge where they had come from.

"What are you doing?"

"We were being honest."

"Let us up."

Shouting from the group grew louder and louder as the lift pulled further away from the center.

"So I can find out the truth." Regina shouted above the rest and the lift stopped. The team was now looking at her waiting for the rest of her confession. "I want to seek the truth from the Grand Master. I think because I don't know the truth about myself and my family, I-I cannot fully trust those around me."

The lift moved back to the center and the voice spoke one last time. "Truth has been told, you may proceed." The platform was now moving up towards the opening. Blank faces stared at Regina. Their sad eyes buried themselves deep into her own. The only eyes that had understanding in them were Tyler's.

"Regina we had no idea." Thack placed a sympathetic hand on Regina's shoulder.

"Yeah, well it is hard to trust when your whole life has been covered in lies. Even in this realm the truth has been covered up." Regina avoided making eye contact with the others.

"What do you mean? Everyone has been completely honest with you." Maggie was offended by what Regina had said.

"How come no one told us that my grandfather, the king, was killed by Midnight Smoke?" Regina looked up to see their reactions.

Genuine gasps of shock came from the group.

"Midnight Smoke killed the king?" Maggie held a hand to her mouth.

"I cannot believe she killed him." Said Ravi.

"My dear, where did you get this information from? No one knew what happened to the king." Thack asked desperately hoping that her information was wrong.

"Barney told me." Regina looked away as she said this. She didn't feel right betraying his confidence in her.

"Barnabas told you? He knew this whole time?" Thack grabbed the hand rail to steady him.

"Yeah, I guess so." Regina was starting to feel awful. They truly didn't know about the king's death and she just blurted it out like nothing. They had been honest with her this whole time and this is how she repaid them.

"I'm sorry. I-I thought you knew the king had died and you just weren't telling me and Tyler to, I don't know, protect us from the truth or something." The lift was close to the top now. Regina could feel the warmth of the sun on her skin. She knew she had to tell them now.

"There is something else I must tell you." Tyler grabbed his sister's hand for support. "Zahari told me 'Your worst enemy may be closer to you then you may think. If this is so, the outcome will be fatal.' But that is only one possible outcome of my future. She did not tell me anything about my other potential future."

No one said a word. The lift reached the top and Thack opened the gate. The sun hit Regina square in the face, almost blinding her. They all stepped off the lift before the silence was broken.

"Well there goes my plan to take you out." Tucker smiled and winked at Regina.

They all laughed, they laughed until their ribs were sore and they could laugh no more. Their laughter was not just about what Tucker had said, it was about everything,

everything that they had faced up until this moment. And it wasn't until Regina said it out loud to the group that made her realize how ridiculous it really was. Regina took in a deep breath of fresh air and laughed some more.

The lift had taken them to the top of a mountain ridge that overlooked a beautiful ravine. Across from where they were standing was a waterfall that lead straight down into the ravine and created a small river that ran through the middle of a mossy green forest. The river water collected into a reasonably deep pond just below where they stood.

"I say we jump from here into the pond." Regina couldn't tell if Maggie was joking or not.

"Are you mad?" Ravi looked over the edge of the cliff. "We are at least 30 meters from the pond. I'm pretty sure that will kill you."

"Not if Regina uses her magic to cushion the impact."

"Wait, what? Maggie you must have gone mad. I can't control my magic."

"Your magic comes out of pure instinct. You saved yourself and Tucker from being impaled by the sharp rocks." Maggie said trying to encourage Regina.

"She is right. You saved me from being smashed under that crate. I think she has a point." Tucker gave Regina an encouraging smile.

"There is no guarantee that my magic will work. Plus, that is a lot of people I have to stop from hitting the water." Regina looked over the edge and back at the group.

"I can transform into a wolf and easily scale down the hill side on my own." Said Thack.

Tyler placed his wingboard at in front of him. "I will use my wingboard to fly down. It will just be you, Maggie, Ravi, Tucker and Vaul that you will have to get down safely."

"Is that all?" Regina responded sarcastically.

Ravi, Maggie and Tucker gathered together. Tucker grabbed Regina's hands and said, "We believe in you Reg."

Regina noticed Vaul's absences from the group's support and so did the rest of the team. Ravi glared at him and gestured with his head to join them.

"Nos. I'm sorrys Regina, buts I will climbs downs myself." Vaul pulled a rope and some hooks from his coat.

"Fine, but we won't wait for you when we safely make it to the bottom." Maggie joined in on Ravi's glare and shook her head in disappointment.

Thack had already started making his own way down. Tyler pulled out his wingboard and flew down to the bottom in no time.

"We all should really get one of those." Ravi looked over the edge in slight jealousy.

Vaul dug in the first hook and climbed over the edge with the rope tied firmly to his waist. "See yous on the other sides."

"Alright are you ready to do this?" Maggie said enthusiastically to Regina.

"Not really." Regina felt her heart pounding heavily in her chest.

"Great!" Maggie completely ignored Regina.

"We should all hold hands so it will make it easier for Regina." Ravi eagerly suggested as he quickly grabbed Maggie's hand.

"Okay, on three we will all jump." Tucker joined in and grabbed Regina's hand. "1…2…3!"

The four of them jumped off the edge. For a brief moment, Regina enjoyed the exhilarating sensation of flying. The wind was swiftly blowing through her hair and she did not have a care in the world, that is, until she looked down.

That flying sensation quickly turned into a heavy knot in her stomach as the water was now rapidly approaching them. Regina panicked and let go of Tucker and Maggie's hands. A flash of light came from her hands and for a moment a bubble had formed just below her feet. They hit the bubble and then it vanished only slowing their fall a little bit.

Regina's toes hit the water first. A few seconds after she hit the water she heard three other splashes around her. The last splash was hard and she was sure she heard someone scream under the water; it was muffled but the pain of it sent shivers down her spine. She resurfaced and looked around for the rest of them. Tucker was the next to resurface, followed by Maggie and finally Ravi.

Ravi was clutching his shoulder as he bobbed in the water. "Ugh, my shoulder. I think it is dislocated."

Maggie swam to Ravi and helped him get to shore. She called over her shoulder to Regina. "I'm sorry Regina. I shouldn't have pressured you to do that."

From halfway down the mountain side Vaul shouted to them. "I tolds yous that wouldn'ts wor-" Vaul's rope snapped under the tension of his weight and he fell into the water. His head popped up out of the water. "I'm okays, buts I coulds use a little helps swimming to the shores." It was weird to see a wolf roll its eyes, but Thack swam out to help Vaul get to land.

They all gathered together at the river's edge.

"Is everyone all right?" Thack asked back in his human form.

"Ravi's shoulder is dislocated, but other than that just a few bumps and bruises nothing too bad." Maggie was still supporting Ravi, who didn't seem to mind.

"The Grand Master should be able to heal that up." Thack looked at the map and smiled. "If we follow this river upstream we will be there in no time."

Now that Fox Squad had reached the bottom of the ravine there was a sense of excitement that flowed through each of the members. Regina was not sure if she was in awe because they had finally made it or because of the breath taking views that surrounded her. The floor of the ravine was covered with green grass that had sprinkles of little blue and white flowers throughout. Dense rows of trees covered in Spanish moss sat on either side of the river. The large trees stood their grounds gently dancing their hundred-year-old dance while pink flowers flourished in the air twisting and turning to a rhythmic flow before they turned into rays of light that swept up and joined the heavens.

The river flowing through the middle played a calming melody of trickling water and blossoming life. A fish jumped out of the crystal clear river and a streak of gold and white ran to the river to catch it. A tiger or something a bit smaller than that stood by the water and waited for the next fish to pop out.

Tyler was completely mesmerized by the creature. "What is that?"

"That is a golden tigre, they are extremely rare and even more difficult to kill." Maggie showed Tyler the description on her tablet.

"Parts of its fur are made of gold?" Asked Tyler; not entirely believing what he had just read.

"Yep, that is why it is hard to kill one. They harden their fur when under attack. Not much can penetrate it." Maggie stopped to watch the golden tigre with Tyler. "It is such a majestic creature. I wonder what it is doing out here?" Maggie scanned the pages of her tablet. "It says here that Golden tigres are usually found in the India jungle realms. Although, the tigres can adapt to most climates. Tigres are skittish creatures that do not like to be pursued. If a tigre feels threatened, it will attack."

Maggie looked up from her tablet to where Tyler was standing. He had long moved from his spot and was now heading towards the tigre. Maggie's eyes widen with fear. She was about to yell for Tyler to stop, but a hand clasped over her mouth.

"Don't you will scare it." Regina could feel Maggie's warm breath being let out through the gaps around her hand. "Tyler will be fine. Just watch."

Tyler was only inches away from the tigre who had been watching him curiously. Tyler had his hand stretched out ready to touch the top of the tigre's head when Tucker ran up behind him.

"Tyler don't!"

Regina and Tyler tried to quickly and calmly tell Tucker to back up, that it would be alright, but it was too late. The tigre turned its attention to Tucker. A low growl emanated from the gold and white stripped tigre. Its ears were pinned back and its eyes had narrowed. The back legs had squatted themselves into a pouncing position. The tigre was about to strike and strike hard.

Tyler was all of a sudden behind the tigre stroking it's back. It turned on a dime and was now facing towards Tyler, but he did not back away. He moved forward closer and closer to the tigre. In a swift fluid motion, the tigre lunged at him. While in the air, Tyler made a circular gesture with his hands. The tigre twisted in its attack. Somehow Tyler anticipated the lunge and in his own tactical maneuver he had used his powers to flip the giant cat onto its back.

Tyler pounced on to the belly of the tigre. The tigre did not move. The shock kept the beast frozen more than anything else. After the shock wore off, the tigre squirmed under Tyler's weight. Even though the tigre was twice Tyler's size, it could not get out from underneath him. Tyler had managed to put some kind of magical resistance spell on the tigre. The tigre struggled and struggled to get free, but nothing it did worked. Finally, it gave in and Tyler had become the tigre's alpha; the winner of their fight.

Tyler let the tigre up; it did not run and it did not attack. It sat next to Tyler as an obedient follower waiting for its leader's commands. The tigre let out a soft purr as Tyler stroked its head.

"I see that you have captured Orwell's devotion." On top of a wooden bridge stood a scrawny man with honey colored eyes and dark gray hair. His clothes looked like a mishmash of fashion trends of the early 20th century. He wore a black top hat a fashion trend of the 1900s, a blue and yellow polka dotted bowtie from the 1920s, houndstooth tweed jacket from the 1930s and oversized high-waisted beige pants that were being held up by red suspenders a trend from the 1910s.

His face was mostly hidden behind his thick square-framed glasses. He walked with a black walking stick to help hide his slight limp. He had a wide smile and an energetic demeanor, but the lines around his eyes told a different story. His eyes held the wisdom of a thousand years or more; a lifetime of pain and happiness, loss and regret, of failure and success. This was the man they had been looking for, the man that would make Regina into a full fledge sorcerer; the Grand Master.

Chapter 12 The Grand Master

"Welcome, welcome. I am Marco Perpetcho." He raised one hand in the air and placed the other to his stomach and bent low into a bow. "I am the Grand Master you seek." A poof of red violet smoke billowed around him and when it disappeared he was no longer standing on the bridge.

"Where did he go?" Before Regina could properly look around, Marco's voice came from behind her.

"I am right here of course." He grabbed Regina's hand and shook it vigorously. His stare shifted over to Maggie and with another poof of smoke he was standing in front of her.

"On chante my sweet." He kissed the back of her hand. Maggie pulled her hand away as soon as he let up.

Regina noticed the red violet color that came from his smoke cloud, was also the same color that created a glowing effect around him. It looked like a wispy smolder was about to engulf him, but it never did.

Marco poofed in front of Thack and shook his hand, "Nice to meet ya." He repeated this rapid greeting with Vaul, Tucker and Tyler.

"Aren't you a big fella?" *Poof!*
"Pleasure." *Poof!*
"Hello sonny!" *Poof!*

He poofed in front of Ravi and touched his shoulder. *CRACK!* "Ouch!" Ravi's shoulder was popped back into place. "Hey you fixed it." Ravi was pleasantly surprised when he rotated his shoulder and there was no more pain.

"Thanks mate."

Marco did a dance with his eyebrows. "I do what I can." He winked and poofed next to Maggie again. "Shall we?" He offered her his arm and gestured ahead with the other. Maggie went on ahead without taking Marco's arm. Marco did not react to Maggie's rebuff, but instead did a fantastical jog/skip to the front and lead them the rest of the way.

He took them to his quaint little cottage located under a wooden bridge. The cottage was covered with moss on the backside, which made it virtually undetectable. Overgrown wisteria vines that started on the bridge and hung over the edge, covered most of the front side of the house. The cottage stood upon a large strip of land that parted the river. The group had to walk across large sturdy stepping stones in order to reach the front of the cottage.

"Welcome to my humble abode!" Marco opened the doors to reveal an overly crowded inside. Large amounts of trinkets sat lifeless on dusty shelves. Large stacks of books lounged about in different corners of the house. None of the furniture matched and there was an excessive amount of lamps throughout. In the far corner a large open chest caught Regina's eye. It was full of treasures that would be kept in a museum; ancient coins, golden jewelry, a bronze bottle with engraved writing, a golden goblet with small red rubies, and a steel dagger among other things. This was one of the few areas in the house that was not covered in dust.

"Uh, nice place you've got." Tucker waded through to a seat, trying not to knock anything over.

Vaul, being twice the width of Tucker, had a much harder time getting through.

"Sorrys." A stack of books fell over. "Excuse mes." He nearly stepped on Thack's foot. "Could yous makes some rooms?" He finally made it to a seat by squeezing himself into a spot between Tucker and Ravi. Ravi switched seats with the much smaller Tyler to give himself some breathing room.

"As I am sure you know, we are here to help Regina discover the full potential of her powers." Thack took charge of the conversation, but faltered on how to phrase the next part. "Uh, how would you proce-, I mean, what would be…"

"What can you do to help us?" Maggie finished Thack's thought.

"No one ever comes to just visit they always want something." Marco mumbled under his breath, but it was a little bit more audible than he intended it to be.

"Please help us sir. My sister's life depends on this." Tyler flashed Marco his sad eyes, a look only an innocent child could pull off.

"I thought you were here to find out the truth?" The Grand Master had a quizzical look on his face.

"Yes I would, but it might be best if we save that for another time. The Mad Sister needs to be stopped before she hurts anyone else and I can't defeat her without knowing how to use my powers."

Marco stared at Regina, as if he were trying to solve a riddle. "Who says you are the one who has to defeat her?"

"You, did, didn't you? You know the anti-curse you preformed." Regina was not sure of what to make of the Grand Master. She was beginning to think it was a mistake to come here at all.

Marco laughed. "The anti-curse. That was not a prophecy girly and nowhere in it did I say you were the one to defeat Duchess Orlean…or maybe you are destined to defeat the Mad Sister. Who knows?"

"But…"

"Let's not fret over small matters. Who would like some tea? Marco did not notice the angry faces in the room because at that moment someone else walked through the Grand Master's door.

"I got those berries you were asking for." A young boy walked into the room with a basket full of bright red raspberries. He paused once he entered through the door. He scanned the room and looked into the eyes of everyone staring back at him.

"Perfection! Tea and jam! Tea and jam! Kolben go ahead and place the basket here." Marco indicated to one of the few small bits of open counter space in the kitchen. "Kolben feel free to introduce yourself to the savior."

Kolben did nothing, he leaned against the wall and looked tensely at Regina.

"Hi I'm Regina." Regina stood up to shake Kolben's hand, but only made it halfway towards him before he spoke.

"It is about time you got here." There was so much anger in his face. Regina looked blankly to the rest of the group, searching their faces for any other reaction besides shock. She found it in Vaul's livid demeanor and she too felt the same.

"Excus-"

"I have been here a couple of days now." Kolben cut across Regina. "I am smarter, faster and more powerful than you will ever be. I am going to beat Duchess Orlean."

"Why do you call her Duchess Orlean instead of the Mad Sister?" Maggie looked distrustfully at him.

"That is what the people of Kazny call her." Kolben said in a matter of fact tone.

The group all stood up at once. "Why would somebody from Kazny want to kill their leader, their Wolf Queen?" Maggie had her fists clinched.

"She is no Queen of mine." The disdain on Kolben's face grew stronger. "Not everyone from Kazny worships the devil in disguise." Kolben went to the door to leave shouldering Regina on his way out. He intentionally made contact with her, but he did not do it in an aggressive manner, only one of frustration.

Regina watched him from the window. He summoned wood and axe from the side of the house and began chopping away at the logs. Regina could tell that he was manually chopping the wood not because he could not do it with magic, but because he had a lot of hatred that needed to be let out.

"The boy is only seventeen and he is stronger willed then most people twice his age." Marco was spreading the jam he had made with the raspberries on a piece of toast. While the tea he had made was pouring itself into a mug. "I think he will do well to defeat the Mad Sister." He paused as he took a bite from his toast. "Tea is ready."

"Seventeen?" Regina thought to herself. He was only a little bit older than her, but he behaved so much older than he actually was. He had confidence in the way he walked and presented himself, however, his over confidence made him look cocky. He also looked perpetually angry, with scowl lines that were already creating wrinkles on his forehead.

Regina noticed that even though he had been chopping wood for twenty minutes, he was hardly breaking a sweat. Kolben looked like he was use to hard labor, like he had done it all his life. His face was muddy and his clothes were tattered. He had dried lips, bronze skin and callus hands. Despite his faulty attitude, he definitely worked hard, Regina had to give him that.

"Grand Master, when will we start our training?"

"Did the girly say we?" Marco was picking his teeth with his fingernail trying to remove the seeds from the raspberry jam that got lodged in between his two front teeth.

"Yes sir." Tyler joined his sister. "I would like to get better too."

"You want to get better, yes, but she needs to learn. That will require two entirely different training methods."

"So does that mean you won't help us?" Asked Regina.

"What?" Marco had strayed away from the conversation; he had been watching a bug run across the kitchen windowsill. "Oh…yes I can help. Of course I will help…" *Poof!* "…anything for this pretty lady." He was sitting next to Maggie raising his eyebrows at her.

"Great! When do you plan on training them? Soon? Like right now?" Maggie asked hoping he would leave to get their training started.

"No, no, right now is too soon. We shall start in the morning after a good night's rest. You can stay in my room." Marco winked at Maggie.

Ravi quickly got up from his seat and pulled Maggie towards him. "I think it will be best if we set up camp outside. We don't want to be a bother." Ravi walked out the door with Maggie before Marco could interject.

"Thank you." Maggie whispered in Ravi's ear.

Everyone was happy to leave the cramped house, except for Thack, who was enjoying looking through the Grand Master's historical items. Regina was the last to leave; she hoped that Marco would have more to say to her, but he carried on like she was not there. A hand grabbed at Regina's upper arm as she shut the door behind her.

"I don't care what you do, just stay out of my way; both here and on the battle field." Kolben let go of her arm and walked over to the river.

Regina was more startled by Kolben's sudden grab than anything else. She wanted to hate him, but his motivation to keep fighting in the worst of situations was something she could relate to. He was already here and there was nothing she could do about it. She would do her best to work with him, but she would not let him run all over her.

Regina crossed the stepping stones and joined the others. Ravi was setting up the huts while the rest of the group talked in low whispers.

"This guy is nuts." Tucker began.

"Yous thinks he cans really helps us?" Vaul added.

"We came all this way." Ravi finished setting up and joined in on the conversation. "We should at least give him a chance I guess."

"I don't care what happens as long as I don't have to deal with him anymore." Maggie shook her entire body trying to get the image of Marco winking at her out of her mind.

"Thack, Vaul, have either of you actually seen him use his magic, I mean like really use his magic?" Regina looked to the two of them hoping to get some kind of reassurance.

"I-s has never seens him."

"Technically yes, I was a wolf at the time, but this was before I knew how to control it. So I only remember bits and pieces." Thack twiddled his fingers and puffed on his wooden pipe.

"How do we know this guy is not a fake?" Asked Regina.

"My dear, I don't actually remember seeing any of his magic at work, but I can recall feeling utterly amazed at the time. We should at least give him a chance."

***

Regina was deep asleep when rays of light from the sunrise hit her face. She tossed in bed to escape the light and closed her eyes in hopes of getting an extra hour of sleep. She began drifting off again when she heard rustling just outside her hut. Regina reached for her cudgel and peaked out the window; it was Kolben. He was sitting by the river letting his feet dangle in the water while he was reading a book. Panic set in. *"Am I late? Is he trying to make me look bad?"*

After a quick change, Regina tried to wake up her brother.

"Ugh, fifteen more minutes." He threw his head on the pillow. Regina tapped his foot a few more times. "Okay, okay I'm coming."

Regina ran out of the hut, but Tyler threw the covers over his head and went back to sleep.

When she reached Kolben she looked around for the Grand Master. "Where is he? Wher-" Her voice trailed off when she saw Kolben's face. His eyebrows were curved downward and his grey blue eyes looked at Regina like she was crazy.

Through the Grand Master's window Regina could see him dancing in his kitchen while the tea was making itself. Purple silk pajamas swayed in unisons with Mozart's Symphony No. 40. One hand was holding a piece of toast while the other conducted the music. He let sparks fly from his fingers at the crescendos.

"He does that every morning." The sound of Kolben's voice startled Regina.

"What?" She looked at Kolben again.

"The music and dancing, he does that every morning. So far it just been Mozart, but I have seen other composers in his collection."

"Oh! I see." Regina contemplated whether or not to go back to the hut or wait around for the Grand Master.

"He doesn't help much…with the training." Kolben said staring at the water.

"What do you mean?"

"He just gives me vague things to do, mostly chores, and he just told me to read this book." Kolben held up the book to her.

Regina walked over next to Kolben and sat with him. The tips of her toes curled as the cold water rippled at her touch. "What is it about?"

"I'm not sure he just gave it to me this morning before he started doing that." He nudged a head towards the Grand Master's house. "It is old and the text is hard to read. It is called *Light of the Dark*."

"*Light of the Dark*? Can I see it?" Regina reached for the book.

Kolben pulled the book close to his chest. "When I am done with it you can have it."

"How good is it to you, if you can hardly read it?" Her arms were crossed waiting for his response.

He looked at her for a minute before he gave in. "Fine I guess we can read it together."

Kolben laid the book flat on his lap so she could see. The pages were yellowed and tattered, corners folded in on some pages and others had smeared ink across the page. The text was small and hand written.

"I see what you mean about it being hard to read." Regina squinted to see if that would help make out the writing. Maybe we can use some kind of magic to make it more readable?"

"If I knew some kind of magic that would make this easier to read I would have done it already." He looked at her with an annoyed frown.

"Okay genius, what do you suggest we should do?"

"I don't think there is anything we can do. We will have to make do with what we got."

The Grand Master came stumbling out of his home at that moment. He had tripped over the long trousers he was wearing. Dust kicked into the air as he scrambled to recover, but it was too late, his whole body was heading towards the ground. Regina waited for the thud. *Poof!* Suddenly, the Grand Master was standing next to her.

"Nice save." Regina smiled impressed by his magical recovery.

The Grand Master gave a small bow. "Have you started reading yet?"

"Uh, not really. This book is kind of hard to read." Regina felt a little embarrassed saying this out loud to the Grand Master.

"Hmm…let me take a look." Kolben handed him the book. "Well here is your problem…" Marco waved his hand over the book three times. He hopped on one foot and then switched to the other. He spun around counterclockwise and then threw the book on the ground and stomped on it twice. Finally, he threw a bit of dirt onto the book before handing it back to them. "That should do it."

"Thanks?" Regina said unsure if he actually helped or not.

Marco looked over his shoulder before he walked back into the house. "Be very careful with that book." Marco lowered his voice so no one else could hear. "It is really old." Regina and Kolben looked at one another and then at the book that was just stomped on. Marco went through his front door and disappeared for the rest of the morning.

Kolben, amazed, opened the book to find that everything had changed. "How did he do that?"

"Who knows, but at least we can start reading it now." The large book, which laid across both their laps, seemed anew and oddly full of life. Regina swore she felt a tremble as she opened the book to the first page. She cleared her throat and began to read aloud.

"20 January, 1345- My wife and I must find refuge. The hunt has taken place here and it is no longer safe for us."

"This looks like a diary. I don't understand how this is going to help." Regina waited for Kolben to reply, but he just shrugged and gave a gesture for her to continue reading.

"It has been two years since the illness has taken hold of the land. I fear it won't be long before it reaches my family."

The book shook violently in their laps. The landscape around them began to vanish and with a gut wrenching thrust they were in a new land. Regina and Kolben strained to look around for one another, but quickly realized they were seeing the world through another's eyes. A hand, their hand, reached out to grab a woman's arm.

"Alana pull your cloak up and stay in the shadows."

"Yes, my love." The young beautiful wife pulled the hood of her cloak up over her head and followed closely behind her husband.

"We must gather as much as we can and then we will head east. We need to get out of the city." The man paused for a moment and looked around to make sure no one was watching or listening in. "The others have created a small settlement a few days walk from here. We shall be safe there."

The husband and wife weaved their way in and out of the crowd. The streets were lined with the ill. Several bodies collapsed to the floor while others carried on and did their best to avoid them. They turned into an alleyway lite by a single torch. The floor was wet with muck and the smell of death filled their nostrils. The man held his wife close as rats scurried passed them.

Alana took a deep breath and whispered, "We must get home to the children." She braved forward; hiked up her dress and waded through the muck.

After several more blocks they finally reached the outskirts of the city. They walked up to a small dingy house that was poorly pieced together. Seeing through the man's eyes they watched as if their own hand was reaching out for the wife's check. They could feel her soft supple skin. Her dark brown eyes were full of tears. Bits of her black hair slipped out from her hood as she lurched forward and grabbed at her stomach.

The husband gently rubbed his wife's stomach. "The baby! Are you alright?"

His wife took in a few deep breaths and stood upright. "I am alright, love. The baby is just upset with me that is all."

He looked his wife up and down and an aching pain ripped at his heart. His wife was not getting enough food to support herself and the growing life that was inside of her.

"We will find a better place for all of us. Some place where you can eat to your hearts content. I promise."

A sad smile appeared on her face. "Don't make promises you cannot keep." He watched her disappear through their front door.

All their belongings sat on a wagon all ready to go. He gathered his sheep and tied the horse to the wagon. He walked into his home and was greeted with open arms by his son.

"Papa! Papa!"

He lifted his five-year-old son straight into the air and spun him around. A tug at his pants indicated that his daughter wanted a turn. He lifted her up, but gave her kisses instead.

A tiny giggle came from her lips. "Pa-pa!" She leaned forward to kiss him back.

He set her down and waved his hand into a fist and reopened it. A bright pink rose laid in his palm. "For you my sweet." The little girl grabbed the rose and ran off to show her brother.

"Alana, everything is ready to go." His wife came out from the back room. Her face was pale and her body was dripping with sweat. "Alana?"

She walked passed him and ran out the door. A few seconds later he could hear his wife heaving into the bushes. She calmly walked back inside and said softly, "Shall we."

He helped his kids up into the wagon one by one. His wife placed her hand on her husband's shoulder for leverage, but he stopped her before she joined the kids in the wagon.

"There is a shaman, he can treat you once we have arrived." She nodded bravely and kissed her husband on the cheek before she climbed into the wagon. She took the reins and followed her husband as he led the sheep forward.

A force pulling from behind swept Regina and Kolben out of that world and back into theirs. It took a few moments for Regina's vision to clear. Once she could see again, she looked down at the book to find it at the end of the diary's first entry.

"What just happened?" Kolben was in shock.

"I think we entered into the book somehow. How will that help us though?" Regina let out a deep breath. "Nothing makes sense here."

"What is this old kook trying to do to us?" Kolben kicked at the water. Some of it splashed onto Regina.

Regina looked down at her jeans that were now soaked and waited for Kolben to apologize. Kolben glanced at her pants, but did not say anything. "Can I ask you something?" Regina continued before he could respond. "Why are you so angry? No, better yet, why do you hate me?"

"Don't think you are special. I'm like this with everyone and it is none of your business why I am angry. It is my right and I will be angry if I want to." Kolben stood up and turned to walk away. Regina grabbed the neckline of his black long-sleeved shirt. She pulled at it to force him to turn back around and in doing so it revealed a small part of a fresh scar on his upper shoulder.

"Hey Reg!" Tyler called out to his sister from the huts. Regina let go of Kolben's shirt at the sound of her brother's voice. Kolben stomped off without looking back. He grabbed the axe from the side of the house and walked into the forest.

"What was that about?" Tyler was now standing beside his sister.

"Nothing. Just Kolben being a jerk again."

"Oh. I-I kind of like him." Tyler looked at the floor when he said it.

"What? Why? Not only has he been mean to me, but he has been mean to the whole group. From the moment we met him he has been this way, what did we do to deserve this?" Regina spoke more loudly than she had intended to.

"I don't know, when I talked to him he was pretty cool."

"Cool?" It hurt Regina a little to hear that her brother liked Kolben, a person who Regina was starting to consider as her enemy. "When did you even get the chance to talk to him?"

"Last night after you went to bed. He actually came over and apologized to the rest of us. We all hung out by the fire for an hour or so and well, we had fun. He even taught me how to do this." Tyler grabbed a leaf from the ground and rubbed it between his hands. He opened his palms to reveal a tiny bird made out of the leaf. It flew around a couple of times before it turned back into the leaf. "Kolben's was a dragon. He said with practice you can learn to make it into all kinds of different things." Tyler trailed off once he noticed the upset look on his sister's face.

Regina was pacing back and forth in frustration. How could someone like Kolben get under her skin so much?

"Hey guys. What's going on?" Tucker took a sip of his coffee and nonchalantly walked over to them. He paused next to Tyler when he noticed Regina. "What is she upset about?"

"She is upset about Kolben." Tyler tried to whisper so Regina would not hear.

"Kolben, I love that guy." Tucker said in an audible voice; clearly not getting Tyler's subtlety.

Regina's stopped mid-pace and jerked her head towards Tucker. "What? You too? What's so great about him?"

Maggie walked over. "Just about everything. Kolben is awesome."

"UGH!" Regina threw her hands in the air and walked away. She went across the stepping stones muttering angry words under her breath. "Smug...arrogant self-loving-" Regina looked up from the rock she had been kicking. She had somehow wondered off in the same direction Kolben had gone to. He was beside the pond getting ready to dive in. Regina was ready to march on over and give him a piece of her mind. Maybe even push him into the pond, but she came to a halt after Kolben took his shirt off. He ran his hand through his thick black hair and stopped at his shoulder. He was rubbing at a scar that was in the shape of an X. The scar had blisters that were just barely forming over the branded skin. Kolben looked over his shoulder to take a look at the scar when he noticed Regina standing behind him.

Regina was developing a better understanding of why Kolben was so angry now, but she needed to know more. "When did you get that?"

Kolben picked his shirt up from the ground and tried to put it back on, but Regina stopped him. He turned away from her. "Almost two weeks ago. Duchess Orlean didn't take long to start weeding out the non-followers."

Regina remained silent, fearful she would say something wrong and Kolben would never tell her what happened. He was the closest thing she had to knowing the actual truths about the real Mad Sister and about the people of Kazny. One side of the story never paints a full picture.

"The night after you and your brother came out of the Fox Tree the Duchess made her return to Kazny. It only took a few hours before all of Kazny knew of her return. All of her followers, the Carnagers, gathered in the town square to celebrate their Queen's revival. Most of Kazny showed up, followers and non-followers a like. My family knew it would be best to show up to the rally, for the fear of being named as unworthy."

"Unworthy?" Regina didn't mean to interrupt; the question just spilled out of her mouth.

"The Duchess does not consider those who do not follow her as traitors or enemies, but as unworthies. These people are not demeaned fit for her world so she believes that they are better off not being in the world at all.

"So some of the people of Kazny pretend to follow her because they are afraid of the alternative?" Regina grimaced at the thought of being forced to cheer for an awful leader.

"Unfortunately, most of the people are happy to support their Wolf Queen. They want to fight for her, they want to die for her."

"But I don't understand. How can so many people want to follow a person who has done so many terrible things? What has she done for them to make them so devoted to her?" Regina asked.

"Because Kazny has always been the outsiders, the forgotten. After the war of Two Brothers, where the kingdom of Nahtovia defeated the kingdom of Kazny and took their lands, Nahtovia started sending all the poor and homeless to Kazny. We were the defeated people that no one cared to think twice about. Many people starved and became ill. Very few could sustain a halfway decent living for their family." Kolben paused. Regina saw how beaten down Kolben looked. He sat on a nearby rock and continued his story.

"For a while after the war, people would travel to see the king of Nahtovia and they would plead to him. They desperately begged for him to send food, to send building supplies to send shamans to help the sick, to send money or anything that would help save the lives of the many who lived there. Those who asked for his help came back beaten and bloodied and they were told that it was the king's goodwill that they were allowed to go back at all."

"This went on for decades and then out of nowhere, Duchess Orlean was sent to rule us. She helped the people at first. She brought back food and supplies, she talked to the lowest of the people and heard what they had to say, and she was slowly improving living conditions all across Kazny. Soon she became the mother to the people, the bringer of good fortunes. Once she had the trust of Kazny, she turned them into an army; an army so loyal and true that they would not second guess any command she gave. She promised them once she won the war that there would be mounds of fortune for all those who helped her get there. Who could refuse that offer?"

"She started out with small victories. Her reign over the land was growing larger with each passing day. It wasn't until the attack on Rapantheon did things begin to change. The fight against the sirens was brutal and made many question their blind faith towards the Wolf Queen. Slowly, some of her followers began to fade from the war; she did not like this and started a crusade on all those who abandoned her. She created a dedicated team, the Carnagers, to track down every last sorcerer who deserted her cause. Once the sorcerers were found she ordered the Carnagers to not only kill them, but everyone in their family, including their children."

"How could her followers still believe in her cause after she ordered the killing of children? They couldn't all be evil, right?" Regina trembled when Kolben faced away from her, not wanting to respond.

"Unfortunately, many of her closest followers were that corrupt and evil and for everyone else this was also the same time when she started calling those she had killed as the unworthies. The Duchess also began a new campaign for her war, a promise to create a stronger magic throughout the land and the unworthies had inferior blood; they were the ones who would stop the progression of magic."

"That makes no sense!" said Regina with a heated passion.

"Any normal sane person would say the same thing, but those who witnessed her power thought she was telling the truth. Her power was getting stronger, she was the most powerful sorcerer anyone had ever seen and the elaborate stories that were being told only helped her case. Her army grew smaller, but it was the strongest it had ever been. Eventually, the fear of Duchess Orlean actually having a chance to take over, became large enough for Broadcove and Nahtovia to get involved. Well you know the rest after that."

Regina sat down next to Kolben and took it all in. She waited a minute or two before she spoke. "That still doesn't explain how you got that X branded onto your back."

"Well, once you broke the curse on the Fox Tree, all magic spells were removed and the Parting Trees worked like they used to, loyalty spells and all. The Duchess ordered the Carnagers to round up the people of Kazny and take them in groups to the Parting Trees. My family was packed and ready to leave when the Carnagers knocked on our door. They forced us out of the house and made us join five other families that were being marched to the Parting Trees.

Once we arrived, one of the Carnagers thought it would be funny to put on his wolf mask and start terrorizing all the children that were there. My brother was already terrified before that guy started harassing him. My brother began to cry so I told him to join my parents who were up ahead and once my brother left I punched that stupid Carnager right in his stupid face. He made me pay for that. He had one of the other Carnagers hold my arms while he punched me in the gut a few times. He also made sure that my family and I were in two different groups."

"I watched the groups ahead of me go into the Wolf Tree one by one. Every single one of them went to the other side and back. My families' group was next. I watched as our neighbor, Dehendren, stepped into the tree. Being loyal to Kazny meant being loyal to its ruler as well, Dehendren was the first to have the traitors mark branded into his skin. The Carnagers blindfolded him and pulled him aside. Most people in that group were branded. I watched the tears roll down my mother's eyes as she stepped into the tree with my younger brother, both of them were branded. My mother held my brother's hand when they stepped out and even when the Carnagers began to blindfold them. My father stepped into the tree, but he did not flinch or even show any sign of pain when he was branded. He was the last of that group. He was placed next to my mom, he grabbed her hand and waited for them to blindfold him. He looked me in the eyes before they tied the cloth around his face."

Regina was shocked to see that tears had formed in Kolben's eyes. His muscles tensed as he took a deep breath in. "My father was good at expressing himself through his looks and that look was no different. His eyes told me everything was going to be okay, that I was going to be okay. He told me he loved me and that he was proud of me all in that one look."

"I watched my family be taken away with the rest of the branded people. I try to watch as long as I could, but I was shoved into the tree. The hot burn felt like nothing because the pain in my heart was so much worse. I searched for my family once I was pulled out of the tree. The Carnagers had forced them to their knees. A hand was pulling me to the side of the tree. The blindfold was being pulled out to go around my face. That same Carnager that had punched me earlier had his mask off and was standing above my brother. He looked up at me and smiled. I screamed for them to stop, but it was too late." Kolben paused for a moment before he continued. "I don't know how, but I managed to escape the Carnager that was about to blindfold me. I punched out two other Carnagers before I was able to reach my family. I held my lifeless brother in my arms. I ripped of the cloth that was over his eyes and looked into them, hoping that there was still some life left in them. His eyes were open, but there was nothing behind them, no light, no fear, no happiness, just death. The Carnager that tortured my brother before he killed him, stood there laughing as I cried for my family. He told me 'the unworthy do not deserve any tears.' I couldn't hold back any longer; all I could see was red and I flung myself on him. I punched and punched until his face was as red as his mask."

Regina gasped. "That must have been the same guy that killed this woman I knew, Ellie."

"He is the Wolf Queen's new commander, Viktor Vallian." Kolben unconsciously made a fist when he said Viktor's name.

"How did you manage to escape?"

"Luckily, one of my powers is speed. I can out run anyone, but only for a short distance." Kolben's solemn demeanor returned. "That was my only family, my brother was only seven and that monster did not hesitate. My whole life has changed and it is all because that vile woman gave the order to take out anyone who was not loyal. I swear that I will do anything and everything to get my revenge." Kolben stood up and threw the rock he was sitting on into the water. He yelled into the open air until he could yell no more. Regina grabbed his hand and stood in silence next to him. They just stood there and watched the wind blow flowers into the water.

A distant sound made Regina let go of Kolben's hand. "Regina! Regina!"

"Over here Ravi." She called back.

Ravi appeared from behind the tree line. "You better come quickly."

Regina ran back to the huts with Kolben in toe. "What is going on Ravi?"

Ravi said in a grim voice. "The Mad Sister has taken over Broadcove."

Chapter 13 The Power Struggle

Regina ran after Ravi until they reached the huts. Nita was in the mirror waiting for their return. "Nita, is everything okay back at home?" Regina was surprised how easy it was for her to call Nahtovia home and how she could only think about Reynold and Ann's safety.

"Everything is fine here." Regina pulled out her locket to double check. "It has been quiet lately and now we know why. I just received word from Broadcove that the Wolf Queen now sits on the throne. Apparently, the King of Broadcove brokered a deal with the Mad Sister. She told him to send his army to Nahtovia and take over the castle.

In return, she promised not to attack Broadcove and that they would split the lands evenly between the two of them."

"I don't understand, why would Broadcove send an army to take over the castle in Nahtovia? There is nobody guarding it." Regina remembered the empty run down castle that they stayed in.

"We made sure to properly spread rumors over the years that the castle was still heavily guarded. Plus, we had someone tamper with a Deception Projection to display a guarded castle instead of a wrecked home to anyone who came to oppose us." Nita answered.

"What happened to the royal family of Broadcove?" asked Ravi.

"They were able to escape before the Mad Sister went back on their deal and breached their castle anyway. They are in hiding, but nobody knows where, which is for the best. Half of Broadcove's army returned to help take the thrown back. The other half agreed to stay and help defend Nahtovia."

"They agreed to stay even though they were sent there to take it over? How can we trust them?" A vein in Nita's forehead began to throb when Tucker asked his question.

"We can't, Sheriff, but they are the only thing that can stop the Mad Sister from completely taking over this entire realm. So not to add any pressure…" Nita's teeth were clenched and she was doing her best to stay in control of her emotions. "…we need Regina at full power as soon as possible. She needs to be the beacon of hope for the people, the savior that will bring armies together so we can once and for all beat the Mad Sister." Nita slammed her fist down onto her desk. "Let me know when you are ready. The realm is counting on you Fox Squad."

The mirror turned back to normal and everyone there stood in silence. No one had expected this to happen at least not this soon. The weight of this new burden was weighing heavily on all of them.

"What does she expect from us? We just got here yesterday." Tucker walked over to Regina and stood next to her. "For goodness sakes, she is only fifteen."

"Joan of Arc was only seventeen when she received control over the French army and she went on to be very successful in her following campaigns." Said Thack in his superior '*I am always right*' voice.

"Yeah and she died two years later by being burnt at the stake." Everyone looked at Tucker in surprise. "What? I know my history too."

"Alexander the Great was only a teenager when he began leading small armies and many considered him to be the greatest military commander to have ever lived." Thack added to his argument.

"He was pretty ruthless, but I guess you are right on that one." Tucker was annoyed by Thack's smug victory. Thack rocked back and forth on his feet trying to hold in a smile.

"Oh come off it Thack." Ravi's nostrils flared. "We still have to come up with a plan on what we will do once Regina has come into full power. The Mad Sister knows Regina is in this realm and it is only a matter of time before she figures out where we are exactly, if she hasn't already."

"Watches will begin immediately. There will be a night shift and a day shift. Someone will watch that half for incoming intruders-" Maggie pointed to the side where they had come from. "-and will have someone posted on this half to do the same."

"What do you want to use as a signal?" Asked Tucker.

"Remember the pouches of green sand I gave you earlier? I will see if the Grand Master can create a third identical pouch for us so someone on the ground can see it as well." Maggie held out her hand so Tucker could give her back the pouch.

"Hows are wes going tos gets up theres?" Vaul asked.

"You can use my wingboard." Tyler grabbed his board and handed it to Maggie.

"Perfect! I'll take the first shift as soon as the third pouch is ready, does anyone want to volunteer to take the other side?"

"I'll take it my dear."

"Thanks Thack. Alright we'll see what the Grand Master can do about this third pouch."

"Uh, I can help watch that side with you if you want?" Ravi did his best to act casual about his offer to Maggie.

"I can handle that side on my own, thanks for offering though." She placed a hand on his arm. "You should probably rest up; somebody needs to take the night shift." She disappeared behind the huts so she could go speak with the Grand Master.

She returned only after a few minutes. "Here you go Tucker." She handed him a third identical pouch. "Keep an eye out, you're the only one on the ground who can see the smoke as long as you have that pouch with you."

"Wow that was quick." Tucker placed the pouch into the pocket of his shirt and patted it lightly.

"Tyler, the Grand Master would like to see you." Maggie grabbed the wingboard and headed towards the pond. "I'll take good care of this for you." She gave Tyler a broad smile before she zoomed off.

"Hey, we should probably keep reading that book." Kolben nodded his head away from the huts so they could read in peace. Regina just stood there with a far off gaze. Kolben tapped her shoulder. "Regina, did you hear me?"

"Huh. Oh yeah right, let's go do that."

Kolben grabbed the book and lead Regina away from the huts. He began walking towards the other side of the ravine. Regina hardly payed any attention to where her feet were leading her. She was so wrapped up by the news that she nearly walked straight into the river.

"Hey!" Kolben pulled her away before she stepped into the water. "Watch where you are going."

Regina's heart was pounding in her chest and the world was no longer glazed over in her eyes. She looked around her and realized she did not recognize the area.

"Where are you taking us?" She asked.

"Somewhere away from all the chaos. We need to focus on getting you ready."

"We?" Regina was thrown off by Kolben's sudden eagerness to help her.

He walked a few steps before he replied. "As much as I hate to admit it, but that lady in the mirror was right."

"Nita." Regina interrupted.

"What?"

"The lady in the mirror, her name is Nita."

"Nita…" He stopped to face Regina. "Nita is right. Now more than ever this realm needs a reason to come together and I think you are the one to do it."

"I don't know if you have noticed, but I have no idea what I am doing. So far the Grand Master really hasn't done much to help with that."

They continued walking until they reached the waterfall. Kolben and Regina were a little sweaty from the walk. It was a hot day and the sun reflecting off the water only made it feel hotter. Regina wanted to go back to the pond and take a nice long swim. She thought back fondly to a time when her parents took Tyler and her to the beach one very hot summer day.

It was an impulse trip that her dad decided to do. The beach was two hours away and every minute it took to get there felt like a lifetime to her. She was eight and Tyler was three; it was the first time ever that they had gone to the beach. Regina rushed out of the car once they got there. Her mother spent a good five minutes rubbing sunblock on her, while her dad inflated the floaties. She was finally all lathered up and safely protected. The floaties were uncomfortably large around her upper arms and they chaffed the side of her ribs, but she didn't care. She placed one foot in the sand and quickly withdrew it. She figured if she ran fast enough to the water that she wouldn't even notice the hot sand below her feet and that is exactly what she did. She ran as fast as she could towards the water. The cool water rushed over her toes and receded back again. She chased the water and then let the water chase her. An arm swooped her up in the air, her father had lifted her over his shoulders and started walking further into the ocean. He walked a good twenty feet before the water even came up to his hips. He placed her in the water and watched her float for a little while.

"Would you like to learn how to swim?" He said with such an exuberant smile.

Regina nodded her head yes. Her father taught her how to doggy paddle and float on her back before he took off her floaties. The ocean was unusually calm that day as if it was told to behave so Regina could learn how to swim. It didn't take Regina long to catch on and once she got the hang of it she wanted to show off for her mom. The whole family was in the water now. Regina swam circles around her mother while Tyler clapped in approval for his sister. It was a great day that Regina wished would never end.

"Hey Regina, Regina!"

"What?" Regina said this a little more sharply than she had intended to. She had been enjoying the memory of that day, of her mother and father and Kolben ripped her away from her daze.

"Man, what is with you?" He waited for Regina to respond, but she said nothing. "Come on. I know a nice quiet place where no one will bother us."

Kolben took her to a boulder that was next to the waterfall. He placed his hands on its surface feeling his way around for something. Eventually, he stuck his hand into a crevice on the boulder and pulled out a large stick from within. He climbed up the boulder with the stick in hand.

"Let me help you up." He reached out and helped pull Regina on top of the boulder. "Here." Kolben handed Regina the stick. "Tap the wall twice."

Regina looked at Kolben strangely. She thought to herself, *"Is this some kind of joke?"* She shrugged and did it anyways. The boulder shook slightly and a blue flash of light erupted from it. Regina stepped back awkwardly and almost fell into the rushing water of the river. Kolben caught her before she fell and held her close to his chest.

"Thanks." Regina quickly moved out of his arms and brushed herself off. When she turned back around to face the waterfall she saw that it was no longer there. Instead, there was a staircase; it started from the boulder and lead up to a cave that was hidden behind the waterfall. Regina cautiously walked up the stairs. Once both of them were in the cave, the waterfall resumed and the stairs disappeared.

"How do we get back?" Regina asked.

Kolben pulled the stick from behind him. "We tap the cave wall twice, same concept."

The cave was hidden from the sun and the mist from the waterfall kept them nice and cool. Regina sat down and placed the book on her lap. The entire cave was completely smooth to the touch, as if water ran through the shallow cave for hundreds of years, polishing off any imperfections it once had. Regina enjoyed only hearing the sound of water falling from the sky and crashing into the ground below.

"How did you know about this place?"

"I saw the Grand Master come here on my first day. He had asked me to pick pink flowers for some brew he was working on. I was on the other side of the river when he snuck out here. He looked like he was trying to sneak his way up here, but I'm pretty sure he wanted me to find this."

"What makes you say that?"

"Because he made sure that I picked the flowers that only grew on this side of the ravine." Kolben let out a small chuckle. "Plus, I'm pretty sure he checked to see if I was here before he came out from behind the tree lines."

Regina let out a small smile and then made it quickly fade away. She appreciated that Kolben was finally warming up to her and she knew it took a lot of guts for him to tell her about his family, but she still felt the leftover disdain for him creep back into her brain. Her first encounter with him was not pleasant and his overall arrogance annoyed her. A thought popped into Regina's head, *"Why is Kolben here?"* Regina saw him use his magic to summon the axe after he stormed out of the Grand Master's place; he obviously had control over his magic.

"Why are you here?" Regina blurted out the question and was surprised to hear the words coming out of her mouth.

Kolben was taken aback too, "What do you mean? I thought we already discussed this?"

"Yes, but you know how to use your magic. I saw you summon the wood and the axe yesterday. So why are you sitting with me going over an old book that we are not even sure has anything to do with making our powers stronger or whatever?"

"Oh that." Kolben's face turned slightly red. His eyes adverted hers. "Well it's none of your business okay!"

Regina looked at Kolben and decided to let it go. "Fine, let's just start reading then."

They sat down as they did before, the book across both their laps; ready to dive into another adventure.

"21 January, 1345- The night was long and cold, but we made it through. It will be another day's walk before we reach our destination. I fear for my wife's well-being, but she is strong and her spirits seem brighter today. I take joy in the small things, like the beautiful rolling hills, the burning glow of the sunset and all the sheep are healthy and accounted for; in dark times like this it is the little bits of happiness along the way that keep you going."

"Why isn't anything happening? How come we are not being pulled in like before?" Kolben grabbed the book from Regina's lap. "Let me see it." He quickly read the following lines in the book mumbling the words as he went along.

    Regina pulled the book back roughly, "Nothing will happen if you read it like that." She looked down at the page and noticed a red blotch on the top right corner. She ran a finger over it and most of the blotch came off, but it left a red stain behind. It took her a second to realize what it was. She turned to Kolben and saw a cut that ran along his forearm.

    "Was tha- was that from me?" Regina instantly felt guilty.

    "Yeah, thanks for that. You didn't have to be so rough." Kolben got up and walked to the opening of the cave and ran his arm under the water.

    "I'm so sorry. I didn't mean to." Regina walked over to him and helped him wash off the blood, but Kolben pulled his arm away. "I'm just trying to help." Regina said impatiently.

    "I can do this myself."

    "Fine. Whatever." Regina leaned against the opposite wall from Kolben. "So why do you think the book didn't work this time?"

    "I don't know." He finished washing the blood off from his paper cut and thought for a moment. "That was a really boring entry anyways. I say we just skim through it and move on to the next important entry."

    Regina didn't find anything wrong in his plan. They were on a time crunch and skipping the minute details couldn't hurt. So they sat back down and silently skimmed through the next two entries.

    "Okay, so basically they traveled to the new town without any problems; like you said very uneventful. Are you ready to move on to the next entry?" Regina asked Kolben who responded with a simple nod of the head.

    "23 January, 1345- The trip was longer than had been expected, but we have finally arrived. The illness has not touched ground in this area and our kind will do its best to make sure it stays that way."

The book raddled in their laps and once again they were seeing the story play out through the shepherd's eyes.

"The people here have said great things about this shaman, they said he would take great care of you and the baby." He waited for his wife to respond, but there was no answer. He walked into their bedroom to find his wife silently sobbing on the bed. "Alana?" He rushed to her side. Regina and Kolben could feel the man's growing concern for his wife and at that moment they knew something was very wrong. They somehow knew that Alana never cried; that she was a strong woman and kept her emotions buried under the surface.

He climbed into the bed with his wife and cradled her head in his lap. He stroked her hair, "Everything will be alright. We can get through this." He feared what hid under the sheets, he knew that once the sheets were pulled off there would be no going back. So he sat with his wife a little while longer appreciating the ignorant truth; that his wife and his unborn child were fine, that things would truly be okay. However, the fates felt like being cruel and the blood from his wife's miscarriage soaked through the sheets.

A knock came from the front door; the shaman had arrived. "Please, my wife, she needs you. Quickly, she is in the bedroom."

Regina and Kolben were back in the cave. Regina's heart was beating fast and her forehead was covered in sweat. Regina's concern for Alana still weighed heavily on her chest. "Poor Alana. I can't help this overwhelming feeling of despair that I feel for her."

"You are just feeling what the shepherd felt." Kolben replied rather nonchalantly.

"It's not just the shepherd's feelings, but my own feelings too. You don't feel the same?"

"Not really, it's just a story. You are just being too emotional." Kolben said the last part in a joking manner, but Regina did not think it was funny.

"Maybe, I'm not as cold hearted as you are." Regina teased back, hoping she would push his buttons for once.

Kolben said nothing, he just stared at her as if he were trying to size her up. After a few moments he spoke, "Don't act like you know me now because I told you about my family."

"Maybe if you weren't so abrasive I would take the time to get to know you, but instead you choose to be mean and callu-" Before Regina could finish her sentence Kolben quickly strode up to her, grabbed her close and kissed her. Regina felt herself give in for a brief second, but all of a sudden Gramm popped into her mind and she pulled away.

"What are you doing?" Even with her angered response she couldn't hide the small part of her that enjoyed it. She placed a hand to her lips and watched Kolben's face turn to shame.

"I'm sorry. I thought you-"

"You thought what?" Regina was now furious. She just had her first kiss and it was with Kolben and they were just arguing. *"What made him think that was an appropriate time to do that?"* She thought.

"I'll leave." Kolben picked up the stick and tapped the cave wall twice. The waterfall stopped midstream and the stairs reappeared. He left the stick in the cave with Regina and quickly ran down the steps. As soon as he jumped off the boulder the stairs disappeared and the waterfall began to flow over the cave again.

"I don't need him." Regina said aloud to herself. She sat back down and opened up the book where they had left off, but she did not read it. All she could think about was that kiss; she could still feel it on her lips. Just when she thought she was getting a better understanding of Kolben he goes and does something like that. Regina scoffed and began reading the book. She knew there were bigger issues to worry about and very little time to figure them out.

So Regina read the next few entries, but it was nothing of importance. When she was not pulled into those entries either she had come to the conclusion that the book only pulls someone in when the entry is significant. Regina tested her magic in the cave for a little while, but nothing happened and she started to wonder what the book was really for.

The sun began to set and Regina was tired of trying to make her magic work. She tapped the cave twice with the stick, just like Kolben did before and made her way down the stairs. She made sure to place the stick back exactly where they had found it, in the large crevice of the boulder, and headed back to the huts.

The clouds gathered quickly overhead turning the sky into a dark black mass; rain was sure to follow soon. Light droplets began falling from the sky and Regina desperately needed someone to talk to. She got back just in time; Maggie and Ravi were trading shifts and Thack would be coming back soon to trade places with Tucker. She grabbed Tucker and pulled him aside.

"Can I talk to you for a second?" Regina began before he could even answer. "What does it mean when a um, when a uh maybe…I should talk to Maggie about this."

"What is it kiddo? You know you can always talk to me?" Said Tucker.

"Kolben kissed me." Regina blurted out.

"HE DID WHAT?" Tucker's face turned red and his fist clenched. "Where is he?"

"I knew I should have talked to Maggie." Regina sighed.

Tucker tried to back track, but it was too late. "Oh no it's not like that. I just want to talk to him. You know man to man."

Maggie overheard Tucker's outburst and quickly swooped in. "Hey Tucker, your shift will be starting soon, you should probably start heading up there."

"I'm going. I'm just going to make a quick stop at the Grand Master's cottage. I need to do something." Tucker thought he was being inconspicuous, but Maggie knew exactly what he was doing.

"Tucker!" She pointed to the top of the ravine. "Now!"

"Thank you Maggie." Once Tucker had disappeared out of sight Regina explained to Maggie what happened. "What do you think that means?"

"Well, that means he likes you." Maggie simply put it.

Regina still confused said, "But we were arguing when he…when he kissed me."

"Kolben is a little rough around the edges."

"A little?" Regina protested.

"A lot in your case, but I think he has a hard time explaining how he feels." Maggie placed an arm around Regina.

"He could try a little harder."

"If you don't feel the same way you need to be honest and tell him the truth, no matter how difficult it may be. And if you do feel the same way…well that is something you need to figure out on your own. Honesty is always a good way to go." Maggie smiled and left Regina to think about her feelings for Kolben.

The next day, Regina avoided Kolben and Kolben avoided her. Regina knew there was no way she liked Kolben, yet she could not bring herself to say it out loud. So she thought it would be best to avoid speaking to him all together. She spent the day reading more entries from the book, but grew tired of it after several of the entries turned out to be uneventful. She insisted on taking a shift on top of the ravine, but was forced to be accompanied by Vaul. He made sure that she always stayed behind him and that she was never allowed to wonder off on her own. Regina sat behind a boulder and tried to practice her magic on a paper airplane. As before, she had no luck. Vaul was watching her attempts but said nothing, until Regina gave up after her tenth try and started crumpling up the paper.

"I-s thinks yous are thinking toos much." Vaul grabbed the crumpled up paper and began smoothing it out as best as he could with his stubby fingers. "Don'ts thinks, just dos." Vaul handed back the reconstructed paper airplane to Regina.

Regina stared back at Vaul; she did not understand what he had meant. She tried again, following Vaul's advice of just doing, but nothing happened.

Vaul pointed to his chest, "In heres. Yous haves to dos in heres." Vaul cracked a small smile and then walked away.

Regina placed her hand on her chest and felt the rhythm of her heart beating. She repeated Vaul's words to herself. "I have to do in here." She understood what Vaul meant and tried again, but this time she closed her eyes, took a deep breath and listened to her heart. When she opened her eyes the paper airplane was floating in her hand. She lifted the plane higher and higher until the wind swept it away.

She smiled at Vaul and said "Thank you." She then hopped onto her brother's wingboard and headed to the huts. Regina slept soundly that night; a spark of light struck inside her and a new path was beginning to reveal itself.

The following morning Regina did not feel like reading from the book, instead, she wanted to spend the day trying to learn more about the Grand Master. Vaul was able to help her discover more about her powers in one simple conversation than anything she had learned from the book, which was nothing. She felt that Marco was holding something back from her and she wanted to know what it was.

"Tyler, what did the Grand Master want with you the other day?" Regina finished eating her breakfast, eggs and toast with jam, when she remembered the Grand Master had summoned her brother after Nita told them about Broadcove's attack.

"He wants me to work with Orwell. He thinks the best way for me to train and work on my powers is if I train the tigre."

"Did he say anything else?" Asked Regina.

"No, not really. He was too busy polishing that bottle that he keeps on top of the chest." Tyler finished his plate and went into the forest to find Orwell so he could do some more training.

Regina snuck over to the Grand Master's cottage and peaked through the window. Kolben was sitting on the couch reading some book and Marco was in the kitchen eating jam straight from the jar. Kolben looked up from his book and turned his head towards the window Regina was looking through. She quickly ducked down and moved away slowly to the other side of the cottage. Kolben stepped out the front door; he swore he had saw something at the window, but when he came out there was nothing there. He looked around for a few seconds and then headed back inside. Regina climbed up a tree across the river and waited for the Grand Master to come out of his house. An hour and a half went by before anything happened. The sun had shifted to shine directly through a break in the leaves. Every minute grew more excruciating between the burning pain of the sun and the pressure that was building in her legs for squatting awkwardly for so long. Finally, the Grand Master came out of his cottage. Kolben left a few seconds after, but went in the opposite direction.

Regina slid down the tree and followed the Grand Master from a distance. He was being very conspicuous, whistling loudly, making sure he stopped to say hello to Maggie and then scaring Ravi by poofing right next to him. It was not until he past the huts did he become stealthy and suspicious. He was gripping a silver bag close to his chest. He poofed from one spot to the next until Regina lost track of him. She made her way to a small clearing, hoping that this was his destination, but when she got there he was nowhere to be found. She turned around to head back to the huts and found Marco standing directly in front of her without the silver bag in hand.

"If you have a question, you can just ask me. There is no need for spying." He tapped his foot in disapproval at first, but it quickly turned into a rhythmic beat that almost distracted him entirely.

"I want to know what you are not telling me." Regina demanded. There was a bit of anger in her voice, mostly because she was mad at herself for getting caught so quickly.

"I'm sorry girly, but I'm not sure what you mean."

"You know exactly what I mean." Regina pointed demandingly at the Grand Master. What is it that you are not telling me? People are counting on me and every day, every hour and every minute I spend trying to learn how to use my magic, I am letting the Mad Sister get that much closer to taking over the whole realm."

"I see. Shall we discuss this over some fazzle tazzle beignets?" Macro wiggled his eyebrows excitedly.

"Sure." Regina did not expect Marco to give in so easily. They walked side by side through the trees back towards the cottage. "What are fazzel tazzle beignets?"

"They are the most delicious treat in the world!" The Grand Master raised his black walking stick in the air in a celebratory manner. He looked down at Regina and waited for her reaction. His thick squared framed glasses slid down to the tip of his nose; it was only then did Regina realize that he did not have any lenses in his glasses. Regina decided to just smile in response and pretend like she did not notice.

The silence between them felt unnerving to Regina as they slowly made their way back. "So, how come you live all the way out here on your own?" She asked to break the awkwardness, but she grew genuinely curious after asking.

The Grand Master raised one of his hands signaling her to stop and with the other, he placed a finger to his lips. "Listen." He said quietly.

Regina stood still and waited for something to happen, but she heard nothing. "What are we listening for?" She whispered.

"Nothing." Marco replied.

"Nothing?"

"Precisely." He continued walking. "The only noise out here is nature. It is one of the few places in my many years of travel that has felt like home to me. Everything here is pristine and untouched."

"How long have you lived here?"

"Too many years to count girly."

"You don't miss other people?" Asked Regina.

"I have found that coexisting has rarely worked out for humanity. It is in our nature to lash out at our neighbors due to conflicting views and what have you. I realize that I am not of the uh, normal sort, shall we say, and to force a neighbor to have me as a constant in their lives, well, I have chosen to seek solitude instead."

Regina was surprised of the Grand Master's self-awareness and how honest he was about it. It couldn't be easy to come to the conclusion that you are an annoyance to society. Regina thought to herself, *"Maybe he is not as crazy as he seems."*

"Do you have any kids?" Regina asked.

"No, I do not." The lines on his face creased and he turned away for a brief second. He poofed away to the other side of the river. He bent down to pick up something from the ground. *Poof!* He reappeared next to her. "For you girly." He handed her a blackish grey rock.

"Uh, thanks." Regina slipped the rock in her pocket not wanting to offend the Grand Master.

They crossed the stepping stones and walked up to the front of the cottage, Regina pulled the door open hoping that Kolben would not be inside. She looked around and was relived to find the place empty.

"Sorry girly, Kolben will not be back for a while." He said with a wink.

Regina's face grew flush and she felt a wave of heat rush over her. "I don't care where he is." Regina could hear it in her own voice how unconvincing she was and the Grand Master's face reflected the same thought.

Marco waved a hand sideways in front of his sofa, the clutter moved itself from the sofa and scattered to different places throughout the cottage, but Regina noticed something. The sleeves of his jacket raised to reveal a bright silver cuff. There was some kind of writing on it, but before Regina could read the text the Grand Master pulled his sleeves back down.

"Take a seat while I grab the fazzle tazzle beignets." He disappeared into the kitchen while Regina looked around in his living room. She could hear the banging of cabinet doors and the Grand Master was mumbling tirelessly to himself as he riffled through the kitchen. She found a picture of the Grand Master dressed up as a cowboy in an old timey looking picture. She sat down on the cleared off sofa and waited patiently for Marco to return with the fazzle tazzle beignets.

"Bon appetite." He handed her a plate and when she looked down, she found a half-eaten fazzle tazzle beignet.

"Uh, did you take a bite out of this?" Regina held out the beignet at arm's length with a discussed look on her face.

"I searched the kitchen high and low and apparently someone ate the rest of them. So I could not let you have the last one without taking a little nibble for myself." Marco licked the powder sugar and cinnamon from his fingers. Regina, feeling uninterested all of a sudden, pushed her plate to the side. "Are you going to eat that?" Marco asked eagerly.

"It is all yours." Regina watched Marco devour the remaining half of the beignet, she was a little disappointed that she did not get to try it because the aroma of it made her mouth swell with saliva, but she remembered that she was here to discuss more important things.

"So what did you want to talk about?" Marco padded his lips with a napkin and swallowed the last bit of food that was in his mouth.

"You were going to tell me what you have been keeping from me since we got here." Regina said feeling a little annoyed.

"Oh right." The Grand Master formed a triangle with his hands and looked at her pointedly. "So what is it that you think I am keeping from you?"

"I don't know because you will not tell me."

"Well there has to be some reason why you feel this way." Marco frowned.

"My powers!" Regina blurted out. "I need my powers so I can defeat the Mad Sister. I have been here a couple of days now and I learned more from Vaul than I have from YOU." Regina really emphasized the last part, which seem to have caught Marco's attention.

"Hmmm…" Marco stared off for a moment. "It seems to me you have an issue with the quickness of your progression or rather, the lack of progress."

Regina rolled her eyes, "Yes, exactly."

"Have you been reading the book?"

"Yes!"

"With Kolben?" He quickly replied.

Regina was taken by surprise, "Why do I need to read it with Kolben?"

"Just answer the question girly."

"At first, yes, but I been reading it alone lately."

"Progress cannot be made alone. Keep reading the book together and the results will follow soon after."

This was the last thing Regina wanted to hear. She had been doing her best to avoid him and now she would have to be reliant on him. She was about to ask the Grand Master why, but Kolben walked in.

"Just the fellow we were talking about."

Regina wished with all her might that she could be anywhere else but there. She saw Ravi out the window and thought to herself, *"If only I had Ravi's powers, I could become invisible right now and disappear without having to deal with this humiliation."*

However, Kolben seemed to have no reaction at all. "Why wouldn't you be talking about me?"

The Grand Master rolled with laughter. "This guy is always cracking me up." Marco continued laughing as he walked into the hallway and disappeared into the bedroom.

The room grew silent. Regina looked around for any kind of escape, but she had no such luck. Finally, Kolben broke the tension, "So...um what were you two really talking about?"

"My powers."

"No luck yet with the book?" Kolben asked.

"That was why we were talking about you. According to the Grand Master, you and I have to keep reading the book together; that is the only way I will see any results." Regina was tapping her foot nervously.

"Hmm..."Kolben had a smug smile on his face. "So you need me? Interesting. Well, I guess you and I will be spending lots of time together."

"Does not mean I have to like it and he did not say anything about me being nice to you." Regina jabbed back.

"If you want me to work with yo-"

Regina cut him off; she already knew what he was going to say. "Yeah, yeah, I'll play nice." Annoyed and frustrated, Regina wanted to wipe the smug look off of Kolben's face. "I'm not attracted to you and I never will be."

"You'll come around." Kolben opened the door, did a half bow and gestured Regina through. As soon as Regina passed through he continued. "They always come around."

They were back in the cave with the book in their laps ready to power through. Regina was about to read out loud when Kolben asked her a question. "Did I miss anything?"

"Not really. Just them settling in the new place and Alana and her husband dealing with the miscarriage. Also, it sounds like the new town they are in is only occupied by magias."

"Magias?"

"Oh yeah, that is what the shepherd has been calling the magical folk." Regina's expression changed all of the sudden; she was frowning.

"What's a matter?" Kolben asked noticing the change in Regina's demeanor.

"This book doesn't make any sense." She answered.

"How so?"

"I thought magic did not exist in the world Tyler and I came from; so how can the shaman or any of the rest of them use magic if they are in our world?"

"Magic did exist in your world until…" Kolben scrunched his face trying to remember. "…uh I think it wasn't until the first realm was created in the late 1300s."

"So Alana and her family did not have a magical realm to escape to?"

"No, I don't think so." Kolben seemed to be sadden for the first time about the book, but he did not let it linger for very long.

Regina began to read aloud. *"15 February, 1345-It has been awhile since my last entry. The family is adjusting to their new surroundings and Alana has been recovering since the loss of our baby."* The book shook and they were swept in.

A flurry of clothes swam around the room. Alana was next to a wooden tub full of suds. The clothes dove into the water, scrubbed themselves a few times, wrung themselves out and flew across the yard to be hung on the clothes line.

From a distance the shepherd could hear his son urgently calling, "Papa, papa!"

"Paolo!" A poof of smoke appeared around them and when it cleared the shepherd was next to his son. "What happened?" His son held up a limp arm. "Oh Paolo, I told you to stay out of the river; those rocks are much too slippery for you to cross on."

"I'm swrry papa." Tears began to fill in his son's eyes.

He gently ruffled his son's hair and kissed his cheek. "It's okay Paolo, let's go home and see what we can do to fix you up." He scooped his son into his arms and they *poofed* back to the house.

"Paolito what happened?" Alana rushed over to her son.

"I okay mamma." Paolo weakly held up his arm.

"I will fetch for the Shaman."

"No my love. We cannot afford the Shaman." Alana grabbed her husband's shoulder before he could leave.

"But Paolo needs his arm to be fixed."

"Paolo also needs food to live and so does little Almita. The Shaman cost us too much the last time he was here." Alana took a deep breath and looked at her son. "I can conjure up some brews to help with the pain and I will do my best to heal his arm on my own."

The shepherd carried his son into the house followed by his wife and his young daughter, Almita. He gently placed Paolo on the table and stroked his dark black hair while he waited for his wife to make the brew. After about ten minutes Alana had the brew ready.

"Drink this Paolo, it will help with the pain." She raised the brew to his lips; a purplish green liquid ran down the side of his chin.

Paolo pushed the brew away. "I don't want it."

"I know it taste bad, but you have to drink it all." Alana tilt the brew into his mouth until it was all gone. She waited a few seconds for the brew to kick in. "Did the pain go away?" Her son nodded. "Good. This next part is going to hurt a little, but I need you to be brave. Can you do that for me?" He nodded again.

Alana waved her hands in a circular motion over Paolo's broken arm. She looked to her husband giving him a silent signal that the next part was going to hurt. As gently as she possibly could, she straightened Paolo's arm.

"Oww mamma." Young Paolo grabbed his father's hand.

Alana said nothing she had to keep her focus and continue fixing his arm. Once his arm was completely straight she now had to work on mending the broken bone. A stream of white light came from her finger tips. Cracking sounds came from his arm and Paolo cried out in pain.

"AHH! P-please stop!" Tears ran down his cheeks and onto the floor.

There was one final loud crack and the light from Alana's fingers stopped. "It's done." She wiped the sweat from her forehead and held her crying son.

Regina and Kolben watched from the shepherd's eyes his son holding tightly onto his mother. They could see his hand reaching out for his son, but they could no longer hear him crying; Alana was moving her lips, but they could not hear what she was saying; Instead they heard water hitting the rocks and birds chirping from a distance. The warmth of the cottage disappeared and cool mist hit their faces. The scene quickly pulled away and they were sitting back in the cave.

"What happened?" Kolben asked. "We didn't get to finish the entry."

"I'm not sure." A buzz on Regina's chest pulled her attention.

"What is that green flash?" Kolben pointed to the spot where Regina's locket laid under her shirt.

The locket stopped buzzing and flashing once she opened it. The mirror read "In distress." The words faded and Reynold's face appeared. She could see panic in his eyes, "Midnight Smoke is here. She got Ann and disappeared I think she is comin-" Purple mist surrounded Reynold and soon that was all that Regina could see. A small outline of Reynold's face remained in the mirror. Regina watched helplessly as a hand drew out from the mist over Reynold's mouth. There was a muffled shout and the display cut off.

Chapter 14 All Alone

"I have to go tell the others!" Regina slammed the book shut and grabbed the stick to get out of the cave. She did not bother to wait for Kolben once the stairs appeared, although she could hear he was following closely behind. When she reached the huts she found everyone gathered together in the same area. Their glum faces told Regina that somehow they already knew.

"How do you kn-"

"Nita." Ravi answered. "She was there when it happened."

"Is she alright?" Asked Regina.

"Yeah, she's alright. She has a bit of a bump on her noggin. She was at the front door when Midnight Smoke burst through dragging Reynold along. The door hit her straight on and knocked her unconscious."

"We have to go back there and find them?" Regina held the locket firmly in her hand.

"Nita has already sent out a search team. Apparently, they have been searching for Midnight Smoke since we had that incident with her." Maggie paused for a moment. "Reynold and Ann were not the only ones taken, people have been disappearing all over town."

"Midnight Smoke is doing all of this?"

"All the evidence is pointing to her." Thack answered Regina's question.

"Wait a second." Tucker interrupted. "She can't be doing all of this on her own, she must have a group of people helping her. Reynold is a big guy, there is no way she could carry him on her own."

"Nots if she is usings the magics." Vaul interjected.

"Yeah, but there have been too many people disappearing. I think Tucker is right she must be getting help from someone." Thack added.

"You think the Carnagers are helping?" Tyler asked.

"Yeah probably." Said Maggie.

"I don't think so. Nita's little birds in Kazny have said that the Carnagers are off terrorizing Broadcove. So it cannot be them." Ravi stroked his chin.

"How trust worthy are her little birds?" Tucker said skeptically.

"Very trust worthy." Kolben spoke out. "My father had been helping Nahtovia since the Mad Hysteria."

Everyone looked shocked except for Thack. "I thought you looked familiar. My dear boy, you look just like him." Kolben now looked as shocked as everybody else did. Thack continued. "I was your father's contact for many years before and during the war. I told him he was much too young to be involved, but your father was stubborn." Thack gave a small chuckle. "How is your father doing these days?"

Kolben looked to his feet and softly shook his head.

"Oh I'm-I am sorry to hear that." Thack patted Kolben on the shoulder.

Regina felt the urge to comfort Kolben, but she refused to give in. That taunting thought that lingered in the back of her head would not win, not today. She could not let herself show the slightest bit of caring towards him in fear that it would reveal a much bigger problem in her heart.

Luckily, Tucker broke the tension. "I guess I should be heading up for my shift."

"Yes, we must be especially vigilant right now. Who knows how long it will take for someone to figure out we are out here." Thack transformed into a wolf and joined Tucker on his way up to their post.

Tyler grabbed his sister and pulled her aside. "I really feel like we should be out there looking for Reynold and Ann. They took us in when we needed it the most; they are family."

"I know and I agree, but what can I do to help look for them? I still don't know how to use my powers." Regina looked absently at her hands.

"What if the group splits up?" Tyler suggested.

"No! Tyler, you and I never split up."

"Please Regina, hear me out."

Regina did not want to hear it, but Tyler seemed determined and Regina knew eventually she would at least have to listen to what he had to say. "Oh alright, tell me why you think it is a good idea for us to split up?"

"I have actually gotten pretty good at using my powers. I have half of the animals here keeping watch out there for us and the other half have been helping us gather food and materials."

"I wondered why my fish had a large bite mark on it." Regina interrupted.

"Exactly! I don't think I can learn anything else from Marco."

"Wait. What?" Said Regina trying to hide her anger. "He has actually been helping you?"

Tyler's face lit up. "Oh yeah! He has been tons of help. Every day, he helped me train Orwell. He even helped me learn how to speak several different animal languages."

Regina was now speaking through clenched teeth. "He did, did he?"

"Look, I really think I can be useful. I just don't want anything bad to happen to Ann and Reynold."

"And it won't." Regina bent down to be at eye level with her brother, but when she did so she noticed he had grown since they entered this realm and she didn't have to bend as far down as she used to. "I trust Nita."

"Really?" Tyler gave his sister a sideways look.

"Well, I trust her with protecting her own town and she is not about to let it up and disappear."

"But, Regina."

"Please Tyler, you need to give me a little more time. I don't think I can do this without you here. I want to find Reynold and Ann as much as you do, but I can't do anything to help without my powers. I especially can't learn how to use my powers if I am constantly wondering if you are okay out there. So please stay."

Tyler said nothing. Regina knew he was furious with her, but he would not say it to her face. Not now when the whole world seemed to be in complete chaos. He just nodded bravely and walked away.

"Hey Tyler." Regina stopped Tyler before he entered their hut. "I know you will do great things with those powers of yours and I want you by my side when you do."

Tyler smiled and that was all she needed.

"Come on Kolben, we have some reading to do." Regina waved Kolben along.

Back in the cave they scanned through several entries that had little importance, except for a single name that kept being repeated through whispers that rode on the backs of destruction and chaos; Black Death.

"Do you think they are referring to the Black Plague?" Asked Regina.

"The what?"

"I forgot, two different worlds, uh, right. So The Black Plague was a vicious illness that occurred about the same time as the entry dates in this book, it killed a lot of people, but it was also known as Black Death."

"That sounds terrible…" Kolben thought for a moment. "…but the entries are almost describing Black Death as if it were a person."

"Yeah that was what I was thinking. Whatever it is, it sounds like it is getting closer to wherever they are." Regina could not explain the anxious bubble that was growing inside her, but she had a feeling it was going to pop soon and the aftermath would be devastating.

"26 October, 1345-" Regina began to read again.

"This entry is several months after the last one we read. I wonder why there is such a big gap."

Regina shrugged and continued reading. *"It has been two months since Almita has passed."*

"Oooh…that explains it." Kolben said somberly as he braced himself for the plunge.

"Alana has been inconsolable. She lies in bed day and night and I struggle everyday trying to get her to eat."

Regina felt her insides lurch, her surroundings fade to dark and reappear in a blistering new world.

"Alana, please eat something." His wife rolled over to the other side of the bed. He sat next to her and began stroking her hair. "I know it has been a rough year, but we have to keep moving; Paolo still needs his mother." He waited for a response, but still she said nothing. "*Sigh*, Almita would not want you to be sad." He kissed the back of Alana's head and walked out the door.

"Is mamma going to be alright?" Paolo asked his father; almost looking as frail as his mother.

He grabbed his son's shoulders and ran his hands down the length of his arms to his hands; being extra careful not to put too much pressure on the arm that did not properly heal. "She just needs more time Paolito."

Time began to speed up all around them. Blurs of images swirled past them until it all came to an abrupt stop. The shepherd was watching his son being chased around by his mother on a large field of green grass while the sun shone brightly up above. Paolo looked as if he grew an inch taller and his hair was longer.

"I'm going to get you!" Alana giggled and pretended she couldn't quite reach her son as she chased him around the field. Then she finally grabbed him and tickled him to the ground.

"Mamma!" Paolo shouted with laughter.

Just beyond them was a large hill that overlooked their small village. The shepherd saw a hooded figure starring down at his wife and his son. A chill went down his spine as he watched the figure look straight at him. He poofed himself to the bottom of the hill, but the hooded figure vanished out of sight. He spent a minute or so of looking for the phantom but found nothing. When he rejoined his family he found Nicholas the merchant was with them.

"Hello, Nicholas. What brings you here?" The shepherd said cheerfully not noticing Nicholas' glum demeanor.

"I'm afraid I have some bad news..." Nicholas paused and let out a deep sight. "...Black Death has reached the boarders of our village."

"We have the barrier up; Black Death cannot get in right?" Alana was visibly shaken by this news.

"There have been breaches in other magical communities, but our magical barrier should be stronger than theirs." Nicolas sighed and rubbed the back of his thick neck. He had been balding for a while, but more recently, it had become especially bad on top. "Well keep an eye out. Let us know if you see anything." He waved his chubby hand goodbye and poofed away in a thick yellow cloud of smoke.

"Where did you go just before Nicolas arrived?" asked Alana.

He starred at her for a moment and thought to himself. She had been happy these last few months and she was eating again. Her face was beginning to look fuller and her hair was getting back its shine. But her eyes still lacked the bright light that was once there, the light that began to dim after the miscarriage; the same light that almost completely vanished after the loss of their beautiful baby girl, Almita.

His hand gently grabbed her cheek. "Nowhere, I thought I saw something but it was nothing." Alana seemed hesitant, but eventually accepted his lie and he did too, for he was unsure himself if he really did see anything.

Wind swept across, speeding along time itself. When it stopped, they found themselves looking out a window watching the dark skies deliver heavy amounts of rain. From behind them they could hear noises coming from the bedroom.

"Alana, my sweet, what are you doing?" He was very concerned as he watched his wife direct flying clothes into different bags on the bed.

"I'm packing!" She said angrily. Her upper lip curled and her eyes narrowed. "We should have done this weeks ago. When Nicolas first told us about it."

"Our people have the strongest magic around. The barrier will hold."

"The barrier is cracking!" Her chest was heaving heavily. "It is only a matter of time before Black Death takes us all down. We need to take our one remaining child out of this place and find somewhere else to hide from this, this monster."

Screams echoed from the distance. Alana let the clothes drop to the ground as she rushed out the door. Blacked flamed horses came barreling through houses leaving trails of ashes behind them. Streaks of light ran across the village as the magias tried to wade off the invading force, but it was too late; the barrier had been breached.

Paolo ran outside and tugged on his mother's frayed dress. "What's happening mamma?"

She turned around and bent down to her son's eye level. "Paolo, get inside and hide. Do not come out for any reason. Do you understand me?"

He gave a brave little nod and ran back into the house.

"What are you going to do?" He watched as bright red flames rose from her palms.

"I'm going to fight fire with fire."

"Alana don't!" He reached out to grab her but it was too late, only a purple cloud of smoke remained.

He was about to go after her when he noticed his son was staring out the window of their home. He ran inside, his heart was beating heavily in his chest. "Paolo, I need you to listen to me. Stay away from the windows, I don't want anyone to know that you are in here and if someone other than your mother or myself enters the house hide and don't come out." He kissed his son on the forehead. "I love you Paolo." He took one last look at his son before he joined his wife in the fight.

He poofed himself onto the battle field. He quickly dodged right as a stream of ice flew past him. He did a forward roll to dodge another oncoming round of icicles. He managed to hit the icicle wielding enemy with a blast of sleeping powder to the face; knocking him out cold.

Sleets of rain came crashing down, making it difficult to search for his wife. He noticed as he scanned the battle field that it was tough to tell foe apart from ally. Lightning struck up above followed by a thunderous boom that shook the ground. Again a bolt struck, but this time it came from below. One after another bolts of lightning came powering through the crowds of people. Screams echoed all around him.

"Alana!" He called out for his wife. "Alana, where are you?" His desperation was growing. He vanished into his cloud of red violet smoke and reappeared on the other side of the field. He continued to bounce around the battle until he spotted his wife.

"Alana!" He grabbed his wife's wrist before she threw her red ball of flames. She turned to face him, her eyes were a blazed and she was ready to strike. "Alana, I'm sorry. You were right. Let's grab Paolo and leave. We will start over again in a new city far, far away from here."

"It is too late for that. We have to stay and fight. If we leave, Black Death will follow. All of us need to end this now."

He was still holding onto her wrist when he tried to poof away. Two clouds of smoke billowed up around them, one was his red violet smoke and the other was her purple smoke. He tried pulling them back to the house, but his effort was met with resistance. The two clouds moved together a few feet, but eventually the purple cloud split off and he poofed back to the house alone.

He was about to rejoin his wife when something heavy knocked him off his feet. A small army of gargoyles had flanked the backside of the village. One of the gargoyles saw him reappear next to his house, the same house he was about to burn down. A large wing struck his back making the shepherd fly forward. Another winged blow to his arm made him tumble sideways. The shepherd raised his palm to shoot the gargoyle in the face with a blast of sand, but he only managed to produce a small amount of sand and it only flew a few inches from his palm.

"Bwahaha, I'll tell the Sovereign not to bother collecting from you." The gargoyle gave another deep throated laugh, but was cut off when his left wing caught on fire. Half the villagers split off from the battle to help fight off the gargoyles that were destroying homes on the far side of the village, one of them was Alana, who saw that her husband was in trouble.

She sent another ball of flame to the right wing of the gargoyle. The gargoyle swished around quickly to see who was attacking him. His eyes narrowed on Alana as she attempted to hit him again. He flapped his wings furiously as he tried to put out the flames. With his wings still on fire the gargoyle lowered his head to point his two long horns at Alana and charged.

She narrowly missed the full brunt of the nasty beast's attack, but he did manage to clip her abdomen with one of his horns. The gargoyle turned back around to have another go, except this time Alana was ready for him. She began sprinting towards the gray scaled beast. About half way there she disappeared into her smoke which threw the gargoyle off balance. She reappeared a few feet in front of him, still at full speed, leapt up and grabbed both of his horns. With his weight off balance, she was able to flip the gargoyle up to his back with a crushing thud. He grunted and snarled on his back, but before he could get up Alana did a magical blow that knocked him unconscious.

The shepherd helped his wife down from the gargoyle and embraced her in a passionate kiss. The rain came to a sudden stop and deafening silence pulled them back to their surroundings.

A strange deep voice came from behind them. "That was impressive." They slowly turned around to see who was behind them. A man in a black hooded cloak sat on a giant boar.

The shepherd instantly recognized him. "You." He stepped forward pointing a finger. "It was you that I saw on the hill, wasn't it?"

"Yes, it was I." The man pulled his hood off; he was tall and strikingly handsome. He had a cleft chin paired with a devilish smile, along with dirty blonde hair and piercing green eyes. He slipped off his large boar and sauntered over to Alana. "My lady." He forcefully grabbed her hand and kissed it. Still in a bow over her hand, he looked up and said, "Allow me to introduce myself." He straightened himself back up. "My name is Zefarious, but you may better know me as Black Death." Behind Zefarious was the last of the villagers; they were being forced by gargoyles to get on their knees with their heads facing towards the ground.

"What are you going to do with them?" Alana glared at him.

"Some of them will become my enslaved prisoners and others, well let's just say, it will be collection time for them." Zefarious turned to look at the villagers when Alana tried to throw a lightning strike at him. With one flick of the wrist Zefarious froze Alana in place.

"Alana!" The shepherd cried out.

"Tisk, tisk, tisk." Zefarious shook his head in displeasure as he walked over to her. Alana struggled to break free of her invisible restraints. He grabbed her chin with his leather glove and continued, "Alana I thought we could be friends. I have been watching you and I have to say, your powers are quite remarkable. I've become rather keen of you so I will give you one more chance." He flicked his wrist again and the invisible restraints were removed from Alana. He walked back to his boar and reached for a satchel. "Either you can join me freely or…" He paused to look over at the captured villagers. "…or you can join your friends."

"I will never join you." Alana reached out for her husband's hand and stood beside him waiting for the oncoming blows.

"Very well then. Borris!" Zefarious threw a rock at the unconscious gargoyle. "Borris!" The gargoyle awoke and stood up slowly. "Will you grab Alana and her husband for me? Much appreciated."

"With pleasure Sovereign." The gargoyle stomped over to Alana and the shepherd and grabbed them tightly around the waist.

Zefarious reached into his satchel. "It is such a shame it has to be this way, you and I would have made such a great team." He pulled out a bronze bottle and pointed it at the group of villagers that were kneeling behind him. White beams of light were being drained out of the mouths and eyes of the villagers. Alana and the shepherd watched in horror as the white light left their bodies and turned into black energy before it went into the bottle Zefarious was holding. The last bit of light was being drawn as their bodies went limp and fell to the floor. Zefarious now had a black smolder glow around him as he sealed the bottle.

Alana pushed the gargoyle off of her and bent down next to one of the villagers, "What have you done to them?" She asked as she held the lifeless body in her arms.

"I stole their powers. Well actually, their life force to be exact." He rolled up the sleeves of his cloak to reveal two gold cuffs. "These cuffs and this bottle are connected. The bottle steals their powers and the cuffs transfers those powers to me." An evil grin spread across his face. "You see, I have been hunting down your kind for some time now. Jins! Who knew you guys were so powerful, I think you might even be the most powerful group out of all the magias, except for me, of course. Too bad you two are the last free Jins remaining in the whole entire world." He threw his head back and gave a menacing laugh. A vein in his forehead pulsed and his eyes grew wide; they darted back and forth and they began to bulged outwards from his head.

"You're a monster." Alana shouted at Zefarious.

Zefarious marched over to Alana grabbed her by the arm and tossed her to another gargoyle standing next to Borris. "I think it is time to make you two my slaves now. What do you think?"

Borris interrupted Zefarious before he could continue. "Sovereign, sir."

"What?" Zefarious turned sharply to face Borris.

Borris cowered and took a step back before he went on. "This Jin…" He pushed the shepherd to the ground. "…his powers are weak and not worthy to be part of your controlled massed."

"That's alright, I was really only thinking about taking his wife anyways. He can watch as I make her my slave." Zefarious pointed the bronze bottle at Alana and opened the seal. A silver light came barreling out of the bottle heading straight towards Alana. The shepherd jumped out in front of his wife and took the full brunt of the hit. Alana reached for a dagger she had hidden under her sleeve and quickly threw it towards Zefarious. He sidestep the blade and shot off another silver light towards Alana and this time it made contact with her.

Alana and her husband were doubled over on the ground as Zefarious circled around them. "It didn't have to be this way. Alana, you could have come quietly and I would have given your husband a quick death, but now you will both suffer under my control." Zefarious placed two fingers to his cheek and ran them across a deep cut. He starred intensely as he rubbed his own blood between his fingers. He chuckled to himself and said, "Oh, you are good! That dagger- clearly I did not see that one coming. You will be a perfect addition to my little army, my controlled massed. I think this has made me even more found of you."

Zefarious tucked the bottle under his arm and stood in a dictator stance. A devilish grin suddenly appeared on his face. "So this is what is going to happen now. Alana, dear, I want you to slap your husband."

Alana was surprised to see her own hand rise in the air. Before she knew it, her hand swung downwards hard across her husband's face.

"Everyone is shocked at first, but you will get used to it. See those silver shackles on your wrist?" Zefarious waited for them to look. "Those shackles let me control your every move. I unfortunately, cannot control how and what you think or even what you say, but your arms, your legs, your hands and feet those are mine."

"Alana, stand up." Without a moment of hesitation Alana was on her feet. "Alana, why don't you help your poor husband up?" Alana's hand reached out to her husband and pulled him off the ground. "Good. Now, I want you to punch him in the gut." Her fist went flying into her husband's stomach. "Do a double punch." Two more hard blows hit the shepherd's stomach. "Now kick him to the ground." Alana, swept the legs right out from underneath him. "Hit him with one of your lightning bolts." Every muscle in his body tensed as the shock coursed through his body.

Alana resisted as much as she could, but she could not stop herself no matter how hard she tried. Tears rolled down her face as she begged for Zefarious to stop. "Please, stop doing this. You are hurting him. P-please stop!"

"Alright, since you asked nicely. Just one more punch to the face and we can stop." Alana punched her husband directly on the jaw and then fell to her knees.

"I'm so sorry my love." She placed her husband's head on her lap and stroked his hair. Her tears landed on his face and smeared his blood as they ran down his chin.

"Papa! Papa?" Paolo came running out of the house and towards his parents.

"No Paolo no!" Alana's heart sank as Paolo came running closer to them. She did not want her son to see his father like this and she prayed that her son did not see she was the one who did it.

Paolo grabbed his father's hand and placed his head on his chest. Alana grabbed her son to comfort him, but Paolo quickly shrugged her off. "Why did you do this to papa?" The shepherd could see that his wife's heart was breaking into a million pieces.

"Paolo." The shepherd said with a weak voice. "Your mother did not do this to me, she would never hurt any of us."

"But I saw her." Paolo said through violent sobs.

Before either of them could respond, Zefarious grabbed Paolo and dragged him away from his parents. "I almost forgot you had a son." Zefarious used the bottle to put shackles on Paolo too. He lightly tapped the top of Paolo's head. "I think I will raise him as my own son, how does that sound?"

"No!" Alana shouted.

Zefarious snapped his fingers at Alana and pointed to the spot next to him. She immediately left her husband and walked over to his side. Zefarious placed his arms around Paolo and Alana, "Don't we make a good looking family. Yes, I think this suits me nicely."

"Stay away from my family." The shepherd was weak and could feel every ache in his body as he tried to stand up.

"Oh but this is my family now." Zefarious pointed to the ground. "Get back down."

The shepherd's arms slipped out from underneath him. He laid momentarily on the ground to catch his breath and then made another attempt to get back up.

"I don't think you understood me, get back down and stay there." The shepherd slipped again, but this time he did not wait to catch his breath, instead he placed his arms on the ground and pushed himself up. He began walking towards Zefarious and his family.

"Stop!" Zefarious shouted with a little bit of fear in his voice.

The shepherd kept moving forward, his feet dragging across the floor as if they were carrying heavy weights.

"I said stop!" Zefarious shouted again, this time with more anger than fear. "Stop! Stop!" But the shepherd was still moving forward and he was picking up the pace.

Zefarious deflected a fire ball thrown by the shepherd. His nostrils flared and his eyes narrowed on him, but he had little time to be angry because the shepherd threw another spell at him. Zefarious continued to block the shepherd's weak attacks, but with each throw Zefarious felt the spells growing stronger and stronger. Until finally, a bright yellow blast that Zefarious tried to block pushed him back leaving a trail in front of him where his feet dug into the ground.

Once the dust settled, the shepherd could clearly see Zefarious' face and he was terrified. "How is this possible?" The shepherd looked at his own shackles and wondered the same thing. "Alana, attack your husband."

The first spell narrowly missed the shepherd. He continued to deflect his wife's spells and managed to throw a few at Zefarious at the same time.

Finally, having enough Zefarious yelled at the gargoyles who were standing by with dumbfounded looks on their faces. "Borris! Don't just stand there, attack. All of you idiots attack."

The gargoyles crowded around the shepherd and through the cracks he could see that Alana was ordered to stop attacking. The shepherd hit the first oncoming gargoyle straight in the face with a sleeping spell, the second he blasted with fire. The shepherd found himself fighting the gargoyles off with ease, but Zefarious noticed that too.

The shepherd poofed to the outside of the dogpile in time to watch Zefarious drag his son next to his wife. Alana stretched out her hand and cried out, "Marco, my love!" and poof, they disappeared in a cloud of black smoke leaving the shepherd all alone.

Chapter 15 Night Sparks

Regina and Kolben were wrenched from the battle field and found themselves back in the cave. Their palms were moist and their breathing was heavy; Regina could even feel a slight ache in her jaw. She let out a heavy breath as a brief surge of power ran through her. The book fluttered its pages, sending a whoosh of air up into their faces until it slammed itself shut.

"M-Marco? The Gr-grand Master? But th-that would make him..." Regina stumbled over her words as she tried to make sense of what they just saw.

"That would make him 700 years old, give or take a few years." Kolben finished for her.

"But are we sure The Grand Master and the shepherd are the same person? I mean we never even saw his face."

"Come on Regina. It has to be him. It would actually explain a lot now that I think about it."

"Why don't we just ask him?" Regina looked outside the cave and notice for the first time that it was pitch dark out. "Oh, I didn't realize how late it was. I guess we can ask him tomorrow?"

"Nah, he stays up pretty late. It will be fine." Kolben waved her along as he tapped the side of the cave.

As they walked back to the Grand Master's cottage loud chirping noises echoed through the ravine.

"What is that about?" Regina asked.

"Why would I know?"

"Never mind." Regina rolled her eyes and sighed.

They walked into the Grand Master's cottage and found him sitting on the sofa like he was waiting for their arrival.

"Were you waiting for us?" Regina asked.

"Well it was only a matter of time before you two would end up at my door, although it did take a little longer than I had expected it would." A sudden smile and raised eye brows swept across his face. "Oh, I see. Were you two…" He clamped his fingers together and butted the tips of his hands against one another while he made kissing noises.

"Ugh! No!" Regina exclaimed. "It is not like that."

"Not yet you mean." Kolben added with a big grin on his face.

Again Regina just rolled her eyes. "Why didn't you just tell us that this book was about you?"

"I can neither confirm nor deny that the book is about moi." The Grand Master said with a mischievous smile on his face.

"But that bottle is the same…" Regina pointed to the bottle that sat on top of a chest.

"Sorry, no comment." The Grand Master interrupted.

"Fine, so this person who may or may not be you, what happened to his family and what happened to Zefarious?"

"That is a story for another day." The Grand Master gave them a broad wink. "We must focus on what is important, your powers. Did you notice anything after you finished the book?"

"Yeah, now that you mention it." Regina remembered the weird surge of energy that ran through her body. She was unsure of it then, but now things were starting to make sense. "The book, it gave me this, this…"

"Quick wave of energy." Kolben finished for her.

"Exactly. Wait, you felt it too?" Regina asked Kolben who simply nodded his head in response.

"You are wrong girly." The Grand Master gave a sly smile.

"But I did feel a wave of energy." Regina began to protest.

"No not about that, but about where the energy came from. It wasn't necessarily from the book, but the feelings that the book made you feel."

"So you are saying our feelings for the shepherd created that wave of energy?" Asked an unconvinced Kolben.

The Grand Master shook his head. "Whatever personal feelings you had for the shepherd are irrelevant, it was the feelings you had as the shepherd that gave you a surge, not of energy, but of your true powers."

"Huh?"

"Yeah I agree with Kolben and the elegant way that he put it, huh?" Regina gave Kolben a playful jab.

"Girly, it is quite simple actually. The shepherd truly believed he had lost everything he ever cared about. In that moment you felt his despair, his anguish, but there is something else that you felt; that he felt growing inside of him. He found his inner strength when things seem to be at its worst. The shepherd never fully believed in himself or in his abilities. The shepherd had extraordinary power and he didn't even know it." The Grand Master passionately gestured with his hands.

Kolben scoffed and said, "So are you saying that the key to obtaining incredible power is as simple as truly believing in yourself?"

"No it is not that simple I'm afraid. Those who have this great potential hidden deep inside them are tested by the fates."

"What do you mean?" Regina asked.

"I mean.." Marco pushed up his fake glasses to the bridge of his nose." "…the fates are cruel. Time and time again, those who have tremendous powers are tested with tragic loss. In the darkest of hours they are meant to search for the light."

"Um what happens to those who don't search for the light?" Kolben seemed shaky and almost nervous.

"They are DOOOMED." Marco said in a haunting voice.

"Doomed?" Kolben gulped.

"Yes. These dark seekers will go down a path that will spiral out of control not just for them, but the unfortunate souls who get pulled into their descent. The light seekers will always defeat those who failed their test of virtue. They were meant to fight for the forces of good, but they turned their backs on it and tipped the scales in the other direction."

"Wait. So the fates feed into both sides of good and evil?" Asked Regina.

"Unfortunately, yes. There is also the test of paradise. The great powers of evil, like Zefarious, are tested with an extraordinary amounts of good fortune…"

"But they try to create misery or something like that. Right?" Regina finished for the Grand Master.

"Correct. There will always be those who seek out the light in complete darkness as there will be those who search for the dark in the brightest of lights. Good versus evil, light versus dark; ultimately it's just different ways to balance life and death." Marco said with a grim face.

All of a sudden, loud squawking noises came from outside. Regina peered out the window and watched as hundreds of birds flooded out of the ravine. The cottage door swung open, Tyler's eyes were wide and he was short of breath.

"We're in trouble."

They all ran outside and all the animals in the ravine were trying to escape. Rabbits and arbunks burrowed into the ground, a small pack of wolves began scaling the mountain side and Regina watched as the fish defied gravity and swam up the waterfall.

Orwell jumped from the bridge above the cottage and sat by Tyler's side. "The animals were the first to sense the danger than shortly after Ravi saw green smoke coming from Thack's post. For now, it looks like they are only coming from the North."

"Who is they?" Kolben asked.

"We don't know yet, but there is at least a hundred if not more. They been sending up sparks every two minutes or so. We are not sure what it means but it cannot be good." Regina noticed that her brother's hands were slightly shaking as he petted the top of Orwell's head.

"Where is everybody?" Regina's heart was pounding.

"Thack and Maggie are on watch so they are at the top. Ravi is packing up the huts with Vaul and Tucker umm…" Tyler trailed off.

"Tyler, where is Tucker?" Regina tried to look passed her brother for any sign of Tucker.

"I-I don't know. I think he said he was going to look for you."

Regina's heart sank. "Oh no, he probably went to the waterfall."

"Regina that is the direction they are coming from."

"Tyler get everyone to the top of the ravine and back to the entrance of the caverns. We will meet you there."

"Wait! What?" Tyler tried grabbing his sister, but it was too late.

Regina took off running towards the waterfall before anyone could stop her. She watched the night sky grow brighter with different colors of sparks shooting off into the air. They were close and she knew it would be a narrow escape, if they were lucky to escape at all.

She reached the waterfall and could hear voices directly above her. She found Tucker fumbling around the boulder that held the stick that opened up the path from the boulder to the cave.

"Have you been spying on us?"

Tucker jumped back at the sound of her voice. "What? No! Of course not!"

"Then what are you looking for?" She folded her arms and waited for his response.

"Fine. I was looking for that stupid stick that you guys use. I only spied because I wanted to make sure that boy kept his grubby hands off of you."

Regina felt touched by Tucker's overly protected father gesture, but knew there was no time to revel in the moment. "We will talk about this later. Come on! We have to go!"

Two loud thuds came crashing down from behind them.

"Where do you think you're going?" Said a deep gravelly voice. Regina slowly turned around and saw two figures lingering in the shadows.

One of them stepped forward into the light of the moon. His skin was a brownish yellow, his eyes were small and squinty and he had round droopy ears and a long pointed nose. "Yeah!" He said in a high pitched voice. "Where do you think you're goin?"

Tucker busted out laughing. "Your voice is ridiculous and...ha...you are so small. What are you like three feet tall? Hahaha! If all your friends are like you than we have nothing to worr-"

The second figure stepped out into the light, but he was not like his friend at all. He was twice the size of Tucker. The creature had a thick protruding forehead and a very square jaw. Every inch of him was thick, there was nothing small about him, not even his pinky finger. His orange skin was rough and bumpy and he had a strong musty cheese odor to him.

"Are you making fun of my friend?" He lightly tapped a wood mallet into his open palm.

Tucker raised his nose in the air and sniffed. His face scrunched up and he waved his hand in front of his nose to clear the smell. "What is that stench?"

The smaller creature leaned in and whispered to Tucker and Regina. "That's Gulren, ogres' are sensitive about their smell and the smell only gets stronger when they are stressed."

The ogre sniffed under his armpits. "Javer! We talked about this!"

"See what I mean."

"Oh yeah, well at least I don't step on my own ears." Said Gulren.

"We Churras are proud of our long ears." Javer pushed his ears back over his shoulders.

Gulren and the Javer began to argue amongst themselves. Regina began to slowly back away towards

Tucker. She waved him to move around them stealthily. The two creatures were now yelling at one another.

"I think this is our chance to sneak away." Regina said to Tucker who nodded his head in agreement.

They had just made it past the tree line when they heard several more thuds behind them. Regina took a quick glance back and saw that at least ten more enemies had joined the ogre and the churra. When Regina looked forward again a large branch stood in her path. She took a hard tumble forward causing her locket to slip out from under her shirt. Tucker turned around to help her up, but something caught his eye.

He dove down next to her and whispered. "There is someone coming."

Regina managed to take a quick peak at what was coming for them, but she quickly realized what it was when she caught a whiff of musty cheese. "It is an ogre." She whispered back. "But I don't think it is Gulren. This one looks taller."

A few cracks, like feet stepping on twigs, came from either side of them. They were being surrounded and there was nowhere for them to hide.

"Come out now and we promise to be gentle." Said the large ogre in a commanding voice.

Regina looked at Tucker who was looking around for an escape plan, when something shinny caught her eye. The locket was gleaming in the moonlight. She held it in her hands wishing there was someone on the other side she could talk to. She placed her thumb on the mirror and began talking to it in a low voice. "Tucker and I are about to be taken by what I can only assume are Carnagers, it looks like they are a group of ogres and churras. I think the rest of Fox Squad made it out okay, along with two new additions: The Grand Master and Kolben. Ann, Reynold if you are somehow watching this I just want you to know that the team will find you. As for Tucker and I, we can only hope this is not goodbye."

Regina closed up her locket and tucked it back into her shirt. She could hear tiny footsteps closing in on them.

The ogre called out again. "This is your last chance. You have until the count of three to come out. One…"

Regina and Tucker stood up together. "We are right here. There is no need for you to strain that pretty little head of yours as you figure out how to count to three." Tucker glared at the ogre and braced himself for the oncoming attack.

"Haha this puny human thinks he is funny." The ogre swung his large hand across and hit Tucker square in the chest, knocking him over.

As Regina bent over to lend him a hand back up, Tucker noticed two brew balls remained on Regina's belt. He quickly reached for the green brew ball. He threw it as hard as he could towards the boss orge, but the ogre knocked him over again and the brew ball went flying backwards. A puff of gas burst into the air; about thirty feet behind them.

"Nice try." The boss orge chuckled and gave a signal to his team. Several churras ran over and restrained the two them and confiscated Regina's remaining brew ball.

Regina turned to face Tucker and said in a low whisper. "Thanks for trying."

Javer and Gulren joined the crowed and stood next to the large ogre. "That is her, right boss? I found her for you, boss. Javer did good right, boss?"

"Javer, didn't find her I did boss." Gulren chimed in.

"No I did."

"No it was me." Gulren tried to push Javer over, but Javer scurried around him in circles throwing soft punches every now and again.

"Enough!" The large ogre shouted. "I don't care who found her." He rounded on them and continued. "What I do care about is how both you idiots managed to let them get away."

Javer hid behind Gulren's leg as they both cowered in fear of their boss.

"I will deal with you two later." He turned back around to face Regina and Tucker. "Our queen has great plans for you and your brother. Our orders are to take you back alive."

One of the other churras came forward and saluted the boss. "Sir, there are no signs of the others. I'm sorry sir, but it looks like they got away."

Regina breathed a small sigh of relief, but she still had to worry about how they were going to get out of this situation.

"Thanks for the update Rex. We will have to get the brother some other time. The queen will still be very pleased that we caught the girl."

"What do you want to do with this one sir?" Rex asked, pointing a finger at Tucker.

"The queen said nothing about the others." The boss ogre smiled and licked his lips. "It has been a while since my men and I have had a good meal. He is a little small, but I think he will do just fine."

"Why is everyone trying to eat us? This was never a problem back in our world." Tucker struggled to break loose from the churras, but there were too many holding him back.

Regina tried to break free from her captives while she shouted at the boss ogre. "If you eat him I will fight you every step of the way back to your precious queen, but if you let him go I will come quietly and will do as I am told."

"No Regina! I can't let you do tha-" They stuck a cloth over Tucker's mouth to keep him quite.

The boss ogre rubbed his chin and contemplated Regina's request. "I think I will take my chances." He gave a signal to the churras and they began tying Tucker up with ropes.

"No! You can't do this! You can't take him!" Regina pulled and struggled to break free of the churras that were holding her back, but all she could do was watch helplessly as they dragged Tucker back to the waterfall.

Rex moved in closer to help the other churras escort Regina back to their camp when he stopped mid-step and began flapping his long dangling ears. Then his eyes flashed red and was momentarily put into a trance state. Regina noticed that the rest of the churras were doing the same thing, except for Javer.

"What is the update?" The boss ogre asked Rex.

Rex walked over to the boss ogre along with two other churras. One of the churras did a front flip jump and landed on the other churra's shoulders. Rex did not bother jumping because the bottom churra lowered to his knees so Rex could simply climb to the top. Even with three churras stacked on top of one another the boss ogre still had to bend down so Rex could whisper in his ear.

"What just happened?" Regina asked aloud knowing she wouldn't get a response.

"Churras can communicate telepathically with one another." Regina was surprised that anyone answered. She turned to Javer with his back hunched over still cowering from before. The two churras that were holding her arms rolled their eyes at the sound of Javer's voice.

"Why did all of the other churras flap their ears and flash their eyes, but you didn't?" The churras snickered at Regina's question.

"Because..." Javer began in a low voice. "Because the other churras did not share the message with me."

"Why not?"

"Because they don't like me very much." Javer looked at his feet and kicked the dirt as he said this.

"It looks like we are closing in on the rest of your team. I'm sure your brother is with them right?" The boss ogre paused for a moment and watched Regina for any kind of reaction. "No matter. I'm sure we will find out soon enough." He and the rest of the team went ahead back to the waterfall. While Regina was left with Javer, Gulren and the two churras that were restraining her.

Regina could feel her heart fluttering in her chest, her face felt flush and her stomach was sick. She could not let it all end like this. Everyone she had come to rely on, trust and considered family was about to be captured and most likely become someone's meal. A large lump gathered in her throat; she wanted to break down and scream.

She began to tug away from the churras that were holding her back. There were only two of them, but they had pretty strong grips. One of the churras kicked the back of Regina's knee causing her to buckle and fall to the floor. Their grip loosened with the fall and Regina managed to free an arm, but the churra who knocked her down was still holding on tightly to the other.

The churra glared at her and with his eyes dared her to make the next move. She did not hesitate. Something inside her awoke and all her fears and doubts seemed to have melted away. She would not be bullied by this small ugly creature and she would not let her team down, she would not let the kingdom down. There was no way she was going to let this one churra stop her.

She pointed a single finger at the churra. He looked around and then back at Regina. He pointed to himself and said, "Me?"

Regina nodded. She let out a small grin and released a giant shock wave from the palms of her hands. The churra was thrown back and the entire area quaked. The other churra that was holding her back came running towards her. She placed a force field in front of the churra and stopped him dead in his tracks.

The two churras were now unconscious which left Regina an open path back to Tucker. As she went to leave she felt something tugging on her shirt. She turned quickly ready to fight, but only saw intimidated eyes staring back at her.

"I think you might want to try going this way." Javer said in a hushed voice and pointed in the opposite direction.

"And why should I do that?" Regina asked suspiciously.

"Because they are already waiting for you on the other side."

"He is right." Gulren stepped out from behind a tree. "I saw the boss and the others turn their attention this way after you took out the first churra."

"Why are you telling me all of this? I'm the enemy."

"Because we are not very good at being the bad guys." Javer began.

"Javer and I have talked about this before. I think subconsciously we sabotage ourselves from succeeding in our evil endeavors. So we want to try doing the right thing for once." Gulren bowed his head and let out a deep sigh. "We are outcasts from our own kind... maybe this is the reason."

Regina was surprised by Gulren's insightful words. "Alright, let's go then."

Broad smiles spread across their faces. "Come on this way. You won't regret this princess." Javer grabbed her hand and lead her away from the direction they had dragged Tucker. Regina felt weird being called princess, but figured this was not the time to correct him.

Javer and Gulren had somehow made their way behind the waiting force and as close as they could to a tied up Tucker.

"Javer can untie your friend and I can help you take out the rest of those guys." Gulren suggested.

Regina considered this for a moment. There were about twenty or so churras and the boss ogre that she could see. It would be a lot for her to take on all at once, but she had to trust that her newly found powers could get the job done.

"I appreciate the offer, but if this goes south I don't want you two to get caught."

"But we want to help you princess." Said Javer.

"Please don't call me that."

"Call you what?" Asked Javer

"Don't call me princess."

"But you are the princess are you not?"

"Yes, I guess, but..." Javer did not let Regina finish.

"It is the proper thing to do then."

"Fine." Regina did not want to waste any more time arguing. "Javer untie Tucker and Gulren, you are going to escort me to your boss. Let's make it look like I was trying to escape again and you caught me. I'm gonna have to...um..."

"Whatever it is I can handle it." Gulren gave an encouraging pat on the back that almost knocked Regina over.

"I will hit you with some kind of spell; I'm not sure what yet, but I will do my best to go easy on you. That will be your cue to 'lose your grip' and I will take it from there."

"Why can't we just help?" Gulren asked.

"This might be a lot to ask of you two, but it would be nice to have inside knowledge. So we can plan ahead and keep casualties to a minimum."

"You mean like spies?" Gulren raised an eyebrow.

"You are right. It is too much to ask of you."

"Spies! I love this idea!" Javer was elated by the thought.

"Like we always dreamed to be Javer." Gulren joined his friend in the excitement. "I can't believe this is finally happening." He saluted Regina. "Your Highness you can count on us!"

Regina smiled. "Are you ready?" The two of them nodded vigorously.

Gulren and Regina back tracked a little so they could avoid bringing attention to Javer. "Boss! Look who I found trying to escape again." Gulren nudged Regina forward with his massive hand.

"There still might be hope for you yet, Gulren. Bring her here. I want the pleasure of tying her up." The boss ogre cracked his knuckles.

"No problem boss." Gulren nudged Regina along.

As they got closer to the churras and the boss, Gulren gave her another push forward, but this time he pushed too hard and Regina fell to the ground. She had felt guilty knowing she had to hit Gulren with a spell, but she felt a little less so as she picked herself up from the muddy ground. Regina used her force field ability to surround a nearby stone and moved the force field containing the stone directly towards Gulren's head. She threw the stone hard and fast to make it look like Gulren took a big blow to the head, but she managed to slow the speed right before impact enough to where it only caused Gulren a minor headache.

Gulren clutched his head. "Oww!" He began, "Oh the pain! I-I think my vision is starting to go. Ugh!" He wobbled in circles and then he let his feet slip out from underneath him. Before he closed his eyes he dramatically reached out with his hand, "Why cruel world, why?" His whole body went limp and he was perceivably unconscious.

Regina thought he was over acting, but the others seemed to have bought it. The churras stared in aww and began whispering amongst themselves.

Annoyed by the lack of response, the boss gave them all an order. "Don't just stand there, attack!" The churras hesitated. Boss let out a sigh. "She can't attack you all at once. Go! Go! Go!"

Regina raised her hands in the air as the large horde of chrurras came charging at her. Silence blanketed the ravine. There were no chirps from the crickets, no trickling of water, the trees were silently swaying in the breeze and the sound of stomping feet running towards her disappeared. The churras stopped just short of her, afraid they had all gone deaf, but once their murmurs filled the air they feared there was something much worse going on. But before they could even react Regina swung her hands around and pushed all the sound down into the ground. The land rolled out in waves causing the floor to quake with each passing surge. Churras toppled over one another as they struggled to stay up on their scrawny feet. A few of them bumped heads and were out cold. Some even ran away.

The shaking and rolling lands finally stopped and all that was left standing was the ogre boss. He stood there tall and mean, but a hint of doubt swept across his face and Regina knew that he was not as confident as he was before.

"Enough tricks! You and the rest of your team are coming with us." He took a step forward, but did not dare to go any further.

Regina held her palms out to to the boss ogre. "I'm going to make you one last deal. You leave now and I won't have to hurt you."

The boss ogre forced out a shaky chuckle. "Ha-haa. Again, I think I will take my chances."

"Alright, but you will regret it." Regina ran off into the woods.

"Running away already." The boss let out a deep roar and followed her into the woods. "Come out, come out from where ever you are." He taunted her, but when he passed the first set of trees Regina was nowhere to be found.

Large footsteps smashed their way through low hanging branches and moss covered ground. A noise sounded to the left of him, he quickly swung around but nothing was there. He walked a few more feet and a loud cracking noise echoed behind him. Again he turned around and nothing was there. He cautiously looked around as he continued to search for her.

"Here!" He jumped at the word because it was whispered into his ear as if someone was standing right next to him, but no one was around. In fact, he was very much alone and he became very aware of that fact.

"What's a matter?" Regina's voice echoed through the trees.

"Where are you?" He shouted in fear.

"Behind you." Regina's voice whispered from behind the ogre.

He turned around throwing punches at the air. "Stop it!"

"But why?" Her voice spun around him again and again, repeating the same two words. "But why? But why?"

A tree cracked in half as the ogre began smashing everything in sight. He ripped a bush from the ground and spilt a stump in two. Mud was splashing everywhere as he stomped his way through.

Regina continued to taunt him. She was controlling the sound of her voice and the direction in which it went. She whispered in his ear and then she would shout from afar. She made it sound like she was above him and below him at the same time. Finally, as he ran back to the waterfall, Regina created a sound bubble that completely surrounded him. He hit the bubble wall and fell to his knees. Regina then sucked all the sound from the bubble; he couldn't even hear himself whimpering.

"I'm SORRY! I'm sorry. Pleaseeee, I just want my mamma!" The boss ogre looked up and saw several small squinty eyes looking up at him. All of the churras were watching him with disgusted looks on their faces.

He stood up and dusted himself off. "Guys, I'm just ki-kidding around. It's just a joke." He took a step forward and hit the bubble wall again. He let out a small sigh. "Alright, I give up." He was completely defeated, warn down and done.

Regina walked out in between the churras and the boss. "Leave now and you will be shown mercy." The ogre nodded in agreement and Regina popped the bubble.

He and the churras began walking towards the waterfall. Like little acrobats the churras formed a chain that reached the top of the ravine. They were slowly making their way to the top when they suddenly stopped. Their ears began to flap and their eyes were flashing red.

The boss noticed and stopped climbing as well. An evil grin spread across his face and he began climbing back down along with the churras.

"What are they doing?" Tucker had been untied by Javer and was now by Regina's side.

"I don't know, but I have a feeling that whatever it is, it probably isn't good for us."

Bright lights shot off overhead. The boss touched down along with the churras. He stood by the wall not daring to move forward at least not quite yet.

Several ropes dropped down around them. The boss began to walk forward still flashing his evil grin. "Reinforcements have arrived." Hundreds of churras scaled down the ravine wall along with a handful of ogres.

The sound of small marching feet came from the woods. Lights flashed through the tree lines as another small army of churras came from behind, leaving Tucker and Regina completely surrounded.

"I don't think you can get out of this one. So how about you come quietly this time and we won't eat your friend. Is that a deal?" The boss said this with a crooked smile on his face.

Regina's every instinct was telling her not to trust him. She knew she would be better off fighting then to end up in their capture. She just needed to find a weak point.

"Psst. Look at the group behind us." Tucker gestured his head to the army that came from the woods. The churras look exhausted and several of them had scorched marks on their clothes. There was not a single churra that didn't look completely battered. "The team must have done a real number on them." Tucker laughed to himself. "We might have a good chance of getting away if we go through them."

Rex stepped forward to address the boss. "What's the latest report Rex?"

"They got away sir." Afraid of the boss's retaliation, all the churras cowered except for the churras who saw him whimpering only moments ago, they did not react at all. It was subtle but all the other churras took notice.

"Your friends got away and all I have left is the two of you." The boss paused to stare Regina down. "So what is it going to be, will you give yourself up or are you going to put up a fight again?"

Regina turned to Tucker and waited for him to give her some kind of a signal. It was a small motion and Regina wasn't even sure he actually did it, but the quick glance and slight nod was everything she needed to move forward. "So you call that fighting? Weird, I thought it was just me kicking your-"

"CHARGE!" The boss ordered his army forward.

Regina and Tucker stood back to back prepared to fight a losing battle. Churras were rushing from all sides and a few more ogres dropped down to join the battle. It was seemingly hopeless odds, even with Regina's new found powers, but they continued to stand strong as their enemies grew closer.

Tucker's fist were up and Regina was ready to release a wave of magic when a loud roar came from up above.

Everyone looked up to see what it could be, but the dark night sky revealed nothing. Regina scanned the skies hoping to see what she thought it could be; it was hardly visible, but she saw a blue light heading their way. Regina whispered to herself, "Eydis!"

"Eydis?" Repeated Tucker.

The roar got louder and the blue light was much closer now. Regina grabbed Tucker by the arm and shouted, "Get down!"

The air around them erupted into flames. The boss ogre was the first to run screaming followed by Rex and the other ogres. Eydis landed beside them wrapping her tail around to keep them protected. She let out another burst of fire as the remaining churras tried to attack.

"Quick! Let's hop on." Regina tugged on Tucker's shirt.

"You want us to go up there?" Tucker pointed to the short spikes on Eydis' back.

Regina was already climbing up. "Come on." She shouted over her shoulder.

They had to stay low to avoid the rocks that were being thrown at them. Churras started launching themselves, in their acrobatic fashion, to keep them from leaving, but Eydis was quick enough to bat them away with her tail or send them flying with a swift kick.

Regina and Tucker were now firmly mounted at the top of Eydis' back. Regina looked around for Gulren and Javer. She spotted them in the back pretending to throw rocks so they would not draw attention to themselves. She gave them a small nod before Eydis flapped her wings and took off into the starry night sky.

Chapter 16 Shadow Lighters

"Wh-where is-s-s sh-she tak-ak-ing us?" Tucker yelled through chattering teeth even though Regina was sitting right in front of him. They were flying amongst the clouds bracing themselves against the heavy wind. It had been a particularly warm night, but the higher elevation proved to be much colder. Regina placed a force field around her and Tucker to block the wind and to kick out the cold air.

"Probably wherever Ann and Reynold are. They are the only ones who could have sent her." Regina placed her hand over her locket.

"And where are they?"

"That is a good question." Regina was sure that her message would not get through to anyone, at least not to Reynold or Ann who were just taken from their home. Yet, Regina was sitting on proof that Reynold and Ann did get her message after all. But if it was not them who sent Eydis then who did?

Regina struggled to stay awake after the exhausting battle with the churras and the boss ogre. The adrenaline and overall excitement kept her alert for a while, but she quickly learned that using her powers as much as she just did can really take its toll.

"I think she is circling."

"How can you tell?" Regina looked around and all she could see were clouds.

"It has been subtle, but she has gradually been making right turns for the last twenty minutes or so." Tucker had a quizzical look on his face. "Do you think it is possible she is making sure we are not being followed?"

Regina patted Eydis on the head. "She is a pretty smart dragon." Eydis did a quick circle and then dropped into a steep dive towards the ground pulling up only a few feet before they hit the ground.

"What was that about?" Tucker was clenching tightly to the dragon's back.

"Eydis has a flare for the dramatic."

Eydis touched down behind an old abandoned library. She waited for Tucker and Regina to get off before she slumped down and almost instantly fell asleep.

"Where are we?" Regina looked around trying to find any kind of landmark that could tell her where they were at.

Tucker examined the exterior of the library. "This place should be bulldozed. It looks like it is one gentle breeze away from falling down."

"I wonder why Eydis brought us here. It doesn't look like anyone is here or even within miles of here."

"Should we check inside?" Tucker pointed to a door that was slightly cracked open.

They slowly walked through the creaking door. The inside looked just as bad as the outside. Dust covered every inch of the place; books were scattered everywhere, chairs were broken and some walls had gaping holes in them.

Tucker glanced around the spooky library. "Are there ghosts in this realm?"

"Not that I know of. Why?" Regina responded.

"Just checking."

They continued making their way through until they reached the rows of bookshelves in the middle of the first floor. Tucker tripped over several books that were laying on the ground, kicking up a bunch of dust in the process. "Geeze this place is a mess. *Ah-choo!*" Tucker let out a loud sneeze.

"Shhh…" Regina looked around. "We might not be the only ones in here."

"Sorry. It's not like I can control it." He threw is head back again. "AH-AH-" But the rest of the sneeze did not make a sound.

"This new power really comes in handy." Regina had her hands up and flashed a smile at Tucker.

"Show off." Tucker replied.

They walked further along the rows of books. It came to Regina's surprise that many of the books were still in decent condition, actually in too good of condition. "Hey Tucker, come check this out."

"What is it?"

"Do you don't notice anything strange about these books?" Regina ran a finger across the spine of a book.

Tucker shrugged. "No. Should I?"

"Look!" Regina handed him one of the books from the *Magical Creatures* section. "There is no dust on it. None of these books have dust on them."

"You're right. Someone or someones is still using this library."

Regina looked at the hardwood floor and noticed they had been leaving footprints in the dust, but theirs were the only footprints there. "If someone has been checking out the books than how are they getting around without leaving any tracks?"

Tucker's eyes were wide when Regina looked back up at him. "Because they glide around through a smoky mist." Tucker pointed to something directly behind her.

Regina turned around and saw a smoky mist in the distance. On impulse, Regina threw a shock wave in the smoky mist's direction, but it just went through her.

"Oh no, run!" Regina and Tucker jumped over a pile of books and ran back to the door that they had come through. They ran through the door and shut it behind them, but when they turned back around there was a smoky mist right in front of them and from it came Midnight Smoke. She laid her hand flat in front of her and blew a gold powder in their faces.

Regina's eyelids grew heavy and her whole body began to sink to the ground. She tried to resist, but the powder was too strong. She rested her head against Tucker's and slowly closed her eyes. The last thing she saw was Midnight Smoke pulling off her hood as she stood over them.

"Regina, are you alright?" Tucker's voice came from somewhere next to her, but she was still too tired to open her eyes. His voice kept fading in out of her conscious mind. "Regina, can you hear me?"

Finally, she awoke. "Yeah I can hear you."

They were in a dark windowless room with two cots laid out on opposite ends. A giant floating lantern was their only source of light.

"Did you happen to see where they took us?" Regina began to feel around, looking for any kind of weak spot or a way to escape.

"No. I woke up in here about twenty minutes ago." Tucker leaned against the wall. "What do you think happened to the others?"

"I don't know. My best guess is that they went looking for Ann and Reynold. I mean they had to have seen Eydis. Tyler would have made the connection and assumed that somehow Ann and Reynold escaped and that we would be with them." Regina let out a chuckle and turned around to face Tucker. "I wonder what that smug jerk thought about Eydis." Tucker gave her a puzzled look. "I'm talking about Kolben."

Tucker scratched at his head. "Oh right, I'm sure that really freaked her out."

"Did you say her?"

"Whoops, I meant to say him. I think the sleeping powder is still wearing off."

Regina went back to searching for an escape while Tucker moved over to one of the cots and sat down. "So what were your parents like?"

"What? Why are you asking?"

"I'm just curious that's all." Tucker leaned against the cold wall waiting for her response.

Regina stopped and sat down on the opposite cot. "They wer- they were wonderful. They would read to us every night and they made sure to tuck us in tight and gave us goodnight kisses. They went to every school event: science fairs, talent shows, plays, swim meets for me and little league football for Tyler."

"My mom loved to cook. She would always be cooking up something delicious in the kitchen and dad would be right there next to her thinking he was helping, but in reality he was an awful cook. But somehow my mom would always turn it around for him and I don't think my dad was ever the wiser."

"My dad was really into music. I always thought it was funny that he would be so intrigued by every song that came on the radio; like he never heard anything like it before. Which I guess makes sense now. He also liked to play the guitar. One of his favorite songs that he liked to play for us was *My Serene Love.*" Regina thought she saw Tucker mouth the words of the song before she had even said it, but shrugged it off and blamed it on the bad lighting. "He said he learned that song from his mom."

Regina sighed. "I really wish I could have met her. He always talked so warmly about her. I guess that is a wish for a different day. Right now, I wish we could find a way out of here."

"Will figure something out." Tucker got up from the cot and lazily searched his side of the room.

Regina paused to sniff the air. "That is odd."

"What is?"

She sniffed some more. "Do you smell that? It smells like Ann's strawberry pie."

Tucker sniffed the air. "I don't smell anything. AH-AH-"

Regina silenced the last part of his sneeze again, but this time Tucker looked startled and unsure. "What just happened?"

"I used my powers to cover the sound of your sneeze like last time." Regina's confused look at Tucker seemed to trigger something in him.

"Haha. Just kidding." Tucker looked uncomfortable and was avoiding eye contact with Regina.

"Are you alright? You seem a little off."

The door flung open. "I told you she would catch on." Midnight Smoke stood in the doorway and directed her attention to Tucker.

"What is going on?" Demanded Regina.

A woman's voice came from Tucker. "She was convinced for the first half of the conversation."

"Nah, she was suspicious of you as soon as she woke up. She is a clever girl; I like that." Midnight winked at Regina.

"Indeed she is." A flash of green smoke billowed up around Tucker and once it cleared an old lady was standing were he was just standing.

"Ta-Da! That is what they say in your realm right?" The old lady smiled and waited for some kind of response from Regina.

"So you're the Mad Sister? You don't look so scary to me." Regina scoffed.

The older lady had an awkward look on her face. She pushed back her long silvery hair and glanced at Midnight Smoke. The wrinkles on her forehead furrowed along with the lines around her thin lips. Her emerald green eyes narrowed on Regina. "I'm not the Mad Sister."

"I think it might be time for introductions." Midnight Smoke responded. "I'm-" She began, but Regina cut her off.

"Yeah, yeah I know who you are. You are Midnight Smoke."

Midnight Smoke shifted her weight. "Yes, I am, but my real name is Naveen."

"Why should I care what your real name is? You are about to hand me over to the Mad Sister anyways, right? So you can get a pat on the head and a nice little treat as a reward." Regina walked forward to Midnight with her hands held together in front of her. "Come on, let's get this over with already."

"I think I should let you handle this, Ez." Midnight Smoke closed the door and left Regina alone with the older lady.

"Is this the part where you try to get information out of me or something?" Regina asked defiantly.

"I already got the information I needed from you."

"Oh yeah, and what information was that?" Regina's heart sank a little in her chest.

"For being such a smart girl I'm surprised you have not figured it out yet, but I guess you know very little about this world and of me. We brought you here so we could confirm that you are who you say you are. I pretended to be your friend Tucker so I could easily get information about your father...who is also my son."

"Your son? Wait, Ez is that short for Esme as in Queen Esme who is also my grandmother?"

A tear spilled out from the corner of her eye as she smiled and nodded at Regina. "I have waited so long for this moment and it is finally here." Esme opened her arms wide ready to embrace Regina in a hug.

"I'm sorry, but how can I believe that it really is you? I mean you can change your appearance to whoever you want."

"Ah, you are skeptical too. I'm learning so much about you already." She stood up and wiped the tear that had rolled down her cheek. "Alright, I will figure out some way to prove it to you. In the meantime, I want to catch you up on a few things." She opened the door and gestured Regina through. "Shall we go for a little stroll?"

Regina kept her distance as they walked through an old industrial looking building held up by brick walls and metal posts.

"Where are we? Regina looked around and noticed there were no windows.

"We are in a basement located directly under the library you were in earlier."

"Is that safe? The library looked like it was about to fall apart."

"Have you ever heard of a deception projection?"

"Yes, yes I have." Regina thought about Reynold and Ann and then she remembered the message she received right before they were kidnapped by Midnight Smoke. "If you are who you say you are, why are you working with someone like Midnight Smoke?"

Esme hesitated for a moment. "Naveen, is a complicated story...she is not that person anymore."

"Okay, but what did she do with Ann and Reynold?"

"You will see soon enough." Esme continued walking. "This secret base was created shortly after the Mad Hysteria. This library was attacked in one of the first battles, but it was not severely damaged, in fact it held up pretty well. It was left abandon for about a year or so until one of Zahari's people found it."

"You are working with the sirens too?"

"Of course. The sirens have important background knowledge on the Mad Sister. They may not be the easiest to work with, but they have been very dedicated. Zahari told me she spoke to you. She is uh…" Esme paused a moment; she was searching her mind for the right word to say. "…interesting huh?"

"If that is what you want to call it." Regina shivered a little remembering Zahari's more terrifying side.

"Zahari wanted to run the day to day operations here, but she wasn't exactly the best leader to the non-sirens. She absolutely terrified anyone who made a mistake, which kept productivity high, but morale was pretty dismal. I took over once I returned to this realm."

"Where were you at the beginning of all of this?" Regina gestured to the entire factory, to the assembly line and the magnificent weapons that they had stocked piled below.

"I was with your father and Naveen trying to find safety in the other world."

"You and my dad were with Naveen."

"Like I said, Naveen is a complicated story. One day she might just tell you everything or she might never tell you. She does not like to talk about her past and who she shares her story with is entirely up to her." Esme placed a hand on Regina's shoulder. "Hopefully, I can earn your trust and you will believe me when I say she is not a threat, at least not to her friends, I cannot say the same for her enemies."

"So what made you come back?"

"There were many reasons for me to come back, but for starters, I basically abandoned the kingdom. I was trying to be a good mother and protect my son, but in doing so, I left behind a lot of people here who needed protecting too. It was inevitable that the Mad Sister would make her return and I wanted to be there and stop her before she could do any more harm to this land and the people in it." Esme let out a deep sigh. "Your father wanted us to stay with him in your world, but I knew this is where I needed to be."

Esme opened a swinging door that lead into a kitchen that looked like it came out of a five-star restaurant. There were sparkling clean stainless steel appliances, cooper pans that hung down from the ceiling, plenty of fresh herbs growing out of different pots throughout and knives a plenty. The sweet smell of pie wafted into Regina's nose as she took a deep breath in. Her eyes scanned the room looking for the small blonde woman that was responsible for the delicious pies baking in the oven.

"Ann!" Regina was excited and relieved at the same time.

"Oh my goodness. Reynold!" Ann called over to the burly man tending to the herbs. Ann's arms wrapped around Regina and held her tight. It was not too long before a large pair of arms enveloped around the both of them and gave a big squeeze.

Ann's hands swept the hair out of Regina's face. "We are so glad that y'all are alright."

"You're glad? I thought you two would be locked up in some dark cell?" Regina looked at the both of them still shocked that they were unharmed and safe.

"Oh that." Reynold rolled his eyes. "Yeah we didn't appreciate being kidnapped either. We were pretty upset until we found out that the Queen was behind all of this. Once she explained everything we were eager to help out in any way possible."

"Sorry we didn't send y'all a message through the locket, but Naveen was worried that someone else might intercept the message and all. When we got your message though…" Ann placed a hand on her matching locket. "…we sent Eydis to come get ya." Ann gave Regina another big hug. "We are so glad that you made it out okay."

"Me too." Regina looked over her shoulder at Esme. "You truly believe that is the queen?" Reynold and Ann nodded yes. "How can you be so sure?"

"Well she seemed to know a lot about ya and ya father and ya mother." Reynold smiled.

"What about Naveen?" Asked Regina.

"We were hesitant at first, there was a lot of awful stories about Midnight Smoke during the Mad Hysteria, but she has been very pleasant to us."

"Ya mean since after she scared us and took us from our home?" Reynold raised an eyebrow at Ann.

"Will ya let it go?" Ann crossed her arms. "We were fine. She was very gentle with us and the Queen herself told us we could trust her. Besides, we were not the only ones in town being taken from their homes."

"What happened to all those people?" Regina asked.

"The Queen and Midnight Smoke have been bringin them here." Ann responded.

"Why would they do that?"

"The Queen is tryin to quickly build up her army and protect those who cannot fight since the war will probably begin soon." Ann looked around the room at all the familiar Nahtovians. "Apparently, she has been recruitin people for years now; just a little at a time so she could avoid drawin attention to her secret compound."

Reynold chimed in. "Any who, I think it is safe to trust her and all considering she did keep her promise."

"What promise?" Asked Regina.

"That she would bring ya and ya brother back safely. Where is Tyler by the way?" Reynold looked around over the top of Regina's head.

"Uh we kind of got separated. Tucker and I....Tucker!" Regina's eyes grew wide.

"What about him?" Reynold tried to get an answer, but Regina rushed back over to Esme.

"Where is Tucker?" Regina demanded.

The swinging doors opened. "I'm right here. Thanks for remembering about me." Tucker said the last part sarcastically.

Regina's cheeks grew red; she felt guilty that she had forgotten about Tucker. "Sorry. I have been dealing with some pretty huge stuff here."

Esme explained Tucker's absence. "He just woke up. We let you two sleep until the powder wore off."

"How long were we asleep for?" Regina just realized she had no idea what time it was or even what day it might be.

Esme responded. "A week."

"We slept for a week!" Regina and Tucker said in unison.

"Hehe I'm just kidding."

Tucker scowled. "Who is this lady anyways?"

"I'll explain later." Regina sighed.

"Let's see." Esme began to mumble to herself. "Naveen brought you in about the same time as the Bumple Fest began..."

"Bumple Fest?" Tucker whispered to Regina who just shrugged.

"...then we- plus the carving...I would say you were a sleep for about sixteen hours." Esme finished.

"Have you been looking for Tyler and the rest of the team?" Regina asked

"Of course. What kind of grandmother would I be?"

"She is your grandmother?" Tucker's mouth gapped open as he put together all the pieces. "That means-"

"Not now Tucker." Regina lightly nudged him with her elbow.

"Zahari's son intercepted them in the caverns." Esme looked at her watch. "They should be here shortly."

An hour passed as they sat around the table picking at strawberry pie. Nervous legs tapped rapidly as they waited for the rest of the team to show up. Tucker drummed his fingers on the table, Ann bit at her lip and Reynold chewed on his nails. Regina and Esme were the only two not showing any signs of anxiety.

"So she is your grandmother. Huh?" Tucker said breaking the silence.

"That is yet to be determined." Regina did not look at Esme when she said this.

"Weird. Old Barnabas made it sound like you were dead." Tucker added.

"Oh sweet Barney! Yes, to him, it really did seem like I was dead." Esme said with a sigh. "I didn't want anyone that I was close to know that I was still alive. For their protection. He was in the dark until Naveen visited the castle. I believe you were all there for that."

"Yeah we were there." Regina answered, but made it clear she was not happy with that run in.

The room grew silent and awkwardness filled the air. Regina was frustrated with the new developments and Esme knew that everything she said was only making Regina more irritated.

"In normal circumstances I would be the last one to ask this, but where is Nita? She is not here? Is she?" Tucker looked around just to make sure.

"No." Ann began. "She is runnin Nahtovia's prison."

"She is a warden now?" Tucker rubbed his hands together and laughed. "I bet she loves doing that."

"Yeah, she wasn't too happy about that, but the Queen needed someone tough to handle the potential new comers." Ann frowned. "I don't know what our town is going to do without her."

"I think we are better off now honestly." Reynold thought for a moment. "Maybe, I will run for mayor when this is all over."

"I think ya will make a great mayor Reynold." Ann smiled again.

The cheerful moment quickly passed and another five minutes of silence hit the room.

"How far are the caverns from here anyway?" Tucker asked.

Before Esme could answer, Naveen walked through the door with the rest of Fox Squad. "Sorry, it took a while to convince them to follow me here."

Tyler ran over to his sister and gave her a big hug. "We tried going back for you and Tucker, but we got ambushed by the churras."

"It was insane; you should have seen the Grand Master. He was brilliant!" Ravi chimed in.

"It really is you." Thack knelt in front of the queen and bowed his head. "My Queen, you have not changed a bit."

"Thack, you were always such the charmer. The rest of the team bowed including the Grand Master and Kolben. "Please, that is not necessary. I have not been a queen in twenty-three years."

The Grand Master poofed next to Esme. "My lady, your granddaughter has great potential, I believe her powers will come in soon."

"Oh, but they already have." Esme responded.

"I told you girly." Marco poofed next to Tyler. "And this one, he takes after you."

"I could not be prouder of my grandchildren." Esme gleamed.

"So you are my grandmother?" Tyler asked.

"Yes, I am your grandmother." Esme smiled, but did not reach out for a hug; remembering Regina's rebuff from their first meeting. However, Tyler was more trusting and did not hesitate to embrace his grandmother. "I see that you do not take after your sister."

"In my defense, I was just kidnapped by the notorious Midnight Smoke and then I woke up in a dark room with a person disguised as Tucker. So excuse me if I seem hesitant to accept you or everything else going on around here with open arms." Regina stormed out of the room.

"She does have a point." Tucker said before he followed Regina.

Regina placed a sound bubble around her so she could scream without being heard. She screamed until she was red in the face and then she screamed some more. She found a bench and flung herself on it. A large lump had gathered in her throat and her stomach was heavy with anger.

Tucker sat beside her, "So do you want to tell me what is going on because I have known you for some time now kiddo and I have never seen you act like this before. But I also cannot say that I blame you for feeling this way, I know I would."

Regina took a deep breath in as she tried to get rid of her anger. "It is just that this woman…"

"Who you have never met before; claims to be your grandmother." Tucker finished for her.

"Yes, but it is so much more than just that. I'm thrilled that she is alive and I have a link to my father again, but I can't trust her. I mean who kidnaps their own grandchild."

"I was not a huge fan of that either." Said Tucker.

"Exactly! She has also been hiding in this underground compound; she is working with a known enemy; she had Ann and Reynold taken from their home and finally, she can disguise herself as whomever she likes." Regina ran her hands through her silky hair in an attempt to gather herself.

"Yeah, that is suspicious." Tucker agreed.

"But most of all, if she really is who she says she is, then why was she not there when my parents died?"

Tucker did not know how to respond so he wrapped his arm around her shoulders and sat there until she was ready.

Tyler stomped over to Tucker and Regina. "What is wrong with you?"

"Tyler you don't understand." Regina stood up from the bench. "You weren't there; you didn't see what I saw."

"But she is our grandmother." Tyler protested.

"Maybe, we don't know that for sure. Besides there are too many unanswered questions for me to fully trust anything she says right now." Regina jumped when a blaring alarm sounded off next to her.

Tyler covered his ears and shouted, "WHAT IS GOING ON?"

The three of them ran back into the kitchen where the others were gathering up their things.

"WHATS WITH THE AL-" Tucker began to shout, but realized half way through that Regina placed a sound bubble around them blocking out the alarm noise.

"Thank you Regina." Esme smiled at her, but Regina did not bother to return the gesture.

"Whoa." Kolben said to himself, while the rest of the group stared in awe as they too were equally impressed with Regina's powers.

"The alarm is sounded when we are under attack and unfortunately this is not a drill." Esme looked to Naveen. "Gather everyone and bring them here." She pulled a small tablet from her pocket. "We have twenty minutes before they get here, so there is no time to waste."

Naveen touched her temple. Her eyes squinted as if she were in pain. "She is with them." She looked distressed as she watched Esme for her next orders.

"Alert Zahari as well. We need all hands on deck if she is here." Esme continued to hand out orders as Naveen disappeared through the now crowded kitchen. Regina couldn't help but be a little bit impressed in the way Esme commanded and how quickly she reacted. Not a single person questioned her commands and every one of them obeyed completely. She knew how to be a leader and that was something Regina could respect and learn from.

"Regina, dear." Esme placed a hand on her granddaughter's shoulder. "I know I might not be your most favorite person right now, but I need your help. I need you to stick by me and command your team. Can you do that for me?"

Regina had no time to respond. Esme stood up on the nearest bench and called for order. The room went silent as they waited for their Queen to speak.

"The night is approaching and along with it comes the darkness that we have long feared. Tonight we stand up and look that fear in its eyes and say no more. No more will I run from you, no more will I hide from you and no more will I let you terrorize me."

"Fifteen minutes." Naveen whispered to Esme.

"Take note here and now because history is about to be made. Future generations will say that this battle was the turning point in the war. The first battle where the Mad Sister saw the beginning of the end."

Naveen was looking at her tablet. "There are about four hundred of them."

"This will not be an easy fight; they out number us two to one. But we have more to lose than they do. Our freedom and our children's freedoms are at stake. So we must fight as one and show them we will not let the darkness win! We are the lights in the shadows!"

The crowded room chanted. "Shadow Lighters! Shadow Lighters!"

"Shadow Lighters?" Regina asked aloud.

"That is the name we have been calling ourselves. We fight the shadows or darkness by bringing the light." Naveen answered.

"That is a little ironic coming from you, isn't it?"

"I would not call it irony more like an unfortunate coincidence." Naveen began to walk away, but she turned back around to re-engage Regina. "You know, Esme, who yes is really your grandmother, is a wonderful and caring woman. You have no idea what she has been through and what she has done for her family. So I suggest you layoff her and try to get to know her a little better."

"And you expect me to trust this from the woman who murdered my grandfather?" Regina could feel the heat coming off her.

Naveen, still upset, looked around to see if anyone had heard what Regina had just said. Fortunately, no one had. "Who told you that? You know what it does not matter. It was a situation that I had no control over and it is something that I have to live with."

"What do you mean you had no control?"

Naveen laughed. "Ha! You have no idea. You don't have to trust me, but you should really get all the facts first before you make any kind of judgments." Naveen stormed out of the room.

Regina had to shake off what Naveen had just said. She had to prepare herself and Fox Squad for the oncoming attack. She walked over to the group ready to take command, but Naveen's comment lingered in the back of her mind. *"Do I really know all the facts?"*

"Hey girly, what is your plan?" The Grand Master looked at her eagerly awaiting her answer.

"Cool moves by the way." Kolben chimed in.

"Uh thanks." Regina answered.

"You guys should have seen her take on all those churras and the ogre, man he did not know what hit him." Tucker had a boastful smile on his face.

"Okay we need to focus." Regina enjoyed the impressed looks all around, but time was running short. "Esme wanted us close by her. Let's see what we are dealing with first." Regina looked to her brother, "Is Orwell here?"

"Yeah he is outside with Edyis."

"Good. We may need both of them."

Tucker raised his hand in the air. "What do you want me to do? I'm not sure if I will be of any use, you know not having any magical powers and all."

"I'm kinda in the same boat as Tucker. My inclination deals with plants remember." Reynold looked around helplessly.

"I think I overheard someone say something about an armory. Reynold and Tucker why don't you two see what you can find and meet up with us when you can." Regina turned to direct the others." The rest of you stay close and watch for my commands. Let's show the Mad Sister what we are made of!"

Chapter 17 Battle of the Queens

"How are we going to defend this place?" Regina was running alongside Queen Esme to the top of the run down library.

"Dear, we have been planning this attack for a very long time now; please have a little faith."

They reached the top of the stairs that lead to the roof of the library. A large wall was now surrounding the hidden compound. Four look out towers rounded out the corners of the wall along with two watchmen in each one.

"When did thi- but how?" Tucker stumbled through his utter amazement.

"This is epic! I cannot believe this is even real." Ravi pinched himself for reassurance.

Groups of sorcerers were gathering below behind the wall. They were in rows of eight by six. Nervous energy had them pacing in place. Some tried to shake off the nerves, but the sound of marching feet from the oncoming enemy made it difficult for them to clear their minds.

Regina noticed each of them had belts on, armed with green, blue and yellow brew balls. "Ann are those yours?"

"Yeah I have been working on them since we were taken here. I gave them the recipes for the green and the blue brew balls which ya are already familiar with, but the yellow one, well the yellow one is special. I had been working on that one for some time now."

"What does it do?"

Ann bounced a metallic yellow ball in her hand. "This one is a little bit tricky, but if it is aimed correctly it can be very helpful. A yellow goo will pour out of the ball and wrap itself around the nearest object. Slowly it begins to harden makin it nearly impossible to move."

Regina smiled. "Yeah that should come in handy. Let's hope everyone has good aim."

"Regina!" Tucker and Reynold came running dragging large heavy bags behind them.

"We gathered as much as we could." Reynold opened the bag to reveal several items from the armory.

"I'll just take this." Maggie pulled out a double sided katana. She ran her finger along the back side of the blade. "I think I'm in love."

"Oohs I wants that's!" Vaul took the large axe that Tucker was holding.

"Hey, I was planning to use that." Tucker reached out to grab the axe back, but Vaul swung the axe around a few times and threw it at a nearby wooden post that split in two. "Okay never mind you can have it." Vaul gave Tucker a hardy laugh before he went to retrieve the axe.

"Here Ravi." Reynold handed him a shield. "We thought this would be perfect for you. It was made by glints. It can mimic your powers so when you become invisible it will too. It also reflects incoming spells."

"Fantastic! Thanks mates." Ravi grabbed the shield and vanished with it a few times.

"We also found these." Tucker opened his palm to reveal eleven silver earbuds.

"What are those?" Regina asked

"They are communication devices. There is enough for all of us." Tucker handed one to each of them. "This way we can be on the ground while you give us commands from up here."

"Up here?" Regina was confused.

"Regina we need to keep ya safe." Reynold responded. "Ya too Tyler."

"I'm not staying up here." Regina and Tyler said in unison.

"If I am going to be any kind of leader to those people down there, they need to know that I am willing to fight for them." Regina added.

"Yeah!" Tyler agreed. "I'm a prince right?" A few of them nodded. "Then I should help protect them too."

"With all due respect girly, this is not your battle. This is her battle." The Grand Master pointed to Queen Esme. "So you do what she tells you."

"Hey grandma." Tyler called out. Regina couldn't help but roll her eyes.

"Oh that is so wonderful to hear." Esme was grinning ear to ear.

"Where do you want me and Regina?" Tyler asked.

"Right here beside me of course. You are both too young to be out there on the battle field."

"But I took out like twenty or so churras on my own and a really big ogre." Regina protested.

"I don't care. You two will stay next to me and that is final."

Regina didn't dare to argue anymore. Esme was very good at making Regina feel like a disobedient child that needed to listen.

"She told you." Kolben taunted her.

"Shut it Kolben." Kolben couldn't help but smirk because he knew he got a rise out of her.

"Fine!" Regina folded her arms. "I guess I will command from up here, but don't expect me to like it."

They each grabbed a belt filled with brew balls on their way out. Kolben lingered behind the rest of the group. "Don't worry, I will make sure to take out a couple just for you." Kolben winked at Regina.

Queen Esme overheard Kolben. "Is this your boyfriend?"

Kolben threw his arm around Regina before she could answer. "Not yet, but I can tell she is coming around." He kissed Regina on the cheek. "Wish me good luck." He bowed to both of them before he left.

"I like him." Esme said walking back to her post. "He reminds me of your grandfather."

Regina looked around and noticed Ann and Reynold had not left yet. Ann was strapping a large belt with several different colored brew balls around her waist. Reynold placed a hand on the buckle before Ann could finish putting it on.

"Maybe ya should sit this one out too." He stared into her eyes looking concerned.

Ann sighed. "I suppose ya are right." She handed him the belt and kissed him goodbye. The belt was not nearly large enough to fit around his muscular waist so he flung it over his shoulder and went off to join the others.

"What can I help out with here?" Ann's worried smile did not fool anyone.

"Are you alright?" Regina asked.

"Oh yea, I'm fine."

Regina was still not convinced but she could tell that Ann did not want to talk about it. "Alright. Why don't you make some more brew balls downstairs in case we run out?"

Ann was grateful for the gesture. "I'm on it." She smiled and did a little curtsied.

"What was that for?"

"Ya are royalty remember." Ann laughed to herself as she headed for the stairs.

Regina sighed. "Ugh, don't remind me."

The enemy finally came into sight. They had spread themselves across the horizon; they were only three deep, but their spread was far and intimidating to the much smaller army below.

"Good it is only sorcerers." Esme was clearly relieved, but just then an orange glow came from over the hill just right of the oncoming enemy forces.

"Someone tell me what that is?" Esme pointed to the increasingly bright orange glow.

"Your highness." One of the watchmen from the towers called over to the Queen. "It appears to be a sizeable army of churras and ogres.

"Oh no." Esme said to herself.

"Uh, your highness. Many of them appear to be pretty tired and beat up though. Some of them looked scorched too."

Tyler chuckled. "The scorched ones are the Grand Master's doing."

"And the others?" Esme asked.

"That was my doing." Regina said looking straight ahead.

"Oh!" Esme was pleasantly surprised. "Maybe you should be down there."

"Wait does that mean…?" Regina looked hopeful, but was quickly dismissed.

"No. You are too important to me." Esme looked at her with so much love in her eyes.

It was then that Regina saw how much Esme really did care. That look was the same look her father gave her when she was being defiant with him. She would argue and he would say, *"It must be a pain to be so loved by me."* Regina could never argue back after he said that. He would give that same look and waited for her to give in and it worked every time.

"I'm…" Regina let out a deep breath. "…I'm sorry."

Esme gave her a big hug and kissed her head. BANG! An ogre had reached the wall and was pounding on it with his fist. BANG! BANG!

"I guess we can bond later." She smiled and kissed her again. "Hold steady!" She shouted to the troops below.

Another ogre joined in. The wall was taking heavy hits, but it stood firmly. Regina noticed a few sorcerers below looking up at Esme in anticipation. In answer, Esme ran a hand diagonally along her chest and the sorcerers below swiftly turned to their left and crept quietly along the wall. They stopped just short of where the ogres were trying to break in.

"What are they doing?" Regina asked.

Suddenly the sorcerers split in half. One half stayed in place while the other half moved just on the other side of the ogres.

"Just watch." Esme let a sly smile cross her face.

"Open Apesame!" A man from the first group of sorcerers shouted. The bricks of the wall dislodged themselves to create a large opening. The ogres saw the opening and charged after it, but what they did not realize was that the second group of sorcerers had open their side of the wall as well. The second group of sorcerers snuck up behind the ogres while the first group scaled to the top of the wall. The opening quickly shut just before the ogres could make their way through. It all happened in an instant, but the ogres were now completely surrounded.

"Hit them with the goo." Esme shouted.

Several yellow brew balls hit the bottom of the ogres' feet and before they knew it, they were stuck to the ground.

"You're up next Grand Master."

Marco poofed to the top of the wall. He watched as the ogres panicked trying to move their feet from the ground. Their arms began to flail about trying to keep the sorcerers at bay and remove the goo at the same time.

Regina had not seen the Grand Master really use his magic before, but she knew he could handle more than just two ogres. "Wait." She said quietly to herself as the Grand Master raised his black walking stick into the air. "Wait!" This time Regina yelled out so everyone could hear her.

"What is wrong?" Esme looked concern, but still interested in what Regina had to say.

"The rest of the churra and ogre army are closing in on the wall as we speak. They are already tired and weak. So…"

Maggie, listening through the earbuds, finished the rest of Regina's thought. "You want to wait for the rest of them to get close enough so the Grand Master can take them all out at once."

"Yes exactly." Regina gleamed.

"Clever thinking girly. It will take a lot, but I can do it." The Grand Master replied over the communication system.

"Very clever indeed. That is what we will do then." Esme signaled below for the army to fall back.

The sorcerers atop of the wall scaled back down, but the second group remained on the other side of the wall.

"Hold until the churras and ogres begin their charge." Esme directed those on the outside of the wall.

Soon enough the incoming army began running to the wall. "Now!" Esme shouted.

"Open Apesame." The wall created its opening and closed as soon as the last sorcerer made it through.

"Look they are retreating!" The boss ogre called out to his troops. They reached the wall and the churras went into formation. One by one they began climbing each other, forming a very long chain to reach the top. The boss ogre was the only one who noticed his fellow ogres were trapped to the ground.

"Something is not right." He stopped punching the wall to get a closer look at their feet.

Regina whispered into her hand, "Hello again." She did a windup and let the words fly out of her hand as she thrust it forward towards the boss ogre. The words hit his head like a ton of bricks. His eyes grew wide as the words tickled the hairs inside his ears. He fell over backwards as he tried to run away.

"Grand Master now!" Esme commanded.

Just like that, red violet smoke appeared and there stood Marco on top of the wall. He raised his walking stick in the air once more. Red dust floated in the air as he twirled the stick between his fingers. A large red cloud quickly formed over his head and with a single forward thrust of his walking stick the cloud plummeted down on the enemy. When the cloud dissipated all that remained were tiny figurines of the former churra and ogre army.

"What did you do to them?" Regina asked over the communication system.

Marco poofed next to her and nearly fell to the ground. Regina grabbed onto his arm and held him steady. "Are you alright?"

"I'm fine girly. I'm just a little woozy from performing that spell." He sat on a nearby crate to catch his breath. "I turned them into toys. The spell lasts for about two hours, three tops." He turned to face Esme. "You should probably get them out of here quickly."

"We don't have time for that. The Mad Sister's army is almost here."

"Hoo! Hoo!" Tyler called.

"Hoo!" A call came back from a tree. "Hoo!" Came from another. The leaves began to rustle and soon every tree was echoing with the call. "Hoo! Hoo! Hoo!" A parliament of owls flew out of the trees and circled the sky. One by one they swooped down and grabbed the figurines with their giant talons and then flew back up into a circling formation. Soon the last figurine dangled from the smallest owl who flew back up to join the others.

"Where do you want to put them?" Tyler asked.

"Send them to the prison. Nita will know what to do with them." Esme replied.

"Nita is a warden now?" Ravi replied over the communication system.

"Haha yeah is that just awesome or what?" Tucker couldn't help himself.

"Hoo!" Tyler spoke to the owls.

"Hoo! Hoo!" They responded and took off high up into the sky.

"Ravi dear," The Queen called down. "Will you let Nita know what is coming her way?"

"Of course your majesty." Ravi pulled out the compact mirror.

"AGH!" Naveen knelt to the floor grabbing her head in pain. "Ow!" Esme ran to her side. Naveen took several deep breaths before she looked up at her. "It is stronger. I don't know how, but she has made it stronger."

"Just fight it." Esme was rubbing Naveen's back. "Fight it as much as you can. Don't let her in."

"What is going on? Is she going to be okay?" Tyler stood next to his grandmother and Naveen.

"I'll be alright kiddo." Naveen continued to rub her temples.

"Your highness they are approaching." The watchmen said.

"Do you think you can keep her out?" Esme asked Naveen.

"I don't know." Naveen looked scared. "What if I can't?"

Esme hugged Naveen. "We will figure it out dear."

"Will someone please explain what is going on?" Regina pleaded for some answers.

Esme looked at Regina and then back down at Naveen. "It is up to you if you want to tell her or not."

Naveen sighed. "The rumors about the Mad Sister are true."

"That she can control minds?" Regina responded thinking that there was no way that this was possible.

"Yes." Naveen said coldly.

Regina nearly tumbled over backwards. "How can that be true? With a power like that she could be unstoppable."

"Well it is not as simple as that." Naveen replied.

"How do you know?"

"Because she controlled my mind for years." Naveen took a deep breath. "She was the one who made me do all those terrible things. Including…"

"Killing the King." Regina finished the sentence for her.

Naveen glumly nodded her head. "It took a lot of strength to stop her from controlling me. To be honest, I'm not even sure how I did it, but I broke free of her control. Every day since then I have worked hard to make up for what I have done and now it is my job to put a stop to her evil ways."

"That is terrible." Said Tyler.

"There is still so much more to that story, but now is not the time to get into it." Naveen rubbed her temple. "It takes a long time for her to establish a connection with the person she wishes to control and even after she does make that connection she has to remain in a close proximity to keep her control over her victim's actions."

"Is she attempting to connect with you now? Is that why your head is hurting?" Esme asked.

"That is the weird thing, she's not trying to connect with me. I'm not even sure she is aware that I am here. Also, I should be too far away for her to connect, but I can feel her sending her wave links out there. Her powers have gotten stronger."

Esme began rubbing her on temples. "Are you sure?"

"I'm one-hundred percent sure." Naveen pulled herself from the ground and dusted herself off. "Esme, we may need to consider another option. We might have to retreat."

Esme shook her head. "No, absolutely not."

"But Esme we could be going in blind. We don't know what we are up against." Naveen tried to object, but Esme would not hear it.

"All the more reason we defeat her now. We can't let her get any stronger."

"Hey look." Sparks were flying into the sky; illuminating the four hundred sorcerers below marching in perfect formation. "What is with the sparks? The churras and ogres did that before they attacked too." Asked Regina.

"It is her signature." Naveen responded.

"Her what?"

"Her signature. She likes to think her enemies cower in fear when they see the sparks in the sky." Naveen rolled her eyes.

All of a sudden the on-coming sorcerers below changed direction. They were coming in at an angle now and they had picked up the speed.

"Hey does anyone else notice how in sync they are with one another? It's like they are movin as one." Ann had come back up from brewing. She had a scope in her hand and was watching the oncoming army carefully.

"I think you are just imaging it." Esme waved her off. "Group one, take your positions." A quarter of Esme's army climbed the wall again. "Group two, go on my count. 3...2...1. Go!" Another quarter of the army rushed through an opening in the wall and took to the trees. "Groups three and four wait for my signal."

The Mad Sister's fleet changed directions once more, but this time they spread themselves out creating two deep long lines. Once the lines were formed they moved into a full sprint.

Ann was shaking her head. "I don't know about this. Somethin does not seem right. Did ya see how perfectly they changed formation?"

"Stop being so paranoid Ann." Esme waved Ann off again, but this time she was not as sure of herself.

"No Esme she is right. We still have time to retreat, but we have to do it now!" Naveen desperately looked to the Queen.

"We will win and we will defeat her." Esme began to speak loudly so her army could hear. "This battle will be the end of her terrible reign. Tonight we will be victorious!"

The charging sorcerers were only a few yards out; when they made their final formation change. Regina watched as the ends of the line began to pick up their pace and curl inward. In one fluid motion the line turned into a circle that now surrounded the compound walls.

Esme still in shock managed to shout out an order. "Groups three and four spread out and defend."

The back of the compound was entirely unmanned and completely vulnerable. All sides of the compound were taking hits. The front was well protected, but they still outnumbered them greatly.

Esme awoke from her disbelief. "Group two attack!" Spells were shot form the tree tops. In unison the sorcerers below turned and deflected the spells with their shields. Half of group two shimmied down the trees while the other half continued to send spells towards the enemy army. Once the first half reached the bottom of the trees the second half followed as the first half covered them.

The Mad Sister's army split off at once and began their attack on group two. They would attack as one and then duck behind their shields; again and again they did this. One sorcerer used the leaves from the trees to surround group two; blinding them from oncoming attacks.

Another cast a spell that made the dirt below Esme's army turn into mud.

Esme's army did their best to fend off the attacks, but they were not fast enough. The Mad Sister's army was to uniformed in their assaults. When there was a break in their attacks a few of them would send spells their way, but their shields were already up. Group two was beginning to slowly wither away.

"Ah I can hear her." Naveen clamped her hands over her ears. "I can hear her talking to her army."

Ann looked through her scope. "There she is. She is just behind the third row of trees." Ann gasped loudly. "And she is with that one fella, the one who wears the red wolf mask. That jerk killed my friend."

"Let me take a look." Esme grabbed the scope from Ann. "Yep, there she is surrounded by her group of Carnagers."

Regina signaled that she wanted to look through the scope too. "Where is she again?"

"Ya are looking up too high. Look at the third row of trees, she is standing next to them."

Regina slowly lowered the scope. "Oh yeah, there's the Carnagers." She lowered the scope just a little further over a woman in an oversized black dress. "I see her now, but her face is covered by a jeweled gold wolf mask." Regina stared at her for a while. "Hmm…"

"What is it?" Esme asked.

"Oh nothing. She just looks a little familiar." Regina continued to study the Mad Sister.

"IT IS GETTING LOUDER!" Naveen still had her hands over her ears, but she was starting to look pale and sick.

A dark rhythmic melody played in Naveen's head *"Hush and listen. I'll show you my vision. Together we will fear no reaper. For I am your mind's keeper."*

Naveen fell to her knees. "I don't know if I can fight it off much longer."

"Hush and listen. I'll show you my vision. Together we will fear no reaper. For I am your mind's keeper."

Regina looked around and noticed Naveen was not the only one who seemed to be effected. Group two only had ten sorcerers left standing and they too had their hands clasped over their ears. In fact, the Mad Sister's army was not even bothering to attack them anymore.

"Oh no!" Regina placed a hand over her mouth.

Esme was trying to soothe Naveen. She was doing all that she could to try and help her fight it. "Regina what is happening?"

"She is taking over your army too."

Esme rushed to see what was going on. Group two had completely turned and was now helping the Mad Sister's army. Group one was now on their knees. Soon they too became part of the Mad Sister's army.

"Those who are still with me..." Esme cried out to her remaining fleet. "...retreat! This battle has been lost, but we can still save the compound. Get back inside and hold the doors steady."

Regina spoke through the communication device. "Get inside quickly, but try and hit as many as you can with your brew balls on the way in."

What remained of Esme's army rushed back inside. A few of them doubled over before they could make it to the doors of the compound. Regina watched Fox Squad unleash everything they had. Clusters of brew balls were thrown at group one as they tried to make their way down. Vaul barreled through five of them who got in his way and knocked them unconscious. Maggie took the lead and cleared a path, kicking and punching her way through. Ravi and Thack followed closely behind and Reynold, Kolben and Tucker were the last ones through the door.

"She is movin closer." Ann pointed as she continued to look through her scope.

"What are we going to do?" Tyler looked to Regina and then to his grandmother.

The door burst open. "What in the world is going on?" Tucker waited for the rest of the group to go through before he slammed the door shut. "Quick someone do some kind of magic to keep the door from opening."

Vaul grabbed a steal pipe from the ground. "This shoulds works." He slowly bent the pipe around the double-door handles.

Tyler threw his yellow brew ball at the door. The yellow goo formed and hardened at the bottom.

"Good thinkin Tyler." Ann smiled, but not just for Tyler she was also feeling very proud of her work.

"Everyone has gone mad as a hatter." Ravi bent over to try and catch his breath.

"Naveen!" Tucker rushed to her side. "Is she going to be alright?"

"Duchess Orlean is controlling their minds." Esme was pacing back and forth.

"She is doing what now?" Tucker looked up from rubbing Naveen's back.

"I thought that was just a rumor?" Reynold asked.

"Unfortunately it is not. She has always had the power to control minds, but it was never this strong. She needed to constantly be around someone a long while before she could make a connection." Esme was still pacing.

"How do we stop her?" Thack asked trying not to look too concerned.

"You...ugh...can't." Naveen looked like she was about to pass out. "All of you...ahhh...need to get out of here!" All of sudden she stood up and faced Esme.

"Naveen! No fight it." Esme hands shook.

"Oh no she has turned." Said Regina.

Naveen took a step forward, but Tucker grabbed her hand to hold her back. She turned around and glared at him. Her hand turned into a smoky mist that Tucker could not clasp onto. She began to walk towards Esme. Tucker tried to stop her again by wrapping his arms around her waist. This time her whole body became a smoky mist.

Once she was free of Tucker's grip she doused him in a black cloud.

Tucker started to cough. He fell to the floor and clenched his throat. He began crawling his way out of the cloud when he felt Reynold's hand grab the collar of his shirt and dragged him away.

In an instant Naveen was next to Esme leaving a trail of purple mist behind her. Her hands wrapped themselves around Esme's neck. Tears were streaming down Naveen's face as she squeezed tighter and tighter.

"Naveen, I know you are still in there. You don't want to do this." Regina pleaded for her to stop.

Thack and Ravi tried to pull her hands away, but were forced out by a cloud of smoke Naveen created around her and Esme.

Regina looked around hoping to find something that would snap Naveen out of her trance. The Mad Sister and her Carnagers were now at the wall. Regina felt a heavy weight on her shoulders. She had no idea what to do. She glanced around once more and saw the sirens coming from over the hill.

"The sirens are coming. The sirens-" A connection clicked in Regina's mind; she knew exactly what she needed to do. "Ann I need you to scream."

"What?"

"Just do it." Ann let out a weak little yelp. "Okay, I need you to be louder; much louder." Regina waved her hand to encourage Ann to be louder.

This time Ann gave it all she got. It was loud and high pitched everything that Regina was looking for. Regina raised her hands and pulled the sound from Ann's lips. She swiped her arms across and steered the sound towards Naveen. The scream circled around Naveen's head swimming in and out of her ears. Her eyes flashed open to reveal life behind them once again.

Naveen removed her hands from around Esme's neck and began to sob. "I can't believe-I almost-I thought I would never be controlled by her again."

"She is back!" Tucker said excitedly.

"How did ya know that would work?" Ann asked.

"I didn't, but I saw the sirens and something just clicked." Regina looked at her hands. She still couldn't quite believe she was capable of doing what she just did.

"That means we can use sound to break all of the soldiers from her trance." Kolben gave Regina a big hug. "Isn't she just amazing."

"Uh thanks Kolben…" She peeled his arms off of her, although she did this rather slowly. "…but how am I going to do that to all six hundred or so soldiers who are currently under her control?"

"I know!" Tyler's face lit up. "We can use the compound's alarm to awake those inside."

"I-s thinks I-s can takes them down." Vaul lifted his fist in the air.

Ravi pushed Vaul's fist back down. "I can make us invisible so we can move through undetected. That way we can get to the alarm in no time."

"Lets goes." Vaul and Ravi made their way to the door. Vaul started unbending the metal bar while Ravi stood by preparing for anyone who might try to break through.

"What about all those outside the compound?" Regina looked down at the wall and then back to the group completely petrified. "Uh where did the Mad Sister go?"

A scratching noise came from the other side of the door, but Vaul was too distracted to notice.

"No Vaul wait!" Regina shouted for Vaul to stop, but it was too late. Vaul finished straightening out the last bend when he and Ravi were thrown back by the doors blasting open.

The Mad Sister came gliding out from the door followed in toe by her loyal band of Carnagers. A few of Esme's tranced soldiers managed to make it through the door before Vaul got back up and closed the door again, except this time he had to keep the door closed by pushing his own weight against it.

"Regina, Tyler so nice to see you again." A shiver ran up Regina's spine and Tyler grabbed his sister's hand.

"Oh no." Regina could feel all her breath leaving her.

"The Sheriff is here too; what a happy little reunion." The Mad Sister clapped her hands together.

Regina noticed the flicker of recognition in Tucker and Tyler's faces. The Mad Sister removed her mask to confirm their suspicions.

"Lady Dumontet!" Regina and Tyler said together.

"Lady Dumontet?" Esme asked to herself.

"I told you little brats that I would get you back." With a twist of her wrist Lady Dumontet shot off an electric shock that hit Regina right in the stomach.

"Leave my grandchildren alone!" Esme stood in front of Regina and Tyler.

"I'm their legal guardian and their great aunt so I will do as I wish with them."

"Orlean you know full well that you do not share a single ounce of blood with them."

"Ah Esme, still playing your part as the protector I see. Well you are right, I don't share their precious blood, but she does." Lady Dumontet pointed to Naveen. "Once I am through with you she will be the rightful ruler of Nahtovia."

"I don't want to rule." Naveen said defiantly.

"Hush child!" Lady Dumontet snarled at her. "You do as I tell you or I will make you obedient." She leaned over and looked behind Esme. "Don't worry, I'll make sure they are taken care of too. I haven't decided though if I want to make them my little slaves or just not have them around at all. BAWHAHAHA!"

"You will never win you old hag." Kolben stepped next to Regina who had slowly made her way from behind Esme.

"Vallian!" Lady Dumontet shouted.

The man in the red wolf mask stepped forward. "Yes, my queen." He kept his head down and did not dare to make eye contact with the Wolf Queen.

Orlean pointed a finger at Kolben. "Is this the little brat that you let get away?"

Vallian lifted his head only to get a quick glance at Kolben's face. "Yes, he is the one, my queen." He bowed and stepped back in line with the rest of the Carnagers.

Although they were all wearing their wolf masks Regina could still sense the fear that laid behind them. They all stood in a perfect line behind their queen just waiting to be called upon, like good obedient dogs who feared that they would disappoint their master. However, between the quick glances up and their fidgeting fingers it was obvious that they were also eager beast wanting to be unleashed.

The Mad Sister made a circular movement with her hand and restraints formed around Kolben. "Here." She grabbed the restraints and with a great force flung Kolben towards Vallian. "Now he is yours to play with again."

"Hey, you can't do that." Regina yelled.

At once, all of Fox Squad charged forward. The Carnagers took a defensive stance; ready to fight anyone off for their queen. No one got further than two footsteps before they were all thrown back together. The Mad Sister stomped her foot and pushed her arms outward causing a force that pushed everyone to the ground.

"Don't you see? I am much more powerful than any of you!" She got a glimpse of the Grand Master out of the corner of her eye. He was still weak from fighting off the churras and from his last magical spell that turned the ogre and churra army into a bunch of figurines. "I'm even more powerful than the all mighty Grand Master." She turned to speak directly at him now. "You old fool. Your eternity will finally come to an end."

"Who are you calling old? Your wrinkles have wrinkles." Vallian pulled hard on Kolben's restraints and smacked him across the head trying to keep him quiet, but his reaction was too slow.

The Mad Sister quickly glided over to Kolben. She ran her finger along his cheek; letting her long painted black nail come dangerously close to his eye. "Oh you dumb boy." She suddenly slapped him across the face, but not before she cut him with her sharp nail. The combination stung badly and blood trickled down his cheek. Kolben made sure to stand firm and not show any sign of pain. "I think I will torture you myself. Yes, you will become..."

Regina looked over her shoulder while no one was watching. The sirens were coming, but they were still a good ways off. She needed to do something now while the Mad Sister was distracted with Kolben. She looked around and saw her answer, she just needed a way to communicate with him and then she remembered that they were all still wearing their earbuds.

"Vaul, can you hear me?" Regina waited for his response, but saw that he was nodding his head instead. "Okay good. I need you to open the door."

"Whats?" Vaul said quietly.

"I need you to open the door so Ravi can go in and turn on the alarm. Did you get that Ravi?" Regina now looked to Ravi who was helping Vaul keep the door closed.

"What if someone sees me?" Ravi responded.

"You will be invisible, remember?"

"Oh, right." Ravi's smacked his forehead with his palm.

"As soon as the alarm goes off, I need you to open the door back up." Regina shook out her hands. "I'll try to take care of it from there."

"A distraction would be helpful so we can open the door unnoticed." Ravi added.

"I can help with that." Tucker chimed in.

"Perfect." Regina gave a thumbs up to Tucker. "Maggie how many of those Carnagers do you think you can take out?"

Maggie sized up the row of Carnagers. "Umm, about seven or eight of them."

"Alright, everyone else can help take out the other half." There was a slight nod or hidden thumbs up from everyone who had earbuds on. Esme and Naveen were the only ones unaware of the plan. "Ravi, Vaul go on Tucker's signal." Regina nodded at Tucker. "Whenever you are ready Tucker."

"...You will wish you were dead when I am through with you. Then I will hand you over to Vallian and it will be his turn." Orlean finished her threating Kolben.

"I knew I was right not to trust you." Tucker began. "The moment I laid eyes on you I just knew that you were no good."

"And yet you did nothing. So why don't you just cry me a river." Ravi was about to go through the door, but the Mad Sister was already losing interest.

"You have to do better than that Tucker." Regina said over the earbuds.

"Hey you dirty old witch I'm talking to you!" Tucker raised his voice to really get Orlean's attention.

She rounded on him so quickly that he did not have time to react, luckily he tripped and fell just nearly dodging a staggering amount of electricity that was aimed for his chest. She raised her hands in the air and lite up the sky with lightning.

"Do I look like those silly witches in your world's fictional stories?" A single finger turned into ice. She aimed an icicle at his head and missed just by a few inches. Her eyes flared. "My powers have no bounds. Every day I grow stronger while you all become weaker."

Ravi and Vaul were in the clear now. Ravi made it inside and Vaul was able to keep anyone else from coming out.

"You will learn to bow to your new queen." She turned to address everyone. "You will all learn to bow to me!" Her eyes were wild and the veins in her forehead were pulsing. "Anyone who refuses will be branded by the traitor's mark and will permanently be under my control."

"You can't even gather enough supporters to build an army. Those sorcerers down below, they are Broadcovians. You will never be the leader that this realm wants or needs. Not even your powers can control everyone." Esme jumped in.

The Mad Sister went on the defensive. "They will come around and see the beauty in my way of thinking. Once they get the taste of how strong their powers can truly be they will be begging for me to rule." She paused and then let out an evil grin. "Would you like me to show you what I can do?"

Vallian walked over to her side. She placed her hand on his chest and closed her eyes. A light pulsated from her hands into his body. His muscles grew tight and his veins bulged. The Mad Sister pushed hard against him; Vallian let out a loud scream as a great surge of light passed through her hand into his chest.

She almost stumbled as she stepped away from him. "Vallian show them what you can do."

He placed his hands out in front of him and transformed his nails into wolf claws. He cracked his neck tilting it from the left to right; he let out a deep breath and began his transformation. His nose grew out first; his jaw protruded; his forehead sunk down and his ears grew to a point. Hair began to sprout all over his face and finally, he growled baring his new razor sharp teeth.

There was a collective gasp from the group. "I told ya he only had a wolf's head." Ann said to Thack.

"Ann, sweetheart, now is not the time." Reynold whispered to his wife.

"Vallian now has complete control over his transformation." The Mad Sister looked over Vallian feeling very proud of her work. "Vallian take care of the Sheriff for me."

In a deep husky voice Vallian responded, "It will be my pleasure." He bowed to the Mad Sister "My queen."

He slowly walked towards Tucker; hoping that he would psychologically torture him by dragging out the inevitable. There was a twitch, then another; he could not stand delaying the kill, he had to have it now. He finished his transformation in mid-run and started sprinting on all fours. He was ready to make the lunge and sink his teeth into Tucker when he was knocked sideways. Another large gray wolf stood over him.

"Good boy Thack!" Tucker applauded.

"Seriously." Maggie said folding her arms and frowning at Tucker.

Thack stepped off Vallian and turned to face Tucker. Vallian was back on his feet and the two of them were skulking towards Tucker. Their eyes narrowed and they began to growl.

"Woah," Tucker put his hands out and started backing away. "I'm sorry buddy, I-I didn't mean it."

Regina looked at the Mad Sister and saw that she was concentrating on Thack. "She is controlling him! She is controlling Thack!"

"Uh, well, can somebody do something?" Tucker was being backed into a corner.

"Ah-ah-whooo!" A howl came from behind Regina. Again, "Ah-ah-whooooooo!" The wolves stopped.

"It is working Tyler keep doing it." Regina patted her brother on the back.

He howled again, but this time Thack and Vallian rotated around to face the Mad Sister.

"You little brat." The Mad Sister took a deep breath and blew. A gush of wind hit Regina and Tyler knocking them both over. She turned her attention back on Thack.

Thack and Vallian were now on either side of Tucker. Tucker grabbed his empty brew belt and whipped it at the wolves. They lunged at the belt getting closer and closer with each snap. Thack launched at Tucker knocking him to the ground. He stood over him, drool dripping down the sides of his mouth.

A muffled noise came from behind the door. "Mereep! Mereep!"

"Now Vaul!" Regina shouted.

Vaul swung the door open. "BEEP! BEEP!" The alarm escaped through the door and filled the empty spaces all around them. Thack awoke from his trance and stepped off of Tucker.

Regina spoke through the ear buds. "I need to concentrate all my energy into moving the alarm noise to the turned army below."

"We got you covered Regina!" Maggie sprinted towards the Carnagers. She used her cudgel as a pole vault and launched herself into the air. Two Carnagers took the brunt of her landing. "We can do this the easy way…" Maggie twirled her cudgel around hitting another Carnager square in the jaw. "…or the you get several broken bones way. Your choice."

Kolben was struggling to remove his restraints while a Carnager fought to keep him still. "Reynold, can you help out Kolben please?" Regina asked.

"Aww you do care." Kolben responded.

Regina ignored his comment and focused her attention back on the alarm. She looked down at the Mad Sister's army. There were so many of them and they were still spread out around the compound. She thought maybe she could focus on certain sections at a time, but that would take too long and the Mad Sister could place her spell on them again. If she was going to do this right she would need to wrap the entire compound in a sound bubble.

Meanwhile, Fox Squad were doing their best to fight off the Carnagers. Thack was still in wolf form fighting Vallian. Ann was throwing brew balls to create a path for Reynold to get to Kolben so he could free him from his restraints. Ravi had just returned from setting off the alarm. He saw two Carnagers trying to sneak up on Maggie and attack her from behind. Activating his invisibility, he ran to stop them. He pulled out his shield to block their incoming spells, but before he could Maggie turned around to face them. She used her cudgel to sweep the legs out from underneath the first Carnager. While he was crawling to get up she used him as leverage to jump off his back and body slam the other Carnager.

Maggie smiled in Ravi's direction. "Thanks Ravi for the heads up!"

"Uh sure no problem." An invisible Ravi was confused, but mostly impressed that Maggie knew he was there.

"Hey watch out!" Tucker elbowed a Carnager in the gut and then punched him in the face.

"You are pretty good fighter. I didn't even see him coming." Naveen kissed Tucker on the cheek. "Thanks for having my back."

Tucker's face turned a light shade of pink. "You're welcome."

Naveen created a purple smokescreen around a Carnager that was charging towards her. She stepped into the smoke and after a few seconds she stepped back out again. Once the smoked cleared the Carnager was on the floor incapacitated with restraints around her ankles and wrists.

It was complete chaos on the roof, but they seemed to be pulling out ahead. Tyler was even trying to make it easier for his sister by having Orwell and Edyis herd the soldiers below into a tighter clump. Regina was pulling as much of the noise as she possibly could from the alarm before she created the sound bubble. Even though the battle seemed to be in their favor currently, Regina had to hurry. The Mad Sister was starting to turn all the soldiers at the door back under her control. So Vaul was struggling to keep the door open, but at the same time he had to keep the turned soldiers from escaping and out numbering them in the fight. It was only a matter of time before they managed to break through and the odds would completely shift in the Mad Sister's favor again. Regina looked around for her grandmother to get some support from her, but she was nowhere to be found.

"Regina you need to hurry; I don't think Vaul can hold them off much longer." Ravi said between hitting Carnagers with his invisible shield.

A small bubble began to form at the door; Vaul and Esme's soldiers clamped their hands over their ears. Inch by inch the bubble grew. More sorcerers covered their ears as they became entrapped by the loud rings of the alarm. "BEEP! BEEP!" Soon the whole roof was in the bubble and then the entire compound. "BEEP! BEEP!" Regina, with her eyes closed, had not noticed that the bubble had now surpassed the tree lines. Her arms were stretched out wide and there was not a single sorcerer left under the Mad Sister's control.

Regina was growing weak, but she kept on going. There was a tap on her shoulder. "REGINA YOU DID IT! YOU CAN STOP NOW!" Tyler was trying to scream over the alarm.

"BEEP!" Regina dropped her hands down to her side and just like that the bubble disappeared along with the alarm. She looked around to see that her team was triumphant. All the Carnagers were badly beaten or tied up. Vallian was in a corner licking his wounds and the Mad Sister was distraught.

"No one can defeat me no one!" The Mad Sister screamed. Her eyes were wild. "You think you have won? This was only the beginning."

"Give it up! You have lost. Just look around you." Regina gestured to the Carnagers and the army down below. "No one is under your control anymore and your team is finished."

Ann and Reynold were just about to remove the last of Kolben's restraints when they were flung backwards. The Mad Sister glided to Kolben's side. "I'll take him as my token." Kolben tried to struggle, but she tossed him over to a nearby Carnager and threw sleeping powder in his face.

Vallian was back in his normal form. "The sirens are here my queen." He said in hushed whisper.

"I think it is time for us to leave, but I need to do what I came here for." The Mad Sister stomped her foot. She disappeared and reappeared next to a Carnager that was standing fairly close to Naveen.

"You can teleport without making a smoke cloud?" The Grand Master asked.

The Mad Sister grabbed the Carnager and teleported back next to the other Carnagers. "There are a lot of things I can do old man." She pulled out a dagger from under her sleeve and stabbed the Carnager.

Everyone gasped as the Carnager dropped to the floor, but no one understood why the Mad Sister would stab one of her own.

"Why would you…" Naveen stopped mid-sentence. "Es-Esme?" The Carnager on the floor melted away. Naveen knelt down; brushed the silvery hair from her face and grabbed her hand. "It's gonna be alright. Just keep breathing."

"Child your loyalty is in the wrong place. I just made you a queen and together we can rule." The Mad Sister placed a hand on Naveen's shoulder.

"Get away from them." Regina and Tyler rushed over to their grandmother's side.

Naveen pushed away the Mad Sister's hand. "So be it child." She gave Naveen a cold smile. "I'll be seeing you around." Her and the Carnagers locked arms.

Regina placed a sound bubble around them. "You're not going anywhere."

"You think this little bubble can stop me." Lady Dumontet used her nail to pop the bubble. "Don't worry you'll see me again." She re-linked her arms with the Carnagers and glanced over to Kolben, "But I can't guarantee the same for your little friend." She stomped her foot once more and just like that they were all gone.

Chapter 18 The Dark Clouds Form

"The funeral is tomorrow! Where could she be?" Tucker was pacing the floor.

Nita, Reynold, Tyler and Regina were sitting at the kitchen table while Ann was busy making pancakes at the stove. Regina starred out the window watching the storm clouds roll by. The gloomy weather was worsening, but inside the gloom was much stronger.

"It will be okay Tucker. Fox Squad is looking for her as we speak. Naveen will show up." Regina tried to put Tucker at ease.

Tucker let out a deep sigh. "You are right. I'm just really worried. I mean that look she gave me when I tried to stop her, ugh, you should have seen her face."

"Yeah I saw that look too. It was unquestionably a look of revenge. I hope she doesn't do anythin stupid, I rather liked her." Ann looked down regrettably and shook her head. "I wish there was somethin we could do."

"Has there been any sign of Lady Dum- uh I mean the Mad Sister?" Regina asked Reynold.

"Broadcove has not reported any sightings and Kazny has gone completely dark. It is like a ghost town there. We've set up the White House for Kazny refugees and anyone else who may have suffered at the hands of the Mad Sister, but only a few families have shown up."

"I would've had information for you if I was still mayor." Nita folded her arms and turned her nose up.

"Ugh, Nita we already went over this." Tucker was tired of Nita's complaining. This was the fifth time she had mentioned it since she arrived. "You are the only one who can keep that prison in check. Why don't you create some kind of network within the prison? I'm sure you can figure out something."

"Yeah!" Nita stood from her chair. "Of course! I can do that. I can start a rewards program. I'll have information flowing through that building in no time."

"How do we know the Mad Sister won't show up tomorrow?" Ann was serving the pancakes out to everyone. They all had bacon smiles, strawberry noses and banana eyes.

"The castle will be guarded by the shadow lighters and I had Tucker buy a bunch of noise makers just in case they run into any mind control problems." Regina began cutting into her pancake. "I doubt she will show; she was really thrown by her loss of control."

"After four years of living with her, there is one thing we know for sure and that is she hates not being in control." Tyler stuffed his mouth full of pancake.

"It is so weird to think that this whole time the three of you were under the same roof. I wonder why she didn't just, you know…" Nita was dancing around what she was really trying to say.

"You mean kill Tyler and me while we were living with her?" Regina clarified for Nita.

"Well yes." Nita tugged at the collar of her blouse; feeling very uncomfortable.

"I'm really not sure. We know that she needed us to break the curse on the Parting Trees. Other than that there was no reason for her to keep us alive. She could have thrown us in the Parting Tree and then killed us on the other side if she really wanted to." Regina shrugged. "There are a lot of things that make sense now knowing what we know, but it also brings up a lot more questions."

"We know as much as we can about Lady Dumontet, but we don't know anything about the Mad Sister." Tucker had not touched the full plate of food that sat in front of him. "Did anyone else catch the weird relationship between Naveen and the Mad Sister?"

Echoes of agreement followed: "Yeah!"
"Well of course."
"Pretty obvious."
"Even I knew that and I wasn't even there." Nita finished.

"Oh good, so I wasn't the only one. So does anyone know why? The Mad Sister wanted Naveen to rule, according to her, she was next in line and Esme didn't dispute it." Tucker ran his fingers through his hair, he was beginning to feel overwhelmed.

"Wouldn't technically The Mad Sister be next in line?" Ann chimed in.

"Well yes technically as the King's sister she would be especially now that the Queen is gone…" Reynold awkwardly paused after realizing what he had just said. "…but Esme said something about her not sharing any blood with ya two."

"This is so frustrating!" Regina pushed her plate aside. "None of this makes any sense and we have no idea how Naveen ties into all of this. All I know for sure is that Naveen knows a lot more than she is letting on and she decides to disappear when we need her the most. She might be the only one who can lead us to the Mad Sister, the only one who can help us save Kolben."

"She'll show up tomorrow, she has to." Tucker walked out of the kitchen with his head down. His plate was left untouched, in fact, most of his meals as of late, had gone untouched. It had been a hard week for all of them and Regina didn't know how to make it better for any of them, let alone herself.

A constant struggle was ragging inside her. She didn't know whether she should feel angry, vengeful or sadness. It had become a concern that she was not sadder during this time of grief and mourning. *"How can I truly be sad for someone I had only known for a day? Even though she was my grandmother I just can't seem to grieve for her; maybe it just hasn't hit me yet."* The room felt like it was spinning as these thoughts swam through her head.

Ravi and Maggie walked into the kitchen. "Have you still not learned to lock the door?" Nita said scolding Ann and Reynold.

"We have actually. My beautiful and talented wife placed a locking charm on the door. Only close friends and family are allowed in without us opening the door for them."

"Ah thanks for including us mate." Ravi placed a hand over his heart feeling truly touched by this gesture.

"So what is the stat-" Nita and Reynold started saying together.

"Right. Sorry, force of habit." Nita gestured with her hands, "Go on."

Reynold eyed Nita first to make sure she wouldn't interrupt again before he continued. "What is the status report?"

"No sign of either of them. We will keep looking, but we might have to start considering the possibility that Naveen might have gone through the Parting Trees."

Reynold let out a small sigh. "Thanks Maggie. We will keep that in mind."

"Uh this is a little awkward…" Ravi started tapping the ends of his fingers together. "Nita we need you to give the mirror to Reynold so we have a way to communicate with him."

"Oh!" Nita pulled the mirror from her pocket and extended her arm so Reynold could grab it.

Reynold tried to take the mirror from Nita, but she had a tight grip on it. "Nita ya need to let go."

"Fine!" Nita let go of the mirror and sulked quietly to herself.

"Regina, when are you and Tyler moving into the castle?" Maggie asked.

"The day after the funeral." Regina looked out the kitchen's back window at the sad broken down castle. "We thought it was best to try and bring life back into the castle. You know give people some hope that things will be normal again."

"Tucker will be moving in with us too. He has to go back to our world though and settle a few things with his job first." Tyler leaned in and whispered as if he were telling a secret. "They think he has been on medical leave this whole time."

"Hey since we have mostly everyone here Ann and I have some news." Reynold placed his arm around his tiny wife.

Ann looked like she was ready to burst at the seams with joy. "We are goin to have a baby!"

A thunderous cheer filled the room. There were happy faces all around.

"Congratulations!" Maggie applauded.

"Congrats, mate!" Ravi shook Reynold's hand.

"That is fantastic, I'm so happy for you two." Regina gave Ann a hug.

"Hey, what is going on?" Tucker popped his head in.

"They're gonna have a baby!" Tyler answered.

All their problems were momentarily forgotten. Life seemed normal again; like things might actually turn out alright. Regina wanted to savor in this moment for as long as she could. They all did.

After an hour of celebration things began to die down. "Sorry we can't stay longer, but we really need to head back out." Ravi and Maggie said their goodbyes and left.

Ann, Nita, Tyler and Tucker were at the table still chitchatting and going over different baby names. "How about Henry if it is a boy and Henrietta if it is a girl?"

"Nice try Tucker!" Ann laughed.

Reynold was looking out the window when he saw his crops rustling. "Not again! Come on Tyler. I think Daisy is stealing from my crops. I need ya to tell him to cut it out." Reynold opened the door to find Gramm standing there getting ready to knock. "Hi Gramm! What are ya doing here?"

"Uh I was hoping to talk to Regina." Gramm said nervously.

Regina heard the conversation at the door and felt completely embarrassed; she had forgotten all about Gramm. She whispered into her hand, "Tell him I'm not here." She released the message so it would reach Reynold, but it was too late.

"Hey Regina, Gramm is here to see you!" Reynold called out from the door. A second later the message was whispered in his ear.

Regina came around the corner. "Thanks."

Reynold shrugged, mouthed the word sorry to Regina and continued on his way with Tyler in toe.

"Hi Gramm." She said halfheartedly. She looked into his kind eyes hoping that there might be something there, but all she could think about was Kolben. "What's up?"

"Well, I was hoping we could hang out and catch up. I heard you have done a lot since we last talked." He smiled.

"Yeah sorry, I haven't come over to visit, but there has been a lot going on and I'm kind of tired right now." Regina let out a fake yawn.

"Oh yeah of course. I understand." His back slouched and he dragged his feet on the way out.

"Maybe we can hang out sometime after the funeral tomorrow." Regina felt bad for blowing him off.

Gramm looked happy again. "That would be nice. I will see you tomorrow."

"Uh yeah maybe. Bye Gramm." Regina quickly shut the door before he could say anything else.

She ran upstairs to the library and slumped down into one of the reading nooks. The clouds outside were getting darker, there would for sure be rain tomorrow. She stretched her feet and kicked a book that was laying at the end of the nook. It fell to the floor along with a note that was tucked inside of it. The book was titled *Death and How to Grieve*. "That is a little on the nose." Regina said out loud to herself. She was about to place the note back into the book when suddenly her name appeared across it in blue lettering. Her heart raced as she peeled open the letter.

My dearest Regina,

Another <u>magical</u> year has gone by my young princess and today we celebrate your sixth birthday in style! In true Regina fashion, we are having an outdoor voyage party! You insisted that all guest must bring their sense of adventure and when you blew out your candles you wished for everyone in the world to be happy.

 At your very young age, you already act as if you can mold the world into something greater and I truly believe that you will. Every day you find new ways to make your parents and me proud. You never back down from a challenge and you always go above and beyond. It is a wonder how you manage to shine through the toughest of times, but you wouldn't be you if you didn't. You are an inspiration. That is one of the many reasons why it breaks my heart to leave you.

 Now it is my turn to make you proud and bring back peace and happiness to the people back home. It has been a long time since I had to abandon my responsibilities, but now that I have your spirit as a guide I know that I can bring it back to the wonderful place it once was.

 Please remember that I love you so very much. Take care of your baby brother; you need each other more than you know. I promise *that one day, (hopefully not too long from now) we will reunite.*

Love,
Nana Esme

P.S. This letter and any future letters will be given to you on your eighteenth birthday. Think of it as a time capsule of sorts.

    Tear drops splashed onto the letter. Any suppressed feelings that Regina had, came flooding out. Tension formed in her shoulders, *"I was so mean to her and all she was trying to do was love me."* Regina couldn't get this thought out of her head. "And now she is gone." The words flew out of her mouth.
    She read the letter over and over again, trying to remember anything she could from her sixth birthday, but that felt like a lifetime ago. Only fleeting images flashed in her mind; a small cake with a pirate ship on it; maybe a bouncy house; a few moments of her dad playing the guitar and a small baby crying in the background, (probably Tyler), she thought. As hard as she tried she could not remember her grandmother, but that letter was proof that she was there. Even after she had left she was still rooting her on from afar.
    Regina held the letter close to her heart and felt very thankful that she found it, but it was then that she realized something that should have been so obvious. She let herself get distracted. How did the letter get there and furthermore, who was the one to place it there?

Chapter 19 The Somber Gather

The castle grounds were covered in a sea of black. Rain gently tapped on the heads and umbrellas of the grieving. There was nothing joyous about the day, not even the birds felt like singing.

The turnout, however, was immense. All of Nahtovia showed, along with the sirens and Zahari. Even Broadcove's King and Queen came out of hiding to pay their respects. Vaul lead a group of dwarves to some empty seats; each more sorrow than the last. Regina noticed on a distant hill top there were a small pack of wolves and in front was a familiar large gray wolf.

Reynold and Ann sat down next to Regina. She turned to them with hope of good news. "Any sign of Naveen?"

"No, sorry." Reynold gravely shook his head.

Regina was sure Naveen would at least come to the funeral.

"We have an issue at the back entrance." Regina pulled the sound from a faraway scuffle. "There is an ogre and a churra here that claim they are friends with the princess."

Regina leaned over to Tucker, "Can you go tell the shadow lighters at the back entrance that Javer and Gulren are okay to come in? Please?"

"I can't believe those guys showed. Alright I am on it." Tucker hurried back, he knew it was important for him to be there for Regina and Tyler on this day.

Soft violin music began to play; signaling the start of the funeral procession. Everyone stood to face the back as they watched a single horse pull a beautiful white carriage with gold trimming. Esme laid on top of the intricately carved carriage surrounded by blue and white flowers. A blanket with Nahtovia's insignia was placed over the lower half of her body.

The horse trotted in a circle once it reached the front and stopped at the foot of the Shaman who was conducting the funeral ritual. No words were spoken; the

Shaman hummed quietly to himself and made circles in the air with his staff. The wooden board that Esme was on slowly lifted into the air and was set on top of a pyre.

Since Naveen had disappeared, the one person who knew Esme the most, Regina thought it was best for Barney to give the eulogy. She watched him make his way up the steps to the podium. He had a handkerchief in his front pocket that had clearly already been used to dab away tears. The tip of his nose was red and his eye lids were slightly swollen.

He softly cleared his throat. "Thank you all for coming here today." His hands shook as he pulled his notecards from his pocket. "I know times are troubling and there is a lot to fear as we step out the door every morning. I also know that to many of you, Queen Esme had a been a beacon of light when things had been at their darkest. She had always been a sign of hope and when we thought we had lost her, all those years ago, a part of our hope went with her."

Barney pointed to the castle. "These walls have been empty since that terrible day during the Mad Hysteria, but the light and spirit of this castle has not been lost. Like many of you, I had found out recently that our beloved Queen was still alive and she had not forgotten about us. She had set forth on a path that would bring peace to not only our kingdom, but for this entire realm. She unfortunately lost that battle, but she did not lose the war."

"If you look around you, you will see that she has succeeded in uniting this realm. Even in death she has brought us closer together so we can fight against the truest of evils. Because now when we fight, we will be fighting with hope on our backs and with love in our hearts."

"I loved and cared for this family for a very long time and I can honestly say they were the most kind and caring family that I had ever met. Today I want all of you to hold in your heart not only Queen Esme, but the entire Foxguard family, past and present."

Barney pulled out his handkerchief and dabbed the few tears that had rolled down his cheeks. "Now, Princess Regina would like to say a few words."

Regina would have been nervous if it wasn't for her grief. The crowd burst into hushed whispers. By now, everyone had heard rumors about Queen Esme's grandchildren. Some had heard about their run in with the Cannipers, others heard about their involvement with the most recent battle and some had denied their existence. Whatever stories were being told Regina was there to present herself and her brother as truth. She would soon be leading the fight against the Mad Sister and the people needed to see she was in fact real; the new leader of the kingdom of Nahtovia.

Regina approached the podium and felt her face go numb. Every eye was on her. She was in a new world that she was still getting used to and now she had to stand in front of all these people and convince them she has what it takes to lead them. Regina scanned the crowd. A woman walked through the back entrance and removed her black veil to reveal her face; it was Naveen.

She was moving her lips trying to give Regina a message. Regina discreetly pulled the words towards her. "You can do this. I believe in you; she believed in you." Naveen's words of encouragement were exactly what Regina needed to hear.

"My grandmother was a brave and selfless woman. She not only wished for peace, but she gave up everything to bring it back to this realm. Now it is my turn to follow in her footsteps."

"From this day forth, that castle over there will be filled with new life. A place where hope can be restored and your voices can be heard, but my brother and I cannot do this on our own. We must all continue my grandmother's work to bring peace to this land."

"My brother and I wish we had more time with her, more time with the rest of our family, but everything good in our lives has been ripped apart by that venomous woman known as the Mad Sister." Angry grumbles washed over the crowd. "She has inflicted so much pain in not only our lives, but everyone sitting here today. She needs to be stopped; she will be stopped."

"So we will not cry for our loss, but rejoice in the light of the life that was Queen Esme. And as we go forward in this new journey to destroy the depression that has been forced upon us each day; we will remember to carry the Queen's kindness in our hearts and her wisdom in our minds. My grandmother's wish will come true, there will be peace."

Four royal guards marched forward, with torches in their hands and assumed their positions at the corners of the pyre. In unison, they turned inwards and lit the brush. The fire quickly spread along the sides. The Shaman stood behind with his staff upright waving it back and forth. Suddenly, he slammed his staff to the ground and the entire pyre was engulfed in flames. Beams of light sprung from the body and formed themselves into a prancing fox.

"The light of her spirit will now dance amongst the stars." Said the Shaman.

The prancing fox had a likeness of Queen Esme, in its emerald eyes and in its face. The fox circled above the crowd, leaving a trail of bright sparkling dust behind it. It lingered over Esme's body one last time looking back at Regina and Tyler briefly before it ascended into the sky.

A strong gust of wind blew out the flames leaving nothing behind and just like that the funeral was over. Regina, Tyler, Reynold and Ann stood at the back gate shaking hands and accepting people's condolences as they left.

"I'm glad to see you made it this far child." Zahari's deep voice came from behind Regina. "Your grandmother was very proud of you…" Zahari let the back of her hand stroke Tyler's cheek. "…of both you. Come see me sometime; we have a lot to discuss." Zahari bowed her head slightly and left with the rest of the sirens following closely behind.

"Both of you are so very brave." A woman with lots of jewelry shook Tyler and Regina's hands. Her voice was kind of high pitched and nasally. She had bright blonde hair, brown eyes and a very large nose. "We just can't believe dear Esme is gone." A taller man with a big gold ring on his thumb joined in. The hair on his head was curly and gray. Regina noticed when he talked the giant caterpillars that were his eyebrows seemed to move a lot.

"Esme was always such a good wife to Amos." He leaned forward to whisper and in doing so a gold necklace with a giant ruby at the end fell out. "I'm King Chauncey and this is my wife Queen Gertrude."

"Oh yes, you are Broadcove's king and queen." Regina acknowledged them with a slight bow of her head.

"Ssshh!" King Chauncey shushed Regina louder than she had spoken. "We are trying to be discrete. That is why we are wearing these ridiculous outfits."

"We look absolutely terrible!" Queen Gertrude added.

Regina and Tyler scanned them over. She was wearing a long black gown with a purple collar and diamonds woven into a design on the chest. He had on a very nice black suit with silk gray gloves on.

"Uh yes, you are blending in very well." Tyler said trying not to sound sarcastic.

Queen Gertrude pulled a handkerchief out from her clutch that had a sapphire as its clasp. "Oh I can't believe it!" She began to cry into the handkerchief. "I can't believe we have to live this way." King Chauncey consoled his wife as a servant opened the door to their large purple and silver carriage.

Slowly the funeral emptied. Several people offered their condolences and moved on; others let Regina and Tyler know that they had their support; and a few offered themselves up for the war to come. Overall, Regina felt that they at least accepted her and her brother as the new royalty; which meant she did not have to prove her claim to the throne.

"Are y'all ready to go?" Ann looked to Tyler and Regina.

Regina took one last look at the spot that her grandmother rested; a small statute of remembrance was being put up already. She appreciated how beautiful the ceremony was and it did help put her at ease, but she couldn't help think about all the possible moments that they could have spent together if she were still alive. Regina still had so many questions swimming in her head and her grandmother would have had the answers to a lot of them.

Regina felt another hand inner twine with hers. She patted the back of Tyler's hand. "Okay, I'm ready to go."

They walked out the back entrance with their heads hanging and their hearts heavy. Regina closed the gate and rejoined her brother. He laid his head against her shoulder as they walked. "Happy birthday Regina." He said quietly.

Regina smiled but said nothing.

Chapter 20 It All Ends With A Dagger

After the funeral, Regina walked into Reynold's barn and climbed up to the loft. "So this is where you have been hiding."

"How did you know?" Naveen bit into a panjello.

"It just clicked when I saw you at the funeral. You in all black, it reminded me of the first time I saw you."

Naveen squinted her eyes and tilted her head in confusion. "The first time you saw me was at the castle."

"I saw a mysterious black shadow skulking around Reynold's crops a day after we entered this realm; that was the first time that I saw you."

"Wow impressive."

"Also, Reynold's crops have been disappearing again and Tyler swears it's not Daisy." Regina pointed to the brown fruit Naveen was about to take another bite from. "What is that anyways?"

"This delicious fruit is called a panjello. It looks like a potato, but it tastes like sour apple candy." She took the last bite. "Happy birthday by the way."

"Oh thanks." Regina looked at the floor. "I haven't felt much like celebrating though."

"I can't blame you. Sixteen is a good year though." Naveen said, trying to cheer Regina up.

"How did you know it was my birthday?"

Naveen waved her hands around in a mystical way. "I know everything."

Regina chuckled but then her face got serious. "So are you going to tell me why you been in hiding."

Naveen let out a long sigh. "I haven't been in hiding; I've been looking for my mother."

"Your mother? What?"

"There is a lot that I haven't told you yet. I was hoping that we could know each other a little better before I had to divulge my deepest darkest secrets." Naveen narrowed her eyes and made a threating face. She held if for a few seconds and then laughed. "I'm not serious enough to have such a serious life. I had always wished it to be different, but…" Naveen let out a sigh. "…it is what it is."

"If my grandmother could trust you than so can I. You haven't betrayed my trust so far, plus you already told me that the Mad Sister controlled your mind and made you do a bunch of horrible things. What could be worse than that?" Regina touched Naveen's hand trying to reassure her.

"Okay, but don't say that I didn't warn you." Naveen took a deep breath. "The Mad Sister is my mother."

There was silence along with a long blank stare. "She's your what?" Regina blurted out suddenly.

"She is my mother and that is not all." Naveen paused. "You know there is so much that I would have to explain, why don't we finish this up in the morning? You know, sleep on it; let things soak in." Naveen was doing her best to push off the matter, but Regina was not having it.

"No, I need to know. If I know her and her past better than maybe I will have a greater chance at defeating her. You have to know your enemy in order to defeat your enemy."

"My father was King Amos." Naveen winched awaiting for the blow back.

This new information hit Regina like a ton of bricks. She had to take a moment to catch her breath and gather her thoughts.

"Umm…weren't they brother and sister? Blahh!" Regina made a gaging face.

"Actually, they were not related at all. Esme even said so herself."

Regina thought for a moment. "You are right. She said that Lady Dumontet did not share a single drop of blood with us."

"Exactly!" Naveen said excitedly.

"Sooo…" Regina began. "…why does everyone think that they are brother and sister?"

"I'm a little hazy on the details, but all I know is that it involved a mixture of creative lies and a really big curse. Esme, my father, your father and Orlean were the only ones who knew about it." Naveen leaned back and kicked up her black boots. "I tried to ask Esme about it a couple of times, but she never really wanted to talk about it. I can't say that I blame her."

"I think you need to start from the beginning because I have too many questions and you telling me your whole story will probably make things a lot easier."

Naveen sat herself back up against a post; ready to tell her story, when the barn door opened. A gush of wind blew in, sending waves of cold air throughout. The rain had picked up and was now pounding heavily against the ground while thunder echoed loudly in the distance.

"Hey Regina are you in here?" Tucker called from the bottom floor with Tyler by his side.

Regina looked to Naveen. "Yeah we are up here." Naveen gave in.

"Naveen? Is that you?" Tucker and Tyler climbed up to the loft. "It is you." He ran towards her and gave her a big hug.

"Uh nice to see you too." Naveen awkwardly patted Tucker's back.

"So just a quick recap: Naveen has been looking for her mom who is actually the Mad Sister, who is not really the king's sister, the king who was our grandfather was also Naveen's father. Okay they are all caught up. Now tell your story please."

Tucker and Tyler stared at each other, trying to process the new information.

"So..." Tyler said slowly. "...you are our aunt?" He was still trying to absorb all the new information.

Naveen nodded her head letting out a hint of a smile.

"Wow that is a lot to take in! I know I have a lot of questions and I'm sure Tyler does too..." Tucker noticed Regina's impatient stare. "...you know what, we can wait until after you tell us your story."

"Well I was just telling Regina that I'm not sure how everyone came to know Orlean as the king's sister, but I know it involved some kind of curse. Here is what I know, Orlean was sent to rule over Kazny. She was pregnant with me at that time, but nobody knew except for King Amos, Queen Esme and Orlean of course. King Amos told Orlean to keep the pregnancy a secret, he didn't want anyone to find out that the baby was his."

"That makes sense because people would have thought he had a child with his sister!" Tucker made the same gaging face that Regina had made earlier.

"Tucker let her finish." Regina glared at him.

"Of course he didn't want that but he also didn't want people to know he was unfaithful to Esme. Orlean also wanted to keep it a secret because in her mind, having loved ones makes you weak. So she gave birth to me in secret and she hired someone to raise me so it looked like I was their child and also so she wouldn't get attached. Those are her words, not mine."

"How could she be so cruel to her own child?" Asked Tyler. "What made her that way?"

"Orlean never talked about her past. I honestly only spent, at most, an hour a day with her and even then she hardly paid any attention to me. She never knew this, but I use to watch her from a distance and study her. I thought if I could understand her and even be like her then maybe I could win over her love. The more I watched her though the more I became aware of how awful a person she really was. It was pretty easy to stop caring about my real mother considering I had two other women who were the best surrogate moms a young girl could ever ask for. The lady who helped raise me her name was Addy Dumontet."

"She stole your nanny's name?" Regina asked looking disgusted.

"Yeah, I was in shock when I found out that was the name she had been going by. It really weirds me out and I have no idea why she would have chosen that name. Anyways, Addy was a wonderful person. She taught me right from wrong despite what my real mother was doing. She cared for me when I was sick; loved me when I was sad; scolded me when I was bad; she was always there for me when I needed her the most."

"My other mom..." Naveen continued. "...well that was Esme. Despite everything, Esme thought it was important for me to have a good relationship with the family. Most weekends Addy secretly took me over to the castle; I don't even think Orlean noticed that I was gone. Esme always treated me like a daughter. I was never seen as a burden or a mistake; in her eyes all I saw was love."

"My father, on the other hand rarely looked me in the eye and when he did I could only see the sadness that laid beneath the surface. He was reserved and strict and he seldom showed any affection to your father let alone myself. There was never a moment where I couldn't sense how ashamed he felt to be around me. I was a reminder of what he had done and all he wanted to do was forget."

"Then there was your father, Will. I had to win him over, but he caved eventually. He had enjoyed five years of his life where everything was about him and then I came along. He wanted nothing to do with me and he did everything he could to keep Esme's attention on him, but Esme would not have it. She let him know that as a big brother it was his job to love and protect me no matter what. I was surprised to see how quickly that sunk in. From then on we were inseparable, although we still had the occasional sibling squabbles."

"I had ten blissful years of enjoying my family, but then Orlean suddenly became interested in me and everything started to change. She tried to send me to the Grand Master's so I could learn how to increase my powers, but luckily she did not know how to find him and she didn't have the right influence to get someone who did know where he was to do it for her. I never understood why she had the sudden interest, she didn't even know what my inclination was at the time. She started to bring me along to these creepy meetings that took place at night. I was forced to stand in the back and wear one of those wolf masks. I was thankful that I happened to be pretty tall for my age, so with the mask on no one knew I was a child and I really didn't want to bring any attention to myself at those meetings. I had known that Orlean was not a good person, but to see her be the leader of these terrible plots; it really frightened me. I was obligated to become more involved once she saw what I could do."

"You are pretty scary when you are in Midnight mode." Tucker shivered at the thought. "I could see why she wanted you to do her biddings."

"What you guys saw on the roof was only half of what I can do. I can turn a sunny day into a gloomy one in an instant. I can control dark clouds; I can make myself into a dark cloud. My name shouldn't be Midnight Smoke it should be Midnight Cloud, but I guess Smoke sounds cooler. I can create noxious gas, I can provide cover from incoming attacks and I can travel great lengths very quickly. All of this really appealed to Orlean, but my powers were not the only thing she wanted from me. I had a claim to Nahtovia's throne."

"That's right." Regina looked at her brother. "You are next in line for the throne not Tyler and I."

"Well technically yes, but I don't want it and I didn't want it back then either. Especially because that meant my family would be killed in the process." Naveen looked away trying to conceal the tears building up in her eyes.

"I don't understand. Why wouldn't she just take the throne herself? She would be within her rights to be Queen if she was the one to conquer over the current monarch. You were a, uh a…" Regina was searching for the right word. "…an, an afterthought to her why would she want to give you the title?"

"She didn't want to give me anything and she was hoping it wouldn't come to that, but she needed me as her safety net. She knew there was a good chance that people would try to come together and overthrow her. If the people didn't accept their new ruler with open arms, then I would be her saving grace. I have the blood of the great King Amos. No one would want to overthrow me. That is why she really needed me, but of course I wanted no part of her evil plan. Addy and I were ready to run away and escape to the castle, but that is when I found out what her powers were."

"I remembered grabbing a bag full of my clothes and turning the door knob to leave when I heard her voice. It was the strangest thing, her voice was not coming from behind me or from the side, no her voice was in my head. I couldn't move. My brain kept telling my hand to finish turning the door knob, but nothing was happening. I can't even begin to describe to you how awful it feels to have your body do one thing and your brain is screaming for it to do another. No one knew what her powers were and no one really cared because she wasn't doing evil things at the time. It had clicked right there and then. My father was under her control when he slept with her and he had no idea. This whole time a part of him hated himself for being weak, but it was never his fault."

"My visits to the castle stopped, Addy was shipped off to the prison under false chargers and I was under her control. After two weekends of not showing up, Will snuck into Kazny to come see me. Luckily, Orlean was preoccupied with strategic planning that night so she couldn't control me. Instead she locked me up in my room. He tried breaking me out of the room, but it was no use. I tried to tell him as much as I possibly could; we only had a minute to talk while the guards traded shifts. Will went back and told his parents everything, but at that point it was already too late."

"Orlean attacked the sirens the very next day. She had me completely under her control; I was creating havoc wherever she sent me. I became the nightmare people heard rumors about; that is when I became Midnight Smoke. I didn't see my family again until the breach."

"That's when it happened. You don't have to explain if you don't want to." Said Regina.

"No it's okay. I think I need to get this out of my system. I never blamed my father for the way he acted around me; he had a child that he did not want nor planned for and it really wasn't his fault. I can never forgive Orlean for taking away my free will. I watched helplessly as my own hands stabbed my father in the heart. I was a ghost for the longest time while I was under her spell. I could see what I was doing, but I was helpless in stopping my actions. I just floated along feeling empty inside; fighting back when I had the strength to. My soul bares a heavy weight that it is not responsible for."

The wind and rain created a small leak in the barn's roof. Water began to trickle down on all of them. It was late and they were starting to get cold.

"Come on let's go inside." Tucker made his way to the ladder.

"I think I will stay here. I'm not sure if Ann and Reynold want me in their house considering what happened the last time I was there." Naveen started shaking from the cold wind that was now blowing in through the cracks in the roof.

"Naveen, Ann and Reynold have been just as concerned as the rest of us. They will be excited to see you." Regina gave Naveen a reassuring smile.

"Plus, it is kind of late. So there is a good chance they are asleep already." Tyler added.

Ann and Reynold were still awake and happy to see Naveen walk through the door. After several rounds of hugs; Ann started to make some hot coco on the stove. Tyler had almost been right. Ann was wearing her pink polka dotted pajamas and Reynold was in his red footie pajamas getting milk before they went to bed.

"Nice PJ's man." Tucker said sarcastically, but Reynold missed his sarcasm.

"Thanks!" Reynold had a big grin on his face.

They each grabbed a mug and gathered around the table. Regina summarized Naveen's story as best as she could to Ann and Reynold.

"Oh my goodness, you poor thing." Ann placed a hand on Naveen's shoulder. "I didn't think anyone could be so cruel."

"Well that is exactly what Orlean is; she has no heart and she doesn't understand what it is to love. Anyways, something happened when she made me kill my father; something that made her powers over me weaken. When I saw Esme and Will by the secret tunnel I knew that this was my chance to finally rid her control over me. There was a part of me that was becoming aware again, but I still wasn't in control. I floated down the hallway still in attack mode about to throw Barney across the room and then Will hit him over the head with a vase."

"Why would our father do that?" Asked Tyler.

"If he didn't hit Barney over the head, I might have killed him, I might have killed them all." There was a small silence that gave everyone goosebumps. "I am so grateful that he did. Between the sound of the vase shattering into pieces and the shock of it all I was able to break from her control. Will laid Barney on the ground while Esme kept me from falling over too. Everything that I had ever done while I was under her control hit me all at once. The near exhaustion of it all almost sent me into a coma. Esme kept me awake and helped carry me through the tunnels while Will carried Barney. By the time we reached the Parting Trees, Orlean was already inside the castle. She had won."

"Will and Esme wanted to stay and fight, but I couldn't take it anymore. The thought of being under her control again…" A scared vacant look spread across Naveen's face. "…I just couldn't; I was afraid that if I was sent to that dark place again that I would never come back out. So we decided to run just for a little while. Days, turned into months and months turned into years. We got comfortable living our new lives in a new world. Then reality set in."

"Y'all found out about the curse placed on the Parting Trees and the prophecy, didn't ya?" Ann finished for her.

"Yes and now we were in the same world as that vile woman. By that time your father had already met your mother. They were happy and I didn't want to tear them away from that, so I went searching for Orlean on my own. I had nothing to fear now that she was in the non-magical realm, but Esme insisted on coming with me."

"We traveled the world trying to track her down. We went to different realms, in several different countries and always we got the same responses. People would give us perfect descriptions of her, but they never saw what she was doing and she never stayed anywhere for more than a week. Then one day Orlean's trail went cold. We spent years following her, always a few steps behind and then she just disappeared. No one heard or saw anything it was the strangest thing."

"We had no clues of what she was planning and no trace of where she had gone to next, so we came back home to Will. He married your mom shortly after we returned and then a little while after that you came." Naveen smiled at Regina. "We were joyous and terrified at the same time."

"Because that meant the prophecy was true." Regina looked to Naveen for confirmation.

"Well it was definitely one step closer to being true. There was no chance that we would be able to find her again in that world so we came back here to give you your best shot of defeating her. We left right after your sixth birthday. We came back to look for you two as soon as we found out about your parents. Now we know why we couldn't find you. I still can't believe she had you two this whole time."

"Do you have any idea why she didn't just, uh, break the prophecy?" Tucker asked delicately.

Naveen gave the same answer as Regina had. "Umm…she needed them to break the curse on the Parting Trees, but other than that I really don't know."

"I take it you didn't have any luck finding her." Regina asked, but Naveen sighed and shook her head no.

"Her powers have grown a lot, but I think she is still trying to figure out how to control them." Naveen cringed a little. "Her control over me was different this time. I could feel her in my head, but I could kind of feel the others too; like we were all fighting back as one. I don't know if I am explaining it right, but she spread herself too far, too quickly."

"Do we still think that my powers alone can take her down?" Regina asked feeling inadequate in comparison.

"Regina, I don't think you fully understand how powerful you really are. It has only been, what a week or so since you even had your powers? You have just tapped the surface of what you can do. I mean to have an inclination like that, wow! I think you are our best shot at defeating Orlean."

Tucker nodded in agreement. "You can control sound! I'm sure with practice you can do stuff like listening to heart beats to see if someone is lying, manipulate voices and shatter objects by changing the frequency of a noise."

"Well I'm not sure if I can do all of that."

"Exactly, my point. We have no idea what your limits are or even if that is your only inclination. You can somehow create force fields as well, who knows what else you can do." Said Naveen.

"Regina is really powerful, but there has never, in the history of this realm, ever been a sorcerer as more powerful as the Mad Sister. She must be gettin some kind of help or somethin is helpin her grow stronger." Ann said scratching her head. "Her powers can't still be growin after all these years."

"So where do we go from here? Kolben is out there somewhere..." Regina began to pace the floor. "...I'll train more, but in the meantime what should we do? How do we stop her?"

Red violet smoke billowed in the corner of the kitchen. "Well, girly..." The Grand Master stepped out of the smoke and slammed a book on to the table. It was opened to a page that had a large silver dagger on it. The exact same one that the Mad Sister used to kill Esme with. "...we can start by figuring out how to destroy this dagger!"

To be continued...

Made in the USA
San Bernardino, CA
20 March 2018